Raves for the *Alien* novels:

"For those craving futuristic high-jinks and gripping adventure, Koch is an absolute master!"
—*RT Book Reviews* (top pick)

"Koch still pulls the neat trick of quietly weaving in plot threads that go unrecognized until they start tying together—or snapping. This is a hyperspeed-paced addition to a series that shows no signs of slowing down."
—*Publishers Weekly*

"Aliens, danger, and romance make this a fast-paced, wittily-written sf romantic comedy." —*Library Journal*

"Gini Koch's Kitty Katt series is a great example of the lighter side of science fiction. Told with clever wit and non-stop pacing . . . it blends diplomacy, action and sense of humor into a memorable reading experience." —*Kirkus*

"The action is nonstop, the snark flies fast and furious. . . . Another fantastic addition to an imaginative series!"
—Night Owl Sci-Fi (top pick)

"Ms. Koch has carved a unique niche for herself in the sci-fi-romance category with this series. My only hope is that it lasts for a very long time." —Fresh Fiction

"This delightful romp has many interesting twists and turns as it glances at racism, politics, and religion en route . . . will have fanciers of cinematic sf parodies referencing *Men in Black, Ghost Busters,* and *X-Men.*"
—*Booklist* (starred review)

"It's no secret that I love the series, and wish more people would pick it up and start reading." —Gizmo's Reviews

ALIEN
SEPARATION

GINI KOCH

DAW BOOKS, INC.
DONALD A. WOLLHEIM, FOUNDER
375 Hudson Street, New York, NY 10014

ELIZABETH R. WOLLHEIM
SHEILA E. GILBERT
PUBLISHERS
www.dawbooks.com

First Printing, May 2015
1 2 3 4 5 6 7 8 9

To all my fans at home and around the world—may we never be separated.

ACKNOWLEDGMENTS

Once again all my love and thanks to my fantastic and incredibly patient editor, Sheila Gilbert (she's a saint), and my awesome agent, Cherry Weiner (she's my hero), without whom my career, and sanity, would not be what they are today. (Take that as you will.) Much love and chocolate is in the mail to you both.

Same again to my awesome crit partner, Lisa Dovichi, and to the Fastest Beta Reader in the West, Mary Fiore, who once again came through at the eleventh hour because I was writing up until the eleventh hour, so to speak. (Okay, more than so to speak.) You're the best and I love you both.

My list of those I want to thank gets longer each book, and for that I'm extremely thankful, grateful, and just plain jazzed about. So, once again and in no particular order, here's this book's list of especially awesome folks who made my writing journey that much more special.

Love and thanks to all the good folks at DAW Books and Penguin, to all my fans around the globe, my Hook Me Up! Gang, members of Team Gini new and old, all Alien Collective Members in Very Good Standing, Twitter followers, Facebook fans and friends, Pinterest followers, the fabulous bookstores that support me, and all the wonderful fans who come to my various book signings and conference panels—you're all the best and I wouldn't want to do this without each and every one of you along for the ride.

Special love and extra shout-outs to: my awesome assistants, Joseph Gaxiola and Colette Chmiel for continuing to keep me sane, on time, and efficient; Bob & Mary Rehak for loving support and a fantastic vacation; Adrian & Lisa Payne, Hal & Dee Astell, and Duncan & Andrea Rittschof for continuing to always show up everywhere, with smiling faces and books (and Poofs) in hand, ensuring anywhere I'm at is always a warm, fun place to be; Oliver & Blanca Bernal for always having the welcome mat out and the comfy bed ready whenever I'm in town; Tom & Libby Thomas, Pat & Barbara Michel, Koren Cota, Chrysta Stuckless, Missy Katano, Christina Callahan, Amy Thacker, Jan Robinson, Mariann Asanuma, Koleta Parsley, Mikel Dornhecker, Tina Williams, Terry Smith, Joan Du, Janet Armentani, Colette Chmiel, Anne Taylor, and Shawn Sumrall for bestowing beautiful, wonderful, and delicious things upon me what seems like all the time; Robert Palsma for continuing to like everything I do; Paul Sparks for continuing to send me scientific proof that I know what I'm writing about; Edward Pulley for instantaneous research on minutiae that's driving me nuts; and all members of The Stampeding Herd—Lisa Dovichi, Hal Astell, Barb Tyler, Marcy Rockwell, Lynn Crain, Sue Martin, Terry Smith, Phyllis Hemann, and Teresa Cutler-Broyles, for ensuring that, even though I was the most frighteningly late I've ever been on anything, the Herd kept me running at top speed—this book would not have gotten done without you guys.

Always last in the list but never in my heart, thanks to my husband, Steve, and daughter, Veronica. You're the best in the world and, as always, I'm glad you're mine.

REVENGE IS A DISH BEST SERVED COLD.

Yeah, I have no idea what that means, either. But it's what they say when you're ready to go after someone who's done their best to destroy you. I think it's supposed to mean that you should be levelheaded and calm while plotting your enemy's ultimate, untimely, and ugly demise.

Sound plan. Pity that I work better angry. But then again, I'm pretty angry. So we should be good here.

Of course, that's probably being far too optimistic.

Not sure what was more shocking—discovering that there's a zillion and one universes out there and I'm representing in most of them, or discovering the identity of the Mastermind.

Visiting another universe was kind of cool. Nice to see how the other half was living with basically no aliens on the planet. Not as well in some ways, just dandy in others. It was a "fun" vacation, if we define fun to mean spending a couple weeks unsure if I'd ever get home again or if I was going to spend the rest of my life in Oz, both literally and figuratively.

Coming home was better—always nice to have that "took a trip but boy it's great to sleep in my own bed and have great sex with my mega-sexy alien husband again" feeling.

But while I got to save the day for the other world, I'm not so sure how to manage back in mine. The term "it's complicated" has never been more apt. And, as in the other world, a frontal attack is probably not the right plan.

A battle will be coming, though, one way or the other. Because it's time to take the bull by the horns and ram those horns right into the Mastermind's personal tenders. So to speak.

But at least I won't be fighting this battle with only a small commando force. For this battle, I'm going to ensure I have an army. And, to quote one of my favorite '80s glam rockers, it's time to make the Mastermind Stand and Deliver. For I am a Woman of the Multiverse and I will not allow evil to continue unchecked.

Yeah, fine, fine. Let's go with what's been working all this time. Yo, Mastermind—just thought you should know that Megalomaniac Girl is back and she's madder and badder than ever. So watch your step, 'cause I'm coming for you.

CHAPTER 1

EARLY MORNING AND I are not best buds. I'm not a girl who sees any virtue in watching the sun rise. However, it was the morning after I'd come back from an unintended vacation, and my husband and I had spent the night wide awake and extremely active in the best possible way.

Now we were lying next to each other, relaxing in the afterglow of a night very well spent.

"I know who the Mastermind is." As post-coitus comments went, this was probably not going to go down as the World's Most Romantic Statement.

"Yeah?" Jeff rolled onto his side to face me, leaning on his hand. His other hand stroked my body. It was great to feel his hand on my skin—I'd spent the last couple of weeks wondering if that would ever happen again.

We had music on, and as Weezer's "My Best Friend" hit our airwaves, I shifted likewise so we were face-to-face and I could also stroke Jeff's chest and such. And I could look at him. Considering I hadn't been sure I'd ever see his face again, it was nice to be here, like normal, as if nothing much had gone on.

We were in Sydney Base, so the standard nightlight glow was in the room, meaning we *could* see each other. Aliens, of which Jeff was definitely one, were different from humans in many ways, not all of them physical. As near as I could tell, no A-Cs liked to sleep in the extreme dark. I'd never asked why—and as I'd learned during my foray out of this world, I probably needed to be a bit more curious about many things.

However, since we'd moved into the American Centaurion Embassy in Washington, D.C., I'd gotten used to sleeping in the actual dark again. But this was kind of a nice retro moment. I'd spent my first night after discovering aliens were on the planet in a room very like this one, half of it with Jeff. The best half.

I was willing to stay in bed with Jeff forever but, partially because I'd had a two-week "vacation" in another universe, duty was calling in a loud and insistent manner. Also, Mr. Clock shared that it was six in the morning, and that meant that our daughter was going to be up in an hour, give or take.

"Yeah. Only . . . I don't know if I can tell you."

"Because you're worried I'll give away the fact that I know because I can't lie any better than the rest of the A-Cs, right?"

"Right. You sound like you had this conversation already."

"I did. With you, in that sense."

"Oh. Other Me figured it out?" I'd switched universes with another version of me. Yeah, my life was just that kind of exciting. Hers was, too, now, come to think of it. Oh well, she was me. She'd roll with the punches.

"Pretty much."

"How? I mean, I realize I'm great at looking at accepted truths and quickly spotting the flaws and all that, but she couldn't have had a lot to go on."

"Oh, she didn't. But she had the one key piece of information we've never had. The same new fact I figure you discovered while you were in her universe—her Chuck hates the Mastermind's guts, with good reason."

Other Me was married to my best guy friend since high school, Charles Reynolds. Well, her universe's Charles Reynolds, at any rate. It had been instructive and interesting to see how my life might have been different. Hoped she'd enjoyed seeing how the other universe lived.

"Wow, yeah. So, you know who it is?"

Jeff nodded as "Bad Blood" by Ministry came on. "Almost the worst person it could be."

"Got that right. So, does Chuckie know?"

"No." Jeff sighed. "We've managed to keep it from him. For the whole week and a half that we've known. And only because we've been so busy and focused on fixing things with the Australian government and getting you and your Cosmic Alternate to switch back."

"Did Malcolm already know?" Malcolm Buchanan had Dr. Strange powers. At least as far as I was concerned. If he didn't want you to see him, you didn't see him. If he said it was so, it was probably so. Luckily for me, my mother had assigned him to be my bodyguard when we first got to D.C. She'd assigned the Buchanan in the other universe onto Other Me a lot sooner. Apparently things were dicey wherever I was. Go me.

"Yeah. Buchanan's known for what sounds like three years. But he has no actual proof. None of us here do."

"We had no proof, either, other than the fact that Cliff Goodman was that universe's Charles' lifelong enemy. And the fact that he tried to kill Other Me, their kids, Charles, James, and Malcolm. He'd already ..." Murdered my mother in that world. Along with the rest of her and Buchanan's teams, which included other people I knew and loved in this world.

"I know," Jeff said gently. "We figured it all out. Well, most of it. I'm sure we're both missing parts of the whole nightmare." He grinned. "And I know I don't have the full story of how you kicked butt and saved the day."

"You just assume I did that?" I hadn't really had time to brief everyone on what had happened, in part because Chuckie was here with the group that had come to fix things with Australia and I hadn't wanted to let anything slip.

Jeff kissed me, his typical awesome kiss. "Yeah, that's my default assumption," he said after his lips and tongue had owned mine for a good, long time, emphasis on good. "That you're going to do what has to be done, better than anyone else ever could."

"I could get used to this form of hero worship."

He laughed. "There's nothing wrong with accurate hero worship, baby."

Snuggled my face in between his awesome pecs and rubbed against his chest hair as the Veronicas sang "I Could Get Used To This." "Works for me. After all, I hero worship your bedroom and leadership skills, so we're even."

Jeff chuckled. "Always nice to be appreciated."

"Back atcha. So, what do we do? I don't know how to tell

Chuckie that the guy he thinks is his best friend is the reason his wife is dead. He's normally laid back and able to roll with whatever's thrown at him, but I'm not willing to bet he'll be able to deal rationally under the circumstances."

Naomi Gower-Reynolds wasn't really dead in the technical, universal sense. She'd taken so much pure Surcenthumain—what we called the Superpowers Drug—in order to save Jamie and Chuckie from being destroyed by the Mastermind that she'd become something far more than human or alien. She'd become a superconsciousness. And she was never allowed to come back to Earth. Our Earth. However, she'd found a way around that rule by covering the protection of her beloved goddaughter and husband in every other universe they existed in. And I was the only one who knew this. Well, me, and my daughter Jamie. Daughters Jamie, I guess.

There was a multiverse out there, and I discovered that I'd seen it before. In the past, when I'd seen the Universe Wheel, I'd never remembered it when I'd woken up or come back to life or whatever. But now, after this trip, I remembered it all. And I was pretty sure I did because of Naomi's influence.

I existed in a large number of the universes out there, and in every one I was in, Jamie was there as well. Same birthdate for every Jamie throughout the multiverse, though her father was usually Chuckie, or James Reader. This was the only universe where Jeff was on Earth, so it was the only one with him as her father.

Jamie had learned how to communicate with her other selves. I wasn't sure if it was because my Jamie housed a superconsciousness in her mind now, since ACE had taken up residence there, or if she was just that highly talented. Probably both.

"None of us have a plan for that yet," Jeff admitted. "It needs to be broken to him gently, if that's at all possible."

"There's a slight possibility that I'm wrong about Cliff being the Mastermind in this universe. Very slight."

Jeff shook his head. "No, you're not. Too many pieces fit."

"Yeah, they fit to me, too. I don't know what to do. Other than get a three-way mirror pronto."

The Jamie I'd spent time with in the other universe was also special—she could see every other Jamie in all the other universes. But she needed help to do so—a large three-way mirror set up as if it was in a department store's dressing room. I was pretty sure that she didn't need a magic mirror, but I wasn't completely confident—in my experience it didn't pay to assume.

"Yeah, you told me that when you, ah, came back. I ordered a set. Should be at the Embassy when we get home. But unless those mirrors are going to give us proof that Cliff's the Mastermind, or show us how to break the news to Chuck safely, I don't think they're what we need the most."

"Yeah. What we really need to know is if Cliff and LaRue have a death ray."

"Excuse me?"

Before I could explain what I was talking about, "Trouble" by Pink came on and we were interrupted by a voice on the intercom. "I'm sorry to wake you, Vice President and Ambassador Martini," a woman I'd never heard before said in an Australian accent. "But we have an incoming call from a restricted number."

"Did the caller give a name, Melissa?" Jeff asked as he sat up and turned the music off.

"No, Mister Vice President, he did not." Apparently Melissa was as big on the titles as Walter and William Ward were. Walter ran Embassy Security and, since Gladys Gower's death, his older brother William had taken over as Head of Security out at the Dulce Science Center.

"Why are we taking this call then?" I asked as I sat up as well. This was far too reminiscent of the start of Operation Confusion for my liking.

"Because the caller said it was a matter of life or death, Ambassador."

CHAPTER 2

"IT SO FIGURES. Can we take that call in here . . . Melissa, is it? Or do we have to go somewhere else?"

Jeff shot me the "shut up, shut up" look.

"Yes, Ambassador, it's Melissa. We've met." Her voice was rather icy on the last sentence.

Crap. The reason for the "shut up" look dawned on me. Now that I was back, I'd forgotten that Jeff had told me that everyone had done their best not to let on that Other Me was here instead of Real Me. "Oh. Right. I'm sorry. You just sounded different on the intercom and this early in the morning. We, ah, didn't get a lot of sleep."

"Ah. Well, I can patch the call through to your room, if you'd like." Melissa sounded appeased and Jeff looked relieved, so assumed I'd handled it well enough.

"Just asking . . . why wouldn't we like? It's not a video call or something, is it?" We were naked and I didn't feel like sharing the wonder that was Jeff's naked body with random strangers, restricted calls or not. Frankly, I was a selfish girl and didn't want to share his naked body with anyone. Shoved the worry about how much of his naked body Other Me had seen and/or enjoyed away. Clearly, the game was afoot. Sometimes I hated the game.

"Mister Buchanan feels he should be with you for this call, Ambassador."

"Gotcha."

Jeff zipped out of bed, grabbed our pajamas, and zipped back. He was dressed in a second. Hyperspeed, the savior of decorum. "Give us a minute, no more, Melissa," Jeff said. "Then have him come to our room."

"He's outside, Mister Vice President."

Pulled the pajamas on at human speeds. Didn't need to rip my clothes in half right now. "Now is fine," I said as I pulled the T-shirt down.

We headed into the sitting room portion of the standard A-C transient housing section. All A-C facilities had transient sections and they all resembled a nice, austere hotel setup, just like the regular living quarters did. Aliens had their funny ways, was how I looked at it.

The door opened and Buchanan came in. He was built a lot like Jeff—tall, buff, handsome for a human. Unlike Jeff, his brown hair was straight, not wavy, and he had blue eyes instead of Jeff's light brown. The perks of my job and life were many, and being surrounded by the best looking aliens in the galaxy somehow meant we scored the best looking humans on Earth, too. It wasn't fair, but I wasn't complaining.

"Secured line, Melissa," Buchanan said, without even a howdy-do. "No one else listening in other than those in this room. Caller unaware that I'm in this room, as well."

"Yes, Mister Buchanan." Melissa clearly liked Buchanan more than she liked me. Oh well. I'd have to find the will to go on somehow.

The sound in the room changed to the crackle of a poor connection on a long distance line. "Missus Martini?"

Recognized the voice. "Gideon Cleary, it's been a while. It's Ambassador Martini to you, though, dude."

"Yes, sorry. I wasn't trying to be offensive."

Considered this. His tone didn't sound snide or condescending. Frankly, he sounded worried. "You were trying to be sure it was me."

"Yes." Now he sounded relieved. "It *is* you. Good. We have a problem."

"How is that? And why wouldn't it have been me? You called for me and my husband and it's dawn over on this side of the world. Who were you expecting to be sleeping in our bed, so to speak?"

"No idea, honestly. There have been some . . . rumors these past couple of weeks that you haven't been, ah, yourself."

"A concussion will do that to people," Jeff said dryly.

And before I could blow it again. Though I had remembered that my excuse for anything and everything was supposed to be the concussion I'd gotten falling headfirst onto some concrete stairs at the start of Operation Bizarro World. Of course, I hadn't used said excuse with Melissa. Jeff's intervention made a lot of sense.

"Yes, I know, Mister Vice President." Interesting. Normally when Cleary was speaking to Jeff, he sounded like he was eating the sourest lemon on the planet. Right now, however, he just sounded normal, and still worried. "However, that wasn't my concern. And I don't mean that in an insulting way, Ambassador."

"You were worried that I'd been turned into an unwilling android, weren't you?"

"Frankly, yes. You're clearly still yourself, which is a relief."

Hadn't been hard to guess. Since he'd at least known about if not helped to turn Cameron Maurer into an unwilling android, and Maurer had been Cleary's VP running mate. "Seriously? I know we reached an understanding during the campaign, but I find it hard to believe that you consider yourself a pal of mine, and vice versa."

"Politics makes strange bedfellows."

"Dude, that is like *the* Washington saying, isn't it? But, fine, what do you want us to be in bed with you about, to the point that you've called on the restricted, we can't trace it line?" I had no way of knowing this, though Buchanan nodding at me indicated that I'd guessed correctly.

"Stephanie Valentino is missing, and has been missing for a week."

Let that sit on the air for a bit. Stephanie was Jeff's eldest niece, and the daughter of one of the biggest traitors the A-Cs had ever had. She'd been turned, too, probably for far longer than we'd realized. We'd given up on trying to win her back to the side of right—in part because I'd had to kill her father or let him kill me and a whole lot of other people. But Stephanie wasn't going to ever forgive me or the others for that. Hard to blame her, until I considered all the evil she was doing to make us pay for ending her father's betrayal habits in a very permanent way.

"Have you gone to the police?" Jeff asked.

"Not yet. I don't want to create a scandal if none exists.

I was hoping she'd gone home to visit her mother or other family members."

"We can check." My phone beeped and I got it. Buchanan had sent me a text. Showed it to Jeff. "Ah, we *have* checked. There is no sign of Stephanie anywhere, including with any of her immediate family."

"Are you certain? I know she's considered an outcast and a *persona non grata* in the alien community right now."

"That was her choice," Jeff said sadly. "But we'd let her back if we felt we could trust her. And her mother would never turn her away." He was texting on his phone. "However, I've just asked every immediate member of my family—they swear they think Stephanie is with you, Cleary."

"Did your wife get tired of the affair and kick her out or get into a fight with Stephanie about something else?"

Cleary heaved a sigh that sounded exasperated. "I realize you think that I was sleeping with her. And she's a beautiful young woman, so I admit the temptation is there. However, I truly don't sleep around, let alone with a girl young enough to be my daughter. My wife and I honestly have done our best to take Stephanie into our family. As a daughter. Stephanie's father was murdered—she needs the stability we felt we could offer to her. My wife was even hoping Stephanie and our middle son would connect romantically."

"Since when did your family become pro-alien?" Jeff asked.

"We were never anti-alien," Cleary said. "Surely you understand how politics works by now, don't you?"

"We do. Find a scapegoat, attack the scapegoat to divert attention away from the actual issues that matter, lather, rinse, repeat. But I have a question in regard to Stephanie. What were *you* hoping for when you took her in, Gideon?"

"That I'd have an assistant who could and would give me all the information on your people I could ever want. And I had that. Stephanie, however, has a romantic interest other than my son, despite my advice to the contrary."

I was shocked by his honesty, but it was rather refreshing. I wasn't used to anyone in D.C. ever being honest on the first try. My brain nudged. Who Stephanie's bad romantic choice could be was oh so likely. Why not ask, just for grins and giggles? "She's dating Cliff Goodman, isn't she?"

Jeff stiffened as Buchanan nodded and shot me a look

that said he was pleased that I hadn't lost any steps going
back and forth between universes. There was no need for
any of us to ask why Cliff hadn't shared who his squeeze
was—that would have made Chuckie, and the rest of us,
suspicious. Though Cliff probably could have spun it as his
attempt to get Stephanie back on the side of good.

"She is."

"Why don't you approve? Aside from the fact that he
has to be sneaking around with her, since none of us knew
of this relationship until right now. He's well connected po-
litically."

Cleary took a deep breath and let it out slowly. "I don't
trust him. And not because he appears to be a friend to all of
you. In part because he is indeed sneaking around with
Stephanie and their relationship is a secret to all but a few of
us. There's no reason for that—he could easily say that he
was trying to rebuild the bridge between her and all of you."

Chose not to say that, again, Cleary was impressing me
with his intelligence. I was about 99 percent sure that Cleary
was aware that Cliff was involved with the Mastermind.
Doubted that Cleary knew that Cliff *was* the Mastermind,
but he definitely knew Cliff was involved with our biggest
enemy. So, if Cleary was coming to us with this, he was either trying to determine if we'd figured out that Cliff was
the Bad Guy Supreme, or else he was afraid of Cliff and
afraid for himself and Stephanie.

The word "appears" also indicated that Cleary didn't
think Cliff actually was our friend and might be trying to tell
us so in a safe way. Which was, of course, true. "Makes
sense. So, what are the other parts of why don't you trust
him?" Figured it was safer to ask than guess at this juncture.

"Because Cliff is a master at playing both sides against
each other. Frankly, he's a master at playing everyone
against each other, regardless of side."

"Why don't you want Stephanie dating him?"

"Because I'm certain he doesn't care for or about her.
No one who sneaks around and dates a girl on the down-
low cares about her. And, as I may have mentioned, my
feelings toward her are fatherly."

"Okay, let's say I believe you," Jeff said. "Why are you
coming to us, and not the police? In fact, why aren't you just
asking Cliff where she is?"

"I asked him where she was the first day she didn't come home. He claims that he has no idea and is as worried as I am."

"You think he killed her and dumped her body in the river?"

"I have no idea, Ambassador. Stephanie was acting oddly the week prior to her disappearance."

"That coincides with when we know she murdered eight Secret Service agents in Paris on Goodman's order," Buchanan whispered to me. Apparently I needed to get caught up on what had gone on here, pronto.

"Oddly how?" Jeff asked.

"She seemed furtive and evasive. Her moods went up and down—one moment, she was happy, the next wringing her hands, then laughing, then crying. My wife asked if Stephanie was on drugs or if someone might have slipped some to her. Stephanie insisted she was clean. Your people don't drink and she still follows that rule."

She'd better. Alcohol was deadly to A-Cs, as Jeff could attest—he'd almost died from one swig of vodka way back when. And Stephanie knew about this, so she wouldn't drink. And if she did she'd be convulsing, not acting like the poster girl for Just Say No.

However, while she'd tried to kill all of us during Operation Defection Election, she hadn't actually succeeded. If she'd indeed murdered eight people in cold blood while I was gone, her reactions made a lot of sense.

"What do *you* think has happened, Gideon?"

"I think Cliff has done something with or to her. Whether he had her do something illegal, she's pregnant and he's not willing to do the right thing, or it's something else, I believe he's responsible for her disappearance. She might have willingly disappeared, though, which is why I haven't gone to the police."

"Why would she be willing to disappear on her surrogate family and employer?"

"Or," Jeff said, "to put it another way—what did you, someone in your household, or someone on your staff do or say to her that would make her disappear without a trace?"

CHAPTER 3

"**A**BSOLUTELY NOTHING,**"** Cleary said. "I know you don't want to believe me, but my wife and my chief of staff and I have been over this for the past several days with each other, and we've asked everyone who Stephanie interacts with as well. No one has any idea why she's disappeared, but everyone noted her drastic attitude change and mood swings."

"Does anyone have any theories? Other than yours, I mean."

"No. Her going home to her family for some reason was the only idea any of us could come up with."

"Why should we believe you're not just trying to get us to think you haven't harmed her?" Jeff asked.

"Look, I realize we're not friends. But stop acting self-righteous. You two have killed people in the line of duty. I've done things I'm not proud of along the way as well. No one's hands are clean, especially not in this town. But I'm not calling you in a way that no one could ever verify to create an alibi. I'm calling you because a young woman I care about, whom I think you also care about, is missing, and I have no idea what to do."

"What, exactly, did you say to Cliff and what, exactly, did he say back to you about this? You said you asked him about her the first night she didn't come home—have you talked to him about her since?"

"I called Cliff the morning after Stephanie hadn't returned. As far as we knew, they'd been out together. I said I was just making sure she'd spent the night with him. He said that she hadn't, that he'd dropped her at our house around two in the morning and waited until she was inside, then gone home. He's checked with us every day to see if we've heard from her or not."

The three of us looked at each other. "She's not hiding from the Clearys, is she? She's hiding from Cliff."

Jeff and Buchanan both nodded. "That makes the most sense to me," Jeff said. "If she's alive and this isn't some elaborate setup to make us all think he's innocent of her murder."

"If I report her as missing, then Cliff will be the first person the police suspect," Cleary said.

"Now, Gideon, here we were, getting along, telling each other the truth, and you have to toss in a great big lie."

"What do you mean?" He was trying to sound innocent. Not his best go-to voice.

"Dude, *you* are the first person the police will suspect, for all the reasons we all just talked about, and because Cliff isn't considered Stephanie's boyfriend by anyone but you, your wife, and your close staffers, in other words, people more than likely to lie to protect you. You're calling us because you're scared, and we are your Obi-Wan Kenobis."

"You're not my only hope," he muttered.

"Yes. We are. Or you wouldn't be chatting with us. But I have to say, your getting my reference just made me actually kind of like you. Choose your next words carefully—you don't want to waste my like."

"Oh, fine, yes, you're right."

Buchanan whispered to me again, and I passed along his question. "What else are you worried about or afraid of? We need all the facts before we can actually help you. And that *is* why you're calling, isn't it, Gideon? To ask us to help you?"

He was quiet for a few long seconds. We waited. I'd learned the sales maxim that—once the offer or big question is made—he who speaks first loses, and I'd taught it to Jeff. Buchanan had probably learned this in the womb. The three of us were utterly silent. I examined my nails to pass the time. I needed a manicure in a bad way. Apparently this trans-dimensional stuff was hard on the paws.

But finally Cleary spoke. "Yes, you're right. I am calling to ask for your help. I have no one else I can actually trust in this situation, and yes, I trust you because your reputations are very strong as both reformers and defenders."

"We're flattered," Jeff said in a tone that indicated we really weren't. "But we need the rest of the answer to Kitty's question. What are you afraid of?"

"I'm worried that this could be a setup, to trap me in some way. To force me to do things I don't want to do—change my vote on certain bills, use my influence with lobbyists or my constituents in a way I don't want, commit crimes I find abhorrent or reprehensible."

Managed not to ask for the list of what Cleary—Mr. I Have An Unwilling Android As My Running Mate—would find unsavory. It was too early in the morning to have my stomach that upset.

"That makes sense," Jeff said. "And it might be a trap. We aren't going to alibi you about Stephanie's romantic liaisons, you know."

"I wouldn't ask because I'm aware that your only proof is hearsay from me. I don't want your help in court—I'm praying we don't end up in court over this. I'm hoping Stephanie is alive and unharmed. I just don't believe that it's safe to assume that's the case. Something's happened. Either Cliff has her or, as you just suggested, he did or said something to her that caused her to run away. But no matter what, I know in my bones that she's in danger."

Buchanan whispered to me again and again I passed it right along. "I think we need to see where Stephanie was living. In case there are any clues about where she's gone."

"We've searched her rooms. We didn't find anything."

"Gideon, don't take this the wrong way, but there's no way you've searched like an A-C can search, and there's also no way that you've figured out A-C thought processes in the short time you've had Stephanie with you. Trust me. I've been immersed for years and they still baffle me at times." Ignored the hurt look Jeff shot at me. "So, what's going to be our reason for dropping by your residence? It needs to be believable, especially since said residence is in Florida and we are, currently, in Australia and due back in D.C. pronto."

"Can't you, ah, just take a gate here?"

"No," Jeff said flatly. "We aren't going to be sneaking around to help you out. If we're helping you, it's going to be aboveboard and seen."

Something clicked. "Wait a second. You're in Florida at the Governor's Mansion. Stephanie was in Florida. What the hell was Cliff doing taking her out in Florida? He lives in the D.C. area."

"He keeps an apartment in Florida," Cleary said. "He's from here originally, I believe. He flies down at least once a month, usually more often. Sometimes I'm sure he takes a gate, but most of the time he flies."

"Amazing how he can do that on a government salary," I said quietly to Jeff and Buchanan. "Gideon," I said in a louder voice, "come up with a reason for us to visit. Make it good, and make it something that won't reflect badly on us. If it reflects badly, or you make it sound like *you* are helping *us*, well, we're going feel obligated to mention that the just-out-of-her-teens A-C you snatched away from us has gone missing. And we all know you don't want that."

He sighed. "No, I don't. I'll come up with something."

"Make it fast," Jeff said. "The President expects us to be heading for home in the next few hours."

"Call back on a regular line, too. We'll roll with whatever your reason is, as long as it fits the parameters we just outlined."

"I will do. And . . . thank you. I honestly appreciate this more than you probably will believe."

With that we hung up and the three of us looked at each other. "So, do we think Stephanie's freaked out about murdering people or is there more going on?"

"There's always more going on, Missus Chief," Buchanan said. "I think it's time to call in the one person who has experience with Stephanie as a traitor who is also your friend."

"Really?" Jeff asked. "You want to bring Siler in on this? Now?"

Buchanan nodded. "He's interacted with her and I think she may still believe he's on the Mastermind's side. But even if she knows he's working with us now, he's seen a side of her that none of the rest of us have, and he may be able to predict where she's gone."

"And you just happen to have him on speed dial."

Jeff groaned. "A call to Siler means a call to Kitty's 'uncles.' Do we really want to involve those people in whatever's going on?"

During Operation Defection Election we'd met Benjamin Siler, the child of the Ronald Yates-Mephistopheles in-control superbeing and Madeline Cartwright. They'd done things to Siler and, among other weirdnesses, he didn't age like normal people. His uncle had rescued him from life as his parents' lab rat, and trained Siler in his profession— assassination.

Siler worked frequently with my "uncles," the top assassins in the world. Peter "The Dingo" Kasperoff and his cousin, Victor. Somehow they'd adopted me as their niece and helped me out when they could.

"Frankly, I trust the Dingo Dog and Surly Vic a lot more than I trust most of the politicians in Washington, including the one who just called us on the secret telephone. So if Nightcrawler brings them along, so much the better."

"I'll leave that to his discretion," Buchanan said.

"Is he here already?" Among Siler's abilities was the fact that he could "blend," which made him invisible to humans or A-Cs. It was more of a chameleon effect than real invisibility, but it was effective, even though he couldn't hold his blend for too long. So, the possibility existed that Buchanan had already called in his version of the cavalry and Siler was just hanging out in here, unseen.

Buchanan chuckled. "No, but he's nearby."

"Why?" Jeff asked.

"Because I wanted backup in case Missus Chief didn't come back right away."

Thought about this. "Oh. The Mastermind has upped his game and you were willing to do the stopgap fix and hire a hit on Cliff."

Jeff looked shocked. "We can't condone assassination."

"I'd condone anything that would get Cliff, LaRue, Reid, all their clones, and all their evil dead gone and buried forever."

Buchanan nodded. "I assume the LaRue and Reid clones backed up Goodman's memory and have clones of him on the way. But killing him would give us a little time, and it's time we might need. My gut tells me that he's going to make a big move soon, and if we're not ready, we'll all be destroyed."

CHAPTER 4

"I CAN AGREE WITH THAT. In the other universe, he was definitely making his big move. There were enough parallels that it's really possible he's ready in this universe as well."

"Murdering eight of our Secret Service detail, and they were eight men who reported to him, sounds like moving up a timetable to me," Jeff agreed. "Especially since he was trying to frame Buchanan here."

Who nodded. "I think the Mastermind trying to get me out of the way indicates he's ready to roll out his plan. Whatever it is."

"Seriously, I think he's got a death ray. He had one in the other world, and that was with far fewer scientific resources available to him. Oh, and this is a biggie that you and all the others need to know—LaRue isn't a human. She's an Ancient turncoat working for the Z'porrah."

Both men stared at me. "Why did you wait to tell us this?" Buchanan asked finally.

"Dude, I've been home less than twenty-four hours. It's early morning. So this is me telling you quickly. Besides, Chuckie was there when I came back and I think we all agreed that we didn't want to tell him what's going on until we're sure he can handle it and we can handle him and his reaction."

Jeff nodded. "Let's get dressed and get ready as if it's a normal day. We'll figure out how to break the news to Chuck."

"Figure out how to brief everyone other than Reynolds,"

Buchanan said. "And figure it out fast. Because it sounds like we need your intel and you absolutely need ours, and there's no way the many A-Cs who figured out who the Mastermind is are going to be able to keep that from Reynolds. I'm not even convinced you can keep it from him, Missus Chief. He knows you better than anyone else, and I'm pretty damn sure he knows when you're lying to him."

"Maybe we can focus him on the Stephanie situation?" Jeff asked.

"That would tell him that his supposed best friend is dating your niece on the sly, and I can guarantee that Chuckie will put two and two together immediately because of that."

"We'll think of something," Jeff said, rather desperately. "We only need to keep it from him for a little while anyway, right?"

Buchanan stood up to leave. "Depends on when you want Reynolds on a murderous rampage. Because the minute he knows, I can guarantee that's going to be his reaction."

"He's normally a very calm, controlled person. And I'm saying this based on years of experience with him."

"Yes, and I'm saying this based on an understanding of human motivations and reactions learned over time. And from your mother. He's not going to be the man you're used to."

Jeff nodded. "He's been dealing too long and too poorly with losing Naomi. This is a betrayal of the highest order, baby. We're all prepped to have to lock him into isolation for his own safety."

"Wow. I go away for a couple of weeks and everyone's got delusions of doom going. Fantastic."

Buchanan grinned. "I'm sure you can handle it, Missus Chief." With that he left.

Jeff and I showered and got dressed. Okay, we showered, had a lot of mind-blowing sex, and then dressed. Hey, I'd been gone for *ages*.

Would have said it was nice to be back in my own clothes, but technically I'd never *not* been in my own clothes. Still, I enjoyed my own selection of concert T-shirts. Based on all that was going on, I chose an Aerosmith T-shirt, because it was always wise to go forth with my boys on my chest.

Jeans, my Converse, and a No Doubt hoodie completed my ensemble. Ready for anything. I hoped.

As Jamie woke up there was a knock at our door. I opened the door while Jeff got Jamie to find Chuckie standing there. "Hey, Kitty. How are you?"

"Um, fine? Why are you asking me that at this time of the morning?"

Jeff came out with Jamie. "Hey, Chuck." He looked and sounded guilty. Not good. "What's up?" I trotted over to give Jamie a kiss and hug and hopefully distract Chuckie from Jeff's expression.

"I . . . wanted to talk to Kitty. Alone. For a few minutes."

Jeff and I looked at each other. "Fine by me." I figured I had the best shot of lying and besides, Jeff was about to give away that something was up.

Jeff nodded. "Don't be too long. We need to do a big, fast debrief. And bring you up to speed on our latest early-morning phone call."

Chuckie nodded and spun on his heel, seemingly uninterested in our phone call. I quickly followed him out of the room. "Where to?"

"My room here is fine." He led me a few doors down and we went into a room that looked just like the one we'd just left, only a bit smaller. The A-Cs were all about conformity.

We sat on the couch. "So, what's up?" Figured it was going to be a lot safer for him to lead the conversation.

"A couple of things." Chuckie looked at his hands, which were clasped together, his forearms leaning on his thighs. "What was he like?"

"Who?"

"The me in the world you were in."

Knew he wasn't asking lightly, so I considered my reply before I gave it. "Basically you. With a slightly different life. But you."

"Was he . . . happy?"

"Mostly, yeah. He'd been lying to Other Me for years about what he really did, and that was taking its toll. And he blamed himself for their Jamie's presumed autism. I, ah, fixed both of those, I'm pretty sure. And you guys over here probably did, too."

He nodded but didn't say anything, and he still wasn't looking at me.

"Um, why?"

Chuckie sighed. "Because everyone's hiding something from me, and it started shortly after the other you arrived. I think . . . I'm worried that there's something awful about the man I am in that other universe." He looked up at me. "And if he's got a bad streak, then I do, too."

And here was the problem with everyone lying to the smartest guy in any room—it was too easy for him to come up with believable scenarios that were both wrong and detrimental to his mental and emotional health. And he was just as likely to freak out if he thought he was some kind of monster in another world as he was if he knew what Cliff was really up to.

"There was nothing wrong with the you in that universe, Chuckie. Nothing at all. If I'd had to stay there forever, I'd have found a way to stay happily. As your wife. Because, just like here, you're still one of the greatest guys I've ever known."

Pondered my next statements carefully. Everyone was walking around Chuckie as if they were stepping on eggshells. And I'd been worried about Chuckie's reactions to the truth, too, in part because everyone else was worried. But, despite what Buchanan and Jeff said, I knew Chuckie better than anyone else alive. And while everyone wanted to tell me Chuckie would go all Mr. Hyde on me if he knew what was really going on, I was the one with the life experience with him, and I didn't buy it. Charles in the other universe hadn't flipped out and, as I'd just said, they were basically the same guy. Time to treat my best friend *like* my best friend.

I took his hands in mine. "But I do know why everyone's acting weird around you."

"So, tell me."

"See, here's the thing. Remember when Joey Tucci had asked me to the Senior Prom and you knew he planned to rape me if I didn't say yes to having sex with him somewhere during the night?"

"Yeah," he growled. "I was scared as hell to tell you, because I wasn't sure if you'd believe me, or hate me for ruining your expected good time, but I had to."

"Right. You told me because you loved me and trusted me to listen to you. You told me I couldn't react the way I'd want to. And I did listen to you and I didn't go kick him in the balls or run him over with my dad's car."

"Yeah. You told him you'd gotten asked by someone you liked more and were being kind and not leading him on. Then you asked me instead." He smiled at me. "That's probably my favorite high school memory."

"I'm fond of it, too."

"So, what's the thing you need to tell me that you don't want me overreacting to?"

Sent a small prayer up to ACE, Algar, Naomi, and any other superconciousnesses or superpowered beings who might be listening. "We've figured out who the Mastermind is."

Chuckie was quiet for a few long moments. "No one's told me. And everyone started acting strangely once the other Kitty was here. So, that means there was a Mastermind in the world she was from, doesn't it?"

"Got it in one. It was very *Age of Apocalypse* there. People who were good here were bad there and vice versa. People dead here were alive there and vice versa again. But some people were exactly the same, both good and bad."

"Yes, we got a lot of that from the other you." I could see the wheels turning in Chuckie's brain. "So, the Mastermind there is someone I know here, and probably trust, because otherwise, why keep this information from me?" He looked stricken. "I'm not the Mastermind there, am I? Him, I mean."

"Dude, seriously, why are you so down on yourself? No, of course you're not the Mastermind there, any more than you are here. But to be sure of the overriding theory . . . did you participate in a mail-in chess competition before I met you?"

He nodded. "In grade school. I won. The people who ran the contest were thrilled. They made a huge deal about it, and I told my teacher, who told the class." His face clouded. "And that was when I learned, definitively, that being known as the smartest person around was the fastest way to being the butt of every joke, the focus of every bully, and more, all of it bad."

Well, that was exactly how it had gone down for the Chuckie in the other universe, so this wasn't a surprise. It was, however, a confirmation. And the proof that my last hopeful doubts were going to be dashed. "Let's talk about that some more. Was there anyone who might have, oh, protested your win?"

"Yeah," he said slowly. "I haven't thought about this in years, but now that you mention it, there was someone who was just a little older than me, in high school, I think. He protested my win, for quite a while."

"Did you ever learn his name?"

Chuckie shook his head. "No. We were both minors, so his name was kept out of it. He came in second, but refused to accept, so they never shared his name with me."

"But yours was shared."

"Yes. I won and my parents and I gave them permission. What does this have to do with anything, or are you just enjoying reminiscing?"

"Oh, it's really significant. Same as for your counterpart in the other universe. Probably in all the universes, but I don't have enough data to guess."

The wheels were once again spinning. "You're saying that this person, whoever it was, became the Mastermind?"

"Yeah, I am. He turned that loss into a lifelong hatred of and competition with you, which grew into a full-blown mania by the time he was an adult."

"So, we just need to figure out who that was in this world, and we'll know who the Mastermind is." He looked at me closely. "And everyone else has figured this out. Because the me in that world knew who this guy was, didn't he?"

"He did. And Other Me did, too, therefore. They didn't know he was the Whack-A-Mole King of Lunatic Take Over the World Plans, but they knew who your lifelong enemy was. I mean, they know he was their Mastermind now, because we had to take him out before I came back. But they didn't know until we switched places."

"The Great Mommy Switch, as your counterpart called it, was good for a few things, wasn't it?" He took a deep breath. "I could start guessing, but I think it's going to be better if you tell me straight out who the Mastermind is. And, before you ask, I promise you that I'm going to do what you want—react like you did when you found out what Tucci was planning, not how I'm sure I'm going to want to react."

Took my own deep breath. "Okay. Dude, just remember two things. One—everyone else is going to kill me if you go into Wolverine's Patented Berserker Rage. And two—everyone else loves and cares about you. Everyone. Even the guys who act all tetchy about your authority. They may have the Alpha Male head-butt fights with you, but they still care about you. So, you're not alone in this, okay? We are all, and I do mean all, here for you."

Chuckie looked pale. "This is going to be worse than I think it is, isn't it?"

"Yeah. You're gonna hate it." Sent another prayer up to the various Powers That Be, and then took the plunge. "The Mastermind is, for certain, Cliff Goodman."

CHAPTER 5

CHUCKIE WAS QUIET, which was a good sign. I hoped. Hard as it was not to run my yap nervously, I allowed him to process what I'd said by keeping said yap firmly shut.

After a good long minute, he swallowed. "So, you're saying that the man I think is my best friend, the man I was going to have be my best man at my wedding, the one guy I think 'gets me,' that man is actually the person responsible for my wife's death?"

"And every other action against us and you, specifically. Yes, that's what I'm saying."

"Ah."

Cleared my throat. "Ah, do I have to tackle you before you make a mad dash for The Retribution Railroad?"

He shook his head slowly. "No. I understand why no one wanted to tell me. And . . . I can't tell you how much I appreciate that you were the one to break this news to me. Alone."

"You need to go to a workout room and hit something and maybe scream a lot?"

"No. I want to save the rage. I know that's what you do these days—you use the rage to control your power, to ensure you're mad enough to kill if you have to."

"Yeah, I do—"

The door slammed open, rudely interrupting me, and Jeff, Buchanan, and Gower were there. Gower was built like Jeff and Buchanan—big and buff. He was also black, bald, beautiful, and Reader's husband. More pertinently in this situation, he was the Supreme Pontifex of the A-C's religion. Why he was with Jeff and Buchanan wasn't hard to guess—bring the head religious man when you have someone about to totally lose it.

All of them looked worried and ready to tackle someone. And all three of them came to a screeching halt, looking confused.

Chuckie managed a small smile. "Sorry, Jeff. Yes, I'm sure my emotions are off the charts. But as I just told Kitty, I've spent a lifetime banking anger and turning it into something that works in my favor."

Gower came and sat on Chuckie's other side. "Chuck, seriously, I'm here for you, we all are."

"I know, Paul. And I appreciate that, truly. But Kitty needs to debrief us and we need to do the same for her."

The three other men looked like they didn't believe it could be this easy. "Ah, are you sure?" Jeff asked. "Because, trust me, you don't feel like you're banking anger or turning it into something useful. You're ready to kill."

"I am." Chuckie stood up. "You just have no idea how many times throughout my life I've wanted to kill someone who's wronged me, or Kitty. I know the expectation was that I'd go on a rampage, and, honestly, if Kitty hadn't told me what was going on privately that could have happened. But . . . we have a history of this, of watching each other's backs, of giving each other the bad news the other one doesn't want to hear but has to. I'll be okay."

"Really?" Buchanan sounded no more convinced than Jeff had.

"Really." Chuckie's eyes glittered. "What you all forget is that I'm both an extremely patient person and I've been in covert and clandestine ops for my entire adult life. You don't rise up in the C.I.A. by losing it anytime something goes wrong or someone tries to kill you or kills someone on your team or someone who you care about. You rise up in the Agency by being smart enough to solve problems off-book, without any dirt flying back onto you or anyone else you need to protect."

Gower nodded. "You're much less . . . impulsive than, say, Jeff is."

"Anyone is less impulsive than Jeff," Chuckie said with a laugh. The others laughed, too, and I felt the room relax. "Understand—I'm *going* to kill him. But I'll do it when it's not going to cause us all more problems than it solves. It's going to be slow, horrific, and as painful as I can possibly make it. And I'm going to make sure he knows it's me who's killing him, and that I know why he deserves to die. *But*, that won't happen until, as I said, it's in a place or a way that doesn't ruin all of us."

"What do you think?" Buchanan asked Jeff.

Who cocked his head. I could tell he was concentrating on Chuckie. Jeff nodded slowly. "When you're with Kitty, you really can't hide your emotions from me. Naomi could, and did, hide them from me when you two were falling in love, and you're pretty good at it when you're not with Kitty. But when you are you're almost as clear a read as she is."

"That's good, I guess," Chuckie said.

Jeff nodded. "It is. Chuck's under control," he said to Buchanan. "For now." He turned back to Chuckie. "But you and we need to be on guard—because that control feels tenuous. And it's going to be tested the moment you see Goodman again."

Chuckie shrugged. "I never did anything to you when you essentially took Kitty from me. I won't do anything to him until it's the right time."

"Hey, I thought we were past that." Jeff sounded hurt.

Chuckie walked over and clapped Jeff on the shoulder. "We are. Well past that. And I was glad of it before but I'm incredibly grateful now that you, not Cliff, were my best man. Thank you for that, Jeff. So much."

Jeff pulled Chuckie in and hugged him tightly. Gower joined them. Group hugs were really an A-C thing, and I didn't mind them. But I knew better than to add into the Bro Hug right now. Chuckie didn't need me there, because I knew without asking that him crying would be a bad thing all the way around, and I was pretty sure he was close to breaking down right now.

Buchanan knew better, too. He stepped closer to me. "This solves the biggest issue. But we still have an entire set of people who cannot lie who know that Goodman is the Mastermind. We have to debrief each other and then move swiftly, before Goodman catches on and escalates whatever it is he's planning now."

"Death ray. I'm telling you, that's what he's working on."

"So you said. However, where the death ray is remains our first mystery."

The others broke apart. "What's this about a death ray?" Chuckie asked.

"Debriefing," Buchanan said in a tone that brooked no argument. "Now. And not here, either. I want everyone back in the Embassy. We can go there first, before any help is offered to Gideon Cleary."

Both Chuckie and Gower looked lost. "What?" Gower asked.

"It's the usual long story. But I agree with Malcolm. Let's tell our stories at home." Looked around. "By the way, where is Jamie?"

"I left her with your parents," Jeff said. "Who also need this debriefing. Just like everyone else."

"What about those who didn't know that Kitty switched universes?" Chuckie asked.

"I'm back. We can share the wonder that was my adventure in another world with them, since it's hugely relevant. They work with us—they'll all roll with the punches."

Jeff hit the intercom button in the room. "We need a voice activated system put into all Bases," he said, more to himself than anyone else.

"Yes, Mister Vice President?" Melissa asked.

"Melissa, please advise Commander Reader that we need all Washington, D.C., NASA Base, Euro Base, and Dulce Base personnel to vacate Sydney Base immediately. Dulce Base personnel should go to the American Centaurion Embassy. All others should go to their home Bases."

"Is everything alright, sir?" Melissa sounded worried.

"Yes, we just need to get back to work on a variety of pressing issues. And the President wants me home, pronto."

"I'll take care of it, Mister Vice President. I'll advise Launch to expect you all."

"Thanks, Melissa." Jeff hit the intercom button again to close the line. "Let's get packed up and back home so we can stay ahead of the latest situation that is laughingly called our normal lives. Ah, baby, why don't you stay here and help Chuck pack up?"

Chuckie laughed. "She doesn't have to ride herd on me, Jeff, but if it'll make you feel better, I'm fine with it."

Jeff gave me a quick kiss, then he and the other men headed out. I shook my head. "I'd ask if I'd jumped into another universe if this wasn't the only one where I know Jeff is on Earth."

"You're sure of that?" Chuckie asked me, as he went to the closet and pulled out a small rolling suitcase.

"As sure as I can be. I've seen what I call the Universe Wheel before—every time I've almost died. But I never remembered it until Operation Bizarro World happened."

"Huh. Well, hopefully that knowledge will give us an edge, even if it's a small one."

"A girl can dream."

"Yeah." He checked the suitcase. As I'd expected, it was already packed. The Operations Team, aka Algar, King of the Elves, was good that way. "Kitty . . . do you think that maybe my role in the greater existence is to be the guy who's never happy?"

Went to him and hugged him tightly. "No. You're happy in all the other universes I saw, even the ones where we aren't married to each other. And, I promise you—you'll be happy again in this universe, too. Even if I have to move heaven and earth for that to happen."

He hugged me back. "Well, as long as you're still my friend, I'm good."

"I'll always be your friend, Chuckie. In this world and all the others."

He kissed my forehead. "And thank God for that."

CHAPTER 6

I'D HAVE LIKED TO have taken a look around Sydney Base, but since Other Me had done the full tour, me wanting one would sort of scream suspicious, concussion excuse or no concussion excuse.

On the other hand, it was nice to be heading home. It would be the afternoon of the day before today. Decided not to worry about it. Also decided that I would be within my jet-lagged rights to ask for one of Jeff's mother's brownies when we arrived. We hadn't had breakfast, after all.

Sydney Base's launch area was just like all the other Bases'—lots and lots of gates, those unlovely contraptions that looked like airport metal detectors but felt like hell on earth to step through, at least for me.

Happily, Jeff carried me though the gate, just like always. And I had to admit, after not knowing if I'd ever use a gate again in my life, even the nausea wasn't as bad as it could have been. Of course, I was also very glad we hadn't eaten yet, because the transfer from Sydney to D.C. was a long one, relatively speaking.

Since anyone at the Embassy who wasn't "in the know" didn't know I'd been gone, our homecoming was somewhat anticlimactic. However, for me, it was great to come back. After all this bouncing around, I was truly able to look at the Embassy as home. Figured that probably meant we'd be moving again soon, because that was always the way things worked for me since I'd joined up with the gang from Alpha Four.

The Embassy was a full city block wide and long, and we

had a raised walkway that attached to the building "next door," which we'd nicknamed the Zoo, meaning we lived in two gigantic multi-story buildings. Normally I found our apartment—which took up half of the top floor of the Embassy—to be overly gigantic. But today it felt normal, possibly because I'd just spent time seeing how large Other Me's house was.

Jamie grabbed my hand and dragged me to the room next to our bedroom. "Mommy, look at my new room!" She flung the door open and pulled me in.

Managed not to gape, but only just. The room was Jamie's typical Shrine to Pink, and had all four dog beds, all the cat and Poof condos, and a lot of sleeping hammocks I realized were for the Peregrines, mostly because some of them were snoozing in said hammocks when we arrived. Those were new, but apparently very much appreciated by the avians.

Before I could give any comment on the room, however, the animals were on me, howling, purring, squawking, and generally letting me know that they'd missed me and I needed to pet each and every one of them right now if not sooner. As I was mobbed, noted that what seemed like every Peregrine or Poof—of which we had an almost uncountable number by now—had joined us in the room.

"The pets missed you, Mommy," Jamie said, presumably in cased I'd missed this somehow.

"I can tell. Give me a second, sweetheart, before I admire your pretty room." Looked over at Jeff as I gave Dudley the Great Dane, and Duke the Labrador vigorous pets. "Other Me approved the new digs?"

He nodded as I moved from the boy dogs to the girl dogs and gave Dottie, our Dalmatian, and Duchess, our Pit Bull, the same enthusiastic petting. "Everyone else says it was past time."

"I'm not complaining." I wasn't. Putting Jamie elsewhere literally hadn't occurred to me as a necessary thing to do. Was glad Other Me had taken care of some Normal Mommy things while we were switched.

Dogs handled, it was time to give the cats some love. Sugarfoot jumped into my arms to demand his snuggles. Once he was somewhat satisfied I handed him off to Jeff and picked up Candy and Kane and gave them lots of snuggling.

Pets from my parents and youth somewhat mollified

first, chose to go for the smaller numbers next. "I see my Peregrines are all in attendance for the Reunion Revival!" Peregrines were Alpha Four birds that looked like peacocks and peahens on steroids. They were bred for protection and could go chameleon along with having the typical A-C hyperspeed.

We had twelve mated pairs hanging out in the Embassy, otherwise known as Earth's Alpha Four Principality, and all twenty-four of them hooted.

"Can I get a bird amen?" I raised my arms up.

More hoots and all wings up and flapping.

"Can I get *another* bird amen?" I waved my hands around, arms still up in the air.

Much louder hoots and all twenty-four flew up a little ways off the ground.

"Awesome! Gimme feather, everyone! Up high, down low, and double dutch!"

The Peregrines landed and trotted to me, one by one, to do hand and wing high fives up, down, and with both hands and wings. Each one got a scritchy-scatch between their wings, too.

This took some time, but the Peregrines, like the dogs and cats, seemed much happier.

This left only the Poofs. Poofs were presumed to be Alpha Four animals, but during Operation Infiltration I'd discovered that they were actually Black Hole Universe animals. This meant they had powers no one but one being fully understood. So far, said powers had saved our butts more than once. Of course said being was a Free Will Fanatic of the highest order, so the Poofs tended to act on their own initiative, and their own initiative was sometimes very different from what we'd all like.

The Poofs were normally small bundles of fluffy fur with no visible ears or tails, tiny paws, and black button eyes. They could also go Jeff-sized in a moment, complete with mouths of razor-sharp teeth. Small, they were the cutest things you'd ever seen in your life. Large, they were among the scariest cute things you'd ever seen in your life.

The Poofs were androgynous and considered to be pets of the Alpha Four Royal Family—of which Jeff's family, Christopher White, and the Gowers were all a part—and supposedly only mated when a Royal Wedding was imminent.

Wouldn't know it from Earth Poofs, though. We had and continued to have a Poof population explosion. Poofs bonded to whoever named them, and they weren't totally discerning about what name they decided was "theirs," meaning we had a lot of people who had their own Poof these days. Most of those weren't here, but some had dropped by to say "Welcome Home." All the unattached Poofs lived in the Embassy, because I said so, meaning there were a *lot* of Poofs in the room. Decided there was only one good way to deal with greeting them all.

Fell back onto Jamie's bed. "Poofies, come to Kitty!"

I was immediately enveloped by a blanket of fluffy adorableness. That was me, always taking one for the team.

While the Poofs and I had a massive Group Snugglefest, I checked out Jamie's room. Looked a lot like her old room, which had been the nursery attached to the master bedroom, but there were some differences. However, none of those differences were anything to worry about from a parental standpoint.

"I think your room is great, Jamie-Kat."

She beamed and joined me and the Poofs on the bed. "I'm so glad you like it, Mommy!" She picked something up and showed it to me—a stuffed, pink, striped cat that said "Paris, je t'aime" in a little heart on its chest. "And look! You and Daddy brought this home to me from Paris! I named him Stripes!"

My throat got tight, for a couple of reasons. The first being the realization that we almost never thought to bring Jamie back anything from anywhere we went while on missions, meaning Other Me was still winning the Good Mother Competition she and I weren't really having with each other. I hadn't realized Jamie wanted a new room, hadn't thought to bring her a present, and pretty much was going to see her for five minutes here then send her to daycare. Well, not today. She was involved in what had happened—probably more than anyone other than me truly realized—and she was going to be with us today, briefing or no briefing. Presuming Jeff didn't freak out about it.

The second realization, however, was that I'd never see Stripes, the awesome, kick-butt cat I'd rescued and made part of the family in the other universe, or anyone else from said other universe ever again.

Felt tears coming and blinked as rapidly as possible to keep them in my eyes and not let Jamie think I was unhappy to be home or with anything she'd done.

Jeff, of course, picked up what was going on immediately. He gently moved the Poofs off of me and picked me up. "It's okay, baby," he said quietly. "It's normal to feel like this."

"But I'm so glad to be home."

"I know. But they were all yours in that other world, too. Your Cosmic Alternate got attached to us, and while I know she's overjoyed to be home, I'm sure she's missing us a little bit, too. It's normal, and it doesn't mean you love any of us less. You attach to people quickly, and they do so with you just as fast. It's a loss, and you're allowed to grieve."

Buried my face in Jeff's chest for a minute and let his heartbeats soothe me like they always did. Finally felt back in some kind of control. "We don't have time for me to miss them right now. Their major problem is handled. Ours is still out there."

He kissed the top of my head. "That's my girl." Jeff sighed. "I know you . . . don't want to send Jamie to Daycare. I'm not so sure that's a good idea."

"Maybe not. But she's more aware of what happened than I think you realize."

"No, we realize. It's just . . ."

"It's okay, Daddy," Jamie said, as she came to us. Jeff picked her up so we could do a family hug. "It won't scare me."

"I'm sure it won't, Jamie-Kat," Jeff lied, as poorly as ever. "But we're going to be discussing grownup things that little girls shouldn't have to worry about."

"You mean like how Mommy was gone and is back?"

I made the coughing sound. "I think, as I said, she's more aware of what went on than you are, Jeff."

He looked worried. "But she's just a little girl." He sounded even more worried. "She shouldn't have these worries shoved onto her."

I leaned up and kissed his cheek. "And you and Christopher shouldn't have had to become men at age ten, either. Sometimes, we can't stop those things, we can only do what we can to protect those who are being forced to grow up too fast."

"I'm taking Stripes with me," Jamie announced. "He's the cat for the job."

This earned her some extremely hurt looks from all the animals, cats especially. "It's okay," I told them. "None of you were with me in the other universe. I found a cool cat, named Stripes, to help cover the kick-butt animal side of things. She saw him, I'm sure. Loving a stuffed animal in no way lessens the love for the real animals. I promise."

Once again, the animals seemed somewhat appeased. Took a good look at them. "Did we lose a Poof somehow?" Had no idea why I thought we were down by one Poof—frankly, we had so many that we could have been down by a hundred Poofs and I shouldn't have been able to tell. But I was sure we were missing one.

Harlie and Poofikins mewled and jumped up and down.

"Oh. Really? Well, that's great then. And kind of awesome, too."

"What's great?" Jeff asked, in the tone of a man who's long since stopped asking himself how his life got this crazy, but still wonders anyway.

"Other Me named and bonded with a Poof, and it went with her into the other universe. Which is great, because now Harlie won't be alone there."

"What? Excuse me?" Jeff was speaking for himself and Harlie both.

Heaved another sigh. "Onward to the briefing. Everyone. Animals, too, I guess."

CHAPTER 7

THE EMBASSY'S CONFERENCE room was a relatively recent addition, created because Pierre—our Concierge Majordomo and the most competent man on the planet— had gotten really tired of us having all of our meetings in the ballroom.

However, since we were doing an all-hands meeting, the ballroom was once again called into service. Nostalgia was good sometimes, right?

By the time we got there the ballroom was packed with people. Thankfully, there was food and drink in evidence, probably because Pierre was clear on how I rolled. Alpha Team, Airborne, all Embassy staff, and my parents were here, along with a few others who were closely attached to Centaurion Division in some way. Hacker International, including the Queen of All Hackers, Chernobog, had even broken down and left their happy home in the Zoo and joined us in person, instead of video conferencing. And, completing our Team Ensemble, Olga and Adriana from the Romanian Embassy and Mr. Joel Oliver were in attendance. Pretty much everyone looked tired and stressed.

Jamie squirmed out of Jeff's arms and ran to Mom and Dad, who were next to Reader and Gower, meaning Jamie was going to bask in the glow of four of her favorite people in the world. Couldn't complain about her choice.

"Where's Bruce Jenkins?" I asked as I completed my headcount and Rajnish Singh, our Embassy Public Relations Minister, handed me a briefing sheet and an envelope.

"We're waiting to brief him," Raj said. "Please read what

I just gave you. I know you never like to read briefing materials, but this time, it'll help."

"Read the letter, too," Buchanan said. "As for Jenkins, Mister Joel Oliver's been proven far longer. Anyone not here isn't here for a reason."

"Um, Christopher and Amy aren't here. And neither is Kevin. Are they not here for a reason?" What had gone on in the time I was away? Kevin Lewis was our Defense Attaché and my mother's right-hand man in the Presidential Terrorism Control Unit. It had been unsurprising to find out that Other Me hadn't known Mom was in covert and clandestine ops. I hadn't known until I'd met the Gang from A-C, after all.

Frankly, I wanted to hug Mom for a long time. And then do the same with half the room, starting with Kevin and his wife, Denise, who was in here. Realized all the Embassy Daycare kids were in here, too, with their parents. Interesting. Buchanan must have come to the same conclusion I had—the kids were targets, involved, more in the know than the adults realized, and needed to be aware of what was coming. This probably put me and Buchanan both on the list of Worst Adults to Care for Children Ever, but we were at war, even if it was a very sneaky, small, focused war.

"They're securing a prisoner," Evalyne, the head of my personal Secret Service detail, shared. "One of our team was determined to be—" She looked at Chuckie and stopped herself. "Anti-alien."

"Malcolm, can I speak safely and freely?"

"Go ahead, Missus Chief."

"Okay. Hey gang, it's great to see you all again." The room quieted. Go me. "For those who might not know, I spent the last couple of weeks in Bizarro World and so did the person who you thought was me. She *was* me, in that sense, but me from another universe. We're both home in our proper universes now, go team. Anyone who didn't know this, raise your hands."

A lot more hands went up than I'd been prepared for, including all of the Secret Service. "Ah. Okay. Those waving your hands in the air like you just don't care, turn to whoever is next to you with no hands up and have them explain what I'm talking about. We'll wait. Oh, and while we wait,

Chuckie already knows the Horrible Truth, so no euphemisms or talking around the issue needed."

"What horrible truth?" Doreen Coleman-Weisman asked. Her hand was up, and she didn't look happy about it. Couldn't blame her. Doreen's parents had been the former heads of the Diplomatic Corps. They were traitors, and had been eaten by our core set of Poofs during Operation Confusion. Doreen wasn't a traitor, however, and she was also the only truly trained diplomat on staff. And yet the rest of the A-Cs, Doreen included, still insisted I remain the Chief of Mission here. Aliens were both weird and sometimes very unaware of the best choices for certain jobs.

"We now know, without a doubt, who the Mastermind is. Oh, and I know other things pretty much no one else does, because other universe and all that. But I'd really like to tell the story of My Amazing Journey once to the team, so I'm waiting for Christopher, Amy, and Kevin. Unless they aren't able to leave our resident bad guy alone."

The Peregrines flapped their wings at me, and then all the males other than Bruno disappeared.

"We're here," Christopher said a few seconds later, as our three missing people zipped into the room. Hyperspeed was the best—and Amy and Kevin, despite being humans, weren't barfing thanks to the Hyperspeed Dramamine that our Embassy doctor, Tito Hernandez, had created. "The Peregrines are handling prisoner guard duty."

"Which prisoner?"

"Sam Travis. He was part of your Secret Service detail, remember?"

"Ah . . ." I'd paid a lot more attention to the gals on my detail than the guys. Go me for not paying attention to things that mattered. Again.

Christopher cocked his head at me. "Oh. Welcome home."

Amy looked at me closely and heaved a sigh. "Really glad you're here."

Looked up at Jeff. "Really? You didn't let them know I was back?"

He rolled his eyes. "Pardon me for being so caught up and relieved that the love of my life was returned to me that I selfishly kept the news to myself for all of twelve hours."

"Well, when you put it like that, all is forgiven."

"I'm so relieved." Jeff's sarcasm knob was heading for eleven on the one-to-ten scale. Chose to not try to up the sarcasm ante, mostly because we really had a lot of briefing to do.

We sat and I threw Raj a bone and read his briefing sheet while others explained the cosmic shift that had taken place.

Along with the usual blah, blah, blah that exemplified why I never read the briefing papers, apparently Other Me had been busy in my absence. We were now besties with the Australian Prime Minister and his wife, Jamie had a dress from them that was a family heirloom of sorts, and Other Me and Jeff had hit Paris to find presents and also apparently discover a new recording artist. I wasn't overly surprised that said artist turned out to be Amadhia—Other Me had owned far too many of that gal's T-shirts for me to believe she wouldn't want to find said recording artist in this world. I mean, if there had been no Aerosmith in her universe I'd have done my best to find them and insist they make up for lost time. And it had apparently worked out, since she, like me, had been at an Amadhia concert when the switch back to our own worlds had happened.

Despite Buchanan's insistence, the letter I chose to save for later. The handwriting was my own, and it was addressed to *My Cosmic Alternate*. I was pretty sure who'd written it. I'd written a letter to Other Me, too. Nice to know we'd both gone out of our way for each other. But then again, we were us, so that was to be expected.

Chose to get back to the briefing before my mind exploded from the contemplation of alternate universes. Also, everyone else was done sharing the wonder that had been the last couple of weeks and they were all looking at me.

"Ah, okay, everyone ready for what went on where I was?"

"Only if it's relevant to the current situation, girlfriend," Reader said, shooting me his cover boy grin. "With Chuck in the know and handling things, we need to formulate plans to take down the Mastermind sooner as opposed to later."

"Most of it's relevant." I'd tell the flyboys later that they were dead in that other world but that their buddy, William

Cox, was alive and on the side of right. Same with telling Tim Crawford, who'd replaced me as Head of Airborne, that instead of kicking butt daily he was a top teacher of little kids in Los Angeles. And, frankly, most of those who were dead in that other world probably didn't need to know about it, and those living other, more sedate lives didn't need to know about those, either.

"I know I'm dead in that world, kitten," Mom said, right on cue. "And we're clear that many who are evil in this world are good in that one, and vice versa."

"We also know there are no aliens there," Jeff said.

Wondered how to say this, but it was actually relevant to the issues at hand. "Ah. As to that, Jeff, you're not quite accurate."

CHAPTER 8

ALWAYS NICE TO GET the full room's attention. "Mind sharing what you mean?" Christopher asked, clearly speaking for everyone.

"Yes. Things on Alpha Four are very different in that universe. Ronald Yates never went to the bad. However, Adolphus' first assassination attempt against him was successful." Decided it would be easiest to keep eye contact with Mom for this next part. "The attack was on a high holy day for the Exonerates. Richard and Lucinda died in that attack, and Terry felt it all and died in Alfred's arms. Therefore, Yates never remarried, so Gladys Gower never existed."

"How do you know that?" Jeff asked quietly.

"I'm impressed she knows the name of our religion," Christopher muttered.

I chose to ignore Christopher, in part because I'd literally learned said name when I was in the other universe and didn't feel he needed that information. "I found the person Adolphus exiled to Earth. After Kitler had had Stanley Gower assassinated for treason, that is."

Cleared my throat and kept looking at my mother, in part because I could feel every A-C in the room tense up. "Alfred is alive and now much more well than he was. He was hiding in the underground tunnel system, but now he's living with Other Me and her family. He's the brains behind literally every advancement for the betterment of mankind that that world, and this one, has had. And that means, Mom, that we need to get the entire Martini clan under lock and key. Because the Mastermind will want what's in Alfred's brain, and I'm pretty sure he's aware that Alfred is the driving force behind most if not all A-C scientific advancements."

Mom nodded and looked to Kevin, who got up and stepped just outside of the room. He was on his phone before he reached the doorway.

"You can look at us," Jeff said quietly again. "Yes, everyone's upset, but that's another world from this one, baby."

"A world our people don't exist in," Christopher added. He sounded both angry and sad. Couldn't blame him.

"True enough. And you're not the only ones who aren't there anymore."

"Yeah. Share that later, baby." Was pretty sure that Jeff had read my mind and emotions and knew who else wasn't alive in Other Me's world.

"On the plus side, Harlie was with Alfred when I found him and, based on the news that a Poof went with Other Me back into her universe, I think they're set up pretty well. Oh, and they're set up because we took out the Mastermind there, also known as Cliff Goodman, as well as his Queen Accomplice, LaRue Pick A Last Name."

"The ... other you said she'd never heard of LaRue," Amy said carefully.

"She hadn't. Over there, we figured that because Yates hadn't hit Earth there wasn't any other alien for her to hook up with and formulate evil plans alongside."

Noted everyone in the room running my last sentence back in their minds. "You mind explaining that?" Chuckie asked, presumably because he'd run the words back the fastest.

"Not at all. LaRue isn't a human. She's an Ancient who is also a Z'porrah spy." Mouths opened. I put my hand up. "I spoke with her. In person and, for the circumstances, at length. Believe me when I tell you that there's at least one Ancient, or Ancient Clone, now left on Earth. And LaRue was the real brains behind what the Mastermind in that world was doing, and that means the likelihood is high that she's also behind most everything that's gone on here."

"That makes sense," Lorraine said. She was still blonde and buxom, sitting next to her human husband, Joe Billings, with their hybrid son Ross on her lap. "She's got the scientific knowhow to have helped the Masterminds and their various associates move forward much more quickly than they could have alone."

Claudia nodded. "Ronald Yates or no Ronald Yates, he was our religious leader, not a scientist." She was a willowy brunette, and like Lorraine, was sitting next to her husband, Randy Muir, who had their son Sean on his lap. "I'm sure he was more advanced than some Earth scientists, but not like an Ancient would be. They're advanced far beyond any of us in either this solar system or our original one."

"But she's a shapeshifter, then," Serene Dwyer pointed out. Like the other two gals, she was next to her husband, Brian, but their son Patrick was crawling all over Matt Hughes, Chip Walker, and Jerry Tucker.

Nice to have all my main Dazzlers on Duty and my five flyboys back within arm's reach. And it was nice to have the sane version of Brian here, too. Decided I'd keep his bizarre fascination with me and flipped-out hatred for Chuckie in the other universe to myself. It was probably better for all concerned.

"So does that mean she could be anyone in this room?" Brian asked nervously. He was an astronaut in this world, and frankly pretty unflappable. But the news I was sharing was bizarre even by our standards, so I could understand where his concern was coming from.

"No. For whatever reason she seems really attached to the shape we're familiar with. Possibly because she's in deep cover and there are empaths around who might pick up her emotions about shifting."

"Makes sense, but you mentioned a death ray," Buchanan said, showing an impressive ability to focus on the key issues. Not that this came as a surprise.

"Yes. They had one. It was scary impressive. Created little piles of dust of whatever thing it zapped. And a gigantic crater when it exploded due to some, ah, malfunctions my team and I caused."

"Is that world safe?" Jeff asked. Wasn't surprised—he was a protector, after all, and even if he wasn't there, his father was, and our daughter was, at least in a sense. And Other Me was, too, and I was willing to bet he'd gotten at least somewhat attached to her.

"Yes, we destroyed Cliff, LaRue, the death ray, and all

the other bad guys. At least the ones we knew about. They're set up better than ever now, because Alfred's with them. They'll all be okay. We, however, cannot say the same."

"We have no proof," Richard White pointed out. He was Christopher's father, the former Supreme Pontifex of the A-Cs, and my partner on the rare occasions when I got to kick butt these days. He was also a younger, hotter version of Timothy Dalton. Realized I'd obviously missed all the gorgeousness I'd become accustomed to these past few weeks. "And we're going to need it, just in case."

Jeff nodded. "The President needs to be warned, if no one else."

"Vander, too," Serene pointed out. "And a host of other politicians near to us like Senator McMillan."

Tim, who was sitting between Jerry and Reader, shook his head. "Reynolds is right—if we don't have proof we're just accusing a high ranking public official who everyone in the world thinks is our friend of treason. That's going to backfire on us."

"Not everyone thinks he's our friend." This earned me everyone's attention again. "Oh, right. Most of you don't know. Gideon Cleary contacted us this morning, or whatever time it was over here when he called. Stephanie's taken off and he thinks she's hiding from her Secret Boyfriend. Who also just happens to be Cliff Goodman."

Most of the room groaned. "Does it get any better than this?" Reader asked.

The intercom came to life. "Excuse me, Ambassador," Walter said politely. "But Governor Cleary is calling for you. He suggested I patch him through via speakerphone."

"Well, James, we're about to find out how much better. Put him through, Walter."

CHAPTER 9

"**AMBASSADOR,** thank you for taking my call." Cleary sounded a little nervous, but nothing like he'd sounded when we'd spoken before.

"What can I do for you, Governor?" I knew he was calling in this way because Jeff had told him to. Assumed he had a bunch of people in the room with him just as I did, because this was the Public Show Call. Hoped Cleary had come up with a good excuse to get us down to Florida, because otherwise he was going to crash and burn in front of a whole lot of people. Mine wouldn't care, but his might.

"I have a problem I'm hoping you and the Vice President will be able and willing to help me solve."

So far so very good. Of course, his answer to my next question was going to determine if we continued to play nicely. "What problem is that, Governor?"

"I'd like to pass a bill that requires our colleges and universities to have better programs in place to ensure the safety of all students, our female ones in particular. My first efforts haven't been met with, shall we say, enthusiasm. I'd like to ensure that my next attempt goes through, and I believe we need to bring in outside help. I understand that you have someone on staff who initiated a similar program in Southern California with considerable success."

"We do indeed." Kyle Constantine, who, along with Len Parker, was one of my permanently assigned C.I.A. bodyguards, had started a variety of programs at USC after we'd met. He and Len had both been on USC's football team—

Len as quarterback and Kyle on the line—and they'd both given up promising NFL careers to work with us.

Kyle looked shocked, but Len grinned and punched him gently in the arm, and Adriana, who was a close friend with both of them, patted his hand.

"I was wondering if you and, perhaps, the Vice President would come down with your resident expert and whoever else you think could provide meaningful input, to help me draft a nonpartisan bill. I feel that it will have a better chance of passing if it has the Vice President's and your approval. And since you, as the wife of the Vice President, need to pick a cause to support, I'm hoping to inspire you to take this one up as yours, not just for my state but for the entire country."

I managed not to ask why I had to have a cause. Even I knew that both the First Lady and the Second Lady, or whatever my ridiculous title really was, had to find something to focus good deeds and such on. Had to hand it to Cleary—he'd chosen something that I actually cared about. And it was a non-alien cause, meaning that it would show that we cared about everyone in the country, not just those with two hearts and amazing good looks. I hated it when my enemies seemed less enemy-like and more like reasonable, potentially decent, people. It made hating them close to impossible.

"Governor, that sounds like a very strong possibility, both the cause and our coming down to assist you. I'm sure that the Vice President will need to ensure that the President can spare him. Let me get back to you, but, in the spirit of partisanship and showing that our administration and yours are able to work for the public good despite the election's outcome, I'll do my best to get us down to you as soon as we possibly can."

"Thank you. I truly appreciate this. Please stay in touch, and we'll be ready for you whenever you can spare the time."

We exchanged the usual call-ending pleasantries, then he hung up. "Caller is offline, Ambassador," Walter shared. "Just the com to Security opened."

"Well," Mom said, "I have to hand it to him—there's almost no way you can say no, and yet it's clear he's asking you for help. It's a win-win for everyone. So, what's the full story behind this?"

Buchanan did the honors and brought everyone else up to speed on our early-in-Australia's-morning call. While he did so, I made a list of who I figured we wanted down in Florida so that we could come up with the reasons why we were bringing them along. Why Chuckie had to come was going to take some explanations, let alone a few others, like the princesses, Rahmi and Rhee.

I wanted them with us for a simple reason: they were the best warriors out of the Alpha Centauri solar system and we might be fighting Cliff, Stephanie, the Death Ray, or God alone knew who or what else.

The princesses had been sent here from their home planet of Beta Twelve right before Jamie turned one, and due to whatever was going on in that solar system they had been left here ever since. I was fairly sure they'd been sent to both help us and protect themselves, but I wasn't a hundred percent sure. I was sure their mother expected me to train them in how to deal with men without killing them on sight, as well as how to deal diplomatically when possible. On Beta Twelve, I was considered incredibly diplomatic, apparently.

The women of Beta Twelve were Amazonian shapeshifters, meaning they had Ancient DNA in them. Also meaning that, realistically, Rahmi and Rhee would be people LaRue would want to get her hands on. Tried to remember if Cliff knew they were from another planet and couldn't. Had to figure he knew by now. One way or another, keeping tabs on the princesses was, if not Job One, certainly in the Job Top Five.

Because they were Queen Renata's daughters, they resembled her—Rahmi was the eldest, tall and brunette to Rhee's shorter blonde. When they'd first come they'd looked like every other woman from Beta Twelve I'd ever seen—very muscular in an attractive way, short, spiky hair, with slightly elongated limbs that looked out of proportion compared to a human or anyone from Alpha Four and larger and more elongated dark purple eyes.

However, I'd had them ensure they looked human while they were here. Over time, they'd altered themselves so that while they still resembled Renata they also—per everyone else, and my own eyes, now that I hadn't seen them for a few weeks—resembled me. It was flattering, really. In a kind of weird way, but that was pretty much par for our particular course.

Realized that while I could maybe say the princesses were attachés of some kind, or even babysitters for Jamie, they weren't going to be able to pass as part of our team of female protection specialists. They were probably the best *at* female protection, so to speak, but while they'd learned a lot since coming here, they weren't really able to pull off the diplomacy required not to ask why the women of Earth didn't just get rid of all the men attacking them, permanently.

Looked at the rest of my list. Sure Cleary wanted us down there and he'd be just fine with me bringing all of Alpha Team, supported by Airborne, along with at least half of the rest of those in the room, but we weren't sneaking down to Florida. We were going in a very obvious and photographable way. Meaning that anyone with half a brain would know something more was going on. And Cliff definitely had a whole, highly functioning brain.

Frankly, to make this work and not alert Cliff that something was going on, anyone past me, Jeff, Kyle, Len, and, possibly Tito was going to be suspect. We could sneak Tito in because he was both our Embassy doctor and a former UFC cage fighter, meaning he'd have professional input. Cliff would expect Buchanan to be with us, and of course Raj would be going to keep me from making my usual faux pas. Beyond that, though, what possible reasons would we have for bringing along everyone else?

Kevin came back in the room, interrupting my fretting. He was a human who gave the A-Cs a run for their money in the looks department. Tall, handsome, dark skinned, and with the best smile going, Kevin also had bags of charisma. He'd been a football player before my mom had recruited him, and still had the athletic build going strong.

He nodded to his wife and seated himself back by her. Denise matched him well—also tall, blonde, and gorgeous, with a matching killer smile and her own bags of charisma. I was only half joking any time I mentioned that if I had to go to Beta Twelve to live forever, Denise would be the mate I'd choose.

Yep, I'd missed all the hotness. And here I'd found all the beauty almost boring as much as a whole month ago. Wondered how Other Me was handling her return to the land of normal-looking people. Then again, she had Reader there, and Alfred, too, along with Buchanan. And Chuckie wasn't a slouch in the looks department, either. Presumed she'd find the will to go on with her concentrated number of close, personal hunks and decided to turn my ever-wandering mind back to the current relative conundrums.

I tried to, but the Lewis kids, Raymond and Rachel, were playing with Jamie, my dad, and Gower now. They were gorgeous, too, a beautiful blend of their parents, and also two of the sweetest kids in the world.

And in the world Other Me was in they were all dead. I couldn't get rid of Cliff Goodman and all his cronies in this world fast enough. Perhaps a frontal "kill 'em all" attack was the way to go.

"Calm down, baby," Jeff said softly. "They're fine here, and we're not going to let anyone take any of our friends from us."

"We've said that before. And been wrong. Dead wrong." We'd hit the Mastermind hard during Operation Infiltration but it had cost us. A lot.

"Wars are filled with casualties," Chuckie said quietly. "And we may be fighting in the shadows, but it's a war, Kitty. You know that."

"True enough." I'd been thinking the same only a few minutes earlier, after all.

"I think the first order of business," White said, "is to share our concerns with the President. Proof or no proof, he's an ally and needs to be on his guard, because if the Mastermind is after us, he's also after the President. Jeffrey, I'm sure Vincent would like you to advise him that you're back in the country, as well."

Jeff sighed. "True enough, Uncle Richard." He kissed my cheek. "Don't start the next offensive without me, baby. I'll be right back." He got up and, like Kevin before him, headed out of the room to make his call.

"Kitty, I know you want to take a big team down there," Serene said, "but I don't see how we can do that without giving away that we know something's up." She sounded like the sweetest airhead in the world saying this. I'd come to realize that Serene was the poster girl for the whole "still waters run deep" maxim. She was an accomplished imageer—so much so that she'd taken over as Head of Imageering when Christopher had come into the Embassy with us. But she was also a troubadour, a fact she kept secret from all but a few people.

Troubadours weren't considered impressive to the average A-C, because they were actors. But, of course, what actors did was lie believably and with conviction. Raj was a troubadour too, and Serene's right-hand man in the clandestine team she'd formed—the A-C version of the C.I.A.

So I recognized now when she was throwing me a leading question. "You're right, Serene. I've been thinking that, too. I guess a few of us should go down openly while the rest of the team goes in covertly. Wouldn't you agree, James?"

Reader been promoted to Head of Field for Centaurion Division at the same time as Serene, replacing Jeff. Jeff had been the Head of Field when I'd first met the gang, but supposedly wiser heads had shoved us into political and public-facing jobs. I still wondered what the hell was wrong with those people, but I'd long since given up complaining that I wanted to go back to my old job.

"I think that's going to be best, yeah," Reader replied. "Frankly, I'd like more information about what was really going on in Florida before we commit a lot of manpower to searching for a traitor who may or may not be having a crisis of conscience or a change of heart. Especially because she could be doing this as part of an elaborate trap."

"She very well might be," a familiar voice said. The entire room jumped, because we hadn't seen him and no one thought he was in the room. Well, everyone other than Buchanan jumped. And every guy who wasn't Buchanan and packed heat had a gun out and pointed at the man who'd spoken.

Benjamin Siler pushed off the wall he'd apparently been leaning against. "But there's a real possibility she's having reactions to having been ordered to murder eight people. And you can't afford to bet a hundred percent either way."

"Nightcrawler, good to see you. Why did you go all chameleon on us?"

He grinned. "Sometimes I like to make an entrance."

CHAPTER 10

EVERYONE PUT THEIR guns away, though not without a lot of glaring. Siler seemed completely unfazed, not that this shocked me.

"Martini let me in," Siler said with a laugh as Jeff returned to the ballroom.

"Yeah, I went to my office to talk to Vince and saw him at the side entrance. Why is everyone so damn tense?"

"Siler slipped in without our knowing," Christopher snapped.

"I knew he was here," Buchanan said calmly, as Christopher shot Patented Glare #3 at him and I enjoyed the comfort of truly being home. No one in Other Me's world was close to matching Christopher in the glaring department.

Jeff shook his head. "He's not our enemy. But he has insight into how some of our enemies think."

"No argument," Reader said. "So, Siler, what's your recommendation on how we handle the Stephanie situation?"

Everyone sat down, though Siler and Buchanan both remained standing. "You need to have a small group that goes down and just deals with the governor and his supposed issue. You need another group that goes down and openly searches. Then you need several small commando teams to do the actual reconnaissance."

"We're not at war," Amy said. Others in the room nodded their heads.

"Wrong," I replied before anyone else could. "We are." As I said this, I felt something heavy on my feet. Whatever it was, it didn't feel like fur, feathers, or Jamie. And I could see Jamie, who'd moved from Mom and Dad over to Gower, who was bouncing her on his knee.

While Siler and others started explaining the war situation to Amy and the others who somehow had a rosy outlook, I risked a look under the table. My purse was on my feet, and since I'd left it in our rooms when we'd gotten back to the Embassy this was likely to mean one thing and one thing only—Algar had deigned to take an interest. But if he was doing so now, that meant something was about to happen. That this something was going to be bad was a given.

"Battle stations!" I shouted as I grabbed my purse and flung it over my neck.

As rallying cries went, this was a good one. For a fort, a submarine, or a battle cruiser. Only we had no actual battle stations in the Embassy. On the other hand, superfast people and those who work with them on a daily basis tend to react swiftly when any kind of cry like this is shouted out.

As everyone started to move, however, something freaky happened. And, considering that nothing normal had happened to me since I'd joined up with Centaurion Division, this was saying a lot.

Light encircled and surrounded me and several of the others. Light from nowhere inside the Embassy. The light was multicolored and flashy, bright but still easy to see through. It didn't hurt, but the light seemed intent on keeping me inside it, as if I was in some sort of tube made of the light.

I couldn't really move, and I could tell that others couldn't, either. But not all the others. Those kept stationary all looked similar—like they were flickering images instead of people. I was in a good position to see pretty much the entire room, which was nice, since my head was also invited to the immobilized portion of the current festivities.

Jeff had tried to lunge for Jamie when I'd shouted—I could tell by where he was looking and how his body was arched when the light surrounded him. He wasn't going anywhere, though. Neither were Christopher, Chuckie, Reader, Gower and Jamie, Tim, Tito, Kevin, the flyboys, Lorraine, Claudia, Serene and Brian, and Abigail Gower, the youngest and now only other remaining Gower sibling.

The princesses were also flickering. Unlike everyone else in the room, however, they didn't look freaked out. They looked worried, and somewhat anticipatory, but not afraid.

Len and Kyle were running for me, Amy was about to grab Christopher, and others were aiming for the rest of us. "No!" Siler thundered, as he body slammed the boys so that they flew into White, who didn't go down, but steadied them. "Don't touch them!"

Those not flickering like an old movie froze. "What's happening to them?" Denise cried out as she held onto Raymond and Rachel and the three of them stared at Kevin with looks of terror on their faces.

"Kitty, is this the death ray?" Buchanan asked, voice shaking just a bit. Noted that Siler had zipped back after knocking the boys aside and was holding him back, presumably to keep Buchanan from diving for me or Jamie.

"Hardly." It was fairly easy to move my mouth. Well, that was nice for me—I worked best when I could run my yap, after all. "We'd be dust piles now. No idea what this is, but it's not from the other universe."

"Yes," Raj said slowly, "I'd bet it probably is. But we've seen it in this one, too. Kitty, think *Star Trek*," Raj sounded soothing, which meant he was working his troubadour magic, because he didn't look relaxed. "You look like you're all being beamed somewhere."

The princesses' expressions told me what I needed to make a very educated guess. "Alpha Centauri." Thought about it. "That's why it's taking so long, isn't it?" Much harder to beam someone from one solar system to another, and I had to assume we didn't have a spaceship floating over Earth because someone would have mentioned that to us. At the top of their lungs.

The A-Cs in the room who weren't in a beam of light all nodded. "That makes sense," White said. "This wasn't something on Alpha Four when we left, however, Missus Martini." White always called me Mrs. Martini when things were rolling. Clearly he was guessing that at least one of us was about to go into action. But, based on the lights, not both of us. Interesting. In a freaky way.

"Why?" Buchanan asked. "Why are they trying to take them? And why not take the entire room? Why these people specifically?" Buchanan was echoing my thoughts, but I didn't have an answer, either.

The reply didn't come from me, the princesses, or White.

It came from Mom. "There's only one reason these specific people would be taken."

"I agree for the most part," White said. Apparently he and Mom were on a wavelength no one else was. Well, go them. "But why Abigail?"

"Not sure . . ." Mom looked at Rahmi. "How bad was the political situation when you left?"

"Bad. Very bad. As Kitty has surmised, it must have been why our mother sent us to you."

"And now she wants you back," White said, sounding as worried as I felt. My daughter was being beamed somewhere, and she wasn't with me or her father. Gower had her in his arms and held against his chest, so at least she wasn't alone. Jamie didn't look scared. Gower did, but she didn't. She looked excited.

"This is not our technology," Rhee said. "Though this was how we were sent to you before."

"Whose tech was it?" White asked.

"The Planetary Council's," Rahmi replied. "But why would others be taken, beyond my sister and me?"

"Because of what's going on and why." Mom replied. "Kitty, the people being taken are significant. You need to be prepared—"

But whatever we needed to be prepped for I was going to have to figure out on my own, because the light stopped flashing, went solid and opaque, and my body tingled as if I was pixelating.

Had to figure I was. Truly, the fun around here never stopped.

CHAPTER 11

REALLY HOPED I'D be put back together correctly when-ever we got wherever we were going, but I didn't count on it.

This was unlike any other way I'd traveled the cosmos in the past. Traveling via ACE remained the most pleasant—just a gentle tug and then you Time Warped wherever and got a lovely view at the same time. The Universe Wheel was weird but weightless, and at least interesting, albeit freaky beyond belief. Superconsciousness Express wasn't so bad when they moved you, too. Even the gates, while nauseat-ing, were, by now, normal. For the freak world I lived in, but whatever, still normal.

This was very different. I definitely wasn't standing on anything, nor was I lying on anything, yet I still couldn't move and was being buffeted about. The feeling now was truly like being in and traveling through a tube, albeit one made of light, like those old fashioned air tubes some banks still used to take drive-through deposits. Only a million times faster, and I was the change rattling around in the plastic container. While still tingling in that weird "I'm be-ing chopped up into a million little pieces" way. I wasn't a fan. Of any of it.

I was less of a fan when the tube sputtered and lost its opacity. As it did so, I was able to look around. Everyone was still within my field of vision, but we were farther apart now. Jeff was farther from me and closer to Jamie and Gower, in that sense, but they were much farther away from both of us than they had been. Everyone was spread out and further away, as if we'd been part of a sphere that had exploded, sending us radiating away from center.

I was closest to Chuckie and I tried to reach for him. As I did so, I realized we were in space and wondered if we were all about to die, fast and ugly. Then the light tube reactivated. Hoped everyone else's had reactivated as well.

Back to being whizzed through a Galactic Pneumatic Tube. Still not a fan. Even less of a fan when the tubes sputtered again. Whatever was going on, it wasn't smooth. Meaning there was probably interference of some kind. This thought wasn't reassuring. At all.

Interference could be caused by a variety of things, but the bottom line was that we were somewhere in the cosmos without spacesuits, spaceships, or helpful space entities. At least as far as I knew.

Then again, because Jamie was one of those taken, we had at least one space entity with us. But I had no idea if this was something that affected ACE negatively or not. Hoped not, and also hoped that ACE's self-preservation would mean that Jamie, and hopefully Gower, survived.

Didn't have too long to worry about it, because I finally felt something under my feet again. Felt like something solid. So, one for the win column. Hey, the win column was totally empty at this moment, so I'd take even the smallest victory.

Of course, "solid" wasn't the same as "steady," "sturdy," or "safe." The light tube disappeared, but the horrible tingling was still going, though it seemed to be dying down. I was able to look around and discovered that what I was standing on was the top of a tall tree.

I'd had a freaky dream about something like this. Only in my dream, the trees weren't all purple and I was, you know, dreaming. Right now I was very much awake. And I was precariously balanced on something that was extremely unlikely to be able to bear my weight.

Sure enough, the moment the tingling finally stopped, gravity decided to take an interest. Nice to know it existed wherever in the cosmos I was. However, gravity was, as so often happened for me, pissed that I'd ignored it for so long. I plummeted down.

Managed to grab a decent-sized branch before I banged through every single branch, twig, and leaf on this tree, but only because I cleverly caught it with my stomach.

Decided to hang there while I tried to get my breath back, the branch having knocked all the wind out of me. Was relieved to realize that I *could* breathe. Took a closer look at the tree. I wasn't the Queen of Arbor Day or anything, but I was pretty sure that Earth didn't possess trees that were literally purple all over. Purple flowers, yes, sure. Purple flowers, leaves, branches, and trunks? No, not so much.

My tree was quite pretty, since each part was a different shade of purple. It also smelled nice, similar to lavender, but different. Nice and sweet, but unlike anything I'd smelled before. It smelled like purple, honestly.

As my breath returned, I considered my options. Climbing down seemed like a wise course of action. Finding the others was definitely up there at the top of the To Do List. Figuring out where in the cosmos we were was also a biggie.

Because Jeff had been given Surcenthumain by some of our enemies, he'd become enhanced. Same thing for Serene and Christopher. Christopher had taken the drug in large doses but most of his enhancement had faded, though he was still potentially the fastest person in the galaxy.

Jeff's and Serene's talent enhancements hadn't faded so far. But there had been another side effect, which was that Jamie had come out extra-special with a side of amazing, and she'd done a mother and child feedback kind of thing inside me so that when she was born, I'd inherited some of the A-C abilities. Meaning that I had hyperspeed, enhanced vision, somewhat enhanced strength, and an ability to heal very fast. Basically I was Wolverine With Boobs.

Meaning that the cuts and bruises I'd just acquired were healing as I looked at them, and I could probably handle myself wherever the hell I actually was, even if I couldn't find the others. However, not finding the others wasn't something I was hoping for. Of course, what I wanted and what was really going on appeared to be, as so often happened, nowhere close to aligning.

Congratulated myself on my foresight, because my purse had stayed with me, even when I'd fallen, but only because I'd put it over my neck. Because I was still wrapped around the branch, it was hanging under me. As I stared at it, it opened and three heads peeped out.

"Harlie, Poofikins, and Bruno! Kitty's so happy to see

you! How did you guys get here? Bruno especially?" The
Poofs weren't a total surprise, but the Peregrine having
managed to make this trip, inside my purse no less, seemed
almost as amazing as the trip itself.

Harlie mewed, purred, and mewed. Poofikins added in.
Then Bruno did his head bob thing and squawked quietly.

I understood this because, in addition to all the other
A-C goodies I'd acquired, I'd somehow become Dr. Doolittle as well. Richard White insisted that I'd always had this
talent and was aware of it now because I had Alpha Four
animals that talked back. Whether I'd had the power all the
time or whether I'd acquired it along with Jamie, I liked the
skill. Jeff wasn't as much of a fan, but he'd learned to accept
it by now. Sort of.

The animals finished their recap. "Huh. Good news." Apparently every person who'd been spirited away had their
own attached Poof with them, other than Jeff, because it
required two Poofs to bring Bruno along. "Well, other than
the fact that Jeff is Poofless."

Poofikins made sounds of protest. Jeff had an unnamed
and unattached Poof with him. Meaning that, very shortly, I
assumed, Jeff was going to have a Poof that had bonded to
him, regardless of Jeff's specific wishes.

"Aha, well done, that Poof."

Technically Harlie was Jeff's. Harlie had been Jeff's father's first, when Alfred was still on Alpha Four. But when
our Poofs came to Earth, Harlie bonded with Jeff. Supposedly. Based on everything that had gone on since then, Harlie was clearly more bonded to me than Jeff.

Frankly, the Poofs were truly bonded to Algar, though I
was the only one who knew this. Meaning they probably
had a way of communicating with him. This was good news,
because I and the others were definitely up the proverbial
creek without any kind of paddle, and any assistance we
could get was probably going to be incredibly helpful.

Of course, Algar was hiding out with the Earth A-Cs for
crimes against Black Hole Universe beliefs or some such.
So his form of helping was extremely low-key. But any port
in a purple sea, sort of thing.

"Is it safe for any of you to do reconnaissance and tell Kitty
if it's safe for Kitty to climb down? As in, are there things
down there that want to eat me, kill me, or enslave me?"

"No. There are things down here that are hoping you have a med kit in your purse." The voice was faint, but I recognized it.

"Christopher! Where are you?"

"He's between us, Kitty." This voice was nearer and one I'd recognize if I was unconscious.

"Chuckie, are you okay? Where are you?"

"Just scratched up. I landed in the middle of a tree."

"I was on top of one. How is it I can hear you?"

"I'm not on the ground, Kitty. Look to your right."

Sure enough, there he was, in another tree just like mine. It was only easy to spot him because he'd adapted to the A-C's formality and wore black Armani suits and white shirts all the time, just like the rest of the men working for Centaurion did. He stood out in the purple tree. I probably did, too.

When I'd taken that fast look around in the middle of space, in addition to Chuckie being nearest to me, Christopher had been fairly near to him as well. So, it made sense that these two were the nearest now. Making as educated a guess as I could, and based on how far away from me Chuckie was now, Christopher had landed even farther away. However, Christopher was so fast that even if he'd landed farther away from us, it would make sense that he'd found us because he could probably search half of this planet in less than a minute.

"Is Jeff here?"

"I don't see him," Chuckie said. "I'd suggest we get down and then look for the others. I'm just worried about breaking something or something stabbing into us on the way down. Me in particular, since you and White have the healing factor and I don't."

"Haven't found Jeff yet," Christopher shouted up to us. "Hang on, though. I have a plan."

"He has a plan." Chuckie didn't sound enthused.

"Dude, he was the Head of Imageering for over a decade, you know. He has the skills."

"Yeah. And in all that time, tell me how often they worked on alien planets or with, in, around, and, most specifically, *on* gigantic trees."

"Wow, you're sure testy."

"I'm sitting high up in a tree, on a branch that's *just* managing to hold my weight, and I can't see another safe branch under me. Yeah, call me the anti-Eagle Scout right now."

"I fell through half a tree to get to my branch. I'm not feeling the sympathies for you at this moment."

"Healing factor."

"Sitting, versus draped like a wet towel, on your branch."

"Keep on bickering," Christopher called up to us. He sounded a little closer. "It's helping me find you."

"Are you building a ladder?" Chuckie asked hopefully.

"No, there aren't enough dry branches of decent size down there."

"Then, um, what *are* you doing?"

Christopher's head bobbed into view. "This."

Had to admit—"this" wasn't something I'd have guessed in a million years.

CHAPTER 12

CHRISTOPHER WAS RIDING on the back of a gigantic, flying bug. The bug looked like a katydid-grasshopper combination, only the size of a pony. Oh, and it was bright yellow. A yellow like a thousand daffodils put together, an almost neon yellow.

The creature had a small head with large eyes and antennae that looked like they were long, delicate eyelashes shooting up and out. Its wings were going so fast they were a blur, just like a hummingbird's, and they made a pleasant humming sound. I couldn't tell for sure, but they looked fairly see-through and very iridescent, just like the eyelash-antennae.

Christopher sat in front of the wings and the two long, bent, and powerful back legs, right behind the head. His feet were resting on the middle two legs that went out to the sides like upside-down L's, almost as if the insect intended them to be stirrups for a rider. The two front legs were in front and under the head and seemed more like arms, albeit arms the insect was going to use to keep its head up when it was on the ground.

"I didn't realize I'd hit my head," Chuckie said, speaking for both of us.

"I'm really glad I'm not a girl who freaks out at bugs. And the two of you should be truly grateful for that, because I can hit a level that'll burst your eardrums if I'm really freaked out."

"I've heard you hit that register, so keep calm and spare

us," Christopher said. "But they're amazingly tame. And strong. And the two of you can stop whining about them."

"Excuse me, 'they,' 'them'? As in, there are more of them?"

Sure enough, as I asked a bright pink one flew over to me while a bright turquoise one went to Chuckie. If Jamie saw the pink one she'd want it for her very own, it was that pink. Clearly we'd landed on Planet Colorful.

Shoved the worry thinking about Jamie raised to the side—Chuckie and I had to get down and be safe. Then he, Christopher, and I could find Jamie, Jeff, and the others.

"How are you controlling them?" Chuckie asked, for both of us.

"I have no idea," Christopher admitted. "But Toby's here." Toby was Christopher's Poof, and I could see it now, riding on the katyhopper's head.

"Poofs to the rescue?" I asked Harlie and Poofikins. I got proud mewls of confirmation, as Poofikins hopped onto the pink one's head. "Okay, the katyhoppers are cool, Chuckie. Poofs at the helm. And all that."

"Katyhoppers?" Christopher asked. "You know what these are?"

"No," Chuckie answered for me. "But they look like a giant cross between katydids and grasshoppers, and this is Kitty we're talking to."

"Oh, good point. Well, it's as good a name as any until we find out what they're really called."

"Thanks so much, I'm *so* glad you two approve."

"Who's testy now?" Chuckie asked, this time just for him. Chose not to reply lest I say something nasty to my oldest friend when we were stranded ACE only knew how many light-years from home.

I could just see him getting onto his giant, blue flying bug, while his Poof, Fluffy, jumped out of his pocket and onto the back of the bug's head. Had to stop thinking of them as bugs—I didn't wig out at bugs, but pony-sized bugs weren't what I was used to. Katyhopper was a good name. It sounded fun and cute. Giant flying bug didn't sound fun *or* cute. Or safe, but that was beside the point—it wasn't safe to be hanging up here in the first place.

Waited to speak until Chuckie was on his katyhopper.

"You both look awesome on the backs of your proud steeds."

"I'll hurt you later," Chuckie said. "Do you need help to get onto yours, or are you just enjoying hanging around like that?"

"Frankly, I think I need help." I wasn't a great tree climber, seeing as I was from the desert, and our kinds of trees were mostly cacti or trees that weren't made for climbing, like Palo Verdes. And my branch was big enough to hold me but not really set up for me to try to use it like a jungle gym. My best options were to flip my lower body forward or my upper body backward. Neither one sounded like a safe plan.

The guys flew over to me somehow and, with a lot of grunting, kvetching, and an almost strangulation when Christopher didn't flip my purse at the same time as Chuckie was pulling me onto my pink katyhopper, I managed to get my butt into the saddle. So to speak.

I'd ridden horses before and they absolutely didn't bob up and down as much as the katyhoppers did. On the other hand, the katyhoppers didn't appear to be into the idea of bucking and throwing us, so that evened them out on the horse to giant flying bug comparison scale. And the humming of their wings was soft and soothing, versus annoying, so that was one for the win column right there.

"Will they be offended if we go onto the ground?" Chuckie asked. "Or hop off with us in tow? Or worse?"

"Beats me," Christopher said.

"Poofikins, is it safe to go down?" The Poof mewled at me and shot me an overly innocent look. I knew what that meant and heaved a sigh. "Gimme a mo', guys."

"Why?" Christopher snapped. "You like it up here?"

"It's okay up here. Beats going splat onto the ground, I can say that for certain. But that's not why I need a second. Now that Chuckie and I are out of danger of plummeting to our deaths the Poofs want, ah, me to get back in, ah, charge."

Both men snorted. "When *aren't* you in charge?" Chuckie asked with a laugh.

"When I'm hanging half upside down in a tree, apparently. Hang on, I need to commune with nature, and I mean that very literally."

By now I'd done the Dr. Doolittle Mind Meld with Poofs, Peregrines, cats, dogs, and parrots, if I could count Bellie the African Grey. Bellie had belonged to one of our insane enemies, then became Jeff's Avian Mistress for what seemed like ages but was only a few months, and mercifully had finally gone on to live with Mr. Joel Oliver to rarely darken my door again. I knew Bellie's motives and she'd been helpful, on occasion, so I chose to count that I could chat with parrots. Let's be optimistic and say I was able to communicate with the entire Avian Kingdom.

However, wings or not, the katyhoppers weren't birds, nor were they horses. They were insects. Huge insects, but insects nonetheless. And I'd never had the inclination or need to talk to insects prior to this precise time.

I concentrated. Nothing. No change in any of our relative positions, and no feedback from the katyhopper, either.

Thought about it. I'd never really *tried* to talk to the animals, it had just happened. "Ah, Kitty would like to go down to the ground, if it's safe to do so."

Nada.

This was not the best time to be less than stellar at the Talking to the Animals Game. Time to stall.

"Christopher, do you have any guess as to what planet we're on?" I knew it wasn't Alpha Four. When we'd been there, briefly, right before Jeff and I had gotten married, and right after the Poofs had eaten Alpha Four's then-king, we'd been shown what that world looked like. Sure, it had been via some weird troubadour-imageer thing King Alexander's mother, Princess Victoria, had done, but in all of her Intergalactic Family Photos Experience there had been nothing that had the level of color that we were surrounded by.

"No idea. I was born on Earth, remember?"

"Paul knows about this solar system."

"So do I. But I doubt Paul has any idea what planet we're on any more than I do."

"Actually," Chuckie said, "if I can make a guess based on where the suns are in relation to each other, I think we're on Beta Eight. I could be wrong, of course."

"I doubt it." Chuckie had spent time learning where the Alpha Centauri planets were in relation to each other and their suns, and had probably asked the Planetary Council members a lot of questions that he'd then memorized and filed away for later use. Like today. The benefits of being best friends with the smartest guy in any room, or on the back of any giant flying bug, were without number.

Tried to remember what I'd heard about Beta Eight. Came up with nothing.

"If you're right," Christopher said, "the natives here aren't very advanced."

"Earth Bronze Age, per the Planetary Council," Chuckie confirmed. "So define 'advanced.' I doubt they have computers and such, but if they're similar to the Ancient Greeks, they likely have a strong civilization, or civilizations, going."

"I see no natives, other than the katyhoppers." Wondered if they were the dominant sentient life on this planet. After all, while many of the inhabited planets here had native beings that were more like humans than not, Betas Thirteen, Fourteen, and Fifteen had Giant Lizards, Major Doggies, and Cat People, respectively. Or, as they preferred to be called, Reptilians, Canus Majorians, and Feliniads.

"Think we could be riding the top sentient life-form on this planet?" Christopher asked.

"Wow. Dude, you're getting as good at the mind reading as Jeff. No idea."

"I don't think so," Chuckie said slowly. "They're too ... docile."

"That's the Poofs' influence, I think," Christopher said.

"Yes, and the Poofs can't influence us in that way," Chuckie pointed out. "Ergo ..."

"Yeah, okay, I can buy that. There's got to be minds, because the Poofs could affect them. But I'm getting nothing."

"I think you're trying too hard," Chuckie said. "Not that you appear to be doing anything, by the way, but from the scrunched up look on your face, you're concentrating. Probably too hard. You could hurt yourself."

"Or the wind could change and my face could stay like this, right? Wow, remind me to hurt you later. But fine, yeah, I'm trying to be mentally telepathic, and it's not working." Had a thought—something else with wings had come along for the bumpy ride. "Bruno, my bird, could you do reconnaissance and let Kitty know if it's safe for us to try to get down onto the ground? If for no other reason than that the katyhoppers' wings have got to be getting tired."

Before Bruno could so much as squawk or the guys

could ask what the Peregrine was doing here, my katyhopper did a slow dive toward the ground. Checked behind me—the katyhoppers with the guys on them were following.

"What did you do?" Christopher shouted.

"No clue. At all."

"She was kind and concerned about the animals," Chuckie called.

"Insects," Christopher said. "At least, I think."

"Whatever they actually are, apparently they appreciate thoughtfulness. Think nice thoughts about the katyhoppers, White. I'm sure you're capable of it if you try."

"I'm with Kitty—I'm going to hurt you later."

Despite the witty banter we landed with little hops and no difficulty. For the first time the katyhoppers' wings were still. Sure enough—iridescent and fairly transparent, the internal veins and such visible and quite pretty, all things considered. The veins, like the rest of them, were the same bright colors. Had no idea if the colors meant male, female, both, neither, or if they were just three examples of the Katyhopper Rainbow.

What hadn't been apparent in the air was that they had three sets of wings, similar to their three sets of legs. So each katyhopper had a small, medium, and large set. But when they were flying they just looked like one big set of wings.

"The wings are fascinating," Chuckie said.

"Dude, you're doing the mind-reading thing, too. I wonder if it's the planet's atmosphere."

"Seems normal." Chuckie looked around. "I mean, for here."

"Yeah, I know what you mean." Refrained from saying that we were in a freak world because, frankly, this was no freakier than the facts that aliens lived on Earth or that we'd somehow taken a magic carpet ride to another solar system.

Contemplated whether or not we should get off. The katyhoppers seemed amenable to passengers and it would be a lot easier if we had transportation. Then again, they'd already done a lot for us, and it probably wasn't right to just assume they wanted to continue to do so.

I was about to dismount when my katyhopper made a sound. I was in no way an Insect Noises Expert, let alone a katyhopper noises expert, but my gut said that the sound wasn't a good one. It was a low kind of screech, as if a metal door that hadn't been oiled in ages was being opened.

Either the katyhopper was calling for reinforcements or it was saying we were in danger. Based on all three of our katyhoppers leaping up into the air, wings going faster than they had before, I went with how our luck rolled and figured on the obvious—we were in danger. Again.

Or, as we called it, routine.

CHAPTER 13

THE KATYHOPPERS DIDN'T really take to the air. They flew us back up into one of the purple trees, then alighted on strong lower branches. Meaning if they panicked and bucked us off, we might not all break something when we hit the ground. So we had that going for us.

Only there was nothing there. At least nothing I could see.

We were next to each other in the tree. "See anything?" I whispered to the guys.

"No," Chuckie said in a low voice. "But the katyhoppers didn't panic for nothing."

"I have the best vision of the three of us, and I don't see anything we should be afraid of," Christopher said softly. "You know, other than being stranded on an alien planet in what we hope is the Alpha Centauri system."

"Maybe whatever's scaring the katyhoppers is invisible." The guys gave me looks I could only think of as withering. "Really? Look around and think back to Operation Defection Election and tell me invisible beings aren't possible. Go ahead. I'll wait."

During the political campaign to get Senator Vincent Armstrong renamed President of the United States, which included Jeff as the Vice Presidential running mate, we'd been visited by some superconciousnesses. They'd been super-powerful and mostly insubstantial. And Siler was able to blend in with his surroundings so as to appear invisible. So I no longer discounted the possibility that we had invisible people out there somewhere. Possibly somewhere here.

But no invisible beings identified themselves. Time for Plan B. "Bruno my bird, is it safe for you to fly off and do reconnaissance?"

Bruno squawked. As far as he could tell, it was safe. He took off. And, to my complete shock, the katyhoppers followed him.

"Was this what you intended?" Christopher shouted to me, as we flew next to each other, the guys on either side of me.

"If it's safe, yes indeedy! If it's not, no way in hell."

"Covering the bases like a good politician," Chuckie said. "Well done."

"Dude, I have no freaking clue right now. Call me Miz Out Of Her Element."

Bruno flew up and around the trees and the katyhoppers followed. So we got a good aerial view of where we were.

Purple was definitely the dominant theme in this area, but I could see off in the distance and there were other colors being represented—they were just far away. However, Bruno wasn't heading for them, he was touring us around Purple Land.

We were away from the purple trees quickly. We weren't flying all that high, so I could see the ground under us pretty well. In addition to the copse of big trees Chuckie and I had landed in, there were some Purple Mountains Majesties scattered about in various directions, all, like the other colors, far away.

Mostly, though, the land was covered with purple plants that looked a lot like lavender, at least from our vantage point. I sniffed. Nope, didn't smell like lavender. Smelled good, just not familiar. As with the trees, they smelled purple, but a different kind of purple. Wondered if we were in some kind of opium field or something.

"Think the scents and local foliage could be affecting our minds?" Chuckie called to Christopher.

"Dude, I was just thinking that. This place smells like purple, but different kinds of purple."

"I'd say that was a Kitty-ism," Christopher replied, "but it smells like that to me, too. The trees smelled different than whatever we're over, but they both smell like purple. Not that I even understand how I'm thinking that."

"I'm thinking it, too," Chuckie said, "and that's why I

asked. By the way, have you also noticed it's not that hard to hear each other?"

Looked down at my katyhopper's antennae. They seemed to be radiating out a little more toward the sides than they had before. Checked out the antennae on the katyhoppers the guys were on. Their antennae were turned more toward me.

"Wow. The katyhoppers are awesome. They're using their antennae to transmit what we're saying to each other."

Chuckie looked at each of the katyhoppers. "I think you're right. Interesting."

"Animal husbandry, or whatever this is, another time," Christopher said. "Something spooked the katyhoppers and we need to be prepared."

"Wow, Christopher, that was worthy of being a Kitty-ism!"

"I'm so proud," he muttered. Not that he sounded proud, but whatever.

In addition to the mountains and ground cover, there were other trees in the distance, scattered all around at various intervals. Some were just single big trees, some were clumped together. None were worthy of being called a forest, nor did they form a barrier or a border. They were simply randomly there.

The plants were less random. They looked too even to have sprouted up accidentally. But unlike lavender fields on Earth, there weren't paths between the rows. The rows were very close together. Meaning there could be things under those plants we couldn't see. Snake things, for example.

"Think there could be snakes under the foliage?" Christopher asked, right on cue.

"The mind reading is getting freaky. But I want to be on record that if there are snakes down there, I'm going to lose it, especially if they're extra-large as far as Earth slitheries are concerned."

Chuckie looked thoughtful. "White, how did you get one of the katyhoppers to help you?"

"No idea. I landed on the ground, in the middle of some of those purple plants. The katyhopper I'm riding flew over to me. I almost ran, but it landed and sort of, I don't know, indicated I should get on its back. I did, and then I heard you two talking. It was faint, but I'd landed near enough to the trees that I had a good guess that's where you two were. I wanted to get to you guys, and then the katyhopper flew up, with the two you're riding joining us."

"So they read your mind. I mean, that's the only explanation for why the katyhoppers knew or cared to come up to us, because we were in the trees as long as you were on the ground."

"Maybe," Chuckie said slowly. "I mean, I agree that they're picking up our thoughts somehow, since we're picking up each other's thoughts somehow and the katyhoppers are clearly sentient."

Took a look at Chuckie's expression. I could see the wheels turning. "But? I mean, there's so obviously a 'but' in there."

He sighed. "White, how close to the trees were you where you landed?"

"Pretty close. Not right under them, but close enough."

"Then I don't buy that the katyhoppers didn't know that Kitty and I were in the trees. I think they did, but you were in greater danger, so they went to help you first. If you'd attacked or run away, maybe they'd have let you. But you wisely held your ground and didn't try to hurt them, so they're helping. Good for you, by the way. I honestly wouldn't have expected it of you, and I don't really mean that in an insulting way."

Christopher looked thoughtful. "No, you're right. We're in a foreign environment and I'm used to killing things that look dangerous. But . . . the katyhopper just didn't *feel* dangerous. But I'm not an empath, so I don't know why that would be. Jeff might have been or might be communing with these things, but how would I have done it?"

"The mind reading. The katyhoppers told you in some way that they were coming to help you, not hurt you." I patted my katyhopper's head. "They rock. But, this gives a lot of support to the idea that there's something, or many things, we won't like in the underbrush. And, I say again, if they're giant snakes or snakelike creatures, you can count me out. I'll stay up in the trees screaming my head off, thank you very much."

Of course, no sooner said than Bruno squawked and flew

for the nearest tree. It was one of the lone giant ones, but we were closer to it than to our original set.

As he did so, we watched the ground start moving. Not like an earthquake, but undulating. Like a sea serpent or a snake.

I opened my mouth to scream.

CHAPTER 14

I MANAGED TO REFRAIN from screaming because, as it turned out, what was under us was neither snake nor sea serpent.

The groundcover was undulating because it wasn't entirely made up of plants. Plants were there, still, and they were purple, yes. But what was moving looked like extra-large butterflies or moths.

"Can those be what's scared the katyhoppers?" I managed to ask, in a relatively normal tone of voice, as the katyhoppers landed on a sturdy branch and Bruno came and perched in front of me to serve as my protective avian shield and to give me something to clutch in case things got freaky.

"Proud of you for not losing it," Chuckie said. "But I doubt it. My guess is that whatever spooked the katyhoppers has just spooked the butterflies. If that's what they are. Presumably they're slower to react or have less sensitive senses."

"Butterflies eat carrion." Why my mind had felt the need to toss this tidbit up from memory I had no guess. Maybe my mind was just ready to freak out and taking whatever opportunities it had. Lucky me.

We were facing our original copse of trees, at least I was pretty sure we were, based on the placement of the mountains and some other trees. And butterflies were leaping into the air in droves, making even the air look purple.

"So do many other things," Christopher said. "But I think I've spotted what's freaking the insects or whatever they actually are out. And, Kitty, it's not a snake, but still, don't freak out either, okay?" He pointed down and off a bit to our left.

I saw what Christopher had and relaxed. "It has legs. Sure, it's a giant Budweiser Lizard, but still, it's a giant Budweiser Lizard with legs. Legs are good."

The animal, or reptile, or whatever it was, was about the size of a Komodo dragon, only it had big, round, bug eyes that stuck out from its head, a long tail that could and did curl up into a spiral, a pointed cowl around the back of its head, and an incredibly long tongue. And colors. Many, many colors.

At least when it jumped up it had colors. When it was on the ground it went back to mostly purple.

"What the hell is a Budweiser Lizard?" Christopher asked.

"It's a giant chameleon," Chuckie and I said in unison.

"Thanks for the chorus," Christopher said, taking time out to shoot Patented Glare #1 at both of us. He was a pro, after all, and always kept in practice. "But here's the big question—do giant chameleons eat people?"

"I doubt it," Chuckie said. "But they would eat the katyhoppers if they could, and the butterflies for certain." As he said this, the chameleon zapped a butterfly out of the air and ate it. The katyhoppers all shuddered.

"So Louie the Lizard down there is a direct predator of our katyhoppers, which is why they helped get us to safety. They're awesome!" I patted my 'hopper again. "And so very brave." Gave the guys the hairy eyeball look, and they followed suit and patted their mounts. I could feel all three katyhoppers relax a bit.

"So, does this mean that we have to sleep in the trees?" Christopher asked as Louie the Lizard romped on. Clearly, he was one happy chameleon, enjoying his whatever time of the day it was snack. "Because while that thing might not be into eating us, it's big enough that it could give it a shot."

I got nothing negative from Louie, but that didn't mean anything. The chameleon reminded me of a big dog, really— he was romping and eating and just enjoying life. I had no guess whether that made him dangerous to us, though. We weren't insects or insectoids. Then again, dogs could and would bite and we were riding on giant insects who were afraid of Louie. Caution was probably going to be the smart watchword.

"Maybe Louie's a danger and maybe he isn't, but the butterflies clearly nest on the ground." Louie kept on going, jumping and romping, but in a reasonably straight line. As soon as he left an area, the butterflies settled back down on the plants, so my saying they nested there was a safe bet. "And the katyhoppers don't appear to nest in trees."

No sooner had I said this than the katyhoppers flew off our branch and headed back toward the trees we'd arrived on and around. Bruno stayed with me and I didn't argue.

I kept an eye on Louie—he seemed to be going far away. Had no idea if that meant he'd be back later, if there were more of his kind around, if they were like tigers and it was one giant Bud Lizard to a territory, or if we'd never see him or one like him again.

"You know what I don't see?" Chuckie asked as we flew back. "I don't see anything that we could rightly say was a dominant sentient species."

"Nothing humanoid," Christopher agreed.

"But what if those butterflies or whatever are a hive mind? It might explain why everyone's reading each other's minds."

The guys actually seemed to give my suggestion consideration. Wondered if they were feeling okay, Christopher in particular.

"Wouldn't we, I don't know, get some feeling that they're there and thinking, though?" he asked finally.

"No idea," Chuckie replied. "Ants and bees are a hive mind and we get nothing from them, so to speak. If their minds are alien enough from ours—like bee and ant minds are, I mean, not just alien in the planetary sense—then we might not know if they're dominant or even highly sentient."

"The katyhoppers have better senses, and they can tell what we're thinking or feeling or something. Wouldn't that make them more highly sentient than the butterflies?"

Chuckie shrugged. "Maybe, but, I say again, if the minds are too alien, we might not recognize the intelligence. And they might not recognize ours."

"We're lost on an alien planet, have no idea where the rest of our people are, and the only things we've got are whatever Kitty has in her purse," Christopher concisely pointed out. "Right now, I don't feel too intelligent. I feel lost, trapped, and out of my element, but not intelligent."

We were near to "our" trees now. "You know, other than the Poofs and Bruno, I haven't taken inventory of what I have in said purse." That there were things in it I was going to be sure I hadn't put in was a given. Algar had essentially handed me my purse before we were all taken, and it was heavier than normal, meaning he'd put in some surprise extras I sincerely hoped were going to help keep us all alive.

If we could find the others, of course.

As we reached the trees, I shoved the worry about Jamie, Jeff, and everyone else aside. Right now, Chuckie, Christopher and I had to be sure we were okay and going to be able to survive in this world. Couldn't save anyone else if we ended up Louie the Lizard Chow.

Once back to our starting point, the katyhoppers landed on the ground underneath the trees we'd landed on.

And then it got weird.

Which was, you know, for what had gone on so far, saying quite a lot.

CHAPTER 15

WE WALKED INTO THE TREES.
Not onto the branches, not into the spaces between the trees, and not into a giant hole in a tree, but *into* the trees. Like we were dryads or something.

"Whoa!" Chuckie said, as we entered Tree Land. "This is like something out of Greek Mythology!"

"No," Christopher said slowly. "It's not. I know what you two think you're seeing, because I think I'm seeing it, too. But, while looking straight ahead, see what you see in your peripheral vision."

I'd done this with the Jamie in Bizarro World. It was how she saw into all the other universes out there where she and I existed. She started straight ahead in the three-way mirror and watched everyone go past out of the corners of her eyes.

So it was easy for me to do what Christopher suggested. Managed not to fall off my katyhopper. "It's an optical illusion. The trees create some kind of barrier that makes it look like nothing's in between them other than ground and what you'd expect to be underneath trees." What I was seeing wasn't what anyone would expect to be underneath a tree, at least, not trees in my world.

"And as if we walked into a tree trunk," Chuckie added.

The illusion didn't last long—as soon as the last part of the last katyhopper crossed whatever weird threshold we had around us, our eyes stopped lying to us.

We were inside the copse of trees, and we could see what was outside of them. But what had merely looked like the ground underneath the trees was actually an elaborate nest setup that went up several stories.

The nests were, shocking no one, made of purple sticks and leaves, and I was fairly certain I saw a few butterfly wings in there, too. Not that I necessarily thought the katy-hoppers were the butterflies' enemies, but then again, for all I knew, they considered the butterflies food, not the plants. Or both. The animal kingdom was really big on the whole Circle of Life thing after all.

But in addition to being purple, it was also intricate and beautiful. The nests were set up like the cave cities of an-cient peoples who'd lived in Arizona thousands of years ago—sort of like a gigantic interconnected apartment building.

It was easy to spot the katyhopper young, because they were both smaller than the katyhoppers we'd been riding and also iridescent. There were some medium-sized katy-hoppers who were colored, but not as richly or brightly col-ored as the larger ones. Meaning they achieved their full color at adulthood.

"Welcome to Katyhopper City, Land of Beauty and En-chantment, and a riot of color. I wish I had a camera with me, and before one of you says that I have my phone, let me mention that it doesn't have a never-ending battery and leave it at that."

Our katyhoppers stopped walking and we all dis-mounted. The Poofs jumped back to each of us and bounded into purse and pockets respectively. Bruno flapped off our katyhopper's back as well and took a look around.

The katyhopper Christopher had been riding started walking around, and Bruno followed. So we followed him.

The trees formed a ragged oval about the size of half of a football field, and three quarters of the interior area was given to the apartment of nests. There were larger ones on the bottom and some smaller up high, but it was hard to be sure, because the trees were tall and the nests went up within them.

Neither Chuckie nor I had seen this katyhopper city when we were in the trees, meaning the illusion was effec-tive from all angles. For all I knew, we'd only been able to get inside because we were on the backs of the katyhoppers.

Katyhoppers were doing things, but they were insect

things and mostly didn't make a lot of sense to me. Unlike the other races we'd met from the Alpha Centauri system, which all felt human even though they were cats, dogs, and lizards, the katyhoppers were definitely still insects. Cocoons were in evidence, and it didn't take genius to guess those held babies. There were piles of leaves and other things I couldn't identify, and since katyhoppers went to these piles—randomly, as far as I could tell, not that this meant anything—and took items from the pile back to their nests, either this was group nesting material or group food. Or something else that didn't compute for me.

However, what did compute was that we were led to several large katyhoppers of various sparkling colors. The three katyhoppers with us did a lot of antennae waving, and these others waved back.

Antennae were waved toward Bruno, and he moved closer and joined the group. He bobbed his head, did some squawking, clawed the ground a bit, and flapped his wings. Only he wasn't talking to me, but to the katyhoppers.

"What's he saying?" Chuckie asked, with a lot more interest and a lot less resignation in his tone than I was used to when anyone other than Richard White asked this kind of question. Then again, this wasn't the world where we were married. Had a feeling that Charles in the other universe was taking a speed course in what his wife now knew and could do and probably had a lot of resignation in his tone going.

Realized I'd really only been back in my own universe less than a day before we were all tossed into an alien solar system. Would have complained to the Powers That Be, but had a feeling that they'd either tell me to pull up my Big Girl Panties and deal or they'd merely been waiting for me to get home to take me on their next version of Ms. Kitty's Wild Ride.

"Bruno's not talking to me. I'm not certain, but I'm pretty sure he's complimenting the katyhoppers on their nest setup. At least, he sounds impressed and seems to be sharing complimentary things. And I'm pretty sure he's talking to the katyhopper elders."

"I don't want to know how you know that," Christopher muttered, clearly doing his best to fill in during Jeff's absence.

"As your father's said many times, White, it's her talent."

"Do you think they grabbed my dad?" Christopher sounded worried, not that I could blame him. All the first Operations I'd been involved with had centered on removing Richard White from power in some way.

Of course, White had retired as Supreme Pontifex when Jamie was born, and Gower had that role now. My gut clenched. "No, I didn't see anything around Richard like was around us. But . . . they don't need Richard now, if they want our head man, religiously. They need Paul." And Gower had Jamie with him. At least, I sincerely hoped she was still with him.

Chuckie put his hand on my shoulder. "I know where you're going with this. And while I realize that our enemies have tried to steal your child from the moment she was born, if whoever brought us here—wherever here really is—had wanted that, why bring the rest of us along?"

"Good point." Did the take a deep breath and let it out slowly thing again. Bruno and the katyhoppers were still deep in conversation. "Okay, you know, Mom was trying to tell me something before we all disappeared. Did either one of you catch it?"

Chuckie shook his head. "Just what you did, I think. Angela felt there was significance to who was being taken."

"So did my dad," Christopher said. "But I don't see it."

I looked around at the katyhopper's hidden city. "Maybe we're looking at it the wrong way."

"Okay, we seem to have some time while Bruno talks to our hosts," Chuckie said. "So, what do we know?"

We went over the list of who'd been taken as far as we knew, to see if one of us had spotted someone the others hadn't. The three of us agreed on everyone taken.

"My dad asked why Abigail was being taken," Christopher reminded us. "I don't know why she would or wouldn't be taken. Then again, I don't know why whoever it is grabbed Tito and didn't take Patrick. I'm inclined to agree with Reynolds—whoever it is isn't necessarily trying to kidnap Jamie, because why not grab Patrick at the same time? And all the other kids, for that matter?"

"It's a safe bet that whoever was taking us knows Queen Renata," Chuckie said. "The princesses said they traveled here by the same means."

"You know . . . could they have really been sent to us as badly as we were pulled here?"

The men both looked at me. "What do you mean?" Christopher asked slowly.

"I mean I thought we were going to die, more than once, when our Space-Age Pneumatic Tubes failed in the middle of space. I get why it would have taken a while to 'grab' us, but once grabbed, shouldn't the process have been stable?"

"The gates never have issues," Christopher said. "But they work differently. At least as far as I could tell. If we can find Lorraine, Claudia, and/or Serene, they'll probably have a better idea about what brought us here. Scientifically, I mean."

"Normally, I would think, once the beam or whatever it was latches on and is set, it should work smoothly. Unless there was interference." Chuckie's eyes narrowed.

"Dude, my turn to read your mind. You think there was interference, don't you? Rahmi said the situation was bad here when she and Rhee were sent to us. What if there's a fight of some kind going on? You know, like in the movies—the, we hope, good guys are trying to pull in their reinforcements and the, we think, bad guys burst in and turn the machine off. Good guys fight and turn it back on, and so forth. The people being transported don't land where they're supposed to because the process was interrupted."

Christopher jerked. "Reinforcements. We've only had significant interaction with people from this solar system twice. The second time was when they came to save us from the Z'porrah attack, and really only Alexander came then. But the first time, the Planetary Council came."

"And stayed for my wedding. Oh, wow. I have Alien Conspiracy Bingo. Think about it—everyone pulled was part of the fight right before Jeff and I got married. That's why they pulled Tito, he was a big part of that battle. Everyone they grabbed was. Everyone except Jamie, Abigail, Rahmi, and Rhee, that is."

"Rahmi and Rhee are Queen Renata's daughters, and I'd bet that she's the one behind pulling us over," Chuckie said. "She's more strategically minded than Alexander is, and if there are problems somewhere in the Alpha Centauri system, pulling in the people who stopped the former King of Alpha Four makes a lot of sense. But why Abigail? She was with the families during that battle and she's not a warrior."

The light dawned. "But Michael's dead, and Abigail is a Gower. And a woman. You're right, Chuckie—Renata, or someone working with her, is who brought us here. A Free Woman would definitely feel that the sister of a fallen male warrior would be an excellent replacement or slot filler or whatever they're doing. Meaning we can probably feel confident we're in the Alpha Centauri system."

"Maybe," Christopher said. "But with the way we traveled, and by the mere fact that none of the others are nearby, I don't think we can be a hundred percent confident yet."

"Why take Jamie, though?" Chuckie asked. "Yes, she was conceived by then, but that's pushing it in terms of saying she was there."

"They know how powerful she is," Christopher suggested.

"Yeah, but . . ."

"I know that look," Chuckie said. "And I have no guess as to what you're thinking, which is almost refreshing based on the past couple of hours."

"I don't think they're bringing her because she has power, at least not that kind of power. I think they took her because she's Jeff's daughter."

"To use against him?" Christopher asked, sounding worried.

"I don't think so. It's because they may need her. There's trouble right here in Alpha Centauri City and that starts with T and that rhymes with C and that stands for 'chain.' As in the chain of succession."

"How and why did you work *The Music Man* into this?" Chuckie asked.

"It's Kitty, why ask why? But Amy loves that movie— I've had to watch it more than once, so I get the Kitty-ism."

"So proud. My musical point is that Jamie could, conceivably, be the new ruler of Alpha Four. Especially if the Free Women have lost their patience with having to listen to King Alexander and Councilor Leonidas."

CHAPTER 16

CHUCKIE SHOOK HIS HEAD. "Renata liked Alexander and respected Leonidas the last time I heard from anyone out here which was, yes, right before the princesses arrived. I can easily believe that someone's against the two of them, but I have trouble buying that it's her unless things have shifted drastically."

"Things shift drastically all the time." Like, Chuckie's presumed best friend had shifted right over to the top of our Most Wanted list.

"We won't know until we find the others and figure out who really brought us here," Christopher said quickly. Figured he'd read my mind or was just thinking the same thing and wanted to keep us off the Cliff Goodman Is Our Mastermind topic. "But I think we need to pay attention to our here and now."

The katyhoppers seemed to be done communing with each other and Bruno. At least I took the bigger ones sort of nodding their antennae at Bruno and wandering off to mean that the chat was over.

Sure enough, Bruno immediately came over to me and did some serious head bobbing, wing flapping, and squawking. "Right you are, Christopher. Bruno says that we have been invited to stay with the katyhoppers. This is a big deal—they don't allow something like this often, but they've never seen anything like us, so they feel that we're here as a test of some kind. Possibly of their hospitality. Anyway, we need to bed down for the night."

"But it's still light out," Chuckie shared. Accurately.

"Yeah, I know, but Bruno says that the katyhoppers say that it's going to get dark fast, and when it does, things that are not as nice as Louie the Lizard will be roaming around. We need to nest with them." Bruno squawked some more. "Really? Wow, that's going to be awkward."

"What is?" Christopher asked with prescient trepidation.

"The katyhoppers consider us a family group. They don't mate like we do, meaning any female and any male, whenever they want, can do the deed. Children are raised by the community."

"It really takes a village I guess," Chuckie said.

I snorted a laugh, but went on. "However, the three who have been escorting us are two females and a male, and they all nest together. Not necessarily as sexual partners," I added quickly, as both guys got looks of panic on their faces. "As in, Jeff isn't going to want to kill us for how we have to spend the night. But their space is limited and they are generously giving us our own family nest, which is a huge honor and we have to treat it as such."

"You got all that from some wing flaps and bird calls?" Christopher asked.

"Actually, I've gotten more. Including the fact that the three who'd given us a lift and, as far as they're concerned, saved our lives from Louie the Lizard, are young adults. If we don't behave appropriately they're going to get in trouble with the community. And that can be bad and mean they're ostracized because of their helping weird strangers."

"Then let's make sure we behave appropriately," Chuckie said.

"I know, I just *know*, I'm going to hate the answer to this question," Christopher said. "But, how do we have to sleep?"

I knew he was going to hate the answer, too, but not as much as Jeff would hate the answer. "Spooned up together." Both guys opened their mouths, but I put my hand up and they didn't speak. "Per what they've told Bruno, it's going to get hella cold about an hour after dark. Cold for a planet that has two suns may not be our version of cold. Then again, it might be worse. This isn't Alpha Four, so I'm betting that Christopher is going to feel like he's freezing once night really hits, and I'm sure Chuckie and I aren't going to be asking to strip down to our skivvies. The Poofs cannot go large here—they will freak our hosts out beyond belief. Ergo, we're spooning and you two can fight about who cuddles up against my back and who gets the front on your own time."

"She moves a lot in her sleep," Chuckie said to Christopher. "I call dibs on her back."

"Jerk," Christopher muttered.

"Wow. I so totally feel the love."

"We're both envisioning what Jeff's going to do to us," Christopher snapped, sharing Patented Glare #2. "There is no win in this situation, and we're both past wanting to grope you."

"Speak for yourself," Chuckie said with a wicked grin. He and I both laughed while Christopher switched it up to Patented Glare #4. "I'm kidding, White. If you'll feel better, I'll take Kitty's front side."

"You two could spoon each other, you know."

"No, we couldn't," Christopher said flatly. "We'll work out who gets which side later."

"Honestly, it doesn't matter," Chuckie said. "I was just having fun at your expense. Seriously, she moves a lot in her sleep. At any time during the night she'll be using one of us for a butt pillow and one for a headrest. Just accept that it won't be fun, because she also hurdles in her sleep, and just roll with it."

"I think I resent all this personal information you're sharing about me. I can't deny it, but I do resent it. And I'm forced to add that Jeff never complains."

"Probably because he knows what's good for him," Chuckie said with another grin.

Wondered if Chuckie was really okay with this. Having just had Other Me around, presumably thinking he was her husband, at least for a little while, had to have been difficult, especially since he hadn't really recovered from losing Naomi and he'd just found out that the guy he thought had his back had been busy shoving knives into it for the past several years.

But right now he seemed fine, and, frankly, we weren't in a situation for him not to be fine. So, decided to err on the side of assuming he was smart enough to not let anything get to him at the moment and roll with things as we had to deal with them.

Our discussing the sleeping arrangements and such didn't seem to be taken amiss by our hosts. "Bruno, my bird, do you know what our katyhopper friends are really called and what their names are?"

Much feather ruffling, head bobbing, and clucking ensued.

"Aha. Well, that's very nice of them."

"What is?" Christopher asked.

"They say that there's no way we can pronounce their names or what they call themselves. They think katyhopper is a nice name and are fine with us calling them by that species name."

"Only you would be in this situation," Christopher pointed out.

"Be glad she is," Chuckie said. "Besides, White, they saved you first."

"True enough. Proved they were sentient. So, what do we call them?" he asked quickly, before Chuckie or I could add a comment. "By name, I mean, versus species."

"They said we could call them whatever we like." The guys gave me the "oh really" looks. "What?"

"It's not like with the Poofs, is it?" Christopher asked. "Where we name them and they're ours for life? Not that I have anything against the katyhoppers, mind you. But, if all goes well, we'll be leaving this planet, and that means leaving them behind, because I'm sure they don't want to go to and probably can't live on Earth."

"Ah. No, not like that at all, at least from what Bruno said. They're sentient for certain, and they know we use names, and they also know we can't manage their names, so, whatever we want to call them, as long as it's not mean or insulting, is fine with them. And they mean if it's mean or insulting to us. They've already said that what offends them and us will be different and they're making allowances."

Chuckie looked thoughtful. "If you're not making this up or just winging it, Kitty, and if they really shared all this with Bruno, they're of a very high sentience level."

"Peregrine's Honor, that's what transpired." At least insofar as Bruno knew, but he seemed confident and who was

I to argue? He'd been born in this solar system, after all.
"Bruno's from here, remember. I'm betting on him having
the skills to translate what's going on properly."

"Then maybe they are the highest sentient life-forms
here and were just being docile because they were trying to
help us."

"Could be. All I know is that it's time to nest."

"Truly, I can't wait," Chuckie said. "I just hope that,
whenever they find out, Jeff and Amy both understand that
we all snuggled together because we had to."

Christopher looked pale. "I hadn't thought about Amy's
reaction to any of this."

I patted him on the shoulder. "Don't worry. I'll tell her
you were great."

CHAPTER 17

TO HIS GREAT CREDIT, Christopher didn't snarl at me for this one. He just shot Patented Glare #4 at me and Chuckie, probably because we were both still snickering.

"Is there a plan past sleeping together?" Chuckie looked around. "Because while it's lovely here, I don't think we're going to be able to stay here too long."

"I don't either, unless this question is answered in the positive—do we get to eat?" Christopher asked quietly. "Because it's been a long time since lunch."

"I'm not sure, and now isn't really the time for us to ask." Due to having started my day in Australia and ended it in another solar system, I had no idea what time it was anywhere. "And at least you had food somewhere in there. Chuckie and I didn't get breakfast, and I can't speak for him, but I didn't get a lot of food in during the few minutes of briefing session before we started our latest Journey Into the Weird."

Bruno clucked at us, then the three katyhoppers we'd been riding indicated we needed to mount up again. Once we were so mounted, they flew us up to a middle section of the gigantic nest apartment.

We dismounted, more antennae were waved about, then our katyhoppers hopped off, but not far.

Our family group of friendly helpers were housing with another young group of katyhoppers in the nest next to the one they put us in, and it was easy to see that the space was crowded.

Despite being made of branches and such, the nest was

comfortable. Cramped if you were pony-sized, but comfortable. For us it was roomy. Once we settled down, Bruno shared some more.

"Those piles of leaves and such are their food," I told the guys quietly. "They know we can't eat it, but they have no food for us and it's too dangerous to let us out to try to find food we can eat anyway."

"How are they talking to Bruno?" Christopher asked. "I mean really? I wouldn't have guessed birds and insects to even be friendly, let alone able to communicate."

"No idea. I'm willing to take the favors as they come to us, though."

"He's smaller than they are," Chuckie pointed out. "Meaning the butterflies or whatever they really are would be Bruno's prey, but not the katyhoppers. He's sentient, so are they. Though, honestly, I'd have expected the Poofs to be doing the communication. Though I couldn't tell you why."

Considered this. "Maybe the Poofs are providing translation services." Looked into my purse. Harlie and Poofikins shot me with their Standard Looks O' Innocence. "Yep, I'm right. Bruno had the natural skills—remember, he talks to a human all the time, and that's as different from an avian as an insect is—and anything else the Poofs are helping with."

Meaning Algar was assisting, or at least the Poofs had decided that the Free Will Manifesto Algar lived by included keeping us all alive on an alien planet that was likely to be hostile territory. We got so few gimmes like this I was more than happy to take this one and just send a big Thanks For Doing Us A Solid out to the cosmos.

Since I was looking in it anyway, decided now was the time to take inventory. I carefully rifled through my purse's contents. I had a good helping of syringes filled with adrenaline, which would be great should we find Jeff and he need to be revived, but whose presence boded. I had my Glock and a lot of clips. I also had some food bars. I never carried food bars, and there were far more syringes of adrenaline than I had in here on a normal basis, so I was sure I'd find more needful things if I kept on digging.

However, I heard stomachs rumbling, and mine was one

of them. "We have a small meal available to us, but no water."

Bruno squawked quietly, then he flapped to the nest next door and had a quiet conversation. The katyhopper I'd been riding flew off and Bruno came back to us.

"Where is he going?" I asked.

"What do you mean 'he'?" Christopher asked. "That's the pink one."

"Yep and they don't have colors assigned to genders, because my katyhopper is the boy. You two are riding the girls." Bruno hadn't told me this, I just knew it. Maybe the Poofs weren't helping Bruno all that much—maybe I was. Or maybe we all were. Maybe ACE was nearby and on the case. And maybe this was all a dream and I'd wake up under a tree and realize that Alice had nothing on me.

But no matter. Watched my katyhopper fly up into the trees. He came back down with three small fruits held in his front legs. He dropped them carefully into my lap and went off again. He came back two more times, so that we had nine of the fruits.

"Thank you so much, Pinky, we really appreciate it."

Pinky rubbed his front legs together to create a pleasant hum. He waved his antennae at us, then he hopped back to the next-door nest.

"I'm not calling mine Yellowy," Christopher muttered.

"Of course not. Yours is named Saffron."

Chuckie grinned as Christopher rolled his eyes. "And mine? Sky? Turkey?"

"I think she'll like Turkey, so sure. Anyway, what Pinky brought us are called, I think, waterfruit, or this world's equivalent. They literally hold liquid more than fruit."

"Is it safe for us to drink?" Chuckie asked. "I mean that seriously. We don't have the same physical makeup as an A-C, let alone a katyhopper."

"I'll try it first," Christopher said. "As long as it's not alcoholic, I should be fine."

"But if it is, or if it metabolizes like that in your system, you'll be having seizures and we have no doctor around, let alone any medicine other than adrenaline. Meaning it's up to me."

So saying I carefully used a fingernail to cut a hole in the purple skin of the fruit. As I did so, I took a deep sniff. "Smells like purple, the same purple from the trees. And it also smells like liquid. And no, I can't say why."

"Maybe there's something in the atmosphere here that makes scents filter into the brain as an image," Chuckie suggested.

"Maybe. Going to take a drink now. So, um, you know, be prepared for me to die and all that. Or not. Really hoping not."

Sure I could have asked Bruno or one of the Poofs to try this, but they had different metabolisms than we did, too. Besides, they weren't my Royal Tasters. They were my pets.

Both guys looked worried and ready to argue. But we were hungry and thirsty, Chuckie was more likely to have read through medical journals for fun than I was, and Christopher was the fastest man alive.

"Down the hatch." And with that, I took a sip.

CHAPTER 18

RESISTED THE URGE to fake dying—hard as it was, based on the guys' worried expressions—in no small part because I wasn't sure if the katyhoppers understood humor like we did and I didn't want them panicking.

"Tastes like purple. Not wine, not grape juice, but like liquid purple. It's really good. Do I look weird? Am I breaking out in spots or shrinking or growing or anything?"

"You're not *Alice in Wonderland*," Chuckie said. "And, no. Thankfully, you look like you." He sniffed. "Only you smell a little purple now."

"Huh. I wonder if the water in this area is what causes all the monochromatic color theme around here along with all the good smells."

Took another sip. The juice or whatever was really good. We waited a few minutes, but I remained me. The guys tried a fruit each—same thing. Tasted purple, none of us died. Handed out food bars, though Bruno and the Poofs passed on eating them. Shared the rest of my waterfruit with Bruno while the guys shared theirs with the Poofs. None of us suggested drinking down the six other fruits we had.

As we ate, night fell. Fast. The katyhoppers hadn't been exaggerating—it was dark by the time we'd finished and I could tell the temperature had already dropped some.

Once we'd eaten Bruno took the fruit skins in his beak and flew them down to the big piles. I shoved the empty wrappers into my purse—no reason to litter. I carefully put the waterfruit in my purse, too, using the wrappers to sort of pad them. They might be the only liquid we could find, and I knew without asking that none of us planned to stay here once daylight returned.

None of us were farmers, and I was as far away from an "early to bed, early to rise" type as you could get. However, the katyhoppers were settling down. And we were treated to a beautiful sight.

The darker it got, the brighter their young glowed. Being inside their hidden nest fortress at night made a lot of sense—why literally have a sign telling predators where your babies were? At least I hoped that no one who wasn't touching a katyhopper could get in here, or even see what was really in here. If they could get in, they'd be able to see all of us easily.

Decided the katyhoppers hadn't built this elaborate nesting complex in a day, and actively chose to relax.

The bright glowing didn't last long. As each baby went to sleep, its glow died down, leaving the lights turned low but not off. It was a lot like sleeping in standard A-C housing, where nightlights were always on in every room. Only in this world, the nightlights were dotted about, since not every family group had a young one. Wondered if the need for low light at night was something this solar system required for some reason, or if there were just more things hiding out here in the dark to be afraid of.

Couldn't tell if the adults were asleep or not, since I couldn't hear them breathing in the first place. And I didn't have a clue if katyhoppers breathed rhythmically when they slept anyway. But if they were asleep, they were silent sleepers who didn't move much. A quick wing flap here or there was all that I could spot, and those were fast, soft, and far between.

Heard a rustling that wasn't katyhopper wings or legs. Wasn't sure what it was, but it seemed far away. "Think that's Louie?" I asked quietly.

Chuckie lay down. "Honestly? I doubt it. Let's not think about what could be out there, okay? There's a reason we're all in here."

"What Reynolds said." Christopher lay down as well. Their Poofs cuddled into their necks.

Considered using my purse as a pillow, but didn't want to squish the waterfruit, and besides, I had a gun in there, too. Put my purse above our heads, then snuggled down in between the guys. Bruno settled at my head, between us and the purse. We were all lying on our backs, well, the guys and I were, and about all I could see above us was a canopy of leaves and branches. "I can barely see the sky."

"Good," Chuckie said softly. "That means predators can barely see us, too."

"Good point."

As we lay there the air around us turned colder. And I could tell by their breathing that no one, not even the Poofs, were asleep. Some, I suspected, due to the unfamiliarity of where we were, but most likely due to cold. I snuggled closer to Chuckie. "Back to back or spooning?" he asked me softly.

"Depends."

"On what?" Christopher asked in kind.

"On how cold it's going to get and how cold you are, honestly."

"I'm okay right now, but I see why the katyhoppers wanted us nesting."

"Yeah. Their nest is snug for them but kind of big for us."

"Hence why they suggested spooning," Chuckie pointed out.

Considered the fact that I'd slept next to Charles in the other universe and managed to keep it chaste. And freezing to death wasn't really in the Smart Wife Handbook at any rate. Rolled onto my side and snuggled my back up against Chuckie, who moved his arm so I could lie on it. "Better?" he asked with a chuckle.

"Yeah. Christopher, snuggle up, it's chilly and I promise not to compromise your virtue."

"Oh, fine." He went onto his side and put his back to me, then shifted closer.

"That's better, or at least a lot warmer. Thanks, guys." Felt bone tired all of a sudden.

"Goodnight, Kitty, Chuck."

"Goodnight, Christopher, Kitty."

Chose not to mention that all of a sudden they were using each other's first names. Bonding happened in different ways for different people. "Night, guys. Sleep tight. Don't let the alien bedbugs, which I'm in no way insinuating our gracious hosts have, bite."

It was definitely warmer this way, and the proof of this was that we all fell asleep.

I woke up and realized I'd moved. Sure enough, just as Chuckie had predicted, my butt was up against Christopher, who was curved around my back, and my head was on Chuckie's chest and he had both arms around me. Figured I'd probably kicked them both a few times, too, but oh well, it hadn't been intentional. Hoped the katyhoppers didn't have some way of taking a picture of this, because I was certain how we were cuddled up together wasn't going to make either Jeff or Amy happy.

Both men were still asleep, snoring quietly. So were the Poofs, all making tiny, adorable little snore sounds. Noted that we were the only ones making sleep noises. Also noted that I didn't hear Bruno. But I felt him. He was snuggled between me and Christopher. Clearly it was cold for everyone. Missed blankets and wondered how the katyhoppers were faring. Probably better than us, since they were used to it.

Frankly, I wasn't that cold, but only because of how we were all dog-piled together. No one was making unusual noises, and I hadn't been dreaming, as far as I recalled. So, why had I woken up?

Listened carefully. No, the only sounds I was hearing were from our little nest. Either the katyhoppers truly slept like the dead—and my knowledge of insect sleeping sounds wouldn't fill even the smallest of thimbles—or they were all gone. Sincerely hoped they weren't all gone.

I was now wide awake. Listened more intently. There had to have been a reason I'd woken up.

No sooner had I thought this than Pinky hopped over, followed by Saffron and Turkey. Each katyhopper settled above the person who'd been riding them earlier. They didn't sit on us so much as sit over us—their legs kept their bodies just above ours. Since we were piled together, they were right next to each other. I could tell they'd stepped on the guys, because I heard quiet grumbling from Christopher, though he sounded like he was still asleep, and Chuckie's breathing changed and I felt him start to wake up.

"This is really sweet of you," I said softly, "but you guys need your sleep and to stay warm, too."

The katyhoppers didn't move. They also didn't provide a lot of warmth, probably because they had chitin instead of skin, and a hard shell rarely equaled the spreading of warmth.

Was about to say that their efforts were great but not doing what they wanted and they should just sleep when I heard something and kept my mouth shut. I heard rustling, like I had before we'd fallen asleep. Only it was louder and seemed much closer. Realized that this sound must have been what had awakened me and probably the katyhoppers, too.

Then I heard a sound I really hadn't wanted to hear, a sound that sent ice through my veins and made me sick to my stomach with fear.

A hiss.

CHAPTER 19

AND NOT JUST ANY HISS. A very loud, very long, very big-sounding hiss. A hiss that sounded like it was coming from the biggest teakettle or, far more likely, the biggest snake around.

The guys and our animals were all awake now. I'd felt them wake up, hear the sound, and freeze. And I could feel the fear—not only from those of us in our nest, but from all the katyhoppers. Whatever kind of snake-thing was out there, it was what the katyhoppers feared the most. So I had that in common with them.

We shifted around so that we were all on our backs, looking up at our katyhoppers. What I wanted to do most was burrow under covers we didn't have and hide. What I wanted to do next most was hide behind Chuckie and Christopher, which, considering we were all lying down, wasn't a workable plan, either. And, what I wanted to do as a third alternate was run away as fast as possible. Of course, I had no idea where I'd run to in the first place, and in the second place, that would leave the katyhoppers alone to deal with this terrifying predator.

However, what I did was force myself to reach up and slowly and quietly drag my purse to me. Got it over my neck and put the Poofs into it. And all the while the rustling and hissing kept on intermittently.

As I moved Bruno onto my stomach, I realized that the rustling sounded like it was coming from above us. Meaning the snake was in the trees. Or snakes.

Chuckie took one of my hands in his and Christopher

took the other. Presumed they'd both either read my mind or were just good guessers about the state of said mind. They both squeezed my hands gently and I clutched them back in a death grip.

The rustling got louder. And closer.

Most of my mind was terrified because I was beyond terrified of snakes. But there was a calm part of my mind, too. Oh, it was a small part, to be sure, but a part nonetheless. And this calm part of my mind wondered if the snake always came around, or if it was coming tonight because we were here.

We had to smell different from anything else on this planet, other than those who'd been brought over with us— if they were even on this planet. And we made noises while we slept, and the katyhoppers didn't.

So it could have smelled us, heard us, or both. But the likelihood that the snake was here because of us seemed awfully high.

And that meant that dealing with it was also up to us, because the katyhoppers had helped us and protected us, and that meant we had to do the same for them.

I had no idea what was really out there, or what would kill it, but I had one thing that was unlikely to be available on this planet—I had my Glock.

Let go of Christopher's hand and slid my hand into my purse, taking time to pet the Poofs along the way, more to comfort myself than to comfort them. Got my gun in my hand and drew it out slowly. The safety was on—proving, as if I needed it, that Algar had had a hand in my purse's contents, because I still forgot to set the safety an easy nine times out of ten—and I didn't take it off, because we were in too close of quarters to risk it.

That Glocks in the other universe I'd visited didn't come with safeties had been a shock. They still worked like a Glock otherwise, though, so I'd been able to stay in practice while I was gone.

Which was hopefully going to be a good thing. I'd faced a giant snake during Operation Fugly, after all. If I'd handled the Serpent without losing it, I could handle whatever was out there in the dark. And Christopher and I had both dealt with a big rattlesnake during Operation Fugly, too. Sure, we'd blown up the apartment building where I'd lived to get rid of it, but that was due to our enemies having set bombs there more than any overkill for one deadly snake.

And maybe if I told myself these things over and over again, I'd believe them — the Little Kitty That Could sort of thing.

I was able to see better, and I realized this meant that the katyhopper young were waking up. This wasn't going to be good.

Let go of Chuckie and gently shoved at Pinky. At first the katyhopper didn't move, but he finally got the hint and moved back a bit so that I could sit up. The guys did the same with their katyhoppers, and we were all able to get up. I hugged Bruno, then put him down.

We all looked around. Unsurprisingly, the A-C spotted what was hunting us first.

Christopher pointed, up as I'd surmised. Focused on where he was indicating and, after a few seconds, I could see it.

It was a lot worse than I'd been imagining.

The snake above us wasn't as big as the Serpent, so we had that going for us. Unfortunately, it was easily triple anaconda-sized, especially in girth. And it also had wings. Lots and lots and lots of little wings on its back. It also had some weird, short, antenna-like protrusions above its eyes.

Basically it was a snake crossed with a centipede, only instead of a ton of little legs on the underside, it had all those wings on top. Presumed it was in the purple family, because it was hard to see and I figured we were only able to catch a glimpse because our eyes were adjusted to the light and all the katyhopper babies were awake.

Though the glow wasn't as light as I would have expected. Risked a look around and saw all the adults with young standing over them, just as Pinky, Saffron, and Turkey had done with us. So they'd been protecting us from the predator.

"Is it inside the nest's protection?" I asked as softly as possible.

Pinky moved his antennae just a little, presumably his way of speaking softly in kind. Snakes were good at catching small movements, too, so he was probably trying to remain unnoticed. But basically, I got the impression that his answer was a terrified "not sure."

Didn't want to, but I forced myself to focus on the snakipede. If I could sense a mind there, maybe I could communicate with it, make it a friend, or at least make it go away.

But I got nothing. Whether this meant that there was no mind there—which I doubted—or that I either had no affinity with said mind, and vice versa, I couldn't say. But my mind melding with the snakipede appeared to be out as a workable option.

There was a good chance the snakipede was sentient to a higher degree than snakes on Earth—the katyhoppers certainly were. But I didn't care. It was threatening our new friends—friends who'd gone out of their way to protect us—and that made it an enemy. And Christopher and I both had something that, potentially, the snakipede didn't—hyperspeed. And I had a gun with a lot of bullets.

The snakipede reared back all of a sudden, hissed in a triumphant manner, and slammed its head toward the nest, jaws open, huge fangs gleaming in the low light. Whatever the illusion was that protected this area, it shattered. Literally. Shards of iridescent something floated down like snowflakes.

The katyhoppers made sounds now, the same sounds that our three had done before—the screeching that sounded like a rusty metal door being opened slowly—only it was all of them, extremely loud and incredibly close.

The sound was painful, but the snakipede wasn't stopped. It sailed in toward the nest.

Mom had spent a lot of time working with me on relaxed, rapid-fire shooting. Christopher had worked with me for several years now, perfecting my ability to get to my inherited A-C skills when I wasn't enraged.

Which was good, because I wasn't mad—I was terrified. But the katyhoppers were more terrified. Each were grabbing young and trying to fly to safety, but the snakipede was fast and above us, and it was striking to keep all of them down and inside. And, unlike a regular snake, because of its wings, it didn't need to land on anything.

I aimed for the snakipede's head, ready to shoot. But it was moving too much and too fast for me to shoot without risking killing a katyhopper. But it was getting closer to them, and one of the next strikes was going to include a katyhopper death—at least one, if not many more. A snake this size could easily eat the entire colony.

CHAPTER 20

AS THE GIANT snakipede flew straight toward us, I ignored everything else and focused on its horrible head.
Took aim—right between its eyes and antenna-like
protrusions—and fired.

Emptied the clip into the snakipede's head, reached into
my purse, pulled out another clip, dropped out the old, put
in the new. At hyperspeed. And without missing a beat.
Then I emptied the new clip into the thing's head, particularly into its gaping, open maw.

The snakipede's head exploded and the Poofs took over.

They went large and in charge, roared, then leaped onto
the rest of the snakipede and devoured it in moments.
Burped discreetly, then went small and back into my purse.
All this only took a couple of seconds. Clearly the Poofs had
been starving.

"Wow, got a double. Killed the terrifying monster and
fed four out of our five animal companions. Go team. Can
I cry, freak out, and throw up now?"

"No, but that was impressive as hell," Chuckie said, voice
shaking just a bit. "Truly."

"I agree, and I just hope to hell you didn't kill the katyhopper's god or something," Christopher added.

It was hard to tell if the katyhoppers were relieved,
freaked out, still frightened, or all three. But the three with
us stayed with us, so that was good. Especially when the
elders flew up and started waving antennae about like antenna waving was going out of style and they needed to use
up their full supply before sunrise.

Pinky, Saffron, and Turkey all waved antennae right back. It didn't take an insect languages genius to realize they were arguing. But I also didn't need Bruno to translate. Meaning I was getting more simpatico with the katyhoppers, which was hopefully a good thing.

"We didn't tell you about the Poofs because we didn't want to scare you," I said, when there was a pause in the antenna waving. "And we know we're what attracted that snakipede thing to your nest. That's why we were the ones who killed it."

"Snakipede?" Christopher asked.

"It's Kitty, why ask why? But if you need a translation, that snake had what looked like a hundred tiny wings instead of legs, which is where the centipede part comes in, I'm sure."

"Right you are, Chuckie. And, guys? Be ready to be tossed out of the nest. I can understand why our hosts are upset with us, even though we had no idea that the snakipede existed, let alone that it would hear the noises all of us make while we're sleeping."

I was saying this far more for the katyhopper elders' benefit than anyone else's and I was happy to note both men seemed to catch on.

"Were any katyhoppers hurt?" Chuckie asked.

Antennae waved. "No, the snakipede spent too much time keeping them in the nests and playing around. Thankfully. And I distracted it just in time."

"Good," Christopher said. "Is there anything we can do to help fix nests or the protective illusion or similar?"

Antennae waved again, but this time with much less agitation. "No. We can't fix anything. Unfortunately, the nest is fouled due to the snakipede's head exploding all over it."

And this was the main point of contention—we may have saved the day, but we'd also destroyed their home in the process.

"I can clean it, in less time than anyone else, if someone tells me what needs to be done to get rid of whatever the snakipede's residue is," Christopher said calmly.

This earned him skeptical antenna waves from the elders.

"He can. He's the fastest being out there, as far as we

know. It's worth a try, isn't it? If he's wrong, what do you lose?"

The elders communed together and finally admitted they'd lose nothing in Christopher making the attempt.

"Okay, they're willing to let you try. It's kind of complex and totally icky, by the way. What you have to do to clean up, I mean. And I'm not sure that Chuckie and I can help."

"Don't need it. I can manage. Just tell me what to do."

Leaves from the trees were brought down, as were waterfruit. Basically, Christopher had to cleanse the nest using the trees. Which made some kind of sense.

Christopher zipped off to do what I could say with confidence was the weirdest housecleaning of his life. Pinky, Saffron, and Turkey went with him. Figured it was going to take him a little longer than normal, but probably not as long as the katyhoppers expected.

"I could understand most of what they were saying," Chuckie said to me while we waited. "Not as much as you could, but then animal communication isn't my talent."

"No, being the smartest guy in the purple is. So, why do you think we can commune so easily with an alien race that has almost nothing in common with us, physically at least?"

"My guess is the air and the water are charged with something that enhances psionic ability. Meaning that your husband, if he's here, may be able to find us if you just concentrate on him."

"I'll try that once we've fixed things with the katyhoppers. Besides, I don't want Jeff or anyone else coming around here in the dark—the snakipedes are nocturnal. And there are definitely more of them."

Elder antennae waved at this. There were many more of them, and I'd been correct in my assumption—the snakipedes were this area's top predator. But they did offer some reassurances that I, personally, appreciated.

"Interesting," Chuckie said. "Did I interpret correctly? They just told you that the snakipedes, as you've so aptly named them, aren't intelligent like we, the Poofs, Bruno, and the katyhoppers themselves are?"

"That's indeed what they shared. I'm glad. I was a little worried that I was killing something really smart. Then again, I've killed smart people. A lot, if I stop to count."

"Yeah, let's not list your carnage abilities for our new friends right now. Especially because we really want to keep them as our friends."

"Well, that was gross," Christopher said as he rejoined us. The katyhopper elders seemed shocked. Nice to know they didn't have hyperspeed. "Now what?"

Pinky, Saffron, and Turkey arrived as he asked this. But before any katyhopper could wave an antenna at us, they all turned and looked up. So we did the same.

A large, ancient katyhopper was slowly descending from a nest above ours. I could tell it was old not only because of how slowly it was moving, but because its chitin was multicolored. It stopped at the nest above ours and began to wave its antennae at us.

Did the interpretation, just in case. "This is the colony's, oh wow, matriarch. Or shaman. Or both. I think both. Every katyhopper here is related to her in some way and she's been in this nest colony for, gosh, if I'm understanding this right, a thousand years."

Chuckie whistled softly. "It's possible. Based on coloration, shaman or similar is also a good bet."

"She's thanking us for saving the nest and you, in particular, Christopher, for cleansing it so well."

"Ah, tell her I was happy to do it."

"She can understand us. They all can. Their antennae take the sound waves and translate them into their heads. The Matriarch is tasking us with an important job, though."

She waved antennae and even got her legs and wings into the action. Once I got what she was saying, though, I understood why.

"There is danger from above. And not just the snakipedes. The Matriarch has seen something they haven't seen before in the skies. The other Matriarchs of the other katyhopper colonies that are, apparently, scattered throughout this part of the world, the purple part, all have seen it, too."

"What have they seen?" Chuckie asked.

"They can't describe it."

The Matriarch hopped down to me and put her antennae against my temples. And I could see exactly what she had. And more. Then she backed away and waited.

"We'll do what we can. All we can. I promise."

The Matriarch waved her antennae, but this time at our

three katyhoppers. Then she bowed to me, turned, and hopped back up to her nest.

"What did she show you?" Chuckie asked.

"What's coming. What's out there."

"And that is?" Christopher asked.

"Spaceships. And lots of them."

CHAPTER 21

DAWN WAS COMING, as fast as night had fallen. But we hadn't slept any more after speaking with the Matriarch. Well, Christopher, Chuckie, and I hadn't. The Poofs were snoozing in my purse and Bruno was on my lap, head tucked under his wing, getting in his forty winks, too.

But the three of us chose to sit and watch the katyhoppers recreate their shield.

"If I'd known we were going through that, I might not have wanted to," Christopher said quietly.

"True enough."

The katyhoppers sprayed a clear liquid out of their butts all over the inner part of their copse of trees. As it solidified, it took on the look of the trees around them, almost in mirror image, so that it made the copse look double its size and also as if there were no easy paths in between the trees.

It took a lot of katyhoppers to do this — all the adults in the colony as near as I could tell. All but our three, who were staying in the nest with us now. But that was because they were now assigned to us by the Matriarch. "I'm choosing to believe it's water, okay?"

"I'm not," Chuckie said. "But I'll spare you what I think it is."

"Thanks, and I mean that, Chuck."

"You suffered enough with the snakipede cleanup, Christopher. I see no reason to share more."

Well, whatever else happened, these two had somehow crossed a bridge, and that was worth much of what we'd gone through.

The katyhoppers finished up and a few of them brought us more waterfruits. We finished up what we already had, and I put these new ones into my purse for later, just in case we couldn't get back here easily. Better to save my special requests for hard-to-find and necessary items, versus something I could pluck off a local tree.

Then it was clearly time to go. We remounted our katyhoppers and they flew us around the nest. We waved our hands to the katyhoppers and they waved their antennae.

"It's nice of them to tell us we always have a home here," Christopher said as our katyhoppers landed on the ground and walked us back through what appeared to be a tree trunk but which we now knew was viscous katyhopper butt fluid.

Once outside the colony, though, Pinky shared that he'd like a destination. And I had no idea. "Um, let's get up high and take a look around, okay?"

We did so, and flew around again, just as we had the day before. This time we flew more toward the mountains in the distance. The land was dotted with more than copses of trees—which were where I assumed the other katyhopper colonies resided. There were hillocks with large holes on their sides, covered with the purple plants but not butterflies. Figured this was where chameleons lived, and when one popped its head out and sent its tongue up at us, that assumption was confirmed.

After about an hour of leisurely flying we passed over a carcass. I had the katyhoppers bring us a little closer so we could examine it.

"Is that Louie the Lizard?" I hoped it wasn't. I'd kind of gotten attached. But it was clear that the chameleon had been attacked by a snakipede, based on the fang marks, and a few other telltale signs, including what looked like a couple of snakipede wings. The chameleon had put up a fight. Good.

"Not sure," Chuckie said. "But probably not. We've flown much farther than yesterday."

"The chameleons are more sentient than the snakipedes." Per the Matriarch, anyway, and I had no reason to disbelieve her.

"I'm sorry, Kitty," Chuckie said gently, as we flew back up to where we had a better view of the horizon. "But we're in an animal kingdom, and we ourselves eat animals that are intelligent."

"I know. I just . . ."

"You just get attached easily. I know." Chuckie jerked. "Hey, look." He pointed off into the distance, where there was what looked like a different mountain range than the one we were heading for. "Christopher, is that dust being thrown up into the air?"

Christopher and I both squinted where Chuckie was pointing. "Yes, I think so," Christopher said slowly.

"Wow, Eagle Eyes Reynolds, come on down." It was dust—if the dust on this planet was a reddish-ochre color. Based on the riot of color around me that was a safe bet. After all, this might be the Purple Land, but the Matriarch had definitely insinuated there were plenty of other lands on Planet Colorful.

"That color wasn't there a minute ago that I could see, that's all," Chuckie said. "But thanks for my Old West Name."

"So, do we keep on going toward these purple mountains, or do we head for the brownish mountains where we think something's going on?" Christopher asked.

Petted Bruno to wake him up. "Bruno my bird, are you up to some reconnaissance?"

He nuzzled me and gave me the head bob, meaning he was well rested and more than up to it. Bruno lifted off of Pinky's back, but to my surprise, the katyhoppers all followed him.

"Pinky, my proud steed, why are we all changing course?" Pinky waved back at me. We had no real destination, so one mountain range was as good as another.

Saffron waved her antennae, too. They'd never been allowed out of the Purple Lands and all three of them were excited about the adventure.

Made sense that we'd landed with the brave, adventuresome katyhoppers. Who else would have tried to save us versus run away or eat us, after all?

Bruno was flying pretty fast, certainly faster than we'd gone yesterday or had been going today, and the katyhoppers were having no trouble keeping up with him. "Katyhopper Express is the way to go. Are they using hyperspeed, do you think?"

In my experience, every being from the Alpha Centauri system was super-speedy. But the katyhoppers hadn't shown any ability with this so far, and they'd been hella impressed by Christopher's hyperspeed cleaning of their nest.

"Not quite," Christopher said. "Not supersonic, either. Frankly, I just think they're fast when they want or need to be, but not as fast as we are."

"If they were A-C fast, they wouldn't have been afraid of the snakipede," Chuckie pointed out.

"So does that mean no beings on this planet have hyperspeed? And, if so, wouldn't that be weird? Everyone else from this neck of the galactic woods has been super-fast."

I'd just spent time going at supersonic speeds during Operation Bizarro World, so I could admit that this probably wasn't that fast, and Christopher was our Resident Hyperspeed Expert.

But I knew the Peregrines had hyperspeed, and I also knew Bruno was going fast, and faster than I felt I'd seen him go on Earth. So, if he wasn't using hyperspeed, but was still zipping along here, maybe Bruno could fly faster here at "normal" speeds for some reason. But I didn't feel either more or less weighty, and my knowledge of physics said that if there was a stronger or lesser gravitational pull on a planet, I'd feel lighter or heavier.

"Christopher, do you have any idea if there is more gravitational pull on some of the planets than others?" Chuckie asked.

"Wow, the mind-reading thing is getting freaky."

"It's just a logical question under the circumstances," Chuckie said.

"Yeah, it is," Christopher said. "The question being logical and the mind reading being freaky, I mean. I have no idea about the gravitational pull, though. As with other things, if we can find Lorraine, Claudia, or Serene, they may know. But I don't. And I don't feel any different here than on Earth."

"You mean besides being able to read each other's minds and commune with the katyhoppers, right?"

Christopher barked a laugh. "Right."

We flew on toward the brownish mountains. Despite our moving swiftly it was far away. We had to stop at a lone tree and have a rest, during which time the guys and I ate food bars and we all had some more waterfruit, which thankfully every tree in this region produced in abundance. Still, I took more, just in case. We were heading toward a different color scheme, and it might not be as generous with the life-sustaining plant life as this one was.

We took off again and finally could see where we were heading. It was far more like the dust—a reddish-ochre—than the mountains, which were mostly browns. As such, this area didn't look nearly as inviting as what we were leaving. However, as with Purple Land, the colors were vibrant.

Finally, though, we left the purpleness fully and crossed over into reddish-ochre land. Didn't feel any different here, and the katyhoppers seemed fine, so that was one for the win column.

There was less plant life here and more dirt, but the plants and trees and such were all reds, browns, tawny yellows and oranges, and the like. The plants were far more scattered here than in the Purple Land, though there were more trees, and many more rocks and boulders than I'd seen on this planet so far. Some of the trees sort of looked like citrus trees, but only just.

The biggest similarity to the Purple Land was that the plants were all monochromatic within their color of choice. If a plant was yellow-brown, it was all yellow-brown. If a tree was orange, all of it was orange, from bark to fruit. But nothing here smelled like oranges.

As with the purple part of this world, this area didn't smell bad. But here the scent wasn't sweet—it was the smell of burning wood without the actual burning and sunsets. Mostly sunsets, really. Though, as with purple, before now I wouldn't have said sunsets had a smell.

Chuckie cleared his throat. "Ah, do you two think this area smells like, ah, sunsets?"

"Yeah, I do. Along with burning wood that isn't burned. And should I be glad we're still able to read each other's minds in this part of the world or not?"

"I get the smell of a cigarette before it's lit along with, yes, sunsets," Christopher said. "But worry about the smells and the mind-reading stuff later." He sounded tense but not snarky. Wasn't sure if that was a win or not, so decided to table that decision for later. "I can see what we're heading toward. It's a caravan of some kind."

"How long before we intercept it?" Chuckie asked.

"Probably a couple of minutes. I don't think they're moving as fast as we are. Honestly, I don't think they're moving quickly at all. I'm pretty positive they're at a fast walk, not any kind of run. And by fast walk I mean for a human, not an A-C."

"Regular speed? Normalcy? Come on, I don't think that's exactly on the docket."

Christopher managed a chuckle. "No, probably not. But we need to assume that they have projectile weapons of some kind with them, if only because giant flying snake-things exist in at least one part of this world and I can say that if whoever's coming toward us is capable of it, making a weapon that could get rid of flying snakes while they were in the air would be the first thing I'd do."

"Good point. But we don't look like snakipedes. At least, I don't think. Thank God."

"No, but we have no idea if we look normal or threatening for around here."

"Snakipede resemblance or not, I'd assume we look threatening," Chuckie said. "Since even if the natives of this part of the world routinely ride on katyhoppers—which seems unlikely since our three friends have never left or been allowed to leave their region before—the Peregrine probably doesn't look like native birds, and none of us have a hope of being dressed normally for around here."

Bruno looked over his shoulder at me, winked, then turned back and flew on.

"Um, Chuckie? If we look at Bruno's coloration, we have to ask ourselves if he would not, in fact, look totally like he belongs here on Planet Colorful."

"Good point," he conceded. "But whether that helps us, hinders us, or makes no difference at all for whatever's coming is something we're going to be finding out. And I truly doubt that the three of us can get away with blending in. We haven't blended yet."

"I think we're about to find out," Christopher said, voice tense. "Because I can see the caravan more clearly, and they have catapults. Incoming!"

He was right. Something was flying up from the caravan toward us. Something moving very fast.

"Um, guys? Is that what I think it is? Because if it is, I have one thing to shout. Bruno! Abort! Abort! Get to Kitty *now!*"

CHAPTER 22

WHAT WAS FLYING up toward us wasn't a projectile, in that sense. What whoever on the ground had put into their catapult and tossed to us was, as far as I could tell, a cat.

Hyperspeed and my shouted warning or not, Bruno wasn't able to get out of the way. The cat hit my Peregrine and flipped itself around so it was on Bruno's back.

I didn't think about it. Bruno was under attack and that meant he needed help. I jumped up onto the back of my katyhopper and, with Chuckie and Christopher both shouting at me, leaped toward the Peregrine.

Hit the bird and was able to grab the cat by the scruff of its neck and get it away from Bruno. I was able to hold the cat out and away from me with one hand while I got Bruno tucked under my other arm. Did this all at hyperspeed, go me.

Of course, the problem was that I wasn't able to fly, neither was the struggling and yowling cat I was now holding, nor was Bruno, because I was holding him. I was also pretty sure he was hurt—the cat had big claws.

The cat was also, typical for the area we were now in, a rusty orange color, with some blacks, browns, and yellows for highlights. Elongated, pointy ears, and extremely bright blue eyes. It looked a little foxy and a lot like a caracal, but in the same way that Bruno looked a lot like a peacock—similar and yet stronger, a lot more human-level intelligent, and just a little more alien.

I could have let go of the cat, of course, but as far as I knew it had been thrown into the air much against its will.

Most cats didn't think flying was da bomb, after all, and falling even less so. I could relate. However, like it or not, I was plummeting downward, and I had no chance if I didn't do something.

So I pulled the cat into my body. "Please don't claw Kitty, Ginger. This is going to hurt badly enough when we land."

In point of fact, the cat didn't claw me. It looked up—well, relatively, based on the fact that we were kind of tumbling through the air—and gave me a very intelligent, very satisfied, and rather pleased look.

Checked Bruno. He seemed okay. Shaken, but okay. However, I wasn't sure that he was able to fly right now, since he wasn't trying to get away and take back to the air. "Hang on Bruno, my bird. And Ginger, you hang on, too. Just without your claws if at all possible, both of you, please and thank you. Kitty hopes these aren't going to be her last words, by the way."

Memory nudged. I had Poofs on Board, meaning I could ask for Poof assistance. The last time I'd fallen from great height, down a long garbage shaft during Operation Assassination, the Poofs had provided a soft, safe landing.

But before I could speak, we hit, but not the ground.

We hit something, or rather, someone.

"Ooof!"

"Wow. If we're not about to be killed, and if tossing Ginger up into the air wasn't some sort of attack or, even worse, some sort of bizarre Start The Fighting Now ritual, this is really kind of romantic. If I ignore the 'ooof,' that is."

Jeff grinned as relief that he was here and okay washed over me. "You fell a long way, baby, that's all. And your purse is even heavier than normal." Then he kissed me, and I didn't think about anything else for a good long moment.

Sadly, "moment" was accurate. Our kiss wasn't long. In part because I had two struggling and, now that we were on the ground, heavy animals in my arms, and in other part because I heard a lot of shouting.

Jeff heard it, too, of course. He ended our kiss and put me down. "It's okay, baby. They're friendly."

"The natives around here throw cats up into the air via catapult to say 'welcome to the neighborhood'?"

"No. The Lecanora I'm traveling with launched the ocellar before I could stop them. Hang on, I need to make sure they let Christopher and Chuck land." He trotted off before I could ask him who the Lecanora were or how he was traveling with them. Of course, I was traveling with katyhoppers, so I was in no position to pass judgment.

I put Ginger onto the ground then did a fast examination of Bruno. Bruno seemed okay—a little bleeding, but as with everyone from Alpha Four, he was healing quickly. Once I was done he nudged his head up under my chin and I gave him a big hug. "Kitty's glad her big brave bird is okay." Bruno shared that I was the best in his book, too.

Interestingly, Ginger didn't run off, but sat at my feet, in front of me. Now that we were on the ground I could verify Ginger's actual size. She—and I was sure it was a female in the same way I known Bruno was a boy when we'd first met—was about the size of a Peregrine without the tail feathers. So, smaller than a full-grown Earth caracal would be, but still, significantly larger than a housecat. So, fox-caracal was kind of right. Wondered if I should come up with a species name, then figured that Jeff had sort of insinuated that this was an ocellar, and decided to go with that for now and focus on more pressing concerns.

"Bruno, is it safe to put you down next to Ginger?"

Bruno eyed the big cat, who eyed him back. They had an animal conversation that I couldn't really catch, new mind-reading abilities notwithstanding, but finally Bruno kind of shrugged his wings, which I took to mean that he was willing to risk it but that if Ginger started something, Bruno was now prepared to finish it.

Put the bird down and he and the cat sized each other up. Then Ginger leaned toward Bruno and gently head-butted him. Bruno seemed surprised, but he head-butted back. Then they both settled at my feet.

Animal war averted, I looked to see what they were looking at. They weren't actually watching Jeff but Chuckie and Christopher and the three katyhoppers, all of whom were landing near to us but away from the caravan, which meant Bruno, Ginger, and I were between them and whoever Jeff was with. Based on this particular greeting, could not blame them.

Christopher and Chuckie dismounted and came over to me. The katyhoppers hopped along behind them. Planet Colorful was full of interesting and, happily so far, mostly friendly animal life. Hoped this trend would continue. One snakipede was enough for my entire lifetime.

"Thanks for taking yet more years off of our lives," Chuckie said as they reached us.

"What Chuck said," Christopher chimed in, gracing me with Patented Glare #5. "Why did you decide to jump off of Pinky instead of asking him to go faster?"

Knew they weren't going to like my answer. "I didn't want the katyhoppers to get hurt any more than I wanted Bruno to get hurt."

The katyhoppers all nudged up to me and gave me their equivalent of gentle head butts—meaning I got antennae strokes along my arms.

Chuckie nudged me when they were done and had moved back a bit. "It's empathy more than mind reading, though I'm sure that's in there somewhere, too. That's why the animals become so instantly loyal to you. Your own form of empathy, I mean. Not like Jeff's."

"I'm assuming you mean my special form of empathy is why I can talk to the animals, any and all animals. Maybe, I guess. But there are a lot of people out there who love and adore and are beyond empathetic with animals and they aren't having conversations with them in the way I tend to. I had no success with the snakipede, by the way. And I have no idea about the loyalty."

"Whatever it is," Christopher said quietly, "please keep on doing it. And Chuck, I can now confirm that we are definitely on Beta Eight."

He was looking toward where Jeff had gone and I finally decided it might be a good idea to see just who my husband was hanging with, so I took a good long look.

Who Jeff was with was less of a shock than Chuckie and I landing on the tops of trees had been, or Christopher riding to save us on a katyhopper, or, really, anything else that had happened on this planet so far. So we had that going for us.

CHAPTER 23

JEFF WAS HANGING with beings that looked remarkably like humanoid rodents. But not just any kind of rodents.

"They look like a cross between humans and mustelidae," Chuckie said.

"All our natural sciences classes in college that you didn't want to take but I did have sure paid off, haven't they? Yeah, they do. All of the animals in that group, I might add."

Well, the ones that were walking on two legs and were clearly the top of the sentience food chain, at least in the Brownish Lands, did. The animals drawing the caravans looked like brontosaurus horses, only small brontos and big horses. In addition to more animals that looked a lot like Ginger, which I assumed were ocellars, there were also animals that looked like pig-dogs. These were bigger than the ocellars and smaller than the bronto-horses.

"What are mustelidae?" Christopher asked.

"Our world's genus name for the carnivorous rodents that include weasels, badgers, skunks, minks, ferrets, and wolverines," Chuckie replied.

There were a lot of those beings bustling around the caravans, and while they all looked like humanoids, they were covering every mustelidae type Chuckie had just named and then some, both in body structures, fur, and markings.

"And otters." The being Jeff was leading to us looked like he was a human otter. "The guy with Jeff looks kind of like Benedict Cumberbatch, doesn't he?" If Cumberbatch was really a six-foot-plus-tall otter walking upright, that is.

"Who?" Christopher asked as Chuckie started laughing his head off. "Chuck, stop laughing. Whoever Jeff's with, he's the head of this group, you can tell by what he's wearing on his head."

"He has two branches that look like antlers on his head. Seriously, that proves he's the top man around here?"

He did have a lovely thick coat of brown fur. He wasn't wearing a lot of clothing, but he had a sword and sword belt, knee-high—or the otter equivalent—boots that allowed his four long, sharp claws to stick out from each paw, a Tarzan-like loincloth—presumably for modesty's sake—and a cape made out of what looked like leaves. Clearly these natives were earthy types. Hoped that meant they weren't going to try to attack or eat the katyhoppers.

"Bronze Age culture," Chuckie said, as he managed to stop laughing. "There have been stranger things used to denote leadership, Kitty."

"Good point. Okay, so Jeff seems chummy with King Benny there. That's good, right?"

"Maybe." Christopher sounded worried. "Only they may trust Jeff and not us."

"Guess we'll find out. Only Jeff and King Benny are coming over. Is that good?"

Chuckie looked around. "We're not surrounded, unless the katyhoppers are on the side of these others."

Looked where he was to see Saffron share that there was no way they were on the side of whatever these things were, particularly if these things were against us. Turkey shared that they'd play nicely with others, though, unless Chuckie, Christopher, or I gave the "attack" sign, and then they were up for the fight.

"The katyhoppers are on our side, whatever side that happens to be."

"Wish we knew what side we were on," Christopher muttered.

I'd have followed this particular thought longer, but Jeff and King Benny reached us.

King Benny looked at Ginger and said something to her in a language I didn't recognize. She didn't budge. He said whatever it was more strongly. Ginger remained firmly at my feet. He tried again, with emphasis in tone and hand gestures. Ginger yawned. Yeah, she was a cat.

"Ah, excuse me, but I think Ginger is kind of planning to hang out with me a little longer."

Jeff shot me the "shut up, shut up" look, but King Benny looked at me sharply. "She belongs to me," he said in perfect English.

"Okay, time out. That I had no idea what King Benny was saying to Ginger here makes total sense. But there's no way in the world he can speak my language." Animals were one thing. Highly sentient animals were another. Then again, the katyhoppers were clearly highly sentient, so maybe it was just my thing no matter what, where, who, or what.

"Now isn't the time," Jeff said quickly. "This is my mate, Kitty, my blood relative, Christopher, and our boon companion, Charles." Wondered if he'd said Charles instead of Chuck because there were woodchucks walking on their hind legs in the caravan and I'd just missed spotting them. Gave it at least a fifty-fifty shot. Why he was giving us old-fashioned titles I had less of a guess, though figured the answer would be Bronze Age Culture and so didn't comment. "This is Clan Leader Musgraff. Clan Leader, my family, like me, would like to help you."

"Honestly, I'd really like to know how it is that King Benny understands a word you're saying, Jeff. Along with how I can understand him. Before we agree to anything else."

"Jeff said not now, Kitty," Christopher snapped.

King Benny gave Christopher a long look. "The Mate of the Messenger of the Gods should not be dismissed, even if you are blood kin."

Couldn't speak for the guys, but I did a fast mindset change. "Thank you, Clan Leader Musgraff."

He shook his head. "I am not insulted by your use of an affectionate name for me, Mate of the Messenger of the Gods."

"Ah, I'd prefer that you call me Kitty, King Benny."

He nodded. "As you wish . . . Kitty. But I wonder, why do the Gods question their ability to understand us?"

"Ah . . ." Had no good answer for this one. Honestly wasn't prepared to be a God or God Mate or whatever.

"She is surprised you understand us," Chuckie said quickly. "We are impressed and your wisdom proves your leadership."

Wasn't sure how otters showed they were pleased, but had a good guess that King Benny was, because his eyes lit up at the compliment and he smiled. At least, I was pretty sure it was a smile of pleasure, not aggression. He had a lot of sharp, pointy teeth, just like an otter would, so it was hard to be positive. "The Gods are said to be wise." He cocked his head at Jeff. "I believe you have deceived us."

"Me?" Jeff looked hugely guilty, of course. A-Cs couldn't lie, well, most of them anyway, and Jeff was usually the shining example of their lack of fabrication skills. Today was no exception.

King Benny nodded, then bowed deeply to all of us. "It is clear to me that you are more than messengers from the Gods. You are the Gods themselves. I will not share this with my people if you do not wish it, but I do not understand why you would not wish it."

"Because we need your people to work with us willingly," Chuckie replied. "Not just to blindly follow our requests. This is how your people will learn and grow."

"Ah." King Benny nodded, making his tree antlers move in a kind of funny way. Controlled the Inner Hyena because I was focused. Go me. "You are wise. I see you for who you are now, Alcalla."

"Alcalla?" I couldn't stop myself from asking.

"The God of Wisdom," King Benny said. "You can test me all you want, Shealla, I will not fail you, any more than we have failed Leoalla, your mate and King of the Gods."

Took a wild one and guessed that Shealla was the Queen of the Gods. Always nice to be appreciated. "No testing is intended, King Benny. But, I would like to speak with my mate and our family in private, for just a short while."

"As the Gods wish it, so it will be." King Benny bowed again, then backed away. After he was a few feet from us, King Benny turned and walked back to his caravan. He had a short, thick tail but I was fairly sure it was prehensile, based on the fact that it was curled around a short sword. Meaning he'd been ready to attack if necessary. Good thing he'd decided we were all Gods.

Waited to speak until he was back with his people. "Okay, clearly these people think we're Gods. Go team. But I want some answers, Jeff, and I want them now."

CHAPTER 24

"**L**ET'S START WITH how in the hell King Benny and I can understand each other perfectly, and go from there. Please and thank you and chop chop time's a wastin'. *If* that's alright with you, Christopher, and all that."

"Fine," Christopher said, sounding like it wasn't.

"She won't stop until it's explained anyway," Chuckie said with a laugh. "But, Kitty, I'd just like to point out that you had no issue with the Planetary Council speaking English."

"Because Crazy Moira of the Free Women made the point that radio waves traveled, and that was confirmed by the rest. The beings in the Planetary Council are all Space Aged or more. That they learned our languages or whatever before they dropped by for a visit I can believe. Not buying it with King Benny there, unless Bronze Age in this world means interstellar communications capable."

Jeff sighed and ran his hand through his hair. "Implants."

"King Benny has implants?"

"No," Christopher snapped. "You do. We all do. Universal communication chips. They hear enough words and they translate that to your brain."

"We all have them," Chuckie added. "I honestly thought you knew that."

"By 'we all' do you mean everyone on Earth, everyone working with Centaurion Division, or everyone in our extended family group? And yes, it's news to me. I like to focus on the bigger picture and all that. And I pointedly don't remember this implant being installed. Just sayin.'"

"Everyone working with Centaurion," Chuckie answered.

"Unreal. Really glad I like to learn and all that."

"It was in the briefing books," Christopher added. In a tone that was far more accusatory than I personally thought the situation warranted.

"I read those! I mean, finally. But I did read them. I distinctly do not remember the Universal Translator chapter."

"You probably skimmed it," Jeff said. "And the implants were put in when you were unconscious, Kitty. At the same time as the tracking devices were installed."

"And other things I don't know about?" Refrained from mentioning that the tracking devices had been disabled by our enemies. Clearly, said enemies had left the universal translator functions alone. For which I'd thank them one day. Maybe.

"Probably," Chuckie said. "But they're all there for our protection and assistance."

"Glad to know you're one with the Centaurion Party Line."

"Does it matter?" Jeff asked. "I mean, really, right now? We need to find our daughter and the rest of our people who were brought here."

I wanted that, too, but I wanted answers more. And logic told me that the three of us knowing all that Jeff did immediately would be better than finding it out when we were surrounded by giant, walking and talking, carnivorous rodent people.

"Kitty's right," Christopher said. "We need to know all that you know right now, Jeff."

"Excuse me?" Jeff looked confused. "She didn't say that."

"No, but I thought it. Okay, I'm just putting this out here right now—the Purple Land portion of this planet enables mind reading. Period. Maybe it's all the weird smells, maybe it's all the colors, it's probably the water and plant life that everyone there eats in some way, which the three of us have, too. But Chuckie, Christopher, and I have been reading each other's minds, and we've communed with the katyhoppers. Yet, if King Benny can do it, he didn't let on."

Jeff shook his head. "I'm having trouble reading emotions here, let alone minds. I only had an idea of where to head because I felt all three of you so filled with terror last night that I could get a general idea of where you were."

"The snakipede, yeah, that makes sense. But this means, then, that at least part of Planet Colorful is also Planet Telepathic. Maybe each color section enhances or detracts from a psionic ability."

"I'm with Kitty on this one," Chuckie said. "Jeff, could you tell us what's going on?"

"I'd like to know how they thought you were a Messenger of the Gods," Christopher added.

"And how you become friends with King Benny. I definitely want to know that. And how you managed to lie in any way, shape, or form."

Jeff heaved a sigh. "I landed on a boulder. It happened to be right when this clan was traveling past it. Needless to say, there was a lot of falling to the knees and bowing. I had to hear them talk for a bit, then I could understand them. I did try to tell them I wasn't a God, but then it occurred to me that what Kitty and Chuck would do was try to play along and turn the situation to their advantage."

"And you did?" Hoped I didn't sound incredulous. I just wasn't used to A-Cs in general and Jeff in particular managing being sneaky.

He grinned. "Glad I can still surprise you. Yes. I did what we were all able to do before you showed up and called us on it. I just didn't give them full information."

"So you said, I'm from far away," Christopher said. "And they took that to mean the heavens."

"Right. Anyway, it was better than them attacking me, and I knew I was going to need help to find everyone else."

"Glad all the political crap has been good for something. I'm glad you didn't try to talk them out of their beliefs, by the way."

"Yeah," Chuckie agreed. "When someone asks if you're a god, the golden rule is that you say 'yes.' I'm kind of as shocked as Kitty that you didn't protest more."

"*Ghostbusters* was such a great movie."

Jeff gave us both the "really?" look. "I wasn't sure if it would work, and I figured that my mission was to find all my family and friends, not worry about not telling all the truth to a backward society."

"Don't sell them short," Chuckie said. "With the little

I've seen so far, they're like the Ancient Greeks, and that means they have a civilization and society. Believing in Gods doesn't make them stupid." He was fond of his Ancient Greece theory. Then again, it was knowledge he had and he, like the rest of us, was out of his element. If being able to compare the races on this planet to Agamemnon and Odysseus made him feel better, bring on Athena and Achilles.

"Well, it still seems wrong to lie to someone who wasn't trying to kill me. It was tense for a little while, but you're right—they're not stupid." He shook his head. "I don't understand why you all weren't near me when I landed, though."

"We discussed this amongst ourselves already," Chuckie said. "We were traveling at faster than light speed and something clearly went wrong, because the trip wasn't smooth. We're guessing we were moving apart at some rate of speed that put your landing zone, Jeff—you were heading away from the three of us when we were grabbed, remember—at some distance away from ours. And I think we were put on the nearest solid object. For me and Kitty, that was the treetops. For you two, it was something a little more stable."

"I was trying to get to Jamie when we were taken," Jeff said quietly. "But I can't feel her here."

"That doesn't mean she isn't here," Chuckie said quickly, as my stomach clenched. "You just said that you could barely feel us and only because all three of us were terrified. Based on where we ended up versus where you did, Jeff, Jamie and Paul could easily be on the other side of the world."

"Or on another world," Christopher added, unintentionally unhelpfully.

Chuckie shot him a look that said Christopher could stop speaking any time. "Or else she's with Paul and neither one of them are scared about anything, meaning they're fine and safe."

Reminded myself that panicking wouldn't save anyone, and that if I wanted to get to my daughter, I had to make sure that I and the others were okay and survived first. Four out of the twenty-two taken were okay. Less than one-fifth wasn't a good enough number, meaning I needed to focus.

Took a deep breath and let it out slowly. I was doing that

a lot on this planet. "I'm worried about Jamie, but she has ACE inside her, and I hope that means that, no matter what, she's safe. ACE is allowed to protect himself, and they weren't unconscious. I'm willing to take Chuckie's idea that she's still with Paul and they're both somewhere safe as gospel for the moment. So, do we have anything else we need to discuss in private before we rejoin King Benny and his people?"

"Yeah, I'd like to know how you ended up flying with these bug-things."

"Katyhoppers, Jeff, they're called katyhoppers, at least by us, and it's a long story."

"But he needs to know it, and know it before we join the others," Chuckie said.

We caught Jeff up on all of our excitement. "Seriously?" Jeff asked. "The katyhopper leaders say there are spaceships in the planet's solar space?"

"Yes, and I'm sure they're right. Think about it—there's only one reason we would all have been dragged here without asking."

"Yeah, what the three of you came up with makes the most sense. And I can easily believe that there's fighting going on. It's hard to keep countries working together—it's got to be exponentially harder with planets." Jeff examined the katyhoppers. "They seem . . . smarter than the Lecanora."

Turkey waved her antennae.

"Turkey says they are in some ways and not in others. They have no contact with anyone in this Bronze Land, so it's hard for them to be sure. But they can read the Lecanoras' minds, as well as the other animals'—at least as and how they read them, which isn't word for word, but more images and feelings—and they seem smart enough. She feels the Lecanora are close to katyhopper sentience levels, with their animals more along the Louie the Lizard level—sentient but not as smart as the ones they're domesticated under."

"Are we sure the Lecanora can't read minds?" Christopher asked. "I'd really like to be sure about that before we all align with them. The katyhoppers more than proved they were our friends. Not so sure the Lecanora have done the same yet."

Jeff sighed. "I think them believing we're Gods and not eating us is the best we're going to get right now. Seriously, if they had mind-reading ability, why would they think I was anything other than an alien on their planet?"

Chuckie nodded. "Good point. And I think it's time we joined them. Making our new hosts impatient could be bad for us, considered to be Gods or not."

"Yeah, and you're right—you all have to be introduced to the rest of the clan."

"And the rest of the clan needs to buy in that we're Gods or God Messengers, too," Christopher pointed out.

"What Christopher said." This earned me a nice smile instead of a Patented Glare. Planet Colorful might be good for him. "And, by the way, are they going to sniff us or just say hello?"

Jeff laughed. "Both."

"Oh good. Things were getting far too normal."

CHAPTER 25

WE WALKED TO THE CARAVAN, with Bruno, Ginger, and the katyhoppers coming along.

Jeff kept his arm around my shoulders and I kept mine around his waist, allowing myself to enjoy the relief of knowing he was okay and the joy of being back with him.

The wagons were a lot like the ones Earthlings had used for millennia—wooden, flat on the bottom, four wheels, some open, some enclosed. The woods and colors maintained the color scheme for this section of the world. As with the katyhoppers, the Lecanora used leaves and mud to create natural grout.

King Benny met us at the lead wagon. "The others feel that because my ocellar—Ginger, as you call her—has accepted you, and because of those you travel with," he indicated the katyhoppers, "that you are clearly not as we have been told. You need to share your Godhood with the others, or there may be . . . problems."

"Did anyone stop to figure that, you know, Ginger's got a good guess going that I'm not going to put her into a catapult and shoot her up into the air and maybe that's why she likes me?"

King Benny shrugged. "We would have caught her. Safely. It's something we do frequently." He looked at the katyhoppers. "When we have to."

"Um, the katyhoppers saved us, more than once, and while we returned the favor, they housed us and so forth, so they're our pals. As in, they took in three Gods and didn't question it and so forth. So they are totally off limits in terms of being attacked or eaten or whatever."

"I was not insinuating that the . . . katyhoppers, as you call them, were our enemy. However, we all share a common enemy, which is why our ocellars are used to being catapulted into the air."

The light dawned. "Wow and crap. You have snakipedes in this section of the world, too?"

"Excuse me? I'm not sure I understand you, Shealla."

"So few ever do, King Benny. So few ever do. The giant flying snakes. You have them over here, just like the katyhoppers do?"

"Ah!" He nodded. "We call them the Horrors. And they are venomous as well as hugely dangerous even without their venom. They are not sentient as we are, or even as our bosthoon are. They are animals in the truest sense of the word, their appetites are large, and their methods skillful and deadly."

"Bosthoon?"

"The animals pulling their wagons," Jeff said quickly.

"Ah, the bronto-horses, gotcha." Was *so* glad I hadn't known that the snakipedes were venomous last night. I might not have had the guts to kill the one that attacked us. Of course, I knew now. But I also knew that, as long as I had bullets, the snakipedes could die. Probably didn't have nearly enough bullets for all the snakipedes on the planet.

Chose not to say any of this aloud. Hopefully our guess was right and the Lecanora had no mind-reading abilities. Made a mental note not to give them waterfruit unless we wanted to experiment with the ability or needed to know they could read us.

King Benny cocked his head and stared at me. The tree antlers managed to stay on, but they looked funny and made him cute rather than imposing. Still controlled the Inner Hyena. Gods laughing at your leader tended to be bad for the leader and many times worse for the Gods. "You wish us to call them bronto-horses, Shealla? You are the Giver of Names."

Interesting. So far, our God Names were really lining up with what we did in real life. Wondered what he was going to assign to Christopher. "Ah, no, King Benny. Bosthoon is a good name."

He relaxed and seemed pleased. "Well and good. May I introduce you as you truly are, Leoalla?" he asked Jeff.

Who looked to Chuckie. Who nodded. "It's wise, as you say, King Benny."

King Benny turned and we followed. He still had his short sword held in his tail. The thought occurred that maybe we weren't who he was worried about.

Went on with my examination as we headed toward a group of the Lecanora. Long wooden bars extended from the wagons to attach to harnesses on the bronto-horses. Bosthoon was indeed as good a name, and since that's what the Lecanora called them and I'd graciously told King Benny it was good, I'd break down and do the same.

The bosthoon had little heads and long, thick necks and tails, hence the brontosaurus comparison. Their middles, however, were all horse, all the way, and their thick legs ended in wide, flat hooves. Their coloration was similar to that of horses—all over the place—but they stuck with the color scheme, just as everything in Purple Land had.

The leather looked to be bosthoon, which made sense. Humans used cow and horse leather because in the old days, we'd used every part of our domesticated animals that we could.

Catapults were on uncovered wagons, of course, and this group had five of them. There were twenty-five wagons, not counting those with catapults, so one catapult for every five wagons seemed to be their setup.

Bronze Land continued to smell of burnt wood and sunsets, but there was a definite whiff of animal that hadn't existed in the Purple Land. The smells weren't unpleasant, but it was clear that mammals were more common in this color section. Especially since we were with a big group of them.

Sure enough, there was a hodgepodge of the extended weasel family here. In fact, it was a little too hodgepodge. Took a longer, closer look at the caravan. The wagons weren't of uniform design. Some had more ornamentation than others, some were clearly made from different woods, dirt, and leaves than others, some wagons had one bosthoon, some two, some four, and so on.

The Lecanora were also different, and not just in their coloration or size relative to each other. Some seemed more prosperous than others, some far less so.

King Benny led us to a clutch of Lecanora, all of whom looked worried or suspicious or both. They seemed to represent the full variety of the mustelidae family.

"You have all met him as the Messenger of the Gods," King Benny said without preamble. "But the truth has been revealed to me. We are blessed—the Gods themselves have tested us and found us worthy."

Some of the others looked impressed, some didn't. All of them were sniffing. Surreptitiously, at least somewhat, but definitely sniffing. Had no idea what we smelled like to them, but had a feeling we'd find out soon enough.

Before King Benny could say anything else, though, one of the pig-dogs ran over and started bark-honking at me. The pig-dogs were about the size of an extra-large German Shepherd but with snouts that were more squat and broad than elongated, long claws on their paws, tusks that stuck out just like a boar's, bristles instead of whiskers, and curlicue tails. This one was also kind of goofy looking—I mean, more goofy looking than the pig-dogs already were—and its whooping at me was kind of hilarious and cute, and I didn't pick up any danger. Not that this necessarily meant anything.

"What's your pig-dog's name?"

This earned me some shocked looks from those who'd looked impressed and more suspicious looks from those who already seemed distrustful. Chose not to look at my guys in case they were glaring at me or trying to tell me to shut up.

"It's a chocho," King Benny said.

"Gotcha."

"Why would one of our Gods not know this?" a Lecanora who looked like a walking weasel asked, while he sniffed at us. Not in the dissing you sort of way, but in the "smelling you from a distance" way.

"Because we Gods have different names for things than you do. Obviously, I might add."

"You would question Shealla, who gives the names?" King Benny asked of weasel-dude.

"Ah, no." He looked somewhat uncomfortable.

"It's forgiven. What's the chocho's name?"

"He has no name," King Benny said. "He's not quite . . . right. But he's part of the chocho's pack, and we've all agreed that we will give refuge to any who need it, regardless of their fur."

"Well, that's great to hear. We, ah, approve. In a God-like way." I put my fist out to the chocho. "C'mere, boy. Give us a sniff."

He bounced forward and back as dogs will when they're excited and unsure. But finally the chocho got close enough to sniff my hand. After a few seconds I moved slowly and ran my hand over his head. His fur was thick and a little bristly, but not unpleasant.

The chocho seemed shocked. I was having that effect on the beings in Bronze Land. I continued to pet him. After about half a minute he sat on his haunches and, curlicue tail spinning, proceeded to let me give him vigorous petting like I did with my own dogs.

"Wilbur's a great chocho," I said as I caught Jeff's horrified and worried expression. "He's not going to bite Kitty, is he?" I asked the chocho.

Wilbur made the bark-honk and jumped up.

CHAPTER 26

WILBUR PUT HIS front paws on my shoulders and licked my face. Nope, Wilbur was definitely on Team Kitty.

The Lecanora looked more shocked than they had yet. "He ... he has never allowed anyone to touch him," the beaver representative said. Was pretty sure it was a female. Lush pelts made sexual differentiation difficult and only a few of the males were wearing codpieces. Or all the females had masculine voices. Too early to tell. "And you travel with other creatures none can tame." She pointed webbed fingers toward the katyhoppers.

"Huh. Well, I have a way with animals." Gave Wilbur a last vigorous pet. "Names are also helpful. Helps a creature know who you're talking to and that you think enough of it to name them something specific. And all that."

"Do you still doubt she is Shealla?" King Benny asked, as Wilbur joined Bruno and Ginger at my feet.

"Why does she call herself Kitty?" a skunk representative shared. Pretty sure it was a male, with no codpiece in evidence. However, he had fluffy fur, so his modesty wasn't exactly compromised.

Heaved a sigh. "What you call us and what we call ourselves is different. As your king understands."

"King?" the weasel-dude asked. "Musgraff is our clan leader."

"And as far as we Gods are concerned, Grover, that makes him a king. Is there a problem with that?" Hey, he looked like a Grover to me. He didn't appear to love the name, but he didn't argue about it, either.

Lots of furry heads shook quickly but many furry faces looked worried. Clearly there was a problem with this.

"There does seem to be an issue with the title Shealla has bestowed," Chuckie said.

King Benny nodded. "There is a king, a ruler of all the clans. He . . . does not take kindly to usurpers or those who wish the rule of the land to be more . . . equal. And he does not take advice, or hear things he does not want to. But this is wrong, and we believe that questioning how things are done and being correct should not be a cause for exile." The others nodded emphatically.

The light dawned. "Ah, you're all rebels. You wanted a better situation for your families, or you saw how things could be better, identified a threat the king wanted to ignore, and you were kicked out of your clans because of it." Looked around. "That's why you're here, in a barren area."

"It's as if she reads our hearts and minds!" the skunk-guy exclaimed. The others nodded. Clearly Skunky here had some sway.

Exchanged a pointed glance with Chuckie. This was the-ater, lying, and subterfuge, and Jeff and Christopher weren't going to be up to what was needed. Happily, they were stay-ing quiet, presumably because Jeff was smart enough to keep quiet and Christopher's desire to snark was being sub-dued by being able to tell what Chuckie and I were doing. Via reading our minds. Made a note to not share that the next color over was the Mind Reading Capital of the Solar System.

Chuckie shook his head and sighed. "Such little faith. It saddens me."

"You have disappointed Alcalla," King Benny said to his folks, who all looked ashamed and worried. Good. "And see? Leoalla will not even speak to us now!"

"He said he was the Messenger, not Leoalla," a wood-chuck that I was fairly sure was male said. Good to know that there had indeed been a reason Jeff had used Charles when introducing us to King Benny.

"Well, Brown, as I see it, Leoalla gets to say he's whoever he wants to say he is." As with Grover, the woodchuck-dude didn't seem thrilled with his name, possibly because Chuckie had laughed when I'd bestowed it, but he didn't argue about it, either.

"The Gods do not need to explain their ways to you," King Benny thundered. "Leoalla was testing us. And Sheala, Alcalla, and Binalla all test us now, too. And we are now failing! You need to beg forgiveness for doubting the miracle of Leoalla's appearance, and then Sheala, Alcalla, and Binalla's deigning to join us as well."

Nice to know what Christopher's God-name was. Hoped we'd get some kind of clue for what Binalla was supposed to do before that lack of knowledge blew our cover for us. Figured forging ahead would be wisest. Working for me so far, at any rate.

"You can earn our forgiveness by assisting us." The Lecanora all looked hopeful. "When we came down from the heavens, we were separated from our brethren. We need to find the other Gods. Assist us with this and your lack of faith will be forgiven."

"You travel with strangers," beaver-chick said. "Creatures we have heard of and sometimes seen from a distance but have been warned against. Why?"

Interesting. The katyhoppers hadn't shown any kind of military mindset or setup and they hadn't seemed aggressive or even sort of nasty, either. And I already knew they weren't allowed out of the Purple Land under normal circumstances. Meaning it was likely that the Lecanora had been told to stay away due to the old "we don't know what's there and we don't want you finding out first in case what's there is good" ploy.

"No. We travel with friends. Friends who have helped us, and who we've helped in kind. And we travel with them in part because they know what we do—that there is a greater threat facing you and your world than your interpersonal struggles for supremacy."

Skunky and King Benny exchanged a look. "You mean the ships in the air," Skunky said finally.

"We do," Chuckie said, managing not to sound shocked. Really hoped Jeff and Christopher were looking at their shoes or something.

"We were not . . . believed," beaver-chick said. "When we saw the visions."

"Visions?"

King Benny nodded. "Our people do an annual pilgrimage to the All Seeing Mountain. We ask for the Gods to guide us and show us what is to come, what they want for and from us."

Resolved to both find out where this mountain was and get to it, pronto.

"Ah, yes," Chuckie said smoothly. "Which is right and proper."

"The air of the mountains is rich and blesses some with more clarity than others," Grover said. "Many times this clarity is a blessing. But for all of us . . ."

"We all saw the ships in the sky," Skunky finished. "So many, so strange, so imposing. But our clan leaders and the king would not listen."

Jeff cleared his throat. "Last night, we spoke about this. The Lecanora clans aren't at peace."

"True," King Benny said. "We fight with each other, and the king allows it."

Took another good long look at the caravan. There was another reason they were in an area that was, at least compared to the Purple Land, quite barren. And I'd said it was barren before and none of them had argued.

"You're not well equipped for war, are you?"

The Lecanora were all quiet, but King Benny finally nodded. "No, Shealla, we are not." He looked down. "And so I fail the Gods."

"No," Jeff said strongly. "You do *not* fail us because you're not killing other clans or prepared to destroy your own people, or others, or your planet."

King Benny looked up. "But, how can we help the Gods to save our world? That is why you have come is it not? Because our visions are true and you have come to lead us and to save our world?"

Oh, the tough question. But, conveniently, I had the tough answer.

"Absolutely."

CHAPTER 27

ENSURED I WASN'T looking at any of the men with me. "But first, we need to know all that's going on. And if anyone wants to question why the Gods want this information, it's because we want know what you know, or think you know. We're here to help you, not do it all for you."

King Benny nodded. "As you say, Shealla. Shall we tell you now?"

"No," Chuckie said quickly. "We would like to discuss where we want to go. Why don't you and your people determine where you will house us for the journey?"

The Lecanora all bowed and backed away. Once they were a few steps back, they turned and scurried off to their various wagons.

"I'd say I can't believe we were sent here on purpose to save the world," Christopher said. "But . . ."

"Based on past history, I can believe it," Jeff said.

Chuckie nodded. "Frankly, it's too easy to believe. I just don't know who would send us here, specifically."

"Maybe we were, maybe we weren't." Figured ACE or Algar had something to do with where we'd landed and that we'd absolutely been put here for a reason, and maybe more than one reason. "But I think we need to get to the All Seeing Mountain as fast as possible, if not sooner."

"It would be faster if we just asked the katyhoppers to take us," Chuckie pointed out. "They're going to go faster than a caravan, especially since they can fly over bad terrain or areas with no roads or paths."

"These people need us," Jeff said. "It was clear to me yesterday and it's clearer today."

"I think there's more going on than just the clan wars, and even more than whatever's going on within this system."

All three guys stared at me, but it was my turn to be shocked. Christopher nodded. "I agree with Kitty. Something's off. More than what we're seeing. Starting with how calmly the Lecanora and the katyhoppers accepted us."

Looked at Pinky, who was waving his antennae like mad. "Oh? Really? Interesting. Okay, Pinky says that the katyhoppers have passed down a story, from the first katyhopper Matriarch who gained full sentience. And that story revolves around furless bipeds who look unusual for this world who will arrive out of nowhere and save the world."

That sat on the air for a while. Jeff broke the silence. "So . . . are you saying the katyhoppers think we're Gods, too?"

Saffron waved her antennae, with Turkey and Pinky adding in.

"Ah, no. They're aware we're from another planet. They just have folklore about something like this happening. It's why the Matriarch sent them with us." And why our three katyhoppers were excited and considered it an honor, versus a burden.

"I wonder if they can see the future as well as mind read," Chuckie said musingly.

Pinky waved antennae.

"No," Christopher said. "And I know you got that, too, Chuck. They don't believe they can see the future. However, their Matriarchs make an annual pilgrimage to the All Seeing Mountain, just like the Lecanora do. The Matriarchs go at different times."

"So each will see what the others might have missed," I said, since that's what Saffron was telling us. "No one other than a Matriarch is allowed to go, by the way."

"Meaning Kitty's right and we need to get to that mountain," Christopher said.

"We need to find the others and help these Lecanora, too," Jeff said firmly. "And I don't want us splitting up again, so no one suggest it. And no, I'm not mind reading. I just know the three of you."

"Wow, bitter much? But I agree. We want our scattered group back together, not rescattering to who knows where."

"We have to backtrack, I think," Jeff said. "They weren't headed this way when they found me. We only came down this trail because it was the most direct way to get toward where I felt the three of you."

"Where *were* they heading when they found you?" Chuckie asked.

"I honestly have no idea. I didn't ask."

"We can just ask King Benny," Christopher said. "It may not matter. They don't strike me as actually having a destination."

"What makes you say that?" Chuckie asked. I could see the wheels in his head turning.

Christopher shrugged. "None of them seemed impatient. I didn't hear anyone asking why they were taking this trip, no one was complaining about how they were late or going to miss someone or something."

"They're wandering in the desert looking for a homeland."

The guys all looked at me. "Why are you comparing them to the Israelites?" Chuckie asked.

"They're outcasts for their beliefs." And my suspicion was gelling into certainty that we'd been sent here, to this planet, specifically. And not by whoever had tried to get us into this solar system in the first place. Which begged a big question. Two, really. "If the katyhoppers see ships in space, and so do the Lecanora, what does it mean? And how can they see them?"

"That's why we want to go to the All Seeing Mountain," Christopher replied. "At least to hopefully answer your second question. As for the first one, we've agreed that there's trouble out here and if there's trouble, spaceships being out isn't a surprise."

Chuckie shook his head. "I think the question is, why are they around this planet, specifically?"

"Really?" Jeff asked. "You three are reading minds and talking to sentient katyhoppers who also read minds. Why are you even asking the question?"

"I think we're asking because until the three of us landed in Purple Land, to my knowledge, no one knew about the mind reading. And by no one, Jeff, I mean your dad, Richard, Alexander, Councilor Leonidas, Queen Renata, the rest of the Planetary Council. No one."

"Maybe they just didn't tell us about it," Jeff suggested. "You know, like all the other things they didn't tell us until we were being invaded or something."

"No," Christopher said slowly. "I really think that they'd have told us when we were invaded before your wedding."

"Operation Invasion would have been the prime time, Jeff, especially because we were getting info on all the other inhabited planets."

"While I'd never say that any politician can be fully trusted, present company being literally the only exception," Chuckie said, "I can say that Councilor Leonidas never insinuated that this planet was worth paying attention to. Alpha Four was interested in Alpha Seven and Beta Sixteen, because they were so much closer to being space-ready. But everyone in the Planetary Council felt that Beta Eight should be firmly left alone. So why are the ships here?"

"If they're here," Jeff said. "Keep in mind that there are plenty of reasons people have visions."

"Drugs being only one. I'm inclined to believe the Lecanora but only because of the katyhoppers." Which might have been why Christopher, Chuckie, and I landed there.

All three katyhoppers waved their antennae like mad.

"Pinky, Saffron, and Turkey insist that they don't do drugs. By the way."

"The waterfruit could be considered a drug," Chuckie said. "But that doesn't mean the Matriarchs or the Lecanora, for that matter, haven't seen what they think they have. We don't have enough data to do anything more than guess, so we need to table the speculation and focus on getting to that mountain and finding the others."

"I like that plan of action," Jeff said.

"Well, Chuckie is the God of Wisdom, after all."

Jeff grinned. "Yeah, and you're the Namer of Things and boy, is that accurate."

"Hey, a girl's gotta do what she does best."

"Please don't get us into trouble, or ignore what Jeff, Chuck, or I say," Christopher said. "Because you've already fallen from a great height, so I'm expecting the other two things you do best to be coming soon."

"I'll hurt you later, Christopher."

"Only if you can catch me."

"Yeah, as to that, I have an idea."

"No," Jeff said flatly. "I may be having trouble reading anyone or anything, but up this close to you, I can get your emotions clear enough. Didn't I already say and we all agree that spitting up was a bad idea?"

"You and we did, but Chuckie's right—we're going to be moving much more slowly than we want to. Christopher's the Flash. He can be around the world in far less than eighty minutes, let alone eighty days."

"I don't follow you, Kitty, but I can, yeah."

"And he won't be alone. Bruno can also handle the hyperspeeds, as can the Poofs. With Poofs on Board, if there's trouble, one or more of them can come back and warn us and then we, who also possess hyperspeed, can get to Christopher to provide backup."

"I'm game, Jeff."

"If we assume time is of the essence," Chuckie said, "and I'm sure we should, then this makes a lot of sense. If Bruno and the Poofs will help."

Jeff sighed. "Fine. And, by the way, I have a Poof with me. Not Harlie, but it's been quiet and I have to admit it was nice to not be totally alone here. Not that I didn't meet the Lecanora immediately, but you know what I mean."

"Yeah. Harlie was with me so as to give Poofikins an assist in bringing Bruno along. They told us you weren't Poofless on the journey." A Poof popped out of Jeff's suit pocket and yawned. "Sleepy there seems to be getting all its snoozing in just like the rest of the Poofs."

Interestingly enough, the Poof didn't do anything. Clearly Sleepy wasn't going to be its name.

"Huh. I'm shocked that the Poof didn't attach to Kitty, after that," Chuckie said.

"Oh, ah, yeah." Jeff looked hugely uncomfortable all of a sudden.

I laughed. "What did you call it?"

Jeff mumbled something. Christopher started to laugh. "Revenge. Revenge! This trip's looking up."

"What did he name it?" I asked Christopher, since Jeff was looking all kinds of embarrassed and still wasn't going to say anything audible as near as I could tell.

"Murphy. After *his* stuffed toy when we were little."

Since Christopher's Poof was named Toby after his former beloved stuffed animal—and Jeff had laughed his head off about that when we'd found out—this truly seemed like Ironic Justice. And I still needed someone to make that into a monthly comic.

Saffron nudged Christopher and waved her antennae.

"Saffron thinks she can handle the hyperspeed," he shared. "I'm doubtful, but if we do a fast test and see if she can indeed take it, then it would be good to have her along."

"Super. Then let's do that test and get Christopher's Speedy Circus on the road."

CHAPTER 28

AMAZINGLY ENOUGH, Saffron had no issues at all with hyperspeed. Don't know why I was shocked—after all, every other being we'd ever met from this solar system was super-speedy—but since none of the natives we'd met so far on this planet used hyperspeed, it came as a surprise that the katyhoppers could handle it.

And all three of them could. It took almost no time for Christopher to test them, after all. They used the experience to grab more waterfruit from the Purple Lands, so we scored a double that way.

While they were doing that, Jeff, Chuckie, and I discussed where Christopher should go. Since we were going to head for the All Seeing Mountain, him searching for the rest of our lost tribe sounded like the wisest choice.

We rejoined King Benny and explained that Binalla was going to go see what he could see, so to speak, and that we expected him to rejoin us sooner as opposed to later. King Benny seemed unsurprised by this.

"Binalla flies on the wind," he said solemnly. "What can we provide that you will need for your journey?"

"Directions would be nice," Christopher said, showing amazing restraint in not asking just what his God-powers were aside from wind. "As in, how you're going to travel to get to the All Seeing Mountain. And a small bag to carry supplies." We'd wisely decided that Christopher should take waterfruit with him, just in case.

A well-worn map was found and presented while the search for a bag worthy of a God was begun. While King

Benny and Skunky went over travel options with Christopher and Jeff, who wanted to weigh in on what route we actually took, Chuckie and I studied the map itself.

The world on the map was drawn as a circle. Whether this meant the Lecanora knew the world was a sphere, or if their awareness of their surroundings said they lived on a circular continent or something, I chose not to ask at this time.

The map was divided into seven sections, not all of equal size. The Purple Land, denoted by color, was the smallest of the sections, and had what I took to be "stay away" signs around it.

The most interesting thing about the divisions, though, was that they weren't random-shaped, like the countries on Earth were, and they weren't like slices of a pie, either. They were sort of swirled, like the Yellow Brick Road, only with six other colors, or a big lollipop like you'd get at the fair or an amusement park.

This meant that the center of the map, and possibly the center of the world, or at least the part of the world the Lecanora knew about, was where every land radiated from, or to, depending on your viewpoint. Took a bet with myself and won, because, shocker of shockers, the All Seeing Mountain was the place in the center.

The other colors on the map—in addition to purple and the reddish-ochre that denoted the land we were on right now—were green, blue, black, white, and yellow. Green and blue were the biggest, both bigger than bronze and purple put together. The other three were all larger than the Bronze Lands. Clearly the four of us had landed in the poorer countries, or whatever these various lands were actually considered by the natives.

Then again, Luxembourg was tiny and very affluent. On the other hand, we already knew that the rest of the population left the Purple Lands severely alone, so the idea that anyone else on the planet knew what a goldmine that place actually was seemed unlikely.

Though having flying killer snakes would be good enough reason to never go there again. On the other hand, King Benny had said they had them here, too. Controlled a shudder. Did not want Christopher and his team running into one of those when they were alone.

Had a thought and pulled Pinky aside. "Are the snaki-pedes or Horrors able to do what you all can?" Reply was in the negatory in terms of antenna waving. "Okay, why not?" More waving. "Aha, that makes sense."

Chuckie came over. "You had the same thought and question I did. Good to know that a high enough sentience level is required."

"Yeah, very much so." The others were done and we re-joined them.

"Do you have the map memorized?" Chuckie asked, as the beaver-chick, whose name appeared to be Nanda, handed Christopher a decent-size knapsack made out of what looked to be bosthoon hide. Got this impression this was hers and she'd emptied it out in order to be the one whose bag was used by a God. Hey, whatever made her happy.

"Ah . . . somewhat," Christopher said.

Chuckie and I exchanged a look. "I know you have it committed to memory, dude. Within a minute of looking at it. And we just proved that Turkey can handle all Christo-pher needs to do, too."

"Seriously?" Jeff asked. "You want Chuck to go with Christopher?"

While he was stressing, I took the knapsack from Chris-topher and transferred waterfruit and a couple of food bars in there as surreptitiously as possible.

As I did, noted that I had a lot of food bars. More than I remembered from the night before. Tossed several more into Christopher's knapsack and a few more waterfruit. Wondered if Algar had turned my purse into an "ask and ye shall receive" receptacle, like all A-C refrigerators and most cupboards were.

Decided I'd find out when all the Lecanora weren't standing around watching. Though as a God-like move, it would be hard to beat the whole "ask and ye shall instantly receive" trick. Though I knew how the cosmos enjoyed its little jokes, and the very moment I had an appreciative au-dience for that trick it wouldn't work in a big way.

"It makes sense, Jeff. That way, no one's alone." Chuckie grinned. "Try not to miss us while we're gone and you two have some alone time. You know, just you and everyone else here."

"The romantic ambiance is overwhelming. Yeah, Christopher, you good with it?" I was. It made more sense, and I had to figure that Chuckie had always figured he'd go with Christopher and had just let Jeff get acclimated to the idea slowly. Plus they'd have plenty of food and waterfruit. Sadly, my purse wasn't tossing up extra guns and ammo. Maybe Algar wanted a formal request.

"I am. Let's get going. We don't have a lot of light left."

"Speaking of which," Chuckie said, "based on where we are and who we'll be with, if we have to spend the night somewhere, we will, so don't panic if we don't come back immediately."

"You're sure you'll be safe?" Jeff looked at the katyhoppers. "Not that I'm insinuating that your traveling companions are wrong."

Turkey and Saffron waved antennae.

"They'll be fine," I said quietly. "The katyhoppers now know the sounds we make when we sleep, and they have ways to muffle us and mask our scents. They just hadn't realized they'd need to do so last night."

"I don't want to know," Christopher muttered. "Because I'm just sure it involves them spraying things out of their rear ends."

It did, so I didn't share. He'd find out soon enough.

Hugs all around, then I handed the knapsack to Christopher and Bruno to Chuckie. The katyhoppers reared up on their hind legs, grabbed each other with one of their middle legs and their respective guys with the other, and waved to us with their front legs.

Well, for a moment they waved. Then Christopher kicked the hyperspeed up to eleven and they all disappeared in the blink of an eye.

CHAPTER 29

THERE WERE APPRECIATIVE gasps all around from the Lecanora. Nice to keep the locals entertained and impressed.

A thought nudged—I'd known how the Alpha Four force would show up during Operation Invasion in part because I knew they'd want to impress the backwater idiots they'd decided we were on Earth. Gave myself a stern reminder that the Lecanora weren't stupid—and we had to watch ourselves, because my dad loved the movie and therefore forced me to watch *The Man Who Would Be King* many more times than once, and I didn't want anyone trying to cut off Jeff's head and use it as a soccer ball.

This led me to another thought—if the katyhoppers and Lecanora were right, and there were spaceships amassing in their orbital space, then there was a high probability that an impressive arrival meant to awe and terrify the yokels was being planned. Hoped Christopher and Chuckie would be able to find at least some of our scattered team before that happened.

Happily, coming to find us hadn't put the caravan off course too badly on its way to the All Seeing Mountain. Unhappily, the caravan's wagons were pretty well filled with Lecanora, meaning there weren't a lot of places for us to sit, and Jeff point-blank refused to allow any of the Lecanora to walk in order to give us their seats.

"They're not just ostracized," Jeff said quietly after we'd looked at the last of the packed wagons and once again said we weren't making anyone else walk so we could sit. "They're refugees."

"Yeah." I'd seen how basically ragged everything looked up close, too. Nanda's bag had looked pretty good. So she'd given one of her best possessions to Christopher. Really hoped the bag would make it back in good shape. "Meaning that we're aligned with the least likely people on this planet that anyone will listen to."

"Are you suggesting we leave them?" He sounded shocked and more than a little bit protective.

Managed not to snort a laugh, but only because it would probably be considered un-Godlike. "Hardly. I'm just saying that we shouldn't expect to be greeted like saviors by anyone else we meet, and if we need to convince those in power that we're right—about anything—then it's going to take more than just saying that we have the trust of these folks to do it."

Amidst a lot of murmurings about the goodness of Leoalla and all that, Jeff and I opted to ride on one of the catapult wagons. There was actually a lot of room, at least by comparison to the cramped covered wagons. And until it got dark and cold and we needed to be inside, it was also a lot less odiferous. Which was a nice way of saying that a lot of the weasel family smooshed in together created a very musky odor.

Ginger and Wilbur joined us on the wagon. Most of the ocellars and chochos were trotting along next to their respective wagons or, in the case of some of the ocellars, hanging about on the catapult wagons. But Ginger was the only ocellar on ours. Got the distinct impression she'd told all the other fox-cats to back off, which impression was made stronger by the fact that she snarled and hissed at a couple of ocellars who tried to join us.

"Is this their catapult?" I asked her.

She gave me a look that said she didn't particularly care, because she'd traded up and *I* was *hers* now, thank you very much. Decided not to argue.

Wilbur was just jazzed about being on the show, basically. Had no idea why he'd been considered weird or dangerous, since he was acting like the happiest pig-dog in the galaxy about being with people who actually petted him.

Pinky was a little problematic. I didn't want the katyhopper to get tired out, especially in case we needed to fly off to help Christopher and Chuckie. But there wasn't room in the catapult wagon for a pony-sized insect, especially with the rest of us in it.

We compromised and Pinky sat on the top of King Benny's wagon, which was enclosed. Pinky was good with this, especially since it meant he could be on watch.

All set up to look like a bizarre traveling circus, we trundled along at a pace that wasn't glacial, but certainly wasn't what Jeff and I were used to. Ignoring hyperspeed, bicycles went faster than this caravan managed to, and the less said about the comparison between a car and a bosthoon-pulled wagon the better. Oxen were faster than bosthoon.

Jeff leaned against the side of our wagon and put his arm around me. "We'll get there, baby. Just try to enjoy the journey."

"I am. Somewhat. You seem a lot less worried than you were earlier."

He sighed. "I've forced myself to accept that Jamie's likely to be safe. ACE will protect her and so will Paul, and vice versa. It helps that you think she was pulled to be an option for the Alpha Four throne. I'm hoping that Alexander is okay, and all of us being yanked here just means Renata or someone else we know wants our help, versus our enemies having kidnapped all of us."

Leaned against him as Ginger settled herself into my lap and Wilbur snuggled up on my other side. "We were taken away at a bad time."

"There's never a good time. Your mother will advise Vince about what we know."

"What, you think Mom's going to tell the President that her daughter did a universal body switch with her daughter in another universe and therefore we now know who the Mastermind is?"

"Frankly, yes. Out of all the politicians out there, Vince is the one who's been through the most with us, if you think about it. He knows what's going on more than most, and he's bound himself to us tightly enough that he staked his entire political career on our being a help to him, rather than a hindrance. And if it's you, me, or your mother telling him, he'll believe it."

"Okay, great. So she tells him. What, if anything, can anyone do? And what about Gideon Cleary and the situation with Stephanie?"

"No idea what they'll do about Goodman. Probably what we would if we were at home—determine where he is and watch him, then wait for him to make a mistake while searching for hard evidence. Frankly, the biggest positive about our being here is that Chuck is here, too, and therefore he's nowhere near Goodman. He'll have some time to process everything before we're back in a situation where he could do something that would ruin his career or his life."

"I suppose. Of course, him being on an alien planet isn't exactly going to give him tons of time to ponder how he'll kill Cliff without any backlash hitting him or anyone else he cares about."

"Exactly. I think he needs the cooling off time. I would, if I were in his place. And despite him being a patient person, he's absolutely got a breaking point. I think we're all better off with him here, as opposed to being at home. As for the situation with Cleary, Uncle Richard and Doreen are at least as capable as you and I are of handling anything diplomatic, and you know it, and hunting for Stephanie was already falling into Siler and Buchanan's bailiwick. They'll handle it until we get back."

"Who are you and what have you done to Jeff?"

He chuckled. "While we were looking at the map, I realized that I had to stop trying to fix what I couldn't and focus on dealing with the situation we're in. We can't find our daughter, family, and friends using our normal methods. I can waste energy railing against that, worrying and complaining, or I can focus on doing the best I can right here and right now."

"Good philosophy."

"It's Vince's. I've honestly learned a lot from him. And he's a good guy—he's not going to turn on our people just because you and I are off-planet. He'll be able to cover for why I'm not visible—and I know your mother will brief him so I also know the story they come up with will fly—and hopefully we'll be back home sooner as opposed to later."

"Yeah. I'm sure more's going on here than we have a clue about. More than what we think, I mean." Algar was being too helpful without my having asked for assistance for me to think otherwise.

Only a few of us knew who and what Algar was. Me, White, and Gower, ACE and the other superconciousnesses out there, so Naomi probably knew, too, at least now. Gladys Gower had known, because she'd been the head of Security for all of Centaurion Division worldwide. William might know about Algar now. I didn't know. In part because I hadn't asked. Had no idea if I hadn't asked because Algar had prevented it or if I was just that blithely uninterested in key facts. Sadly, time in Bizarro World had confirmed the blithely uninterested option.

Couldn't speak for the others, but White, Gower, and I couldn't talk about Algar to anyone else unless Algar allowed it. If William did know, he'd be under the same restriction. Algar also blocked any thoughts we had about him from anyone else somehow. Being a Black Hole Universe Being had its advantages.

Had a thought and dug around in my purse, moving the Poofs gently. Murphy was in my purse now, too. My purse was Poof Snooze Central at all times. I was okay with this, of course.

Found several things I was and wasn't looking for. My iPod, speakers, earbuds, and phone were all here. All fully charged. And I had a snazzy external charger with a fancy USB universal charger cord that meant I could recharge needed things. Which had not been in my purse the last time I'd looked into it any more than the food bars had.

Pulled my iPod and earbuds out and took a listen. Algar liked to give me musical clues, and it might be nice to get some clues while nothing deadly was going on.

Sure enough, there was a new playlist—Traveling Songs. I'd never created that one. Had a listen and laughed as "Everyday Superhero" by Smash Mouth came on.

"Music making you feel better?" Jeff asked.

"Just helping me remember that, regardless of where we are, we always have a job to do. Saving the day, protecting the innocent, and foiling the evil bad guy schemes."

Jeff grinned. "Ah. Or as we call it, routine."

CHAPTER 30

THE SCENERY WASN'T as monotonous as it was in the Purple Land. But the monotony of the Purple Land had been beautiful and serene. Well, mostly. You know, if I didn't think about the snakipedes and dead giant chameleon carcasses.

The landscape here changed more than it did in the Purple Land, so to speak, with different plants, small trees, rocks, and more dotted all over, but it wasn't as pretty. It also wasn't as symmetrically laid out—no straight rows of plants as far as the eye could see here.

However, it was definitely rugged and, in that sense, far more random. More like I was used to wild land being. Frankly, the Bronze Land reminded me a lot of Arizona and New Mexico, though much redder, browner, and so on. The colors on this planet were incredibly vivid.

The bosthoon actually did get up to something faster than a slow walking speed—it just took them a while. A good thirty minutes by my watch. But we were at least trundling along and might have a hope of getting somewhere before we had to stop for the night.

Of course, my watch was useless for telling the real time. I had a guess for what time it was at home on Earth, but that wasn't going be much help here. As far as I could tell in the time we'd been here, the days were longer than ours. But since it hadn't occurred to me to pay attention to my watch pretty much until I was bored with how slowly we were going, I really had no guess for an easy way to determine it. Decided to leave that to Chuckie. More his baili-wick anyway.

My iPod had turned off the moment "Everyday Super-hero" was over, meaning Algar either wanted me to save the battery or felt I needed no musical clues right now. Or my iPod was freaked out by being on an alien planet. Chose to go with Theories Number One and Two.

Not that I minded all that much. I'd missed my husband a lot and we really hadn't had much relaxed alone time to-gether. Sure, a catapult wagon didn't scream "romantic ride" but it was calm right now, and that meant we could just relax a little and be ourselves, so to speak.

Based on the map, we'd run into Jeff and the Lecanora closer to the All Seeing Mountain, aka The Center of the World, than where they'd been when Jeff had landed in front of them. Which was good, because it meant both less travel time for us and an easier path into the other lands for Chuckie and Christopher.

Most of the lands had no border patrols and no restric-tions upon entering or exiting. The exceptions were the Green Land—because that's where the Lecanoras' king resided—and the Black Lands—so named because they were made of sharp, black volcanic rock which, per Skunky, whose people were from that part of the world, made trav-eling there somewhat dangerous. Skunky had a name, but I'd slipped and called him Skunky when we were looking at his wagon and he'd taken that as a special name from Shealla and so now everyone was required to call him Skunky.

"Have you noticed how unpopulated this planet seems to be?" I asked Jeff as we headed for a large outcropping of rocks that we were hoping to reach before dark.

"Depends on what you consider the population, I guess. You said the area you landed in had katyhoppers and other life-forms."

"Yeah, it did, but it was still remarkably ... serene. So is this part. I mean, you didn't mention running into any other Lecanora on your way to meet up with us."

"No, these were the only people I saw. I guess we were both lucky to land near sentient beings who could help."

"I have absolutely no belief in luck like that. First of all, our luck just plain doesn't run that way. And second of all, seriously, if we're in the deserted parts of this world, it's one heck of a coinkydink that not only Chuckie, Christopher, and I landed right by the katyhoppers, but that you landed right by these Lecanora."

"Do you think that means the others might have landed near people who could help them?"

"Maybe, yeah."

"Ah, do you think ACE or . . . Jamie had anything to do with that?"

"I'd like to think so, yeah, but I don't have a good guess." This was a total lie. I had a really good guess. ACE had to feel that he was being watched, based on the fact that the Superconsciousness Supreme Court had paid him a visit during Operation Defection Election. That meant he'd be keeping himself, Jamie, and Gower safe. And sure, he'd have made sure we all landed without dying somewhere. And if I hadn't had my purse with me, I'd have bought the ACE theory all the way.

But I did have my purse. And every one of us had Poofs on Board, per Harlie. Meaning Algar or, more likely, the Poofs on his suggestion, were helping us in ways we couldn't notice.

The question was simple: why?

That Algar liked the A-Cs in general and me in particular had been established. However, he was hiding out on Earth and his dedication to his own personal Free Will Manifesto was pretty impressive.

Meaning there had to be a lot more to all of this than we knew. And that meant there was likely to be a direct threat to Alpha Four, because that was the planet and those were the people Algar had been with for millennia.

Algar had told me that he was responsible for allowing Mephistopheles to destroy his entire solar system, which was against the Black Hole Universe Rules. This was why Algar was a fugitive, and he didn't want to be caught, tried, and put into a sensory deprivation prison for eternity. Could not blame him.

But he was also trying to fix or rectify that mistake in some way, and I had to guess that unrest in this solar system wasn't something he'd want. For a variety of reasons, not wanting to bring yet more attention to our backwater part of the galaxy being the biggest.

And I point-blank knew it was Algar who'd arranged our landings because I desperately wanted to talk to Jeff about all of this and I couldn't. The words literally would not leave my mouth.

Algar being this involved was a rarity. So whatever was coming, he wanted us here, and he wanted us prepared to do something to save the day or similar.

I'd figured out how to kind of work around the whole "Algar won't let me share" thing. It took a heck of a lot of mental and verbal gymnastics, but we had the time and I more than had the desire.

"Jeff, why do you think we're on this planet?"

"Honestly? I think it's a mistake. Like the three of you worked out—whoever was trying to pull us elsewhere, maybe Alpha Four, maybe Beta Twelve, maybe somewhere else, they had some kind of malfunction. Something went wrong in some way and we landed here. Better here than in outer space."

"Yeah. Only . . ."

"Only?" Jeff shifted to look at me. "You think we were meant to come here?"

"I think there has to be more to where we landed than meets the eye."

He cocked his head at me. "I know you think we couldn't have been lucky twice, but it's not out of the realm of possibility. Coincidences do happen, even to us."

"Yeah, I know. Two isn't enough of a sample to be sure." I was about to mention that three would indicate a pattern, but before I could we were interrupted. And not by Christopher and the others coming back.

All the chochos were bark-honking, Wilbur included.

At nothing. At least, nothing I could see.

CHAPTER 31

BUT I COULD HEAR. And it sounded like whooping. Familiar whooping.

Looked up in the sky. Sure enough, there were things flying around up there. Based on my experience and the total weirdness of this world, what they were wasn't a surprise. Or rather, who.

The Lecanora, of course, were racing to toss ocellars into catapults. When we had a moment, I was going to have a severe Shealla Does Not Like This chat with them. I knew Ginger would approve this chat—trained for flying into the air to kill Horrible Snakipedes or not—because she was cuddling against me even harder than she had been.

But Jeff had seen what I had, too.

"Stop!" he bellowed. No one could bellow like my man, and I had to assume he had a lot of pent-up bellowing, based on the last month or so of our lives, let alone our current situation. "They are *not* enemies! No catapults! No attacks!"

The Lecanora froze in their tracks. Apparently, when the Top God bellowed, the Lecanora listened.

So the five giant flying ostrich-pterodactyls were able to land safely. Which was nice, because each one of them had a flyboy riding as either pilot or copilot. Wasn't sure if the ostrich-pterodactyls were of a high sentience level or not yet. Right now, though, my bet was for high.

The flyboys' mounts had ostrich bodies, legs, and necks, but their wings, though covered with feathers, were pterodactyl sized and shaped. Their feet and heads were really combos of both things, though, with more emphasis on pterodactyl in the head—particularly in terms of elongated beaks and eyes set more in front, like predators' were, rather than to the side, like prey—and more ostrich in the feet. Unlike ostriches and what we figured pterodactyls looked like, their skin was a light lemon yellow and their feathers were literally neon yellow, with neon orange and red highlights. It was like the flyboys were all on predatory Big Birds. Yep, they were a Planet Colorful species.

As the flyboys dismounted, I gently moved my current menagerie off my lap—Wilbur had followed Ginger's lead and snuggled much closer than before—and trotted over. Humans didn't group hug as much as the A-Cs did, but we made an exception in this case and had a big group huddle hug.

"I was so worried about you guys," I said when we unclenched and Jeff grabbed each of them individually for hugs. "Are you okay?"

"Yeah," Jerry said with a grin. "We are. We lucked out and landed with the strautruch."

"Really? That's what the ostrich-pterodactyl Big Birds call themselves?" What was I complaining about? I traveled with Poofs, after all, and Lecanora was no better or worse.

"Yeah," Walker said, as he patted the one he'd been riding. "They're great. They can't really speak in a language we can understand."

"But they can draw pictograms," Hughes added. "And they can understand us just fine."

Pictograms meant sentience. Understanding extremely foreign languages meant a higher intelligence, though if I had a universal translator chip, so did the flyboys. Only I was sure they'd known about theirs since they'd been installed.

"We were lucky," Joe said. "We landed in one of their empty nests."

Randy nodded. "Really lucky. They nest on the tops of mountains. They aren't all that high, at least most of them."

"But if their nests weren't large and we didn't land just right, we'd be toast," Jerry said.

Looked at Jeff. "Coinkydink is now out of the question."

He nodded. "I agree, baby. Someone wants us here, and in specific places."

"No argument," Joe said. He looked around. "Uh, where are the others?"

Randy was looking, too. Both of them now looked worried, and no wonder. Their wives had been taken and were nowhere in evidence. And I had no answer that was going to make them feel any better.

"Not with us. Chuckie, Christopher, and I landed with the katyhoppers," I indicated Pinky. "Chuckie and Christopher, along with the katyhoppers who've let them ride on their backs, are off checking out the planet and searching for the rest of our team. Did you see them? Because I kind of assumed they'd told you where we were."

Hughes shook his head. "The strautruch elders suggested that some of their younger members help us search for the rest of our people."

"So we were flying around and spotted dust flying up," Walker said. "Figured that meant something or someone was down here, so we flew closer to take a look."

The Big Bird that Walker had been riding scratched in the dirt. Took a good look.

"Aha. That's the All Seeing Mountain, isn't it?"

It bobbed its head, just like Bruno did. Then it scratched some more, nudged its head toward Jeff, then me, then the flyboys.

Looked around for King Benny, who was waiting nearby, and motioned him over. "King Benny, who are they?" I pointed to the flyboys.

"They are the Winalla, the flying warriors of the Gods." He sighed. "Still you test me, Shealla."

"Just because I know you'll always pass the tests." Looked back to the pictograms while Jeff quietly and quickly brought the flyboys up to speed on our Godhoods. "So, the strautruch also have a history of, ah, Gods like us? Or visitors like us?"

Pinky joined us, antennae focused on the Big Birds. They, in turn, gave him their full attention. And then they all bowed to him. Deeply. In the same way that the Lecanora had bowed to us.

"Mind catching me up on what's going on?" I asked Pinky quietly.

He waved his antennae at me.

"Interesting. Excuse us all, for just a minute," I said to

King Benny and the Big Birds. "Please talk amongst yourselves—we're all headed for the same place, by the way. King Benny, the strautruch are as smart as your people are, so work at the understanding, please." Pulled Jeff and the flyboys aside. Pinky came with us. "Okay, Pinky just had an interesting talk with the strautruch."

"How?" Randy asked. "They didn't speak, and they didn't draw."

Well, no time like the present. "The katyhoppers can read minds. And, frankly, so can Chuckie, Christopher, and I right now. Something in the water or food or whatever in the Purple Land."

"I've never flown faster than we did over the purple part," Jerry said. "They told us it was a forbidden area."

"I think it's forbidden because that's where the mind-reading life-forms and mind-reading food source are, but that's not important now. Well, it is, but not what I'm trying to tell all of you. The strautruch know of the katyhoppers. They worship them as demigods on the planet—that's why they avoid the Purple Lands, so as to not offend them. But the strautruch, like the rest, consider all of *us* to be the embodiment of millennia-old God legends. We're all fitting into the assigned God roles perfectly, too. Which is weird beyond belief, but probably a reason we were sent here."

"Do the katyhoppers consider us Gods?" Jeff asked.

Pinky waved antennae.

"No, they do not. They're really clear that we're aliens from another world. Their Matriarchs are also really clear that other worlds exist, and that they're populated. Look, what I'm trying to say, among other things, is that the top sentient life-forms on this planet are not the Lecanora, though that's what I think all of the rest of the system has decided, because they're bipedal and have wagons and a civilization we can all relate to. But the top minds on Planet Colorful belong to the katyhoppers."

Everyone stared at Pinky. Who, despite not being able to blush, still managed to look embarrassed.

"So," Jeff asked slowly, "what does that mean for us or for what's going on?"

Was about to share my thoughts when Christopher appeared out of nowhere. "Everyone's fine," he said quickly.

"At least right now. Hey, guys, good to see you," he said to the flyboys.

"Why are you back already? Did you find the others?" I asked.

"I'm back because we've found good shelter. Chuck and the others are there. And we need to get this caravan to that shelter as fast as possible, because there are at least twenty snakipedes heading this way."

CHAPTER 32

"THE FLYBOYS AND PINKY can get to shelter fast. But there's no way that we can get this caravan anywhere faster than tortoise pace. Trust me. It took the bosthoon thirty minutes to get up to faster than a Sunday Afternoon Stroll speed."

Christopher looked at Jeff. "I think we can carry a wagon each, if we do it together."

"Not with the bosthoon attached you can't," I said. "They're big, heavy, and unwieldy."

"Then we unhook them and get them if we're able to," Christopher replied briskly. "They're the lowest sentience life-forms we're traveling with, and that means they're the last to be taken care of."

Jeff nodded. "I agree. Let's give it a shot. Kitty, I think the ocellars and chochos can go a lot faster than the bost-hoon can. If Christopher and I really can move the wagons, you and Pinky lead the animals while we get the Lecanora to safety."

"Okay." It wasn't, but I knew they were right—we had to get the majority to safety first. Then I could worry about the slowest. "Keeping in mind that I have no idea where safety is."

Toby popped its head out of Christopher's pocket, mewed, and leaped onto Pinky's head. "Aha, never mind. Poof at the wheel. Okey dokey." Ran over to King Benny. "Binalla has identified a terrible threat. We're going to move your people to safety much faster than you're used to. You need to unhook the bosthoon, get everyone into their wagons, and ensure that they all stay put until one of us tells them it's okay to get out. I'm taking the chochos and ocellars with me."

"What about the bosthoon?" he asked, sounding worried. "Not only are they our transportation, but they have no real natural defenses."

"Leave that to me. Just get your people doing what we need, as fast as possible."

He nodded and trotted off to get his people moving.

I ran back to the others. The flyboys were already mounted up. Kissed Jeff hard. "Get yourself to safety, too, please." Then I went to Pinky, mounted up, and whistled. "All ocellars and chochos, follow Shealla Kitty!"

Interestingly enough, Ginger roared, and the ocellars formed up right behind Pinky, adults holding young ones too small to run fast in their mouths. The chochos, on the other hand, weren't doing so well. Until Wilbur barkhonked louder than I'd thought possible.

It was as if he'd given them the Line Up and March order, because they fell in faster than the ocellars had. As with the ocellars, any chochos too young to run fast were being carried, but on the adults' backs. Decided now wasn't the time to argue or question. "Pinky, my friend, let's fly low and as fast as the slowest of these animals can run."

With that, we took off.

It was probably an interesting sight from the air. Or from space, if someone was looking at us with a really excellent telescope. The flyboys were higher in the air than Pinky and I were, but they were in goose formation and flying behind us—Hughes in the lead, with Walker and Jerry streaming out to the right and Joe and Randy streaming out to the left.

Under them were the mass of ocellars and chochos. I hadn't bothered to count heads in the time we'd been with them, but it seemed like there were at least five chochos and four ocellars per wagon. Really hoped that whatever place Christopher and Chuckie had found was truly big enough to house us all.

The land under us flew by quickly. We passed several large rock outcroppings, but no one was there. Surprise at how very unpopulated the parts of this world we'd seen so far were struck me again. It just didn't seem normal. Then again, nothing else here was normal, either, at least as far as

I saw it. Besides, I hadn't asked the flyboys about their population intel, and we hadn't seen most of this world yet.

It took us a good thirty minutes to reach what I realized was our shelter—a gigantic rock formation. Well, it was gigantic when we got into it. From the air, it just looked like a domed rock about twelve feet high and not all that impressive.

However, as we flew in and landed, I could see that what they'd found was an underground cavern. A huge one.

Jeff and Christopher already had five wagons in here, and by the time we dismounted and checked in with Chuckie, they had another. However, there was no way the bosthoon were going to make it here in time, not if the snakipede herd was close by.

Pinky read my mind, of course, and we both went outside. I was still on Pinky's back anyway, and Toby was still with me, along with Harlie, Poofikins, and Murphy. So we flew up to see what we could see. We still had light from the suns, but we were going to lose it sooner rather than later. Far off on the horizon was a speck that got larger as I looked at it. Safe bet this was the snakipede herd.

"Pinky, what are our options?"

He waved antennae as the five strautruch joined us.

"Aha, good plan and worth a shot. Wow, you guys are strong if you think you can do this."

The Big Birds bobbed their heads. Took this to mean they were going to do their best to be awesome.

"Super. Let's roll, then." We zoomed off, at a far faster speed than I'd flown with Pinky yet. Presumably because we had no reason to go slowly. The strautruch kept up without issue.

We swooped in as Jeff and Christopher returned for another wagon. "What are you doing?" Jeff asked. "I want you back to safety right now." He was using his growly man voice he still persisted in believing I listened to anywhere other than in bed. It was cute.

"Yes, well, I'll go a lot faster if you guys move it. Now, leave me alone. I need to focus."

I was focusing on the bosthoon. They weren't the brightest, but then again, I was Dr. Doolittle, and now was the time to use the skills. Pinky was assisting, so I had high hopes.

"All bosthoon, gather together, please. The nice strautruch are going to fly you to safety, one or two at a time, depending. You need to not struggle. Shealla Kitty promises that you'll be safe this way. The rest of you, follow Shealla Kitty as fast as you can."

The strautruch were actually able to grab and carry two bosthoon at a time, which was amazing. Almost too amazing. Made a mental note to ask about what their part of the world was like.

Ten bosthoon flying off was good, but since we had seventy-five bosthoon if we had one, this wasn't making the dent it could. However, I wasn't willing to just give up.

"We need to herd them, just like cattle," I said to Pinky. "Normally that takes at least three cowboys. We have one, since rider and mount work as one."

Pinky waved antennae. Not to worry—help was on the way.

It was. Saffron and Turkey arrived, with Hughes and Walker riding them. "Need help herding your cows, little lady?" Hughes asked me.

"I do. We need to get them to safety before the rustlers show up. Great to see you guys, how did you know to come here?"

"Jeff just did a drop-off and was shouting at Chuck, as if he was responsible for you doing this. We suggested that we knew what you were going to try to do and that we should help. Chuck said the katyhoppers were in agreement. Everyone else is staying put, per Chuck and Jeff's orders."

"We promised to force you to safety if whatever's coming shows up and there are still animals in danger," Walker added. "So let's get moving."

Pinky and I took the lead, with the bosthoon following us pretty decently. Hughes and Walker did what the cowboys who weren't lead did—herded and encouraged said herd to move a lot faster.

We trundled along, but faster than we had before. The bosthoon were able to move better since they weren't pulling laden wagons. The strautruch returned, grabbed two from the rear each, and took off again.

Based on my limited memory of how to do speed and distance math problems, I had to figure that if it had taken us thirty minutes to fly to our destination at a fast rate of speed, it was going to take at least an hour, maybe more, to get the herd there. And I didn't think we had an hour.

However, we persevered. After about fifteen minutes and one more Big Bird snatch and grab run, Jeff and Christopher showed up with a catapult wagon. They tossed four bosthoon on it, with me doing some serious animal calming talk, and then zipped off. Figured the bosthoon barfing up their cud, or whatever, would still be preferable to them turning into carcasses.

Between all of these efforts, we were a lot closer to our destination and had a lot fewer bosthoon to get to safety. But we still had plenty and I could now see things in the sky. Not clearly, but close enough that I knew we didn't have too long before we were attacked.

Motioned for Hughes to come up to where I was, and he did so. "What's up, Kitty?"

"Did you guys happen to have guns on you when you were snatched into this solar system?"

"Yeah, Chip and I did for sure. We don't have more than one clip each, though. We weren't going out on a mission, we were doing a briefing."

"Yeah, tell me about it. The things that are coming at us from the sky are what I've kind of named snakipedes and the Lecanora we're with call the Horrors."

"We know about them. They're a threat to the strautruch, too."

Really? Interesting. "Did you guys have to deal with any of them yet?"

"No, but we saw one yesterday. It flew below the nest we landed in. The strautruch had us look so we'd know what to fear, basically."

"Well, that's good, I guess. Because according to Christopher, we have a herd of snakipedes coming. They're definitely killed by bullets, but it took a lot. I have plenty of clips in my purse, but I'm not sure that they'll work in your guns."

While I was saying this I was also digging around in my purse. Pulled out a bunch of clips. They were not clips for my Glock. Hughes grabbed them. "Yeah, these will work. I'll get some to Chip. I know you don't want to let these animals die, Kitty, so we'll all do our best to hold the snakipedes off."

Sent a mental thank you to Algar. "Thanks. But you need to know and to tell Chip—in addition to these things being like a triple big anaconda with a zillion little wings, they're also venomous."

"Oh, great. Can't wait." With that, Hughes and Saffron flew over to Walker and Turkey.

"Pinky, is there any way we can get the bosthoon moving more quickly?"

Antenna waves indicated that he doubted it. The Big Birds arrived again and grabbed another ten bosthoon, while Jeff and Christopher arrived with another catapult wagon. Four more bosthoon on, more animal calming work from me, and then they were gone.

The Big Birds were tiring. I could tell because Jeff and Chuckie were back with the third catapult wagon before the strautruch came back. Another four bosthoon were off and the guys were back with the fourth catapult when the strautruch returned for their next set. They were still able to grab two bosthoon each, but all of them were flying lower this time. Didn't figure they could do more than one each next run. If they could even manage a next run.

However, that would work, if we'd get the time. Because we had nine bosthoon left, meaning that the last catapult run and one bosthoon to a Big Bird would mean we got everyone to safety.

Took a look in the sky. I could see the snakipedes. Clearly.

We were out of time.

CHAPTER 33

BECAUSE WE ONLY had nine bosthoon left, Hughes, Walker, and I were close enough that we could shout and hear each other. Plus the katyhoppers were helping with sound transference.

"We need to keep them moving," I told the guys. "But the moment they see the snakipedes I'm pretty sure the bosthoon are going to panic."

"Who the hell can blame them?" Walker said. "I can see them and I'd like to wet myself. And I'm not actually afraid of snakes."

"I am. And if I'm not peeing my pants, you guys don't get to, either."

Jeff and Christopher arrived with the last caravan wagon. "Get to the shelter," Jeff shouted at us. "Leave the last ones and get to safety."

"We will," I totally lied. "But you two get going first, so we can cover you on the way back."

Jeff shot me a look that said he didn't buy it for a New York Minute. But Christopher just nodded. "Jeff, she's right. Let's go."

They disappeared and we moved closer to our five remaining bosthoon. The animals had picked up the scent or something about what was coming. I knew this because I could feel their panic and terror. But we had them in a tight formation, and they didn't break from it.

I could see our destination in the distance. The snakipedes were about as far away from us as the cavern. However, they were going much faster than we were.

The Big Birds arrived and took our last bosthoon in their claws, but they were all flying low and slow. They were going faster than the bosthoon could, but not nearly as fast as they'd been earlier. And not fast enough to beat the snakipedes.

Hughes, Walker, and I didn't talk — we just rose high up in the air to meet the snakipedes before they headed down and at least distract them from their targets.

Of course, one snakipede had been bad. And we were facing twenty of them. They were flying in an altered goose formation, with three in the front and the others behind them. Did another fast count. Oh, goody. We weren't facing twenty. We were facing twenty-one. Naturally.

Wanted to throw up, run away, or just plain scream. But I did none of those things, and neither did Hughes or Walker.

What we all did was start shooting.

We'd each taken one of the lead snakipedes and were firing at them. Wasn't sure if we were too far away for the bullets to hit or not, but as with superbeings, the guns definitely made you feel a little better and like maybe the fight was more even.

One clip emptied, I rummaged around in my purse for another, not that it appeared to be doing any good at this distance. "A machine gun, a machine gun, my kingdom for a machine gun."

And proving that Algar had indeed decided that my purse was now a portable portal, lo and behold, my hand hit a large piece of metal. Pulled out a nice machine gun complete with a long belt of ammo already loaded and ready to go.

"Thank you so very much," I said to my purse. Looked up. The snakipedes were far too close. Aimed and started firing in a broad back-and-forth pattern so I'd hit all three of the lead monsters. "Snakipedes, say hello to my leettle friend!"

If I hadn't been enhanced the recoil would have knocked me off Pinky. As it was, I could just barely stay on his back. On the other hand, the machine gun was doing what I needed it to — cutting through all three lead snakipedes.

Three Horror Heads exploded and three Horror Bods fell to the ground. Kept on firing in the same strafing pattern. Next line was down just like the first. This machine gun was a godsend. Or rather, an Algarsend.

As I started on the third line, registered that Hughes was shouting at me. Risked a look around. Hughes and Walker were okay, and both were indicating that it was time to get out of the air. Checked the ground and saw the last Big Bird fly inside the cavern.

Nodded to the guys. "Start down. Pinky and I will follow you and hold them off!"

All three katyhoppers started to fly toward the cavern's entrance, Saffron and Turkey going faster than Pinky. Unfortunately, the remaining snakipedes saw their prey moving and they broke formation. "Go, go, go!" I shouted, to Pinky and the guys.

We all sped up. I was still firing the machine gun, but it wasn't nearly so easy to shoot turned around on Pinky's back, and I wasn't hitting any one of the snakipedes enough to kill now. And, to make things just that much more exciting, as I tried to aim better and rapid fire at the same time, I lost hold of the gun. Which did not do me a solid and shoot the snakipedes as it was falling to the ground. It didn't shoot any of us, either, so chose to take that as, if not one for the win column, at least not a total failure.

I imagined that I could feel snakipede breath on my neck, but I didn't turn around. I was a sprinter and I'd learned a long time ago that sprinters who turned around while running were sprinters who lost their races. Sure, I wasn't running, but my shifting could affect Pinky, and he and I didn't need that.

All the flyboys and Chuckie were in the cavern mouth, and they were all firing. Ducked down as Pinky and I zoomed in. Flipped off his back and took a look. I hadn't imagined that snake breath on my neck.

The snakipede head exploded just outside of the cavern mouth. As it did so, all three katyhoppers sprayed stuff out of their butts. Realized that they'd covered most of the cavern's mouth already—presumably Turkey and Saffron had done so before Hughes and Walker had joined me—because I could recognize the way the solidified butt juice looked.

The snakipedes were fooled, at least somewhat. They were only trying to get in at the point where Hughes, Walker, and I had come in, not at any other part of the entrance.

Was going to contribute to the gunplay when I heard the sounds of trouble from inside the cavern. Ran back and deeper in to find Jeff holding back a couple of Lecanora. Minks, by the look of them.

"What's wrong?"

"One of their kids is missing," Jeff said, sounding tense and upset. "I have no idea how. Or where. We didn't see anyone out when we were going back and forth."

"Ginger, Wilbur!" The ocellar and chocho ran to me. "Are any animals missing? Any at all?" They ran off to do head counts. "Someone needs to search inside the caverns. Christopher, you'll do that fastest."

He nodded and zipped off.

Wilbur bounded back and bark-honked quietly. "Okay, all chochos are accounted for, even puplets."

"Puplets?" Jeff asked.

"Puppy piglets."

"Why did I ask? Look, we have to do something and find their child." He indicated the mink couple he was holding back. There were several kids of varying sizes standing behind them, all looking worried.

"Boy or girl?"

"Our youngest daughter," the mother mink sobbed, as Ginger returned.

Ginger yowled softly. "Gotcha. So, your daughter likes the ocellars a lot and has a favorite kitten, doesn't she?"

The father mink nodded. "They don't belong to us, though. They are Nanda's."

"Well, one of them is your daughter's now." If I was able to find the two little ones, that was. "What's her name?"

"Patrina."

Christopher returned. "Didn't find her. But there's what looks like a tunnel in here. She might have gone down it, but I doubt it. I ran a good ways and found no one."

"Jeff and Christopher, stay here and keep all the others here. Start getting everyone organized and head them into the tunnel Christopher found. We're going to assume that the tunnel goes somewhere, and even if it doesn't, it'll be easier to fight off the snakipedes one by one."

"The tunnel's narrow enough that we can't get the wagons in, so yeah, it'll limit what the snakipedes can do," Christopher said.

"What are you going to be doing?" Jeff asked in a tone of voice that said he already knew and didn't approve.

"What I do best—improvising." He started to argue and I put up my hand. "I can talk to the animals and you can't. I'm going to find them based on the ocellar kitten that's missing. I can go faster than the snakipedes. And you just said we had to help, and we do."

With that I turned and ran for the cavern's opening, Ginger at my heels.

The guys were holding the snakipedes off and had even killed a couple. But all that meant was that we still had over a dozen alive and seriously pissed.

Grabbed Chuckie. "We have a kid and a kitten missing. I'm going after them. I'm assuming that the kitten got spooked and ran out and the kid ran after it and no one noticed in all the chaos, but I could be wrong. I need cover fire, then you guys need to be ready to run for the back. Christopher found a tunnel and it goes a long way. We're going to bet on it leading somewhere."

"Jeff let you do this?" Chuckie sounded like he didn't believe it.

"Not really. But he's having to deal with the families."

"And I left that to Christopher," Jeff said from behind me. "I'm coming with you."

Made eye contact with Chuckie and told him that Jeff wouldn't be able to protect me from these things and would slow me down. I none too gently suggested Chuckie do his Vulcan Nerve Pinch thing.

Proving that the mind reading was still working, Chuckie reached over, grabbed Jeff's shoulder right by his neck, did something, and then caught Jeff as he went down. "He's going to want to kill me when he wakes up, and if you don't come back safely I'll let him," Chuckie said.

"Things to live for are always good. Ginger, you're staying here, too." She didn't look happy. "Trust me, I'll find them. I promise."

And with that, I ran through the small opening that didn't have katyhopper butt fluid over it yet. Right toward the gaping maw of a snakipede.

CHAPTER 34

HYPERSPEED WAS THE best thing ever. Oh sure, faster healing and regeneration was nothing to complain about, but being faster than anything else around remained the best thing I'd gotten from my enhancement.

Yes, the snakipede was close to me when I left, and yes, it struck as it saw and smelled me moving. But it missed.

Sadly, I heard a cracking sound, meaning that it had hit the katyhopper's shield. That wouldn't hold long, especially with more than one snakipede there. Hoped Chuckie would get the rest of them back with the caravan and through the tunnels, but I didn't have high hopes.

I went for the machine gun first, in part to get away from the mass of writhing snakipedes, and in other part to have an effective weapon with me. Managed to find it because it had fallen near a dead snakipede body and because I could run around really fast until I found it.

Weapon in hand, I ran around the area near to the cavern. So far, the snakipedes hadn't noticed that I was out, but that probably wasn't going to last too long. I had to find the two missing members of King Benny's flock quickly to have a hope of getting them and me back into safety. And I had to do it before we lost the light, and that, based on the long shadows everywhere, was going to be really soon.

Naturally they weren't close by, because that would have been too much like right. On the other hand, not being too close meant I had a hope of finding them before a snakipede did.

Found a boulder bigger than me and hid behind it. Not

because I needed to rest—the adrenaline rush that fight or flight gave me was turned up well past eleven, since I wanted to both fight and flee very badly—but because I needed to concentrate.

Took my all-too-common deep breath and let it out slowly. Didn't want to, but I closed my eyes and sent my mind out.

Nothing.

However, I heard a small, Poofy sound. Looked into my purse to see Poofikins and a waterfruit. "Poofs are the best," I whispered as I took the fruit and ate it quickly.

It was refreshing and helpful. As I ate I again sent my mind out, searching for terror. That was what Jeff had used to find me and the guys, after all, and he'd always said that terror was the sharpest and strongest of the emotions. And Chuckie thought that what we had going on, with me especially, was empathy of a sort.

I heard them, at the edge of my mind. Two minds, both crying for their mothers. But silently. And they were definitely together. And, of course, they were in the opposite direction from the cavern.

Headed toward them at hyperspeed. I could hear them in my mind, but I couldn't see them, and I wasn't an empath. Jeff would have been able to home in on them instantly, and the stupidity of my keeping the strongest empath in the galaxy from helping me loomed large. Only he'd said he could barely feel things in this part of the world, and it might not have occurred to me to give him a waterfruit and see what happened.

Self-recriminations over, forced myself to slow down to human speeds. I knew they were somewhere near me because the voices in my head were much louder. There were a couple of small trees near where I felt them, and I hid behind one while still looking around. If I wasn't careful, though, a snakipede could see me.

"Patrina," I whispered. "Patrina, where are you and the kitten?"

Nothing.

"Patrina, sweetie, I know you're scared. But Shealla Kitty can't help you or the kitten if you don't let me know where you are."

Felt rather than saw that a snakipede had broken off

from the group. The mind was dull and hungry, but there were no revenge-type thoughts. The snakipedes weren't after us because we'd killed some of their number. They were after us because we represented a feast.

The katyhoppers were right—these creatures weren't high on the sentience scale. However, sharks weren't considered to be Rhodes Scholars and yet they were terrifyingly effective killers.

Focused on the cat. I'd have more affinity with the animal. "Come to Shealla Kitty. Shealla Kitty can't find you two and that means Shealla Kitty can't protect you two." Nothing, other than fearful thoughts.

Tried to think like a little girl would. That the kitten had gotten spooked and run out of the cavern and that she'd followed it were givens. So, what would Jamie do, where would she hide, if she and Mous-Mous were lost with terrifying monsters close by? Looked around at the landscape. More to the point, where around here would actually look like someplace safe? To a baby mink and a baby cat?

Both of whom would have claws.

Looked up. The leaves of the trees I was near fit the rest of this area—brown, red, orange, yellow, ochre, and everything else from this particular color palette. But that made them excellent camouflage if you were a reddish fox-cat and a little kid who had dark fur.

I couldn't see them, meaning that the camouflage part was working. However, I was sure that the snakipedes would be able to smell them, and me, sooner as opposed to later.

The option to keep on being nice and soothing was there. But time was of the essence. And in times of stress, the best choice I could always make was to channel Mom.

"Patrina, you and the kitten get down to Shealla Kitty right now!" I said in the sternest soft tone I could manage. "I mean it young lady. This instant! Or you'll be giving me a good answer why."

This worked. Not a surprise. It had always worked when Mom had done it on me or any of my friends. The leaves above me rustled, and a little mink face looked down at me. "I'm scared," she whispered.

"I know. I won't let the monsters hurt you. But I can't do that if you're not here with me. Come down, right now.

Jump into my arms if you can, and be sure you're holding the kitten tightly, too."

She nodded and I put the machine gun down. Just in time, as she jumped into my waiting arms. Managed not to say "oof" but only because I'd been prepared. She was clutching the ocellar kitten in both paws.

Shifted her to the hip opposite where my purse was, grabbed the machine gun, and took a look around. The snakipede was getting closer.

"What's your kitten's name?"

"Pretty Girl. Only she's not really mine," Patrina said sadly.

"I promise that once we're back with everyone else, she's going to be yours, okay?"

"Okay. Pretty Girl and I are really scared."

"Wisely. I want Pretty Girl to hold onto you, and you're going to hold tight to me, okay?"

"Okay." She cuddled the ocellar into her chest and clutched me with her other paw. It was the best we were going to get.

I'd held Jeff's niece, Kimmy, like this when Doreen's crazy mother had attacked me during Operation Drug Addict. And I'd gotten used to holding Jamie this way, too, a lot, especially in times of danger. So precedent existed for me to be successful now. Held Patrina tightly, sent a prayer up to the various Powers That Be, Algar especially, and started running.

Just in time, because the lone snakipede had found us, and it struck as I moved. The tree Patrina and Pretty Girl had been in and I'd been hiding behind crashed down. I didn't stop to mourn its noble sacrifice.

I could outrun the snakipede, with no issue. The problem was that the rest of the snakipede herd was blocking the safe entrance back into the cavern. Which also meant that they were going to break through soon and be able to eat or kill everyone—the cavern was definitely big enough to hold them.

So, I had to save myself, Patrina, and Pretty Girl, and I also had to save everyone else. Well, that's why I had a machine gun, after all. Sure, it didn't have unlimited bullets, but it did have a half-full belt of ammo, due to my having lost my grip on it earlier. I loved it when a plan came together.

Ran us to the top of the boulder that was the cavern's roof. This put us very near to the snakipedes. And the lone one was coming for us, too. No time like the present.

"Hold on," I said to everyone with me. This was important for Patrina and Pretty Girl, because they were gagging. But not barfing, thankfully. From experience, adrenaline highs tended to reduce the nausea hyperspeed caused. And maybe they could handle it just like the katyhoppers because they were Alpha Centauri beings.

Not that this mattered all that much, because I had to do something. So I did. I fired right down on top of the snakipede's heads.

I lucked out and killed one right away—figured that one had been close to dead anyway because of the guys shooting at it. And another couple were down already, again, probably due to the guys.

The rest, however, lost interest in the cavern and turned their entire focus onto me.

Rapid-fired into their nasty faces until I had no more bullets left. Kept a hold of the machine gun—I could use it as a club if I had to—turned, and ran toward the back of the cavern which, since I was on top of it, meant down a rocky slope toward the ground. But at human speeds.

Not for too long, of course. Just long enough for all the snakipedes to see and follow me. Reached the dirt, ran a little farther, turned to my right, saw them all massed there and coming for me, and let terror kick my hyperspeed into overdrive.

Ran a bit in this direction, turned right again, and headed back for the cavern. The lone snakipede was there. Clearly this one was a rebel and just didn't want to do what the others did.

Heard no gunshots, meaning that the guys were either out of ammo or everyone had run off down into the cavern and tunnel. Hoped it was the latter but figured on the former.

Stopped by its tail. Due to how things were, it was hovering at about head height. Swung the machine gun and hit the tail as hard as I could. Which was hard enough that I lost hold of the machine gun once again.

The snakipede spun faster than I'd seen them move yet and lunged at us. Only I'd expected the lunge, though not

CHAPTER 35

JEFF GRABBED ME AND SHOUTED, "Now!"

Lecanora wagons slammed against the katyhopper's barrier, stacked side to side and on top of each other. A Poof might have been able to get through, but nothing bigger.

They were standing there, creating a great barrier. But no one was touching them.

As Jeff put me down I heard the snakipedes slamming their heads against the wagons, but I wasn't looking there. I looked for who was doing this. And I was unsurprised to see the Big Birds all clustered together and obviously concentrating.

"You and I are going to have a talk about this," Jeff said. His voice was shaking and so was he.

Didn't let go of kid and kitten, but hugged him one-armed. Tightly. "Hope you didn't hurt Chuckie."

"The flyboys wouldn't let me," he growled.

"Good. Chuckie's better than you at realizing who's the best person to do a job, Jeff."

"I have no argument about the job you do, baby. I have an argument about my wife running off to face monsters by herself."

"I knew I could find them." I let go of Jeff and hugged Patrina and Pretty Girl. "They were extremely brave."

As I said this, Patrina's parents broke free from whoever had taken on the job of holding them back. They and the rest of their clan swarmed us. I handed Patrina to her mother, then gently moved out of the family circle.

"I need to speak with Nanda," I told Jeff.

"Later. The strautruch can't hold this barrier for long."

"They're telekinetic, aren't they?"

"Yeah, appears so. You seem unsurprised."

"They were carrying the bosthoon with too much ease, and if you have a section of your planet that assists with mind reading, it makes sense that there's a part that helps with other psionic talents, too, and telekinesis is the most likely. Who came up with the barrier idea?"

"Chuck. The wagons wouldn't fit through the tunnel and the Lecanora were making a fuss about leaving them, understandably. Chuck said that the wagons were needed to save Shealla and protect the rest of us, and they shut up and let him have them. As soon as the strautruch realized what he wanted to do, they helped."

"And I'd bet that Leoalla saying 'Do as Alcalla the Wise says' helped a lot."

He sighed. "Yes, it did. And you can stop worrying—I'm not mad at Chuck. Anymore. I know he was following your insane orders."

Pointed to Patrina's family. "I note again that my crazy's working a lot better than your sanity."

Jeff managed a laugh. "True as always." He went over to the mink family. "Okay, folks, you need to hurry up and join the others and follow Binalla down the tunnels. Now," he added sternly, while Patrina's father kept on trying to take Pretty Girl away from her.

"The ocellar is Patrina's," I said in what I sincerely hoped was a Godly tone. "Patrina risked her life to save Pretty Girl, and bravery, love, and loyalty like that should be rewarded. I will clear things with Nanda, but as of right now, that cat is hers, and anyone trying to take it from her will answer to me."

Patrina's father put her and the ocellar down. She ran over to me and hugged my legs. "Thank you, Shealla! Pretty Girl thanks you, too!"

Bent down and hugged her. "It was my pleasure."

Her mother grabbed her paw, then, whole family bowing to me in a really obsequious way, they backed off and ran to do what Jeff had told them to.

This left me, Jeff, and the strautruch in the cavern's entrance. "Where's Bruno?"

"I have him with Christopher, in case of something. He's fine. Same with your new dog and cat. They're with Chuck."

Okay, I could stop worrying a bit about my pets. Checked my purse. Harlie, Poofikins, and Murphy were in my purse. Presumed Toby was back with Christopher and all the other Poofs were with their respective owners. "Great. What's our plan?"

"The moment all of our group, animals included, are far enough into the tunnels that we can feel confident that the snakipedes can't get to them, then everyone holds on and I run us to the others at hyperspeed. All the kids and elderly are on the backs of bosthoon, which supposedly never panic. Based on what we just went through, I'd say that's accurate."

"That's a great plan, only it doesn't cover what we do when the snakipedes reach the tunnel. I could outrun them because I could go anywhere. There's nowhere to go in a tunnel other than through that tunnel. And we can't go fast at all, even if the bosthoon were fleet of foot, which they very much are not."

"I'm open to ideas." Jeff shot a glance at the strautruch. "They can't hold it too much longer, I don't think."

"No, probably not. And I assume we're out of ammo."

He nodded. "The guys kept their guns, just in case but, yeah, we're out of bullets."

Looked around the cavern. There were no convenient boulders in here. Looked at the wagon wall. "So . . . we've told the Lecanora that they're never going to see their wagons again, right?"

"Right. They're fully refugees now. Everything they own is being carried by each one of them. Conveniently they didn't own much." He sighed. "Still, they had homes, albeit traveling ones. They were better off before they met us. All of them were. Because if we fail, they're all going to die. And us, too."

Thought about this. "Maybe, but hold the fatalism at bay for a bit. I know we're here for a reason. And it's always darkest before the suns shows up or some such. We need to come up with another way."

Trotted to one side of the wagon wall and looked out through a little gap between wagon and rock. There was enough light left that I could see that we had a lot of snakipede bodies on the ground. But still had at least a half a dozen or more in the air trying to break their way in.

Trotted back to the Big Birds. "I know you guys are concentrating, but I may have an idea. Can you manipulate things or just move them, make them lighter, or whatever it is you did to move the bosthoon and the wagons? As in, make the wagons fold in on themselves and sort of bite the snakipedes' heads off?"

Received a couple of squawks and a garbled mental reply, but the gist appeared to be that, were they not exhausted, it was a definite maybe. Not good enough to bet on, especially now, however.

Time to come up with a stellar Plan B. Pity I didn't have one.

Wrong thinking. I was stressed and that was never good. Reached into my purse to get my iPod—in times of stress music remained my go-to move, especially if sex with Jeff wasn't possible, which it certainly was not at this precise time.

As I pulled the iPod out I looked at the screen. It was lit and the album cover being displayed was "Elemental" by Tears for Fears. The album that had the song that had saved us from a giant snake what seemed like so long ago now.

Dug out the speakers. They were small but powerful. I knew because they were speakers I'd coveted but hadn't gotten yet because I was the wife of the Vice President and it was probably wrong to be blasting music wherever I went.

Other than here, apparently. Go team.

"Jeff? I have a plan."

CHAPTER 36

PUT THE SONG ON REPEAT, plugged the iPod into the speakers, turned the volume up to my iPod's version of eleven, and hit play.

As "Cold" from Tears for Fears hit the airwaves, I contemplated how we'd keep the wagons in place, then counted and realized that a few of them weren't here.

"Jeff, we need the rest of the wagons."

"Of course we do. I'd complain about the music, but I have a memory. Just hope it works on these things like it did on the Serpent."

"Memories light the corners of my mind. Wagons, we need them, pronto. Unless you're too tired." I'd learned that the fastest way to get any of my men to do something was to ask if they were too weak, sick, or tired to manage it. This had a one hundred percent success rate so far, sometimes even when I actually didn't want them to do whatever thing I felt they were too weak, sick, or tired to do.

"Ha ha ha, aren't you funny?" He zipped off and was back quickly, pushing a wagon in front of him, ensuring my Manipulation Success Rate remained perfect.

We used the remaining wagons to brace the wall while the sounds of snakipede heads slamming against the wagon wall slowed.

Realized I could see well in here, and it wasn't because I was using my enhanced A-C ability to see well in low light. It was because the cavern was lit from the inside somehow. Figured I'd find out how later, if we continued to have a later.

I had the iPod and speakers kind of jammed up against the biggest opening I could easily reach. The cavern created a natural amplifier—if it wasn't in the middle of nowhere, for this world, at least, and if there was any point to it, it would make a great amphitheater. This was wonderful for us—even if we didn't have Aerosmith or Elton John around to play stadium shows on Beta Eight to sold out crowds—because it was helping send my sonic weapon at the snakipedes with a lot more force than my new awesome speakers could alone. There were enough gaps between the wagons that the sound was able to get out, versus bouncing back and deafening those of us in the cavern.

Wanted to ask Algar if I could keep the speakers when we got back home, but decided that would indicate a lack of focus on the matters at hand, and cool prezzies had a habit of disappearing if a person didn't use them wisely.

As we got the last of the wagons stacked and shoved up against the others, the banging was almost down to nothing. Risked another look through a gap and saw that my musical gambit had worked again—the snakipedes piled on top of each other, deaders on the bottom. If I hadn't been terrified of snakes and known how deadly these particular ones were, it would have been almost cute. Almost. In a horrifying way.

The last snakipede landed on it pals and closed its evil eyes as we lost the last bit of natural light outside. Perhaps the snakipedes would freeze to death at night if they weren't flying or eating. A girl could hope, right?

Motioned that the Big Birds could relax, which they did, into a big Big Bird heap. I stayed on guard while Jeff picked up the Big Birds one at a time and trotted them back to the others. Presumed they'd ride on a bosthoon each, at least for a while.

It was a shame that we were going to have to leave the wagons, but we were likely to move faster on foot than we had with the caravan. Even though we had a lot of Lecanora and their animals to get to wherever the tunnel led to. Prayed it led somewhere and somewhere good, versus underwater or right into the lair of evil beings bent on killing us all.

On the plus side, we had five more of our team with us, along with the strautruch, and that was worth a lot. Wondered if I was going to need to give the Big Birds any adrenaline. Then again, had no idea what it would do to them, so probably best not to experiment.

Jeff returned after he'd taken the last Big Bird back. "Everyone's in the tunnel now. Christopher's leading, and if the messages passed back are correct, he hasn't found the end yet. What if the tunnel is a dead end?"

"It won't be," I said with far more conviction than I felt. "Are the strautruch okay?"

"Yeah, I have them on a couple bosthoon. Frankly, we're all in a lot better shape than we probably have any right to be." He hugged me. "You did great, baby. As always."

Hugged him back and leaned my head against his chest. "You did, too, and so did everyone else. Do you need adrenaline?"

"No, not yet. I feel fine, honestly. I kind of expected to feel burned out, but I don't."

Did a health check. "Huh. I feel good, too. Maybe it's surviving death."

He laughed softly. "Maybe. So, what now? Do we have to leave your iPod?"

"No." Wanted to say over my dead body, but felt that would be giving the cosmos too easy an opening. Unclenched from Jeff and walked quietly to my musical weapons. Removed them from where I had them jammed and backed up slowly.

The amphitheater setup assisted, of course. It didn't matter how far back I went, the acoustics ensured that the sound was still flowing out toward the cavern's mouth. Once we were at the back of this part of the cavern, where the underground stuff really started, I turned the volume down, again slowly, so that the sound tapered off gradually.

Figured out how, despite our being underground without flashlights or torches, it was light in here—there was lichen or mold or something that grew on the sides and tops of the rocks, and on the ceilings, too. The cavern's roof was covered with the stuff. Hoped it repelled snakipedes as well as providing light, but didn't bet on it.

Finally I turned the volume all the way down, turned my iPod off, and dropped it and the speakers back into my Purse O' Wonder. Jeff took my hand in his and led me to the tunnel.

It was quite a ways from the cavern's entrance, and there were a variety of natural rooms and what looked like other tunnels that branched off from the main path, so I had hope that if the snakipedes woke up and broke down the barrier, they'd still have to spend a lot of time searching for us. The stuff that grew on the sides and top of the rocks was here in abundance, which was nice, because it meant everyone would be able to see.

Happily, it wasn't freezing cold in here, either. Considering how cold it had been in the Purple Land the night before, I'd have expected the underground cavern and tunnels to be icy, but they weren't. Decided the win column was mighty empty, so placed this happy situation firmly there.

"Wish we could take the time and fit in a quickie."

Jeff started that quiet laughing where the person is likely to snort or bust out a guffaw as much as hold it in. He managed to get control of himself. "It sucks to be me."

He stopped walking, pulled me to him, and kissed me. Long and hard. In no time flat I was up in his arms, my legs wrapped around his waist, and he had one hand on my butt and one at the back of my head, keeping me close and unable to back away. As if I'd want to.

Jeff was pretty much the God of Kissing, and, as always, his lips and tongue owned mine. And, as always, I loved it. His kiss was deep and demanding and I was grinding against him, my hands running through his hair and clutching at his back.

We were both definitely ready and ready to go for it, in the middle of a tunnel that undoubtedly echoed or not, but we also were both aware that we had horrific death on one end and people we had to protect on the other.

Jeff ended our kiss slowly. He had the best expression on his face—where his eyelids were half closed and he just looked like a jungle cat ready to eat me. I loved that look. It was possibly my favorite look of all his looks, and that was saying a lot. It was the look that made me want to rip our clothes off as fast as possible and just go to Sexy Times Town.

He nuzzled my forehead. "Duty calls, baby. So, hold all those thoughts and plans for later."

Heaved a sigh. "I know you're right. I just . . . whenever last night actually was, it wasn't long enough."

Jeff kissed my forehead. "I know. I feel the same. But we have to get back to what we both know we need to be doing instead of enjoying ourselves."

"Being mature adults really sucks sometimes."

Jeff chuckled as he let me slide down his body until my feet were on the ground. This was never a move that took me out of the mood. Wondered if he was being extra sexy right now as my punishment for taking risks to save the bosthoon and Patrina and Pretty Girl.

"Yes," he said with a grin.

"You're able to read my mind again now?"

"Yeah, I am." He jerked. "I am, actually. And it's really the first time since we found each other here."

"I'm going to suggest my hypothesis, which is that we're not under or on the Bronze Land portion of the world anymore. I'm betting we're under the Purple Lands."

"Maybe. I don't have a clear idea where the cavern goes to or which direction the tunnel is heading."

"The lands are set up in a lollipop spiral structure. I think that will mean that the closer we get to the All Seeing Mountain, the easier it will be to cross into other territories."

"I suppose." Jeff took my hand again and we started off. "But that's just the weirdest thing, isn't it? I've never heard of a planet that has regions divided in such an odd way."

"Yeah, there's a lot that's weird about this place."

We walked into the tunnel and stayed at a walk. Neither one of us was tired, but there was no reason to use hyperspeed when we didn't have to. Better to conserve energy now, because it was a sure bet we were going to need that energy later, and perhaps not all that long of a later, either. Besides, we'd catch up to the others soon enough.

Only, we didn't.

After about five minutes of walking, when I'd guessed we'd at least hear everyone else, if not be at the end of the line, there was nothing and no one. Well, not totally nothing. It was clear they'd been here, if only because there was a lot of bosthoon poop to avoid. On the plus side, it was large and easy to spot, because, thankfully, there was plenty of the moss or lichen or whatever that was lighting the way. But other than stepping around the evidence that others had gone this way before, there was no other proof that we weren't the only living things in this tunnel.

"Do you think the moss or whatever that stuff is ate everyone?" I asked Jeff quietly.

"No. Chuck checked it out earlier. He said it's just a natural growth, and the katyhoppers confirmed it."

"Well, that's good. So where is everyone?"

"Maybe they're out already?" Jeff didn't sound like he believed this.

"Christopher ran through this at hyperspeed. His hyperspeed. And he said he went far looking for Patrina, and he found no end. There's no way we've walked as far as Christopher ran, so there's no way they're all out already. We weren't dealing with the snakipedes long enough for all those people and animals to be out of the tunnel by this time."

"I have no idea, baby, but they were here when I brought the strautruch to the rest. I put them onto the backs of bosthoon myself. And it was wall-to-wall people and animals as far as I could see."

"Well it's wall-to-wall you and me only right now. Which is creepy. I know that's obvious, but it needed to be said."

Jeff squeezed my hand as we walked on, just a little faster. "We're together. We'll find them. It'll all be okay."

Which would have been a lot more comforting if, fifteen minutes later, we had found anything other than more bosthoon poop. The bosthoon ate well, I could verify that. What I couldn't verify was the presence of the poop creators.

"Should we speed up?" I asked.

"Maybe. If something's happened, I'm not sure that we want to hit it at hyperspeed."

"Then use the slow hyperspeed." Sounded like an oxymoron, but it wasn't. There was a level of hyperspeed where the human eye couldn't see it, but it was slow compared to the fifty miles in far less than a minute an A-C really running fast could do. "Because this is freaking me out a lot more than the herd of snakipedes did and, trust me, that's saying a lot."

We sped up and ran on for another fifteen minutes. "We should have found someone by now," Jeff said, sounding as worried as I felt. "I think we're beyond the point Christopher went to when he was looking for the lost little girl."

Looked around. "Still nothing but the glow-in-the-dark moss, a ton of bosthoon poop, and us." Looked harder at the tunnel. "But you know, doesn't this tunnel seem really, I don't know, regular to you?"

"I don't spend a lot of time in tunnels, baby. I wouldn't know what a regular tunnel is."

"No, I don't mean ordinary regular. I mean the kind of even regular you get from something that's manmade."

"Maybe." Jeff didn't sound convinced. "But what man would have made this? And why?"

"No guess. I'm still waiting to find something beyond poop. Like the slow-moving things that made the poop."

"Me too."

We trotted on, but other than moss and poop, there was nothing. Until five minutes later.

If you could call a dead end something.

CHAPTER 37

"WHAT THE HELL?" Jeff spoke for both of us.

"I just want to say, to whomever out there in the Greater Cosmos happens to be listening and enjoying the Jeff and Kitty Show, that just about the last thing we needed right now was a locked room mystery, especially on top of everything else."

"A what?"

"A situation where there's no way in or out but someone's either murdered or disappeared. Like, you know, right now."

"Ah, yeah, I'm with you, baby. This is not what we needed."

We confirmed that neither one of us had seen a side tunnel. And the bosthoon poop was confirmation that the people we were with had come this way.

Took another look at the poop. "You know . . ."

"What? I know that look. What's weird with the poop? I can tell that's what you think is odd, so there's that."

"Yeah, glad your skills are back to normal. There's a problem with the poop."

"Aside from how much of it there is?"

"Yeah. We've been able to avoid all the bosthoon patties because they were sitting there, all perfectly formed and undisturbed."

"If that's what you want to call perfectly formed, baby, sure."

"For cow poop, yes, it's right on the money. But there are seventy-five head of bosthoon that were in this tunnel, and easily as many Lecanora. A huge pack of chochos and just as big a pride of ocellars. Seven Earthlings, six of whom were not in the lead and also were not A-Cs able to use hyperspeed. All of whom had to *walk* through this tunnel. And yet, there hasn't been one place where you and I couldn't simply step around the bosthoon patties to avoid getting our shoes mucked up."

"So," Jeff said slowly, "what you're saying is . . . what? That Christopher got everyone in here and they all just . . . stood still?"

Considered this. "Yeah. If I try to align the number of bosthoon with how far we've come I think we'd be at the front of the line, or where Christopher would have been, about here. And maybe the bosthoon didn't poop until they were standing around, waiting. You know, because Christopher had hit a dead end and didn't know what to do next."

"Okay. Let's say you're right. Where the hell did they all go?"

"No idea. But I'm sure that Christopher did or triggered something, which is why they're gone."

"Why would you say that?"

"Because he was the leader and they're all gone. I'm not saying he's evil or a loser or anything like that. But whatever happened, we need to figure that he caused or created it."

"Okay." Jeff didn't sound like he really thought it was okay. "So, where does that leave us? Besides nowhere?"

"Think like Christopher. You know him better than anyone else does. He's here, leading all these people down a tunnel he's found and felt led somewhere. You and I aren't around—we're trying to hold off murderous creatures, call them superbeings if it helps you get into his mindset."

"It does. Go on."

"So, he's here. He's here long enough for an entire herd of Planet Colorful Cows to each take a dump. Meaning what?"

"Meaning he was trying to figure out how to turn everyone around."

"Probably, at first, anyway. But that's out, remember, because we have no exit due to there being superbeings at the only exit we know about. Plus, he's been down this tunnel and he felt it went farther than he'd gone, and I was sure it went somewhere other than nowhere and he didn't argue. So, what's his next move?"

"You mean besides cursing? Ah, he'd call someone using a cell phone that doesn't work here."

"Actually, we haven't tried our phones. Oh, sure, it's probably not the greatest coverage out here, but I'd be willing to check to see if someone could hear me now."

"Hilarious. I guarantee Christopher didn't try that. Chuck wasn't near him, and neither were the flyboys. We had them spread out, with Chuck near the rear, so we had people we could count on keeping the rest calm."

"Where were the katyhoppers?"

"Flying overhead. They fly all the time, and shared with Chuck that they weren't all that tired, even though they'd done a lot. Apparently they rejuvenate that fluid through flight, too, don't ask me how, so they wanted to fly for that reason, as well."

"So whatever happened, it got the katyhoppers, too, meaning it's not something triggered by the floor, and it also means the floor didn't fall out from under them. Though the presence of the poop confirmed that already."

Think, we had to think. Christopher had done something, I knew it, and that something had disappeared everyone in the tunnel. Really prayed that, whatever had happened, it was very good, or at least neutral, versus very bad.

Jeff shook himself. "Okay, I'm Christopher. I'm stuck here, and I have to handle it. I don't want to admit that I just led everyone to a dead end, partly because it'll cause panic, and partly because I'll sound like a moron, and I hate that."

"Sounds like Christopher to me. So, then what?"

"He's the former Head of Imageering, he's been in worse situations than this. There's nothing trying to kill anyone in this tunnel. He considers options. We don't have many." Jeff looked uncomfortable.

"He gets pissed, doesn't he? That's why you look like you don't want to share your next thought. You bellow and let it out, but he doesn't. So he's angry—at the situation, with himself, with me for saving some cows and so letting the snakipedes know where we were, and with me for telling him the tunnel led somewhere when it appears that it does not. What does he do when he's angry, especially when he has no one nearby who he can shout at, snarl at, or snark at?" I was certain he'd been running through all his Patented Glares, though, and possibly created a new one due to this situation.

"You know . . ." Jeff cocked his head and held my hand tightly in his. "There are times when you get so angry you just want to hit something." He stepped us closer to the dead end. "Like the thing that's blocking you."

With that, he pulled his fist back, then slammed it into the wall in front of us.

Results were immediate. And, as with so many things that had happened so far on this planet, it wasn't something I'd have expected in, if not a million years, certainly a good thousand.

CHAPTER 38

THE STONE IN FRONT of us was a circle, and that circle activated. It glowed a bright blue-white and made a humming sound, just like a machine will when it's said to be purring.

The circle didn't touch the sides of the tunnel, but it was close. I didn't have a lot of time to look, however, because blue-white light zoomed out from the rock and went past and through us, just as if the flat circle of light was actually the end of a tube being pushed down the tunnel.

The light enveloped us. There was a distinct feeling of movement, similar to the feeling I got when I walked through a gate only, happily, without the nausea. And then it stopped. And we weren't in the tunnel anymore.

Nor were we alone.

We were in another cavern, but not the one we'd just left. Looked behind me. Yep, there was the tunnel we'd used. Only it looked different. Just a little, but still, different. This cavern was shaped differently than the one we'd been in before, and in fact the tunnel entrance was far closer to this particular amphitheater and therefore the cavern's mouth. All I could see outside was white. The whitest white I'd ever seen. Got the impression I was seeing this world's version of snow, though I didn't feel any colder here than I had before.

Happily, we'd found everyone else, and it was clear that they were waiting for us, based on the expectant looks on everyone's faces, human as well as Lecanora. It was hard to tell with the katyhoppers and Big Birds, expression-wise, but the ocellars and chochos also looked relieved we'd arrived, and I could tell by the way the katyhoppers were waving their antennae and the Big Bird were ruffling their feathers that they'd been worried, too. The bosthoon didn't seem to have an opinion about us one way or the other. Chose not to be bitter.

Bruno flew into my arms and we had a cuddle. He was followed by Ginger and Wilbur, who both demanded their own pets and cuddles. Heard Jeff muttering about how we didn't need to add in more alien animals into our menagerie. Ignored him.

"Really glad you figured out how the warp tunnel worked," Chuckie said. "Almost as glad as I was when Christopher triggered it."

"Warp tunnel?" I managed to ask.

"Where are we?" was Jeff's question.

"That's a great question," Chuckie said. "We have no idea. However, I have a good guess, based on a variety of factors I haven't had time to discuss with you yet."

"The white part of this world," Jerry said. "Based on, you know, looking outside."

"No argument, makes sense. You know what doesn't make sense? How did a warp tunnel get into a world that doesn't have microwave ovens, let alone spaceflight?"

"My guess is outside influence," Chuckie replied. "There's a lot that's unusual with this world."

"We're traveling with beings that can read minds or move things using telekinesis. Let's talk unusual."

"You're married to someone who can run at hyperspeed and knows what everyone around him is feeling, and you talk to animals. I'm talking about unusual for a planet. And I want to discuss this now, right now, because the warp tunnel confirms outside influence, but there are other indicators."

"Chuck thinks this planet is really small," Christopher said. "We had this discussion earlier today, when he and I were going all over. He measured shadows for some reason."

Managed not to say that he was lucky Lorraine, Claudia, and Serene weren't here, because they'd tell him he was an idiot.

"You never paid attention to things that mattered in school," Lorraine said.

Jeff and I both jumped and looked around. Sure enough, there she was, arm around Joe's waist.

Claudia and Randy wandered out from behind the bosthoon they must have been using as a make-out shield. "Eratosthenes used the method effectively over two thousand years ago on Earth," she said. "Chuck just applied it again here."

"It's great to see you guys. Um, anyone else with you?"

"I'm here, Kitty," Serene said, as she came around from behind another bosthoon. "But I don't know where Brian is." I was relieved to see the girls, but she looked ready to cry. I could understand that—her husband was a human with no enhancements. We had several missing humans, and I was worried about all of them.

"We'll find him," I said quickly. "And everyone else. But why were you guys hiding?"

"We weren't," Serene said. "There's something here we were studying while we waited for you two to figure out how to trigger the warp tunnel." She turned and went back to whatever she'd been looking at. The other girls and their husbands did the same.

"How did you all find the girls?" Jeff asked.

"They were investigating this cavern and tunnel when we came through," Jerry said. "They landed in this part of the world. It looks like snow out there because it is. They were cold, they looked for shelter, they found it here."

"We've had time to get the story," Hughes said. "You two took forever."

"Yeah," Walker added. "We were wondering if we were going to have to use the tunnel to get back to show you how it worked."

"Were you having sex?" Jerry asked.

"My money's on yes," Hughes said.

"Nah, we're in the middle of danger, they waited," Walker countered. Accurately. "But I'll bet they made out." Very accurately.

"Hilarious," Jeff said. "Kitty and I are laughing. We're just keeping it all inside."

"Look, you need to hear this. This world is small," Chuckie said, as he indicated we should follow the others. "Far smaller than Earth, about the size of the moon."

Looked toward this cavern's mouth. "It's still light here.

I mean, not like it's high noon, but still, light. I have no idea if that means this world goes clockwise or counterclockwise when it spins, or if it even spins, but night had fallen back in the Bronze Lands, just before we went to the tunnels."

"The moon is still large for us, Kitty," Chuckie said patiently. "But even on a planet this small, yes, you'll have sections that go dark, or light, before others, as the planet turns."

"Okay, if you say so. So it was easy to go all over?"

"No," Christopher said, as we wended our way through animals of various shapes and sizes. "That map is accurate—the continent is pretty much a circle. What the map doesn't show you is that the blue section is all water, and it extends to go around the continent."

"Think of us as being on a round Australia, but an Australia on the moon," Chuckie said. "The issue isn't that. The issue is gravity."

"Having fallen from a great height on this planet, I can promise you that gravity's still working here."

"Yes, it is," Chuckie said patiently. "But not as it should. For the size of this planet—moon-sized, remember—we should be able to jump just like the astronauts did and do when they're there."

"You mean leap tall buildings with a single bound?"

"Yes. And we can't. I feel the same as when we're on Earth, and so does everyone else, I've checked."

"Yeah, I can't run faster or lift more than I can at home," Jeff said. "Though I'm not tiring out as quickly."

"None of us from Earth are," Lorraine said as we reached what she and the other girls were so interested in. It was an orb, about the size of a soccer ball, and it glowed blue-white. It was also floating between two cones, not in contact with the cones' tips. The cones were set in the ground and the roof of the cavern, like a space-aged stalagmite and stalactite set. "I think the air here is oxygen rich."

"That looks just like it's from a movie, where if we touch that orb, we're going to get sucked into another world or universe or something. Or else it'll bounce all over the place causing mass destruction."

"Yes, and we're not sure what it's going to do if we touch it," Claudia said. "So we haven't."

"Yet," Serene added, for honesty's sake, presumably.

"So, while we stare at this thing that is clearly manmade but not by any man on this planet, Chuckie's making some point about gravity and Australia."

"The planet's too small to have the gravitational pull it does. Meaning it's either a manmade planet, which seems unlikely based on our knowledge of this solar system, or else its core is made of heavy metals."

"Like what?" Christopher asked.

"Like plutonium or uranium," Chuckie replied. "You know, what we use to make nuclear weapons."

CHAPTER 39

"EXCUSE ME?" Jeff asked.

"How would you know that?" Christopher asked.

"Plutonium and uranium are heavy metals, the ones at the bottom of the periodic table," Chuckie explained patiently. "In order to have a planet this size duplicate the gravity of a planet six times larger, said planet has to have extremely heavy elements making up its core." Of course, Chuckie was as smart as the Dazzlers. Smarter, really. So this was him being really nice to those slower minds he had to work with.

Chuckie was right as always, of course. We'd needed to know this, me in particular, because this information now gave me a good idea of what was going on. But I needed to ask a couple questions first. "Chuckie and girls, is it possible that a world would naturally form land sections in the spirals that the map the Lecanora have insinuates is the case here?"

"Possible," Claudia said. "There are some planets in other solar systems that have this kind of spiral formation on their crusts. It's rare, but there are some out there."

"Most like that are closer to the galactic core," Lorraine said.

"How do you know that? I mean that seriously. You guys were born and raised on Earth."

The girls shrugged. "We learned about the galaxy in school," Serene said.

"You know, where the guys spent their time focused on honing their talents and running really far, but never studying the things that really matter." Lorraine wasn't trying to hide her disdain for talents and track. Refrained from comment, because this wasn't a new mindset for her or any other Dazzler—it was why most of our younger A-C women wanted to marry humans.

"Besides, the galaxy is one of our hobbies," Claudia added.

Jeff, Christopher, and I all exchanged a look, but we didn't say anything. Only for Dazzlers would math, science, medicine, and engineering be their totally fun jobs and bomb building and the study of the entire galaxy be considered a hobby. Chuckie was only single right now, as far as I could tell, because he was still mourning Naomi's loss. The Dazzler weakness was brains and brain potential. Had to figure there was a line forming in the ranks and that he'd be spoilt for choice the moment one of the Dazzlers with empathic ability could give the "he's ready to date again!" signal.

"Okey dokey. So, back to this planet. Uranium and plutonium are really valuable, right?"

"Very," Chuckie said. "And not in the hugest supply."

"There's no guarantee that Chuck's guess is right," Christopher said.

The three girls and I all looked at him, snorted in unison, then the Dazzlers went back to their study and I went on as if Christopher hadn't spoken. "So, a planet whose core is made of uranium or plutonium, or one of the other desirable 'iums,' would be worth fighting over, wouldn't it?"

Chuckie nodded. "Yes, it would." He cocked his head at me. "You think that's what's going on?"

"Yes, potentially. We still don't have enough information yet. But I'd like to know what powers all the Faster Than Light ships this solar system uses."

"All those 'iums,'" Claudia said. "And I can guarantee that no one here would think that they had enough of them."

"I think someone would have tried to take over Earth for its resources," Serene added, "if not for the fact that they're afraid of you and Jeff, Kitty."

"Always nice to be appreciated or feared. Okay, all that makes sense and so figures. I also think that this planet's been tampered with. We have likely suspects in both the Ancients and the Z'porrah, by the way, though there are other options."

One, in particular. He was helping me just a little too much, more than he ever had before. Meaning that Algar had some sort of vested, emotional interest in what was going on, and my gut said that his interest was in more than the crew who'd been dragged out here from Earth.

"Tampered how?" Christopher asked, sharing Patented Glare #5 with us, in case we might have thought he'd missed the group diss.

"Races uplifted, seeds planted that create special sections that provide special powers to those who reside there, weirdness all the way around. Things like that."

"There's certainly precedent in both of our solar systems," Jeff said. "But what does that mean for us and, more importantly, for all the people we're here to help, the Lecanora in particular?"

"Don't know yet, but we need to get to the All Seeing Mountain as soon as we can. Think the warp tunnel can do that?"

Chuckie shook his head. "It's only made to go from here to there as near as we can tell. We haven't had the time to do a full test, of course, but since there's no way to program a destination—like we can with the gates—it's unlikely that there are other destination options. However, Christopher and I spotted a couple other caverns like the one we sheltered in and this one when we were going all over the planet."

"Did you happen to find any of our other people?" Jeff asked, in a tone of voice that clearly indicated caverns were not on his Top Ten List of priorities.

"No," Christopher said. "We did a search of all the planet and Chuck did his measurements. But we stand out, and we both thought it might not be a good idea for Alcalla and Binalla to appear and then disappear."

"Especially if we weren't actually considered Gods or good guys," Chuckie added.

"Makes sense," I said to Jeff, who grunted.

"However," Chuckie went on, "there were excited activities happening in the Green Land—and trust me, it was like being in the Emerald City over there—and in the Blue Land. That's set up a lot like Venice, by the way, with most of the buildings tied together and floating on the water. And, of course, lots of blue and not just the water. So I think there's a good chance some of our missing team are in those lands."

"I'm sure they are." I was. If there were sentient beings, our people were going to land near them, guaranteed.

"We did sneak around the Blue Land a bit and were able to listen. Caught an old Lecanora telling stories to some little ones, and he was saying that the water went on forever."

"Meaning, as near as we can tell, that everyone on this continent thinks it's the only continent on the world," Christopher said. "We couldn't figure out how to prove it, and while I know I'm fast enough to run on the water, it didn't seem like a smart option at the time."

"That *was* smart. For all we know, they have giant leviathans in their water that can catch someone using hyperspeed. Anything's possible, just as this world having one continent and being otherwise all water is possible. In an infinite multiverse, you'd have the probability of having anything and everything."

Chuckie grinned at me. "Just when I think you never paid attention."

"Always, to everything you ever said. But I have a more pertinent question. If it's hella cold outside the cavern, why isn't it cold inside the cavern? I'd expect it to feel like an icehouse or deep freeze in here, not comfy."

"Oh!" Serene sounded like the light bulb had just gone off. "Of course."

We all stared at her. She was still happily staring at the glowing orb. "Um, Serene? We're all agog to know what you think is an 'of course' sort of thing."

"Oh, I'm sorry, Kitty. What you said about the temperature just made sense."

We waited. That was it.

"Serene? We're not on your wavelength and time is, as it so often is, of the extreme essence. Full sentences, with all the information that no one else has guessed." Not even Claudia and Lorraine, based on their expressions.

"Oh. This isn't dangerous." She pointed to the orb. "Well,

I think it could be, of course, and we shouldn't touch it, but it's not here to do bad things. It's the power source."

"For what?" Christopher asked, taking one for most of the team.

"I think for the entire planet."

CHAPTER 40

"I CALL SHENANIGANS. The power source to keep this cavern warm? Fine. The power source to keep the cavern warm and work the warp tunnel? Okay. The power source for the entire planet? Not buying it."

"I can," Lorraine said slowly. "Especially if Chuck's right—and we know he is—and the core of the planet is loaded with plutonium or uranium or both. I think this is a nuclear generator of some kind."

Every human, Chuckie included, took a giant step back, and dragged whichever A-C they were closest to back with them.

"Let's move away from the source that turns people sterile and gives them horrible cancers, shall we?" It was clear I was speaking for everyone other than the girls, Chuckie included.

Claudia pulled out of Randy's hold. "Don't be ridiculous. It's shielded. But I think Serene's right. Good job on pointing out the warmth, Kitty."

"Wow, always willing to take credit for just saying something randomly that turns out to be right and all that, but radiation isn't a fun thing, girls."

"It's shielded," Lorraine repeated, patience clearly forced. "Trust us. That's why we knew not to touch it."

"Is it a shield you can see?" I really wanted proof. Hey, Chuckie and the flyboys had no regeneration and I knew they all wanted to have kids or more kids, depending, and live long, healthy lives. The rest of us did, too.

"That it's shielded is something we can derive from a

variety of factors," Serene said. "Chuck, you know it's shielded, you can do the math, too."

"I'll take your word on it," Chuckie said. "Though the presence of a power source isn't surprising."

"Why here?" Jeff asked. "Why this cavern in this area?"

"It's really cold and deserted in this part of the world," Claudia said.

"Which would make this cavern more appealing to the life that's out there," I pointed out, "not less. Besides, how is it getting power anywhere? Though the stalagmite and stalactite?"

"Yes." Lorraine sounded extremely pleased with me. "Exactly, Kitty."

Chose to not share that, once again, I was tossing something out that just happened to be right. I knew when to go on sounding brilliant. "I'm with Jeff, then. Why would someone put the power orb here? Or, rather, why only the one?"

"Well, there could be others," Serene admitted. "But I think this one is strong enough to cover the entire world, especially if this is truly the only continent."

"I don't buy it. I'm going to put forward a theory that the moment we find another cavern like the two we've been in already they'll be in another part of the world and they'll have both a warp tunnel and a power orb."

"My bet is at least three power orbs," Chuckie said. "Because I'm with Kitty—even if one is good enough, whoever put it in place must have put in a backup generator, if you will."

"And there are seven sections, but the Purple Land is avoided by all for a variety of reasons. Meaning I think the tunnel we just took moved us from Bronze to White Land while avoiding the Purple parts."

"Yellow is between White and Purple," Christopher said. "And can we call it something other than the White Land? I feel like you're telling me I conquered the place or something."

"Sure. We already have Greenland here, let's call this place Iceland."

Chuckie laughed. "The names would be far more accurate here than they are on Earth."

"Yeah, 'cause we're not Vikings trying to fool everyone else and keep the good parts for ourselves without having to fight for them."

Chuckie sighed. "You know that theory has been debunked."

"Blah, blah, blah."

"It's possible that if we can find other caverns and tunnels that those tunnels will go to the Yellow or Purple Lands," Serene said quickly, probably to forestall a conspiracies theory discussion. "We just have to find them and test."

"We have hundreds of beings who are now homeless because we had to use their homes to save them and ourselves," Jeff said sternly. "All the rest of this can wait. We need to determine what we do with and for the Lecanora and their animals before we do anything else."

A throat cleared behind us and we turned to see King Benny standing there. "The Gods are coming together. There is not one of my people who would wish to be anywhere other than where you are, Leoalla."

"King Benny, who are these women?" I pointed to the girls.

King Benny smiled at me, teeth showing. Decided it was just how otters smiled. "And still Shealla tests me. They are the Muses of Knowledge, Shealla. They give inspiration for creativity and science, and therefore assist the Gods with creation."

"Right you are again," I said cheerfully. "I told the other Gods that King Benny was always right about his God-knowledge."

He beamed at us while the others all nodded quickly. That was one of the nice things about working with smart people—they tended to catch on quickly.

"What do *you* call the different lands?" Claudia asked King Benny. Which made me feel bad—because none of us so far had thought to ask.

"They were originally named for the Gods," he replied.

"Originally?" Chuckie asked.

King Benny nodded. "Our king has demanded the names be changed. But, Shealla, the Giver of Names, is here with us, and whatever Shealla says we should call these lands we will call them. Therefore, we are now in Iceland." Clearly King Benny had been listening to us for far longer than we'd realized.

"We can discuss these things later," Jeff said with finality.

"Right, because the issue is how we move everyone," Jerry said. "Since we had to sacrifice your wagons."

King Benny shrugged. "They are things. You saved what mattered—the lives. All the lives." King Benny bowed to us. "That the Gods would risk all to save the least of their creatures proves that the Gods are good and right and their laws are just."

"Ah, just checking, but you don't think we created the snakipedes, ah, I mean the Horrors?"

"Oh, no, Shealla. We know that they were created by Zenoca."

This was a new one. "Just checking, but who do you think Zenoca is?"

King Benny shrugged. Somehow he still had his antlers on and the shrug moved them again in a humorous way. And again I contained the Inner Hyena. Go me. "He is the creator of all that is evil in our world and all others."

"What does Zenoca look like?" Chuckie asked. "To you, I mean."

"Zenoca can change his appearance, Alcalla, as I know you well know."

"Then how do you know that one of us isn't Zenoca?" Chuckie seemed intent, and I could see the wheels spinning in his head. I just didn't know why they were so spinning.

"Zenoca always travels with the glittering Jewel of the Gods, which he stole from the First Father of the Gods. The Jewel cannot be hidden from our sight, the First Father of the Gods saw to that."

And all of a sudden, I knew exactly why Chuckie was on this line of questioning. "King Benny, does Zenoca sometimes appear as a woman?"

"Yes, Shealla. Many times. Zenoca has much guile, and in one of his incarnations he used his influence to create a King of the Clans of our people."

"Oh?" Jeff asked. "So your people didn't always have a king?"

"No. We had our own clans and clan leaders, and while we interacted, we didn't encroach on each other's ways. But once we were under the rule of the king, we were forced to alter much of our lives."

"How long ago did this happen?" Christopher asked.

"Two of our years ago."

"Years are arbitrary," Claudia said. "On Alpha Four, we counted a year as a revolution around one of the suns, but not both. King Benny, how do you count years here?"

"A full return, Muse. We must travel around both suns before our year is done, so that we honor all the Gods and shirk none."

Did the math. "So, roughly four years ago for us. And you know who was sneaking around over in this solar system behind our backs at that time?" When I was pregnant with Jamie, and while they were setting up Operation Confusion.

Everyone on my team nodded. "The former Diplomatic Corps," Christopher snarled.

"Assisted by Ronaldo al Dejahl," Chuckie added.

"And LaRue, who I believe I've mentioned is a shape shifter. In other words, Zenoca is probably her real name."

"Ronaldo?" King Benny seemed very intent. "That is our king's name."

"Really? That seems far too coincidental to me. What clan did he come from?"

King Benny shook his head. "He is not Lecanora. He looks more like all of you, like the Gods. Zenoca was in female form and convinced most of the clan leaders that we needed a strong king to protect us."

"Protect you from whom?" Jeff asked.

"Threats." King Benny shook his head. "The biggest threat on our world are the Horrors, and no king can protect us from them, especially one who just sits on his throne and does nothing. Some believe he is a God, but my people, we have seen his true heart, and he is of Zenoca."

"And," I said to the others with false cheerfulness, "lucky us, he's probably also a clone."

CHAPTER 41

"**D**OES IT GET ANY** better than this?" Joe asked.

"Probably," Walker said. "Never sell our enemies short."

"So, we have to take down the king then, right, Kitty?" Hughes asked me.

"That will be easier said than done, guys."

Randy shrugged. "We've done harder things."

Jerry laughed. "True enough. But Jeff's issue is still the key one, isn't it? How do we get everyone out of here safely, let alone quickly? It's great to talk about another warp tunnel. Finding another is the hard part."

"Maybe not," King Benny said. "As you know, my people come from all regions where the Lecanora are allowed to live. Some of them may know of caverns such as the two Alcalla and the Muses have found."

"Love how Chuck gets all the credit," Christopher muttered.

Ignored him, because there was a word that King Benny had said that stuck out. "Allowed? Where aren't you allowed to live, and why?"

"We do not live in the Purple Lands, as you call them, or where they," he indicated the Big Birds, "dwell. And none but my clan live in the lands where Leoalla found us."

"Because they're barren or because they're right next to the Purple Land?"

"Both, Shealla. May I fetch the others?"

"Absolutely." Looked back to the others as King Benny trotted off. "I find it hard to believe that LaRue or anyone else knows about the powers in the sections of the world where the katyhoppers and strautruch live."

"Why not?" Jeff asked. "Other than the fact that those lands aren't already destroyed and overfarmed, I mean."

"No one's reading our minds or moving us around against our will at home. However, I'm willing to bet cash money that the dirt or the elements in the Bronze Land that dampened your skills down to nothing is in all the empathic overlays and enhancers that are tormenting us back on Earth."

"That makes sense," Lorraine said. "I wonder if whatever they did to the imageers originated on this planet, as well."

"Potentially," Chuckie replied. "But, there's another thing to consider, and that's the idea that this Ronaldo might not be a clone at all."

Let that sit on the air for a bit. "They said they weren't going to clone more than just LaRue, Leventhal Reid, and the Mastermind," Claudia said finally.

"That doesn't mean they were telling the truth," Chuckie pointed out. "LaRue and Ronaldo went to the Galactic Core, as least as far as we know. They definitely went to the Z'porrah home world. And who knows if the cloning advancements our enemies have made were created on Earth?"

"Does that mean the LaRue that was killed by Esteban Cantu was a clone, too?"

"Why make a clone of her on Earth if that was the case?" Lorraine asked. "When we found the cloning facility underneath Gaultier, neither she nor the Leventhal Reid clone acted as if there was a master around somewhere to worry about."

"We'll find out, I assume," Jeff said. "But I see King Benny coming back with his advisors. Seriously, do we have even the slightest plan for how to get all of from here to there, to any there other than here, I mean?"

"I might," Serene said slowly. She was still staring at the power orb. "Just deal with the natives and see if they can determine where another cavern might be."

Serene was an explosives expert of the highest order—that was her "fun" hobby. Wanted to ask if she thought she could blow us up to get us wherever we needed to go, but didn't in case her answer was "yes."

King Benny rejoined us with the same group of advisors as before, one of whom was Nanda, the beaver-chick, and the ostensible owner of Pretty Girl. I opened my mouth and she put up her paw. "I have already heard your pronouncement, Shealla. And I agree—the ocellar kit will remain with Patrina, and her family will not need to provide me with payment for her."

"What payment do you need from me?"

She laughed. "The Gods ask if we need payment to follow one of their decrees?" She shook her head. "Rescue our world from the evil of Zenoca. That will be payment for anything and everything." The others nodded.

"No pressure," Christopher said quietly.

"Let's start with getting all of us out of this region," Jeff said. "I don't see any of you whose coloration would indicate that you come from around here."

"Which we're calling Iceland to make Binalla Christopher happy," I added in case King Benny hadn't already shared.

The Lecanora all nodded. "We have Lecanora who reside here," King Benny said. "However, they have not fallen out of favor with the king, and so do not join us."

"Really? None of them have seen what the rest of you did? None of them have questioned the status quo, ah, the way things are?"

"Their clan leader is strong, and their clan prefers to remain apart from the rest of the Lecanora. They may all have seen the ships, and they may all chafe under the king's rule. But they will not let any others know if that is the case."

"Got it!" Serene exclaimed. She spun around. "Chuck, Claudia, Lorraine—I need to run some formulas past you." At which point Serene started spouting higher math and my brain said that it refused to hear her words.

Looked at Christopher. "While they discuss this, are you up to doing a search of this region with me?"

"Chuck and I already did."

"Yes, but you were looking for our team, ah, other Gods. I'm not looking for them now, since the Muses are here already. It looks like we have some light left, and I'd like to take care of this before dark for certain and before tomorrow if we can."

He shrugged. "Sure. I think you're going to be cold, though."

"I'm counting on it." Looked up at Jeff, whose mouth was opening. "You need to handle things here. I'll be with Christopher and we won't be gone long, I promise."

Jeff closed his mouth and heaved a sigh. "I should say no, but it's probably bad for my image to have my wife constantly ignoring my orders."

"Probably," I said cheerfully as I leaned up and kissed him. "Order me around the moment we have some alone-time," I whispered. "I promise I'll be obedient then."

He grinned. "I'll hold you to that, baby."

With that, I took Christopher's hand. "Where to?" he asked.

"The borders first, then inward. I literally want to search this entire region." Christopher shrugged and we took off at not-quite-Flash level. "Why so slow?"

"You want to search for something or someone. I can go faster if you want, but I figured you'd like to see."

"Yeah. I went at supersonic speeds in the other universe. It was hella cool."

He laughed. "I can take you that fast, Kitty, but I don't think it's what you actually need or want."

"No, you're right."

We continued on at the slower Flash speed. Still faster than normal hyperspeed but not as fast as Christopher could go. Despite the fact that it was covered in ice and snow and had the temperatures to match, it was less mountainous than I'd expected, and I said as much to Christopher.

"No, that's what you're not realizing. Hang on." We zipped off and stopped. "Look around," he pointed. "That's the ocean that surrounds the continent."

"Okay, I see it. It seems far away, even though we seem to be at the edge of the land here."

"It is and we are." He turned me around and pointed again. "See that point far, far away? I think that's the All Seeing Mountain. We didn't make it there for a variety of reasons, but mostly because we were saving it for last and spotted the snakipedes before we could go check it out.

Chuck's positive it's the highest point on this continent. But we're standing on the next highest. The land here is literally all mountains, though the topography is more like a lot of really tall mesas."

Considered this as I tried not to shiver. "Is it my vision or is this continent sort of . . . tilted?"

"It's not your vision, and that's one of the reasons we didn't get to the All Seeing Mountain—Chuck wanted to look at everything."

"So, all of the Iceland spiral is this high up?"

"Yes."

"Think this weird topography is visible from space?"

"Probably, with the right telescopes, which I'm sure all the spacefaring planets have. Why?"

"I'm wondering why no one from this solar system that we've met has ever mentioned that Beta Eight is so weird."

"Maybe they don't think it is. Lorraine and Claudia said that there are other planets like this out there."

"Far, far away, but yeah, okay."

"I'm freezing and I can tell you are, too. Do you want to keep on going?"

Looked around. "Are we easily spotted up here, do you think?"

"It's not snowing and there's still light, so yeah, probably. Why?"

"I'd like to wait here for a little while. Just in case."

He cocked his head at me. "Oh. You're hoping the Lecanora in the area will spot us, assume we're Gods, and come over to check us out and possibly help us, right?"

"Got it in one! The waterfruit is awesome, isn't it?"

"Yeah. You know, we haven't given it to any of the others yet, or at least I haven't. But Chuck and I both had more when we were racing all over the planet."

"Yeah, it hadn't occurred to me to give Jeff any until I was out running around after Patrina. But when we got back safely, I didn't think about it, either. And I haven't asked him if he's hungry or anything. But I had one when I was out after Patrina."

We were both quiet for a few moments. "That's not normal for us," Christopher said finally. "Or Chuck, because he hasn't suggested we give some to the others, either. I mean, sure, we've all been busy, but . . ."

"But they're addictive, aren't they? I mean, something this great has to have a downside."

"Either that or they'll turn us into katyhoppers."

"Dude, where did you get that idea from?"

"I guess because the katyhoppers are the top sentient form we've met so far, and yet, we didn't think they would be because of their docility."

"Like we said before, I think they were docile because they were able to tell we weren't there to hurt them and, in fact, were afraid of them but got over it because they were helping us and not attacking. I mean, do you feel like you're turning insectanese?"

"No, but I guess I wouldn't know how that felt. But . . . I do know how addiction feels." He cleared his throat. "It feels like this."

"Are you sure? I mean, what if we don't want to share simply because they're awesome?"

"Since when have you not wanted to share something awesome with Jeff?"

"Good point. Well, crap. Do we throw them all away?"

"And risk dying? See, that's the downside—they haven't hurt us at all. They've helped us. So what's wrong with continuing to eat them?"

"The fact that we can't get them when we go home. Or likely grow them at home. And we wouldn't want to grow them at home, would we?"

"No, I don't think we would."

We were quiet for another few moments. "Poofikins suggested I eat the one I had when I was looking for Patrina."

"Huh. I want to think that if the Poofs offer it, it's not dangerous."

"Maybe it isn't."

"Maybe we're relying too much on an animal's opinion, even if it's a really smart, amazing animal."

Several heads popped up out of the snow. They were silvery-white, with blue eyes and light pink noses, and, as they stood up, I could spot some black fur framing their ears, paws, and tips of their tails. I put them as ferrets. Giant ones, to be sure, but still, ferrets.

One of them approached us cautiously, sniffing like mad. "Strangers, you smell like our cousins," she said. It was definitely a she. And I took the leap and assumed she didn't mean actual cousins, but rather the other clans.

"We're traveling with some of them."

Her nose kept on going. "There is only one clan that has all our cousins in it." Yep, I'd called the cousins term right.

"Is that so?"

Her eyes narrowed. "It is. And if you've harmed them, we will be forced to avenge them."

"Forced?" Christopher asked as he took hold of my hand again.

She pulled herself up to her full height, which was about equal to mine. She had beautiful fur, but unlike all the other Lecanora I'd seen so far, she wasn't wearing any clothing or carrying any weapons. "It is our duty."

"Good. I was hoping you'd feel that way. What about if that clan is in need of help? What's your duty then?"

She eyed me. "Who are you?"

"Your cousins call me Shealla." I nodded toward Christopher. "And they call him Binalla."

Interestingly, while all their eyes opened wide, there was no immediate bowing, gasping, or anything else going on. Time to take the plunge.

"And I'm just betting that whatever it is that they call you, what it translates to is 'warrior.'"

CHAPTER 42

THE FERRET NODDED her head formally. "Shealla is said to know her people."

Had to figure this was a test. "Shealla's a lot more interested in finding food and shelter for the people she's protecting. And help protecting them, and the others who are helping them, would also be nice."

"Others?"

"From different regions of your world. The strautruch and the katyhoppers. Well, I call them katyhoppers. They look like giant brightly colored insects. And the strautruch look like giant brightly colored birds. The katyhoppers are from the Purple Land and the strautruch are from the Yellow one."

Finally the ferret seemed impressed. "You travel with those? But they do not speak. We are not certain they think."

"They don't speak your language or in your way, no. But they speak to us. And they definitely think. At your level." Or higher. Kept that one to myself, and Christopher had learned long ago to let me roll and stay quiet.

"You claim you are Shealla, and that he is Binalla. Yet we see no proof."

I shrugged. "I think I'll call you Fancy. And because I'm the Giver of Names, you'll be stuck with Fancy, unless you want to tell me a name you like better. Binalla flies on the wind." I let go of Christopher's hand and he took the hint.

He zipped off. To the Lecanora, of course, it looked like he'd disappeared. This time there were some gasps, but not from Fancy. He was back shortly. "Shealla, night is falling."

"Fancy, we need to leave you and return to those we're protecting."

"Why have you come?" Fancy asked.

"To find warriors." With that, I nodded to her, and started walking. Christopher came with me.

"How did you know they'd be here?" he asked me quietly.

"Just sort of knew. Based on what King Benny said about the natives here."

"Really?"

"We can smell our own, Christopher, okay? Tell you more later."

Fancy did a very ferrety thing and ran in front of us on all fours, then stood up on her hind legs. "Why do the Gods need warriors? Can the Gods not fight themselves?"

"Of course. But then the world will be ours, and not yours."

She stared at me. "You mean to go against the king."

"We do, because we fear he is not just. He has cast out many for speaking the truth. If he rules well, we will leave him be. But it does not appear that he rules well."

"We have all seen the ships in the sky, all my people," Fancy said. "But I would not allow any to say so."

"Because you saw what happened to the others who did speak the truth."

She nodded. "Do you truly travel with them?"

I put my hand out. "Come with us and find out."

She stared at my hand. "And if this is a trap?"

"Bring your warriors with you. Link hands and hold mine."

She made a chittering sound, and the others I'd seen already zipped over. None of them were wearing clothing or carrying weapons. Wondered where Rahmi and Rhee were. Hoped they were safe just like I hoped all the others we still hadn't found were safe. Maybe Rahmi and Rhee were with Jamie and Gower. That would be good for all of them.

Shoved the worry back down. Didn't have the luxury to wallow right now. Fancy's Ferrets linked hands, she put her paw into mine, and then Christopher kicked the hyperspeed up to eleven, and they got to go on Ms. Ferret's Wild Ride.

Of course, the ride didn't take long. We did a fast tour of the entire Iceland Spiral and were back with the others in less than a minute. Had to give it to Fancy's Ferrets—they didn't fall to their paws and start retching, though I was pretty sure a couple of them really wanted to.

The people we were rejoining were expecting me and Christopher to come back, of course. But they weren't expecting us to show up with twenty additional Lecanora. So there was a lot of gasping and jumping going on for a minute or so.

Looked at Fancy. "Note where we are. Why aren't your people in here?"

"It's a place of great danger," she said. "None should ever enter these places."

These places. Chuckie was, as always, right. "Why not? Who gave that decree?"

Fancy sniffed at me. "If you were truly Shealla, you would know."

"Alcalla gave that order," Chuckie said, stepping forward. "In other words, I gave that order. Thousands of years ago." Figured I'd ask later if he'd guessed this was the right thing to say or had learned as much from one of the Lecanora while Christopher and I were gone.

Fancy finally looked like she believed. "Are the Gods truly here with us, Musgraff?"

"Yes, Corzine." King Benny stepped forward. "They have saved us from the Horrors. A gigantic herd of them. All of us, from the highest to the lowest," he indicated a somewhat nearby bosthoon.

Fancy eyed me. "What are the other Gods?"

"You know, King Benny here—that's what I call him, instead of Clan Leader Musgraff, by the way—he didn't need to cheat to pass the God Test."

Her lips quirked. "But then you did not have to pass the test yourselves."

The katyhoppers and strautruch joined us. They sized up Fancy's Ferrets. They felt they could take them. I wasn't so sure.

"This is Saffron, Pinky, and Turkey." Each waved their antennae when named. "They're katyhoppers. All given new God Names by me. These others are strautruch." Crap, hadn't actually had time to learn their names. Well, when in doubt and all that. "Their Shealla names are Tyler, Perry, Whitford, Hamilton, and Kramer." The strautruch nodded their heads. The katyhoppers shared that the Big Birds were cool with getting named after my favorite band in the universe.

While Chuckie and the flyboys practically killed themselves controlling their Inner Hyenas, Jeff walked over, carrying a bosthoon in each hand. "Not sure what else you want as proof, but I have to say, yet again, that what I want is for these people to be safely housed, fed, and moved." He put the bosthoon down. "I'm tired of all the standing around discussing things that we'll handle later. Right now, King Benny's situation is the most important thing and I want it handled, or the rest of the Gods are going to have a discussion with me they're not going to enjoy."

Fancy bowed to him. "You are truly Leoalla." She turned to me and Christopher. "Forgive me, Shealla and Binalla, for not believing."

I shrugged. "You questioned. There's never a problem with questioning authority, even the Gods' authority. The problems are blind obedience or stubborn resistance in the face of the obvious."

"Shealla is wise and speaks the truth. We can provide what our cousins will need for the night's survival. And we can offer the same to the Gods, if you so desire."

"We're with all of you, we so desire. Unless providing for us will cause your own people hardship, and then we'll do without."

"Speak for yourself," Randy muttered. "The Winalla are starving."

Fancy heard this and she laughed. "Never would we refuse to feed fellow warriors."

"Oh, yeah, my God Gang, look at Fancy's Ferrets as this planet's Amazon Fighting Force and act accordingly."

"Fancy's Ferrets?" Joe asked.

"It's Shealla Kitty," Chuckie said. "What did you expect?"

"We wear that name with pride," one of the Ferrets said. "Because we do follow Fancy Corzine into battle."

"See? They're one with the Shealla Naming Plan. The rest of you could take a lesson." Saw that Jeff was ready to pop a vessel. "But enough of that. Let's get our refugee clan fed and bedded and then we can discuss strategies."

CHAPTER 43

WE HAD TO FIND a trail that ran close to the cavern and follow it about a mile, per Fancy, to reach the nearest entrance to her people's homes.

We hurried, because the snakipedes apparently had no issues with cold and, sadly, we'd been shown they weren't strictly nocturnal, either—they were 24/7, or whatever this planet's equivalent was, killers. Apparently they were also willing and able to slither as much as fly, meaning they could get into Fancy's Ferrets' homes if they weren't careful. But hurrying and hyperspeed weren't the same thing.

However, everyone moved quickly and with purpose, which was a refreshing change. Had to admit they were probably moving well not because we'd told them to but, on top of fear of this world's most terrifying predator, it was dark by the time we'd left the cavern and extremely cold. Plus it got darker and colder every minute, even for those with heavy fur coats and those who lived in nests high up on top of mountains. Even the bosthoon, once again loaded up with the young and the old and/or infirm, were hurrying. Well, for them.

The snakipedes really reminded me of sharks, and more than that. They sort of screamed "created monster," especially since they seemingly had no issues with temperature or elevation changes. They also seemed to have no issues with day or night and no natural enemies, and yet they hadn't overtaken the planet. Which again, sort of said Made In A Lab.

Had an easy guess for who'd created them, too, since

LaRue had a Z'porrah power cube and apparently those puppies took you anywhere you could visualize. Meaning she could be routinely leaving Earth and going to the far reaches of space, then returning with more things to use to destroy us.

Needed to determine the range on the power cubes the moment I could convince one of the Poofs to snag one back from Algar, or when I had time to badger Algar in person. Presumed neither were going to happen right now.

As it got darker around us, though, something interesting happened—the snow began to glow. A soft glow, similar to glow-in-the-dark toys, only whitish as opposed to greenish and mixed with black light, so that whites glowed whiter and other colors looked more fluorescent. If you looked down, it was easy to see the ground. If you looked up, the glow went about twelve or fifteen feet above the snowline and then tapered off. Planet Colorful was even pretty at night.

The trail we were following sloped upward on a very gradual incline, meaning we were heading away from the All Seeing Mountain and toward the rim of the continent. If I was correctly remembering Christopher's geography lesson from earlier, at any rate.

We Gods went last, with the katyhoppers and strautruch doing Line Monitor duty. You didn't have to tell me twice that there were little kids and young animals along who didn't necessarily understand or follow the rules, and the katyhoppers and Big Birds both felt they could spot and grab any potential deserters quickly.

The chochos and ocellars—who didn't seem overly bothered by the cold, or at least not yet—were also helping with this form of herding, in no small part because I'd asked Ginger and Wilbur to ensure we didn't have another baby of either of their species wander off to cause problems, and they'd made sure the rest of their pack and pride had gotten the message.

Bruno, like the rest of us, was cold, and I put him in my purse with what looked like all the Poofs of our group here already snuggled in there. "Keep Bruno warm, too," I whispered to all of them. Soft mewls indicated that this was an acceptable request.

So, while we walked at the back and I carted all the animals we'd brought with us to this planet, the Earthlings discussed our situation. The three couples cuddled close together for warmth, the others cuddled close to the couples for the same reason. We were a chummy clutch of cold people.

"I think I can make the power orb essentially create a gate between the other power orbs," Serene said. "The issue is determining where they are with enough accuracy for us to do the calculations."

"I have another idea that doesn't involve one or all of us potentially ending up inside a rock or blown up," Christopher said. "Let's leave the Lecanora here with their relatives, link hands, and just act like the A-Cs and humans able to handle hyperspeed that we are and run wherever we need to go next."

"The katyhoppers are tasked with helping us, and they want to do so," I reminded him.

"And they can all handle hyperspeed. I'm all for Saffron, Pinky, and Turkey coming along. Besides, it's just three of them." Christopher shook his head. "We need to move, and move fast, we all know it. But we've slowed to a crawl because we have a large group of refugees we're trying to take with us. For no good reason I can see."

"The strautruch are also supposed to help us," Jerry said. "They fly fast, and I'm sure they can probably handle the hyperspeed."

"They aren't going to turn tail and go home," Randy added. "Like your katyhoppers, they're excited to be a part of all of this."

"We're responsible for these people," Jeff said with more patience than I'd have expected. "We destroyed their homes."

"Protecting them," Joe pointed out.

"Protection they might not have needed if it wasn't for us," Hughes countered.

Chuckie shook his head. "Frankly, I think the snakipede herd or flock or whatever they call them was headed for King Benny's caravan. From what Jeff said, the Lecanora would have been on the far side of the Bronze Land if they hadn't been coming to meet us. Meaning the snakipedes smelled them and went after a large food source."

"Meaning we're responsible," Jeff said. "I realize we

want to find everyone else, my daughter included, in case anyone's forgotten. I realize we want to solve the problems and fix whatever's going on around here. But while I agree that the katyhoppers are probably the top of the sentience pyramid here, the Lecanora are by far the most populous race on this planet and their so-called king is therefore considered to rule this entire continent. Or, as they think of it, world. And if we want to actually effect positive change, then we cannot leave these people, who are already shoved down to the bottom of their society, in worse circumstances than when we found them."

We all stared at him for a few long moments. "Wow," I said finally. "You've spent a lot longer in D.C. than I realized."

Jeff rolled his eyes. "It's not a political speech. It's reality."

"I told you, he's the only politician I trust," Chuckie said with a sigh. "Jeff, believe me, I understand your position. And I agree with it. But we still have ten people to find, including Jamie, as you said. Most of them are humans, meaning they have none of the advantages that the A-Cs and Kitty have. For all we know, they aren't having nearly as good a time on this planet as we are. And I don't mean that facetiously. All four groups here landed either with friendly natives or in a place where they were left alone and able to find shelter. There's no guarantee that's what's happened for the others."

"You know, I want to know how you knew Fancy would find us when you and I went out," Christopher said to me. "I know that's why you wanted to leave the cavern. And it could be relevant to the issue."

"It is but only sort of. We all landed near friendly natives, as Chuckie said. But the girls didn't, at least as far as they knew."

"Correct," Lorraine said. "We didn't find any living soul. We saw the cavern and headed for it."

"So you landed in view of it?" I asked.

Claudia nodded. "It was far away but we could see it, so that's where we went. We figured we'd find people or animals or something. People we'd talk to, animals we'd deal with."

"You said this aloud, right?"

"Yes," Lorraine said. "We were speaking to each other. Oh, and duh."

"Just checking. And you ran to the cavern at hyperspeed, right?"

"Of course," Serene replied. "It was cold, Kitty. We wanted to get inside before we froze. You know, like right now."

"Right. Only, I'd bet you had to land and make sure each other were okay, look for the rest of us, things like that. In addition to making the plan to run for the cavern, right?" All three Dazzler heads nodded. "Right, then. See, it's cold here, as you've all so astutely pointed out, Christopher took me all over this area and I never saw one home or anything that could be construed as a home, and that means that the natives are likely to be burrowers. Meaning that their homes are underground. They have gorgeous fur, and it blends in beautifully with a snowy landscape. I assumed that whoever lived here spent some time watching the girls."

"Why didn't they help them like the katyhoppers helped us?" Christopher asked.

"Because the girls are really efficient and I'd imagine they weren't scared all that much."

"We weren't," Lorraine confirmed. "We were pissed, but not scared. By the way, since I'm sure you're going to care, we're headed roughly toward where we landed." She pointed at some tracks to our right that I could only see because of the pretty glow and the fact that I had enhanced A-C vision now. "Those are ours."

"And we're definitely going in the same direction we came from," Claudia added.

This surprised me not at all. The girls *had* landed near help. They just hadn't needed it.

"But you knew they were all female," Christopher said. "Fancy's Ferrets, I mean." Knew he'd read my mind. Didn't mention it aloud.

"Yeah. Because males tend to come check on females. But female warriors tend to see if the females are other warriors first. The girls showed that they were, and then they entered a place where Fancy's people have been told for generations not to go because it's dangerous. Meaning they were either dead or brave. They didn't die, and they didn't run away. Meaning brave."

"We used snow for water, too," Claudia said. "In case that was impressive or something."

"It would confirm your resourcefulness and intelligence, so yes. Warriors tend to not be impressed by Gods that don't fight. I'm sure Fancy's people assumed you were the Muses, but they'd have been a lot more excited if the Winalla had landed here."

"Maybe excited in the wrong way, if they're like Rahmi and Rhee," Walker said with a laugh. He shook his head and the smile disappeared. "You know who I'm the most worried about? Them. They don't have a lot of experience and their first reactions are to fight, and to fight men. That could go badly here."

In some ways I agreed with Walker. It was curious that the princesses hadn't been placed in this land. They would have had an instant affinity with Fancy's Ferrets. But as I said all the time, I didn't get to make the plans, I just had to foil the bad ones or make sure the good ones worked.

"Yeah, good point," Christopher said.

"Really?" Jeff asked with extreme politeness. "What point is that?"

CHAPTER 44

DIDN'T LOOK AT CHUCKIE, because I knew he'd also
gotten whatever Christopher had from me. Had no idea
why I didn't want to admit what was going on. Unless, you
know, it was because I was becoming a waterfruit addict.

Followed Dad's sage advice and avoided answering the
question by asking another question instead. "You can't
read me here?"

"I wasn't trying to. But since you didn't say something
aloud, it's clear Christopher read you."

Christopher and I looked at each other. "Ah . . . I did.
Sorry." Christopher looked as guilty as I felt.

"Nothing to apologize for, I guess. But Kitty, for the rest
of us who can't read minds, what point did you make that
Christopher agrees with?" Jeff sounded pleasant and not at
all jealous. This was, frankly, not like him.

"I think it's odd, since we were all carefully placed, that
the princesses weren't the ones who were put here."

"By the way," Chuckie said, "it's not mind reading in the
way you do it with Kitty, Jeff. We're just thinking the same
things at the same time, or sort of feeling each other's
strong thoughts."

"That's exactly how I do it with Kitty." Jeff looked at the
three of us, and I got the feeling he was empathically exam-
ining us. Risked a look at Chuckie out of the side of my
eyes—yep, he looked guilty, too, though only a little bit.
Chuckie had a poker face, so him betraying this much was
a rarity. And indicated that the three of us might be in trouble.

But Jeff's probe was interrupted by our arrival at our destination. It turned out that I was right—Fancy and her folks all lived underground. But not like any burrowing animals on Earth lived underground.

First off, we didn't go down into a hole, which, considering the size of the bosthoon, was probably a good thing. We came to what looked like a dead end. Well, our line of refugees came to a halt and, after waiting for a minute or so, Jeff, Chuckie, and I went forward to find out what was going on. So we got to see the rock that looked like it was part of the mountain rise in front of us.

This was actually an entrance, however—an eight-foot-tall door of rock. Not that you could tell, because it was basically seamlessly fitted to the mountain.

The rock was covered with indentations the size of a fingertip. Fancy tapped some of these indentations in what looked like a random manner but was obviously this world's version of a keypad lock, and the doorway lifted just a bit.

The indentations she'd hit were not close together and they were too small for any creature without fingers or beaks to manage. Meaning that while a normal enemy might figure out how to get in, snakipedes would be out of luck. Unless they were being led by a being with fingers or beaks. Filed this thought away to mull over later.

The bottom of the doorway had pieces of metal on the bottom, just like a portcullis. Lifting this door normally took at least ten of Fancy's Ferrets. Jeff took one look at them straining and went and opened the door himself. Not to increase his Leoalla reputation—though of course that's what happened—but because he didn't want them overdoing it when we were right there to help. Didn't argue—he opened the door far faster than they could, and we had a lot of Snakipede Chow to get into safety.

Chuckie ran the head count, and after everyone had tramped on through he was happily able to confirm that we had no runaways, strays, or wanderers.

Everyone finally inside or underground or whatever we were calling it, Jeff and Christopher dragged the entrance door back down into place using the metal bars attached on the inside. Noted that Jeff had needed Christopher's help, meaning the cold was affecting him, and probably the other A-Cs as well. Not that it wasn't affecting everyone—but I'd never seen the A-Cs in a freezing environment for too long. Sure, we had folks all over the world who were in cold regions—Moscow Base, for example. But they were all dressed for the weather there, living in the A-C underground facilities, and out in the elements only on rare occasions, all of them using hyperspeed.

Once the door was down, I could see that it had similar indentations on this side. Fancy hit a different set of indentations and I heard a locking mechanism go into place. On this side, the only way I could tell this was a doorway were the metal bars sitting on the ground.

None of us were dressed for the weather in this spiral of the world. At least I had jeans, Converse, and a hoodie on. The girls were in the usual female version of the Armani Fatigues—white oxford shirts, black Armani slimskirts, and black pumps. Their look didn't say "adapting to the elements." Jeff, Christopher, and Chuckie were all in the male Armani Fatigues, so at least they all had suit jackets on. The flyboys had come to our meeting in their regular Navy uniforms for whatever reason, meaning they had layers on, but short sleeves and no jackets.

Wanted to ask my purse to cough up some parkas, but figured it would raise questions I both couldn't and didn't want to answer. I had enough of that going on with Jeff already—no need to create more reasons for him to be suspicious of my behavior.

Thankfully, it was warm once the stone door was closed and secured and got warmer as we followed the trail into the mountain. The trail here was much more like a dirt road and much wider than the trail had been on the outside.

We walked for a few minutes, still going up on a gradual incline, and it appeared that all we were going to see was a road and the mountain walls on either side of us. Jeff pulled me, Christopher, and Chuckie to the end of the line, while indicating that he wanted the rest of the Earthlings to go on ahead. Tried not to worry. Failed.

"Now that it's just us, let me see one of them." He put his hand out.

"One of what?" I asked, hoping I sounded reasonably innocent.

"The fruit you three don't want to share with anyone else."

Looked at Chuckie. "You, too?"

He rubbed the back of his neck. "Yeah. I have no idea why."

"I think they're addictive," Christopher shared, as I pulled out a waterfruit and handed it to Jeff. "But Poofikins had Kitty eat one, so maybe not."

Jeff examined the fruit, including sniffing it. "Uh huh. Why do you three think it's addictive?"

"Because we don't want to share it with anyone else," Christopher said. "That's not like Kitty, at all."

"It's not like Chuck to take something, think it's addictive, and keep on taking it, either," Jeff said. "Here's a question, though—why do you think this fruit allows you to read minds?"

"Well . . . honestly, we were reading each other the moment we landed in the Purple Land. But as soon as we ate this fruit the ability got stronger and better."

"I'm sure it did. But baby? I have a request. Tell me what I'm thinking."

Looked at Jeff. He had a very placid and pleasant expression on his face. "Um, that you're mad at us?"

"I know I've made my expression pleasant, so why would you think I'm angry?"

"Because it makes sense that you would be," Christopher offered.

"Maybe. However, I'm not angry. And what I'm thinking and feeling isn't something the three of you seem to be picking up on. If you were really able to read minds, you should be able to read mine."

We all concentrated. "Nothing," Chuckie said. "I can feel Kitty's stress and Christopher's guilt, but nothing from you Jeff. Are you blocking us?"

"No. Eat all of this you want. Don't give it to anyone else." He tossed the fruit to Christopher, who caught it. "You three can't actually read minds. Or emotions."

"Care to explain that? I mean, just so we have a freaking clue as to what you're talking about?"

Jeff grinned. "Sure. I think the katyhoppers gave the waterfruit to the three of you because it makes it easier for *them* to read your minds. While you two," he indicated me and Christopher, "went off to survey the territory and find reinforcements, and Chuck was having an in-depth discussion with the girls, I chatted with the flyboys. We all think that the katyhoppers' antennae work like radio towers—they broadcast and receive. In their case, because they *are* mind readers, they're broadcasting and receiving brain-waves."

"Okay," Christopher said slowly. "Then why just the three of us?"

"And why did it start immediately?"

Chuckie jerked. "It didn't. We'd landed and then Christopher found the katyhoppers, or they found him, and *that's* when it started." He looked at Jeff. "Why didn't I think of this before?"

"They probably didn't want you to," Jeff replied. "From what you've said about them, they know aliens exist. Meaning they know this is a crowded solar system, life-wise. So, the katyhoppers have been waiting for visitors from far, far away. You three dropped in, they wanted to read you, and they did. The side benefit was that you three started reading each other. It helped that the three of you didn't freak out about it, so the katyhoppers knew they'd found kindred spirits, in that sense."

We were quiet for a few more steps. "Kitty's really rubbed off on you," Chuckie said finally. "I mean that as a compliment."

Jeff laughed. "And I take it like one, believe me." He put his arm around my shoulders and hugged me. "Stop worrying, baby. You're all fine and I'm not upset with any of you."

"You're awfully calm about all of this. You sure you're okay?"

"Yeah, I'm fine. Well, freezing like the rest of us, but otherwise, fine."

"Why don't you want anyone else to eat the waterfruit, then?"

He shrugged. "Why allow anyone access into more of our minds than they already have? Frankly, with the three of you, they don't need access to the rest of us."

"Mind explaining that?" Christopher asked.

"Sure. Chuck's the smartest guy we have, and by 'we' I mean Earth."

"There are smarter," Chuckie said, sounding a little em-barrassed.

"Fine. One of the smartest guys on Earth," Jeff said with

a grin. "So they have access to everything you know. Or maybe only access to what you're actively thinking. But they don't need access to the girls because they have access to you."

"Okay, why me then?" I asked.

All three men snorted. "That's easy," Chuckie said. "And I see where Jeff's going with this. You're the leader, Kitty. Yes, technically Jeff is, but we all follow your plans. You're the one who usually instigates the action, comes up with the bizarre ideas that are correct, and so on. They don't need access to our other leaders if they have access to you."

"And me?" Christopher asked, sounding more than a little down. "Why do they need me?"

Based on the thinking going on, this one was easy for me to answer. "You're the military mind. You were the Head of Imageering for years. Sure, you're not in a military position now, but you were the number two guy from a military perspective for over a decade, and every person here other than Jeff answered to you at one time or another. So, you know how we work in a military fashion—both the A-Cs and the humans—and you have knowledge of how this solar system functions, too, right?"

"Yeah, I do." Christopher sounded a little more perky. "We had to learn about it when we started moving up the ranks in Centaurion Division. It's not really taught to us before then."

"You're also an imageer," Chuckie said. "And that means you see things differently. Serene is as well, but as Jeff's pointed out, if they can access the three of us, they don't need to worry about accessing the others."

"You know, I'm convinced that we were literally placed where we landed, including having me and Chuckie land in freaking trees."

"Why so?" Jeff asked as the road finally leveled off. "I mean, I accept that it wasn't a coincidence that we all landed near sentient life-forms. But I think you mean that we were put not only by sentient beings but also by specific beings, based on who we are, right?"

I nodded but it was Chuckie who replied. I could see the wheels turning in his head. "Yes, particularly based on what we just discussed, about us and about the girls' landing, it seems very deliberate. I'd suggest that it was the katyhoppers, only they absolutely aren't the ones who brought us here."

"I don't think whoever brought us here—and by that I mean whoever did the snatch and grab on us when we were on Earth—is who put us onto this planet and into these specific places. I think it was someone else, and that that being wants us to do something with this world, specifically, regardless of what else is going on in this solar system."

But our discussion was put on hold as we rounded a corner that doubled as a T-intersection, because we were all too busy gasping. I wasn't the only one gaping, either.

Fancy turned and smiled at us. "Welcome to Haven."

CHAPTER 45

TURNED OUT FANCY'S Ferrets didn't live in burrows. Fancy's Ferrets lived in a vast, underground complex that bore the same resemblance to a prairie dog or rabbit warren that Jeff did to a slug.

"Wow, it's like we just entered the Dwarf Kingdoms in Middle Earth, isn't it?" I asked Chuckie.

"Somewhat, yes, without the roof being hundreds of feet higher than necessary."

"Depends on your view, dude. Look down and to the left."

"Oh. Wow."

What I'd managed to spot before Chuckie was that the road we were on led down as well as up. He'd been looking up, and as the road went upward, the ceiling, if you will, never got more than about twelve feet high. It wasn't an ornate ceiling, but it was reinforced as far as I could see with thick stone columns. Based on what I'd seen with Christopher, my bet was that the columns and this road, or others like it, went all the way up inside the highest peaks or mesas.

But when you looked down, you saw the complex. And then realized that the ceilings were a hundred feet high if they were an inch, if not more.

While the setup had reminded me of *Lord of the Rings*, everything else was more like something out of Disney's Storybook Land ride, particularly the parts dedicated to *The Wind in the Willows*—lots of thatched huts, quaint and cozy buildings, puffs of smoke coming out of chimneys, and more. There was a river that meandered through, as well.

Clutches of villages were dotted on either side, with a larger town visible off in the distance.

Contrary to what I'd have expected, it didn't smell all that musky, and thankfully it didn't smell dank, either. What it smelled was earthy, with a little smoke and water, and a lot of something that smelled like how wheat looks. The planet was pretty much like what I'd been told a drug trip was like, but without most of the negative side effects. At least so far. And not counting the snakipedes, which were a bad drug trip all on their own.

As my eyes adjusted to the perspective, I realized the entire complex was built on a slope. And part of the river was actually a waterfall. In fact, as we started down the road toward the nearest village, I spotted several waterfalls behind us.

We didn't stop at the first village on the road's side of the river. Or rather, this road's side. Jeff pointed out another road on the other side of what was an interior valley within the mountains—we could make out specks that were Lecanora moving on it, meaning we were very far apart.

And we could see all of this clearly because the interior of the mountain gave off a soft golden glow.

"Do you think it's gold veins?" Chuckie asked me as we examined the wall next to us.

"No, because what would be making them glow? Gold's glow comes from light reflection, and I don't see another light source."

"It must be like the snow outside," Serene said. "I think the snow glows because of cold. Maybe this stone glows because of the lack of cold."

"I don't think so," Jeff said. "Let's worry about it later." He was acting a little funny, but I decided not to ask him about it right now.

We trundled along for another hour until we reached a larger village than any we'd passed yet, on either side of the river. Fancy led us in and—after having the bosthoon that were already in it removed by their owners—had King Benny's people put their bosthoon into a large corral.

Per Fancy, there were males in her clan, and we were meeting a lot of them, but all the warriors were female. The males ran the villages and most of the businesses, but the females handled all the military and most of the government, though Fancy ran the entire clan. Each village had an Under-Clan Leader, assigned by Fancy. She gave this status to males or females depending on her view of their ability to lead, so there were as many male Under-Clan Leaders as female ones.

"Does Haven run within the entire mountain range? Or, rather, as we're calling it, all within and under Iceland?" I asked her.

Fancy nodded. "Yes. The river starts at the edge of the world and runs to the All Seeing Mountain."

"Wouldn't that mean it has to run uphill at some point?" Chuckie asked.

"Yes, particularly near the edge of the world," Fancy said, as if this wasn't odd.

I wanted to ask more about this and I could tell Chuckie did, too, but Jeff changed the subject by requesting that we get down to the business of housing and feeding all of King Benny's people and livestock.

Before this could happen we had to do the Introduce the Gods and Their Amazing Traveling Companions thing, which was just as awkward and embarrassing as you'd imagine. But we were all getting used to being this world's Gods, and the katyhoppers and strautruch seemed unfazed, so we handled it well. Jeff refused to allow the Under-Clan Leader of this particular village, named Karason, to kill a bosthoon for a feast in our honor, which was a relief to many, the bosthoon in particular.

Jeff asked that King Benny's advisors and Under-Clan Leader Karason discuss the logistics, then he pulled me, Chuckie, Christopher, Fancy, and King Benny aside.

"We need to discuss more than what we're going to do for tonight," Jeff said.

"We will sleep and travel with you in a few hours," King Benny said.

"Look," I said without a lot of preamble, "King Benny, you and your people have been great. However, there's trouble here, and we need to move more swiftly than we've been able to. And at the same time, we can't leave you and your people homeless and unprotected. Fancy, what are the protocols for them to move in with you guys? And I'm asking that in an extremely God-like way, with extremely God-like intentions."

Fancy and King Benny looked at each other. "It was my understanding that only your clan is allowed to live here," King Benny said politely.

"Your clan are our cousins," Fancy replied. "And the Gods are requesting that we open our home to our family. I cannot refuse that request."

"Sure you can," I said. "But let me be very clear. I don't want King Benny's people shoved off to the side anymore. I don't want them mistreated, abused, ignored, starved, beaten, tortured, cast aside, or whatever nasty things your king does. He's already caused all of them to become cast-offs and castaways from their original clans. Right now, all they have is each other. They're also the best example of worldwide cooperation you all seem to have. They need to be shown as examples of good, not bad."

"In other words," Chuckie added, "what Shealla means is that unless King Benny's people will be integrated into your clan with love and acceptance, we're not going to be happy."

"That will not be an issue for my people," Fancy said. "We have no quarrel with our cousins, and less with these cousins."

"Because they saw what you did, but unlike you, they said something and suffered for it."

Fancy looked at me sharply. "Yes."

"You have seen the ships in the sky?" King Benny asked her.

"Yes, Musgraff, I have. All our people have. And we said nothing because we saw how the king was dealing with those who spoke the truth. We could not risk him attempting to banish us from Haven."

Attempting. Didn't get the impression Fancy felt that the king would manage that banishment, but I could understand her not wanting to have to find out.

"So, basically, King Benny and all his people are braver than yours," Christopher said.

Fancy stared at him. "How dare you say that to me?"

"He can dare because we've just spent time with your world's version of gypsies, who all faced down the snaki-pedes or the Horrors or whatever it is you guys call those terrifying flying snake-monsters without panicking. And they only had to do that because they were brave enough to speak the truth. You might be smarter than they are, but you're not braver."

Fancy stared at me now, for a few long moments. Then she laughed. "You have a good point. Yes, we are smarter, in that sense. We hid our knowledge."

"And yourselves," Jeff said. "I mean, let's be honest—how many outside of your clan know what Haven really is?"

"Few," Fancy admitted.

"Who built Haven?" Chuckie asked. "Originally, I mean."

"The Gods like to test us," King Benny said. Which told me it was time to give it a good guess, lest we give Fancy reasons to once again think we weren't the real Gods.

"Alcalla does like to see who knows that the Father of the Gods gave them their blessings, it's very true."

Score one for me. Fancy's eyes opened wider and King Benny looked pleased. Hoped the guys were looking like they'd already known this.

"Therefore," Jeff said, without missing a beat, "since Haven was given to you by Our Father, it's not just for you, is it?" I was so proud.

"No, Leolalla, it is not, you are correct." Fancy turned to King Benny. "Musgraff, would you and your people like to join with my clan?"

King Benny looked uncertain. Thought about why. "Ah, Fancy? There is one issue. His people see King Benny as Clan Leader. Not sure if they're going to be okay with the Under-Clan Leader thing."

"No," King Benny said. "They will accept it, because I see no reason to demand an equal position with Corzine. She has protected her clan better than any other Clan Leader and better than I have protected mine."

"That's not true," Fancy said. "You have done more than any other could have or would have. The Outcast were sent to the Barrens to die alone. You brought them together and joined the disparate cousins into one clan that has survived and thrived for two long years when none expected any of you to last a month."

Interesting. So the king was a bastard, but then I'd known that already. But my Israelites comparison was apt and King Benny was more than the Guy With Antlers On His Head—he was Moses, for this world, at least. And Moses was, among other things, a fighter.

"You want to go with us, don't you?" I asked him quietly. "But you don't want to leave your people unguarded. That's why you want to take them all with us, despite the obvious logistical problems. But that's dangerous for everyone, especially the people you want to protect the most."

"Shealla speaks the truth, as always." King Benny looked down. "I am ashamed of my hubris in wanting to continue to accompany the Gods."

"There is no shame in that, Musgraff," Fancy said gently. "I, too, wish to go with them."

"Awesome. Fancy, figure out where King Benny's clan can settle down—and be sure it's not someplace crappy, and also be sure that it's not with others of your clan who will resent their taking up land and such that was someone else's to begin with." Why start an Israel-Palestine issue on this world? Planet Colorful had enough of its own problems, we didn't need to export some of ours to them.

"There is space between this town and the next," Fancy said. "I will ensure that both Under-Clan Leaders understand that their favor with me is dependent upon Musgraff's clan being accepted and integrated in with our clans and into Haven."

"Super. King Benny, put Nanda or Skunky in charge of your clan while you're gone, whichever one of them is the most levelheaded and agrees with your leadership style the most."

He looked shocked. "You wish me to come with you, Shealla?"

"Indeed. You've been far more help to us than you realize. Oh, and Ginger and Wilbur are coming with us, too, but I want to leave the rest of the ocellars and chochos here, along with all the bosthoon. We'll go faster without the bosthoon, and I want to limit the number of additional animals we have along for a variety of reasons, avoiding another Patrina and Pretty Girl scenario being the biggest."

"Skunky will be a better leader than Nanda," King Benny said. "He and I do not see tail-to-tail on everything, but he is more levelheaded and less inclined to make a rash decision that will be regretted later."

"Nanda didn't really strike me as being overly rash."

"She is not, but Skunky is less so."

"It's your clan, you put whoever in charge you think is

best," Jeff said firmly. "Fancy, if you accompany us, who will protect Haven and, more importantly, ensure that King Benny's people are taken care of as we Gods wish them to be?"

"The same people who do so when I lead our raiding parties."

"What do you raid?" Chuckie asked. Hoped the answer wasn't going to be other Lecanora clans, because that would mean we were taking King Benny and all his clan along with us.

Fancy smiled and showed all her teeth. Didn't get the impression it was a ferret thing—definitely got the impression she wanted to show all her teeth.

"We raid the king's palace. All the time."

CHAPTER 46

"AWESOME!" Hey, this was the best news I could hope for.

"We also raid the nests where the Horrors come from," Fancy said. "I believe you will be interested to discover where those nests are."

Decided it was once again time to put the Megalomaniac Girl Guessing Skills into use. "They're somewhere within the king's complex or palace or whatever, aren't they?"

This time, while King Benny looked horrified, Fancy looked hella impressed. "They are indeed."

"How long have the Horrors been around?"

"For as long as we can remember. But the king's palace was built intentionally to be near their nests."

Confirmation, as if I'd needed it by now, that the snaki-pedes were created monsters, not something that this planet had come up with all on its own. Clearly Ronaldo or, more likely, LaRue had wanted easy access and close proximity to their "pets."

"Bring a fighting force with you," was all I said, however.

She nodded. "I will bring those you have met already. They are my best raiders, and it will cause less suspicion in my clan if they are the ones to go with us. Because we will not be sharing with anyone where we are going with the Gods, and Musgraff, I mean you, in particular."

King Benny shook his head. "My people will panic if they know I'm leaving them here. I plan to tell them that we are looking for a suitable place for us to settle, that the Gods wish to join us, and that Clan Leader Corzine has graciously offered to come along and help me find the best place. The way the Gods move, I believe we will be reunited sooner as opposed to later."

"Wise," Chuckie said. "All of it." Both King Benny and Fancy looked pleased by this. Apparently they had no issues believing Chuckie was the God of Wisdom. Couldn't argue with them on that one.

"We need to rest before we head out," Jeff said.

Fancy nodded. "Of course. Preparations are being made."

"We have other Gods we're looking for," I said before we headed back. "Have you heard any rumors or news?"

Fancy shook her head. "Not up here. But we'll be traveling toward the Centerpoint of the World, and some of my clan who live nearer to the center of the world may have heard of more Gods arriving."

King Benny gave me a warm smile. "We will find all your family, Shealla."

Decided I didn't want to argue with this mindset, so we headed back to the others. A nice meal of fish, which came from the River of Dreams—the name of their river, not the Billy Joel album, though now I wanted to listen to that album—and some kind of root vegetables was provided. It all tasted delicious and I hoped we weren't all going to die from allergic reactions later.

Thinking about how the only medical we had was in my purse made me think about Tito, and then worry about Tito, which brought all the worry I had about Jamie to the fore. What if she needed medical attention? What if Tito was hurt and couldn't doctor her even if we found them both? This worry opened the floodgates, and the worry about Kevin, and Brian, and Reader, and Tim, and Abigail came rushing in. Then felt guilty for not worrying at this moment about Rahmi, Rhee, and Gower, so filled out the Missing Set and worried about them, too.

Jeff picked it up. These days, I didn't add "of course" to that. The emotional overlays and enhancers our enemies had created had caused him to focus less and less on his empathic talents. And the Bronze Land had just been a repeat performance, in that sense. But I could tell he was picking up my worry because he took my hand and squeezed it gently. I leaned against him and did my best to relax while we finished eating.

The Ferret Clan did a lot of travel up and down their vast underground country. I was interested to discover that there were more Lecanora here than just ferrets, however. Beavers and otters and many other mustelidae species were represented—easily as many as were in King Benny's Gypsy Clan, possibly more. But to a one, they all had white fur.

Realized they weren't the Ferret Clan so much as they were the Albino Clan. Wondered if albinos were treated badly on this world or if it was just the usual for Planet Colorful—you matched your spiral's main color scheme. I was a betting girl, and I went with the latter.

Dinner over, we were able to use the excuse of having spent a day fighting off danger and go to bed. Well, to room. Because it turned out that the Lecanora didn't really use beds. They were into the "soft stuff on the floor" thing. I wasn't a fan.

However, when in Rome and all that blah, blah, blah meant that we had to smile and say that the mosses and such looked super, especially since we were being housed in Karason's home, which was both kind of him and an honor, in that sense.

The soft stuff on the floor was comfortable, especially as compared to the bare ground—cement wasn't going on in Haven—but nothing like the beds at the Embassy or any other A-C facility, for that matter.

Now I desperately wanted to ask my purse for air mattresses, but I knew that would mean questions I couldn't possibly answer. On the positive side, we were given the nicest sleeping room this particular village had. On the negative side, the Lecanora tended to sleep in chummy family groups, meaning that we were *all* in the nicest sleeping room. Together. Katyhoppers, strautruch, Ginger, and Wilbur included.

This was a bummer because I'd really hoped that, if nothing else, Jeff and I could have some sexy times together. I was used to sleeping and having sex with cats and dogs around, and even Peregrines and Poofs, so Ginger and Wilbur weren't an issue. But doing the deed with everyone else around was out of the question. I could tell Lorraine and Claudia had been hoping for the same with Joe and Randy and, like me, weren't willing to go for it with a large audience.

And Karason's home had enough rooms that we could have split up, especially because he lived alone—his mate had passed away a few years ago and their children lived father up the river. But he hadn't offered that, and, Gods or not, it wasn't wise to risk sounding like whiny, demanding houseguests.

So we all settled down and tried to get to sleep. Frankly, we were all exhausted, so everyone fell asleep right away.

Everyone but me.

I was tired but wide awake. I had a thing where if everyone else was asleep I tended to stay awake. Guarding, I guess, though I'd been like this from well before I'd met the gang from A-C. If Jeff and I had been in our own room, I'd have been able to nod off because I wouldn't know that everyone else was asleep. I didn't have this issue in a place I called home or where I felt protected, but when I wasn't at home and we were in a danger situation, it kicked in. And it kicked in here, big-time.

Hadn't had this problem so much in Bizarro World. Then again, I'd woken up before everyone else there. Six of one, half a dozen of the other. Basically, sleep and I weren't as tight as I liked us to be when I was in action situations.

The golden glow from the rocks never faded—the homes here had dark coverings over all their windows so that they could sleep in the Land of the Midnight Glowing. So our room was dark, so dark that we'd decided to leave the door opened a bit, so we could all see if we woke up earlier than the others. But the glow wasn't what was keeping me awake—I was used to the A-C Nightlight System, after all.

Sex with Jeff would exhaust me happily, but that was out. So was he. He was in a deep sleep and I was cuddled next to him, his arms wrapped around me, my head on his chest listening to his heartbeats. Normally this helped me nod off happily, but not right now. Wondered if I was going to sleep at all or if I was alert for a meaningful reason.

Heard a small noise and decided meaningful reason was the winner. Moved carefully out of Jeff's embrace and looked around. To see a small figure in the doorway. Make that two small figures.

Got up and went to the doorway. "Patrina, what are you and Pretty Girl doing here?" I whispered as I knelt down to be at her eye level.

Patrina, who was holding Pretty Girl, came inside and snuggled near me. "I can't sleep, Shealla." Well, it was going around.

"Why not?" I sat down cross-legged and pulled her and Pretty Girl onto my lap. Ginger, who'd been snuggled next to me, got up and joined us, snuggling right back next to me. Hoped that whoever Jamie was with was taking care of her if she couldn't sleep or was missing her parents or was scared.

"There are no stars here."

"Ah." The Gypsy Clan was used to sleeping outside by now, and Patrina was young enough that it was probably what she knew best. "Well, the stars are still there, Patrina. We're just all inside, in fact, we're inside a gigantic mountain!"

"Really?"

"Really. The Father of the Gods created this to provide a Haven for his people. All his people, not just the ones with white fur."

"The katyhoppers and strautruch, too?"

"Yes. Everything here was created by the Father of the Gods."

"Not the Horrors," she said solemnly.

"No, not the Horrors."

"Can they get us here?"

Wanted to say no, but my brain nudged. We'd left a huge trail, and snow or not, that trail would have scent attached to it. There was no way the snakipedes weren't going to find it. Maybe not the ones who'd attacked us, but others. And I'd already determined that all they'd need to get inside Haven was a being with opposable thumbs to help open the door. Several beings, if they were normally strong for a human or a Lecanora.

But it only took one A-C.

Put Patrina off of my lap. "You and Pretty Girl stay here. If Ginger and I aren't back soon, you wake up Leoalla and tell him we went to make sure the door was locked. Then you wake up Wilbur and tell him to get all the ocellars and chochos ready to fight." Jeff would handle the Lecanora.

"How long is soon?" Patrina asked.

Good question. I was wearing my watch but it had been a present from Jeff and had gone to Bizarro World and back with me, and now was traveling the galaxy with me. I didn't want to risk losing it.

Pinky opened his eyes and came over to us. He waved his antennae—I could move fast enough without him and was strong enough to carry Ginger if we had to run, and he could stay mentally connected to me. If he lost the connection, or too much time passed, they would wake Jeff.

"You rock, Pinky." Hugged Patrina and petted Pretty Girl, then grabbed my purse and slung it over my neck. "Figure I'll be back within fifteen minutes. If I'm gone longer than thirty, sound the alarm. C'mon, Ginger, time to patrol."

With that Ginger and I slipped out of the room.

CHAPTER 47

AS SOON AS WE were out of the room I picked Ginger up and used hyperspeed to get out of the house. Did a fast check of the village also at hyperspeed—everything looked serene. But there were no Lecanora on guard duty.

Of course, there was technically no need. The only ones who lived here were Fancy's Albinos. Once inside Haven, they all considered themselves safe. And they were, under normal circumstances. But the circumstances now were no longer normal.

What my mother called instinct, Jeff called my feminine intuition, and I called my gut were all saying the same thing—we were going to be attacked. Sure, the door was locked from the inside, but all it took was one traitor on this side and that was over.

Had no idea why I suspected a traitor, other than this was the only way the door could be unlocked. But a traitor within the Albino Clan was unlikely—if they were here, Haven would be overrun already.

So if there was a traitor, we'd brought them with us, with King Benny's Gypsy Clan. Only none of the Lecanora had given off anything that would have triggered Jeff. When we were in the Bronze Land this wouldn't have been a surprise. However, his empathic talents were working in the other areas we'd hit so far, and if there was a traitor, focused on me, Christopher, and Chuckie though he'd been, I was sure that Jeff would have noticed.

The katyhoppers and strautruch were in the room with

the rest of us, so they were out as potential door openers and, besides, they didn't have the paws for the job.

Retraced our steps but at a human walk—I didn't want to miss anything and I wanted to conserve energy just in case. Besides, I could speed it up if I needed to and this way, Ginger didn't have to deal with hyperspeed. Though she'd only gagged a little when we'd stopped outside the village.

All of Haven was asleep—clearly they functioned on the same daily clock as the rest of this world did. Had no idea how they managed it, because Patrina was right—looking up I could see no stars. There was nothing but a dark golden glow. At least the rocks ensured that they didn't have to burn torches all over the place, so there was that small blessing.

This land was beautiful. It was hard to connect with the rest of the planet that we'd seen. Not because of its beauty—this was potentially the prettiest planet in the galaxy, if not the universe—but because it looked so normal. Normal for Earth. Normal, from the little I'd seen and the A-Cs had told me, for Alpha Four, too.

I was getting more and more convinced that this world had had more than a little help in its creation. Which made sense considering we'd been so carefully placed here.

As we walked and I noted that there were literally no sentries anywhere, my memory nudged. King Benny had carried a short sword in his tail when he'd first come to meet us. And I'd had the thought that we weren't who he was worried about. So, that meant there was someone in his clan who he didn't trust. Took the leap and assumed it was one of his advisors.

Ruled out Skunky because if King Benny didn't trust him he wouldn't be planning to leave the rest of the Gypsies in Skunky's care.

This left a few options. My top three choices, based on their willingness to speak up, were Nanda the beaver, Grover the weasel, and the woodchuck guy I'd named Brown, for Charlie Brown, a joke that only Chuckie had gotten or appreciated.

On Earth, suspicion would fall firmly onto Grover based on his species. But I was willing to keep an open mind. King Benny hadn't wanted Nanda in charge because of her willingness to be rash. And Brown, once we'd been accepted into the clan as Gods, had basically been quiet and not interacted with us at all.

"Hey." Christopher appeared out of nowhere and I managed not to scream. Only just. Ginger, too, based on her jumping at him and only getting her claws pulled back and her jaws slammed shut at the last moment. "Ack! Get your cat off me!"

"Hey, Ginger has fast reflexes and you scared the crap out of us. What are you doing here?"

"Little kids don't stay quiet, even when they're trying hard. Patrina woke us all up on accident. Pinky told us what you were worried about and where you were going and why. Jeff was going to go after you but Chuck pointed out that the Lecanora are listening to the two of them, Chuck and Jeff, far more than anyone else, and that if we were in trouble, I was the fastest so could get you out the quickest."

"And Jeff listened to reason? Wow. I guess he doesn't care anymore."

Christopher laughed. "No, but he's clear on what you think could be going on, and the destruction of Haven and all the people in it requires him to stay put." He shrugged. "Like when we were running Centaurion Division, he knows when he has to make a choice he doesn't like."

"Sounds a lot more like politics, but either way, works for me." Brought him up to speed on my theory about the potential traitors. Now wasn't the time to discuss this world and why we were in it. "So, it could be one of them or none of them. I have no guess right now."

Christopher picked Ginger up under one arm and took my hand. "Let's find out sooner as opposed to later. I got some sleep and food and I feel fine." With that, he zipped us off at hyperspeed, but at the regular level, not his Flash level, for which I was grateful.

It didn't take us long to get back to the T-intersection where this road met the pathway coming in. We stopped, Christopher handed Ginger to me, and while she settled her stomach as quietly as possible, he zipped around the corner and back. "Clear so far, but I can't see all the way to the doorway."

"We're ready. Who do you think it's going to be? Nanda, Grover, Brown, or someone else? Or no one?"

"I have no idea. That's why we're going to investigate." He took my hand again and we sped down the trail.

To come to the door and remember that it took more than one to move it. "Or," I said conversationally, as we stopped behind them, "it could be all of them."

CHAPTER 48

HAD TO ADMIT, I was surprised to see so many of the Gypsy Clan working together against their king and the people of Haven. However, it was who they were working with that was the complete shocker.

"So, Under-Clan Leader Karason, you're opening the door to let the Horrors in?" I could hear banging on the other side. It was dull and faint, as something banging on rock would be, but it was still distinctly there. "And you're not afraid that they'll eat all of you first?"

The all were the rest of King Benny's advisors, other than Skunky and, I was happy to note, Nanda. But Grover, Brown, and others I hadn't bothered to get to know yet were all here, clustered together, looking hugely guilty.

"Not the Horrors," Karason said. "I would never release them on my own people." The tone was completely honest and believable. But there was a slight emphasis on the words "my own" that was, for me, telling.

Maybe it was because I knew LaRue had been here, and, thanks to my time in Bizarro World, I also knew that LaRue was actually an Ancient, and therefore a shapeshifter. Maybe it was because there were shapeshifters in this solar system, many of whom I knew didn't want to play nicely with others, despite their Queen's views. And maybe it was just because I was so used to this kind of crap that, by now, the idea that anyone or anything was exactly as presented seemed totally out of the realm of possibility.

Whatever it was, what I did was simple. I tossed the animal trained to fly through the air and kill a gigantic, venomous, flying snake right at Karason's head.

Results were, as was so often the case, immediate.

Karason shifted into an Amazon from Beta Twelve, complete with the short spiky hair—in this case, a dirty blonde—and the *Xena: Warrior Princess* outfit. She wasn't one of the tall ones, I put her at about Rhee's height, but that still meant she was taller than me. And, as with all the Free Women, she was very muscular in an attractive way while still being just a bit out of proportion to human eyes.

Speaking of eyes, while hers were the typically Amazonian larger and more elongated, unlike every other Free Woman I'd ever seen, they weren't a dark purple—her eyes were black. With no whites in them at all.

Freaky eyes or no, I'd been expecting a shapeshifter to appear. No one else, including Christopher, had been.

He said one word, "Whoa!" Then he disappeared. Had no idea where he'd gone, but my suspicion wasn't that he'd run off in terror. Had a feeling he was moving so fast that I, and therefore the Amazon, couldn't see him.

The Lecanora panicked. Interestingly enough, this meant that they followed Ginger's lead and attacked the Amazon. Unsurprisingly, even though there were five of them, they weren't a match for her.

She flung them off easily and focused on the real threat—Ginger. This wasn't going to be good for Ginger.

"Ginger, retreat! Come to Kitty!"

She tried, but the Amazon had a good grip on her, one hand on Ginger's throat and one buried in her stomach, and I could tell she planned to rip Ginger apart.

Which was nice, in that sense, because I flipped right into rage, and rage meant I was now a match for a trained Amazon spy.

The Amazon was holding Ginger up, almost over her head. Meaning she was pretty exposed. Also meaning she was either poorly trained or hugely overconfident. Hoped for both.

Bent down, ran, and slammed my shoulder into the Amazon's stomach hard enough that she hit the wall. This loosened her grip on Ginger. Sent a palm-heel strike up to her chin, while my other hand found a pressure point on her arm and squeezed it.

Ginger meanwhile was clawing, and managing to miss me but not the Amazon, and she got a good cut in. The Amazon let her go and focused on me. She swung, I blocked. She tried to sweep my legs. I jumped. She hit me in the chest and I flew away and hit the other wall. She laughed and stepped toward me, and therefore away from the wall she'd been up against.

Which was a mistake, because Christopher had fought as many of the Pissed-Off Amazons during the battle before my wedding as I had. Probably more than I had. And that was before he was the fastest man on Earth and, from all I'd seen, on Beta Eight, too.

Plus, he'd been training me how to use my powers for over three years now, and that meant we knew how to fight together as a team. Which we did.

Christopher reappeared and took the Amazon's back, literally. He had his arm around her neck and had her in a choke hold before she took two steps toward me. He was about her height, which meant he could get her, but he couldn't hope to use his body weight to get her down, like Jeff or even Chuckie would have. But then, that's what I was here for.

She grabbed his arms, meaning her fists were occupied. I'd seen plenty of movies, so when I stepped toward her I was ready for her to lean back against Christopher and try to mule kick me. So I let her try it and jumped out of the way.

She used the falling momentum to try to flip Christopher over her back when she landed. Which would have worked better for her if I hadn't anticipated that, too, and had, therefore, already made a double fist and swung up right at her face as said face came right down to meet my hands.

She went to the ground, Christopher still on her back. The Lecanora, sensing that the Gods and the whatever they thought the Amazon was were occupied, tried to make a dash back up the trail. Ginger, however, was pissed off and she blocked them, snarling and doing the low growl-and-yowl that cats do when they're saying, "yo momma" and "bring it" in feline.

"You five will stop or I will rend you limb from limb," I snarled at them. "Or I'll just let Ginger do it."

"A little ... help," Christopher said through gritted teeth. "She's down but she's not out."

Opened my purse to see what I could use or surreptitiously ask for without Christopher noticing that would allow us to tie her up, and saw Bruno and the Poofs. Shoved the thought that that would be a cool name for a band aside and focused on the situation at hand.

"Bruno, my bird, help Ginger keep the five Lecanora traitors at bay and not doing anything Kitty wouldn't like, please and thank you. Poofs, assemble!"

The Poofs poured out of my purse. Every Poof that corresponded to every person with me in Haven right now showed up. Then, when they had the Lecanora's full attention, and the Amazon's too, they went large and in charge.

The Poofs at normal size were merely adorable bundles of fluffy cuteness. However, when roused and in fighting or protective mode, they were as tall as Jeff, with giant mouths filled with razor sharp teeth. The teeth were there when they were small—anyone watching them devour a fallen foe could attest to that—but you just couldn't see them for all the fluffy fur when they were tiny.

Large, however, the teeth really stood out. Especially when the Poofs bared them and did the same low growl Ginger had been doing. Only there were more of them and their growls were a lot deeper, meaner, louder, and longer. The area we were in, being made of hollowed-out rock and all that, assisted with a lovely echo.

The corresponding screams were, as was so often the case, impressive.

CHAPTER 49

LECANORA SCREAMED LIKE, well, small animals being taken off by a bird of prey. Only the sounds were coming out of human-sized beings, meaning the noises were much louder. And painfully high. Was glad Wilbur and the other chochos weren't here, especially if they had canine-like hearing. As it was, Ginger, Christopher, and I all winced, and Bruno shook his head like crazy.

Of course, after the screaming stopped, other exciting things happened.

Grover flat out fainted. Brown wet himself. The other three whose names I hadn't bothered to get started to cry. They weren't exactly starring in The Brave in Action. And these people had not lost their heads when the snakipedes were attacking. Filed that away, but right up front, for immediate consideration once the Amazon was contained or eaten, depending on her attitude.

She hadn't been prepared for the Poofs, either, but she was a trained warrior, so she only screamed a little bit. But she'd still screamed, meaning she'd never seen a Poof before. Also meaning she'd never hung out on Earth or watched the Earth TV Channel so many of the planets in this system seemed to get on their version of Intergalactic Cable.

She also started struggling even more. Hit her head with a side blade kick and she shut up.

Helped Christopher up while the Poofs surrounded her and us. "Think she's out?"

He shook his head. "Doubtful. You might have stunned her for a second, though."

"Great." Looked into my purse. "Amazonian-level handcuffs, I wonder if I have something like that in here." Dug around and sure enough, came up with some handcuffs. "Thanks," I whispered to my purse. Put them on her, hands behind her back, and closed them tightly. Didn't find a key. I'd pick the lock if events warranted, which I doubted they would.

"How the hell were you carrying something like that?" Christopher asked, as I hauled the Amazon into a sitting position.

I was saved from having to come up with an explanation guaranteed to make him blush by the arrival of Jeff, Chuckie, King Benny, and Fancy Corzine.

"What is going on here?" Fancy asked. Realistically a good question—sincerely doubted our tableau was normal for this world. Frankly, it wasn't really normal for my world, either, though we were all a lot more used to the weird than this world seemed to be.

There was much protesting by those Lecanora who were still conscious that they hadn't been doing anything wrong, Ginger and the Poofs were growling, Bruno was squawking while he helped Ginger keep the Lecanora in place, and Christopher was right—the Amazon wasn't out. Sensing a new audience, she started sharing what she was going to do to us in just a moment. This involved a lot of rending and beating and such.

Jeff listened to all of this for about two seconds, and then he lost it. "Shut UP!" he bellowed.

No one bellowed like my man. The reverberations went on for quite some time, which had the double effect of hurting everyone's ears even more and shutting everyone up, though now all five of the Lecanora traitors were crying, albeit quietly, including Grover, who'd rejoined us in Conscious Land, probably due to Jeff's bellowing. One for the painful win column.

"Now," Jeff said when everyone, Amazon included, quieted. "I want an explanation for what's going on. And I want that from Shealla Kitty only."

"Okay, in a really fast nutshell, this chick is a shapeshifter from another planet. Either she's been pretending to be Karason for a long time or she's killed him off and taken his place." There were gasps of horror from all the Lecanora. "She, as Karason, and the five of King Benny's followers there were trying to open the door to let the Horrors on the other side in."

"No," Brown said. "That is not what we were doing! Under-Clan Leader Karason said that Clan Leader Corzine had cast out some of her people and he wanted to bring them in to join with our clan." He shot a pleading look at King Benny. "We wanted to bring more wanderers under your leadership, Musgraff, not do wrong."

"What the hell do you think is pounding on the other side of this door?" Christopher asked.

"The castouts," Grover said shakily. "At least that's what . . . she told us."

"I'm going to tell you a different story," I said. "One where there are these freaking ginormous monsters that cruise the air and land looking for things to eat. They don't have any problem in any type of climate, and they can *smell* their prey. An absolute *tonnage* of prey just walked through this door. And *my* bet is that what are slamming their horrible heads against this door are not more Lecanora but a whole bunch of hungry Horrors. You pick which story sounds the most believable," I said to Fancy. "I'll wait."

"Shealla is, of course, correct," Fancy said. "I have cast none out of Haven."

"I was going to tell you that you had five traitors, but, honestly, I'm not convinced." Shot a look at Jeff, who nodded. Good, he'd be paying attention empathically. "One of you, and only one of you, explain what you were told," I said to the five who were cowering together, still crying quietly.

"That," Grover said, as he pointed to the Amazon, paw shaking, "we thought was Under-Clan Leader Karason. He told us that Clan Leader Corzine had cast out some of their clan, but since she was accepting ours, hoped that these others would be allowed to return to Haven. He said that he had sent a message to them to return and plead their case and that he would need help to open the door. He didn't want to ask Clan Leader Corzine for permission, since he feared she would say no, but hoped that if we presented the outcasts as being part of our clan, she might reconsider."

"And never, at any time, did it occur to any of you to ask King Benny what he thought?"

Grover shook his head. "Under-Clan Leader Karason said he'd chosen the five of us specifically, based on our positions within the clan."

"So you're saying that the supposed-Karason here didn't ask Skunky and Nanda to join in?"

The five shook their heads. "No," Brown replied. "He said that we were the ones he knew would be most sympathetic."

Rather, the Amazon felt they were the most gullible. Looked at Jeff, who nodded, meaning he believed their story.

Turned to the Amazon. "So, what's your story? Aside from being a Beta Twelve traitor, I mean?"

She sat up straight and sniffed at me. "I am no traitor. I am loyal to the Empire."

We were all quiet for a few long moments. Chuckie broke the silence, and, unsurprisingly, he spoke for all of us.

"Empire?"

The Amazon shot a very derisive look at Chuckie. Not a surprise, really. He was male, after all.

"We'd like an explanation," I said to her. "Or we'll let the Poofs eat you. Alive."

On cue, the Poofs increased their growling. The Amazon looked at them just a little nervously.

"Let's start with your name," I said pleasantly. "Or I'll give you a name I'm certain you won't like."

"My name is Usha, and I have no fear of you 'giving' me a name. I know you are not a real God," she said with a smirk.

"Well, Usha, I know you're not a real Free Woman."

She stared at me. "What do you mean?"

"Your eyes are wrong." In a big way, but that wasn't important at this moment. "And the Free Women are a whole lot more straightforward than this. You're a spy, and I don't think you're a real person." That was a lie. I'd fought supersoldiers and androids as well as Amazons, and she felt real. And, realistically, Kyrellis and Moira had used guerilla tactics, some of which involved subterfuge.

But I knew that Free Women reproduced via a cloning process, and the Mastermind and his nearest and dearest were using a very advanced form of cloning, undoubtedly perfected in this solar system somewhere. And I found it difficult to believe that Queen Renata had a spy in Haven who wanted to destroy all the Lecanora inside. However, the Beta Twelve insurgents had wanted to destroy everyone on all the other planets, at least all the men.

On the other hand, Fancy was female and she was the leader here. Meaning that a Beta Twelve spy who wanted to have women run things would be helping her, not trying to destroy her, in part because spies had specific orders, and I knew that Queen Renata's would not be "kill 'em all."

Having met two of the Beta Twelve insurgent leaders up close and personal, there was no way one of them had managed to hide in here effectively pretending to be a male for as long as I suspected Usha had been in her deep cover. And no Amazon I'd met yet would have ever asked a male for help, even if it was just to lead them to their horrible deaths. And it was five males huddled in front of Bruno and Ginger.

"There is nothing wrong with my eyes," Usha snarled. "My eyes are as they should be."

Of course, there was one other option, and one I hadn't considered before. In part because I'd only just found out that LaRue was an Ancient, and a traitor working for and with the Z'porrah, when I'd been in Bizarro World. You know, the world I'd been back from something like a whopping three days.

Really hoped Jeff was paying emotional attention and that Chuckie was watching for tells and such. Because it was again time to put on my Megalomania Girl Cape and make a guess that fit with my go-to strategy—the crazy.

"Yes, they are . . . for the race we call the Ancients."

CHAPTER 50

IT WAS A HUGE GAMBLE, but my guessing skills remained sharp—Usha jerked, just a little, but I caught it, and I was sure Chuckie had, too.

"I have no idea what you mean," she said. Had to say this for all-black eyes—it was really difficult to tell if they were shifting around or not. She might have been telling the truth. Though, on a scale of one to ten, I gave the likelihood for truth from her to be about a negative two.

"I mean you're not actually from Beta Twelve. You're actually from the galactic core. Or your parents or test tubes or whatever are from there originally. And you're not spying here for any empire we know about. You're spying for the Z'porrah's empire."

Her jaw dropped. "What . . . how did you . . . ?"

"I'm Shealla, and I just get to know these things." Looked over to Chuckie. "You want to use some 'fun' interrogation techniques to get what we want out of her?"

"Happy to," he said with the smooth menace in his tone I was, by now, certain he'd learned in his first week with the C.I.A.

"Let's make sure the door is still secure first," Jeff said, as he zipped over at hyperspeed and verified the lockup. Good thing, too—what Christopher and I hadn't noticed, what with Amazonian Ancient fighting and dealing with the Lecanora, was that the bars that should have been flat on the ground were raised just a tiny bit. Meaning that if the Amazonian Ancient got free, she could slam the door open.

Jeff motioned Chuckie over, and they hit what looked

like the same pattern Fancy had when we'd come in. The bars lowered back and I heard the mechanism lock again.

That the Amazonian Ancient had known the secret codes made sense, since she was impersonating a trusted leader. But having the others along didn't seem necessary. "So, Usha, why did you want to blame your traitorous actions on these Lecanora? I'm willing to believe that they were just pawns in your scheme, but why these five and why now?"

She rolled her eyes—beyond weird in this case since they were all black, but, as she rolled them, I could see shade differentiations, subtle but there—and didn't reply. Shocker.

Jeff was behind her now, though, and I could tell that he was paying emotional attention to her, and I could also tell that he was reading her. We'd done this before, so it was time to pepper her with questions and let Jeff do his thing.

"I'm betting that you wanted fall guys so that no one would make the connection that you'd impersonated Karason."

No reply from Usha, but Jeff nodded.

"So, how long has it been since you murdered Karason?" No answer and nothing from Jeff. Forged on. This was right in my wheelhouse, after all. "I'm betting you were in here for a long time as some Lecanora who was very quiet and so forth. You probably murdered some family's child and took their place so that you could learn the culture."

Usha stared at me. Jeff nodded, expression thunderous.

"And then, once Karason's mate died—excuse me, once you knew things were getting closer to coming to a head and you murdered her—you also murdered him and took his place. Any personality changes or whatever would be put down to mourning on his part."

Jeff nodded again. Had to wonder who was going to want to beat information out of Usha more—him or Chuckie. Jeff seriously looked ready to kill Usha right now. Had a feeling he was reading how she'd killed innocent, helpless people as much as that she'd killed them.

Saved from this guess by Fancy coming to stand next to me. "Karason sent his children off to live in other villages after his mate's death. He said that he wanted them to ensure that all remained true to my leadership. Now it seems that they were sent away to ensure they would not notice that their father was not the same."

"Sounds right to me. So, what's your guess for why she wanted some of King Benny's folks unwittingly involved? I ask because the chances of these five surviving the Horrors seems slim to none to me."

Christopher jerked. "How many other doors are there like this?"

"Five," Fancy replied. She drew in her breath sharply. "Do you think there are other traitors at the doors?"

"It pays to be sure." Grabbed Fancy's paw and Christopher's hand. "Jeff, Chuckie, keep on with the interrogation. Bruno, Ginger, Poofies, ensure that everyone stays here unless Jeff and Chuckie say you all need to leave. Fancy, you lead, we'll handle the speed."

And with that we took off. "Farthest door first," Christopher said.

Fancy nodded and we zoomed up the road that led up into the mountains. Because Christopher was at his Flash Speed Level, I couldn't see much more than a blur. But the architecture, villages, fields, and such all looked similar. The Albino Clan kept to their theme, which was typical for what we'd seen of this planet so far.

Haven was like a gigantic rectangle, with four of its doors at the four corners and the other two roughly in the middle of the long sides. We'd entered Haven though the middle door on the right side of the rectangle.

The river also went all the way up, with waterfalls creating a natural boundary between one large set of villages and farms from the next plateau up or down. But nowhere along the way did we meet any sentries of any kind. Clearly once inside, the Albino Clan considered themselves completely safe.

Unsurprisingly, the farthest door was at the "end" of the world, where we'd first met Fancy. It was secure and undisturbed. Christopher took us back to the intersection where the hallway, so to speak, had broken off the main road to lead to the doorway, and then he mercifully stopped.

While Fancy and I both gagged and I missed having Siler with us, particularly his touch ability to quell the bad side effects of hyperspeed, even and in this case especially Christopher's top speed level, I looked around. This main road went on for a ways, but right here we had a full intersection with the road that went to our left leading across the valley.

I also managed to gasp out a pertinent question. "How did your people near the cavern entrance let you know we were here?" Assumed Fancy had been alerted, since I also figured she'd been looking for oddities when Christopher and I appeared. She just hadn't been surprised to see us, indicating an expectation that we were going to show up somehow.

She put up her paw and a part of the stone detached itself and turned into a golden beetle. "We have a communications network."

"And they're what makes the interior glow, too?"

She stroked the beetle, then returned it to the stone wall. It blended in and I literally couldn't see any beetle outline at all. "Yes, they are. They're our friends. We grow food for them, they provide our light and communications. To kill one, other than out of mercy, is considered as evil as killing one of our own."

Christopher and I looked at each other. "It's like I can read your mind," he said.

"You can."

"Yeah." His brow furrowed. "But, actually not right now."

"We must be too far from the katyhoppers." Not necessarily good news, but at least we now knew they had a range.

"Maybe, but anyway, I know who you want to put onto the throne here."

"Was it that obvious? Or did you read my mind and you're just pretending you can't?"

He grinned. "I've known you a long time now. And no, right now, I honestly have no idea what you're thinking."

"Honestly, I was thinking that. Well, what I assume you think I'm thinking. I'm thinking that. I think."

"Thank God I've gotten used to the Kitty-isms."

"Blah, blah, blah."

Fancy looked back and forth between us. "You truly mean for us to overthrow the king?" she asked, interrupting our witty banter. "And you also want me to take his place?"

"No. I want to get rid of the interloper who's trying to destroy your world and put the best potential ruler into his place. Right now, it's between you and King Benny, but you're ruling a lot more people than he is, so I'm leaning toward you."

She shook her head. "What you speak of is war."

"Civil war. Yeah."

Christopher took our hands again. "Let's discuss politics after we make sure that the rest of the doors are secure."

We took off again and this time went down the road that took us across the valley. We crossed the river this way, of course, and I realized that what I hadn't really noticed was the sound of the water. Normally in a cavern with this much water rushing by that also was loaded with waterfalls, the sound would be quite loud. But the sounds of flowing water were hushed all the way through Haven. Something to ask about when we had less pressing concerns.

We reached the other side and other side's road but went across it and beyond. There was a corresponding door at the end of this road we were on, also thankfully undisturbed and secure.

Since we'd gone a much shorter distance this time, relatively speaking, we raced off for the door that corresponded to the one where Jeff and the others were, only for the other side of Haven. Took a wild guess and figured the other two doors were going to be at the point nearest to the All Seeing Mountain.

This door was also secure and unmolested. As Fancy and I gagged some more, really hoped it was going to be the same at the last two doors. Now that I'd done the top half, so to speak, of both sides of the Haven Valley, I was able to see the curvature of the mountains and the land, especially toward the area we were heading. Even underground the area conformed to the spiral.

Zipped off again, the last door on this side was also safe, and there was another road that intersected the roads that ran on either side of the Valley. "How close to the All Seeing Eye are we here?" I asked Fancy.

"Not as close as we will be. The last door we're checking lets us out closest to the Centerpoint of the World. It's also closest to the king's palace."

"In other words, it's the door you'd expect us all to come out of, right?"

She nodded. "Why?"

"Oh, just my suspicious mind and all that."

"Yeah, I agree," Christopher said. "It's the perfect spot for an ambush."

"And if the snakipedes were in, running down toward these exits would make the most sense."

"Only for half of my people," Fancy pointed out.

"They don't care about your people, babe. They care about *you*. About getting rid of you, I might add."

And King Benny, which might have been why Usha had chosen some of his advisors—even if he'd lived, his key people would have let the snakipedes in to destroy Haven. Any of Fancy's Ferrets who survived would consider it his fault and execute him. A tidy way to get rid of two potential leaders who could bring the world's population together.

"But how would they know where she was?" Christopher asked. "Fancy found us at the edge of the continent. And even if Usha has accomplices inside Haven, how would they get a message to anyone outside about where Fancy was? Let alone the rest of us?"

"The Goldens would have let me know if anyone was conspiring against me through their network," Fancy confirmed.

"Well, where we were was an easy guess based on tracks and smell. That we would only be allowed into Haven under Fancy Corzine's order and, most likely, escort seems to me to be a good bet."

She nodded. "Yes. We don't bring in others without my approval. For safety." She sighed. "Not that this seems to have been effective."

"Trust me, the failure isn't yours. You have enemies. Luckily for you, they're our enemies too."

She cocked her head at us. "The Gods have enemies? More than Zenoca?"

"Working with Zenoca." After all, I was pretty sure LaRue was Zenoca and all of our enemies were working with her. Lucky us.

"Let's go," Christopher said as he took our hands again. "One door left. Let's hope it's secure, too."

"What are the odds?"

"Kitty, I'm with you and we're somehow following one of your plans. I think the odds are really good that whatever's going on at the last door isn't going to be good."

"Or, as we call it, routine." As we raced along to the last door another thought occurred to me. "Fancy, are there beetles like the Goldens on the outside, in the snow?"

"Yes. They glow—"

"Snow white, yeah, we saw them. So, does that mean we were walking on them or something?"

"No. They live several feet under the snowline. Their light is just very strong. We don't have to feed them—they subsist on the snow itself. And we don't interact with them very much—they are not as bound to us as the Goldens are."

"How often does it snow around here?" Christopher asked as we reached the intersection that would take us to the last door.

"Snow? Do you mean as an active thing?" She sounded deeply confused.

"Yeah, snow falls from the sky. It's like super-thick water."

"That does not happen here. The snow is always here, and only here, in our part of the world."

Would have commented about how freaking weird that was, but by now I had a list of the weird going on with this planet so merely added this fact to it and moved on.

Besides, we were at the last door and, true to expectations, it wasn't undisturbed. It was, in point of fact, open.

CHAPTER 51

THANKFULLY, what was in the doorway wasn't a snaki-pede or twenty. What was in the doorway were beings I really hadn't been prepared to see.

"James!" Flung myself at Reader. Which probably would have been better if we hadn't still been going at the Flash hyperspeed level when I'd let go of Christopher's hand.

I hit Reader hard, and we slammed into the other people with him, meaning I took him, Tim, Tito, Brian, and Kevin to the ground. Go me. If we were starring in the WWE.

This wasn't so bad, except that they weren't alone. They were with a lot of Lecanora, most of whom looked a hell of a lot like wolverines, with heavy emphasis on the claws and teeth part of wolverines. And all of them had sharp spears and now all those spears were pointed right at me and moving.

Christopher kept his head, thankfully, so I kept mine. He let go of Fancy, grabbed me, and moved us back to Fancy, who was far enough away that they'd have to throw the spears to hit us. Conveniently for the guys I'd knocked to the ground, they'd sort of connected, so Christopher had moved them away at the same time he'd moved me.

"Stop!" Reader shouted, as said spears hit the ground where we'd all been and the six of us untangled in a decidedly ungodlike and very undignified way. "These are our friends!" The Lecanora with the spears froze.

"What the hell are you guys doing breaking into Haven? Oh, and it's great to see you and I'm so glad you're all okay. And all that."

"Long story," Tim said. "Starts with James and me landing in the blue part of this world, which is—"

"All water like Venice, we know."

He shot me a dirty look. "We got help," he nodded toward a couple of Lecanora in the back, who looked like they were part of King Benny's original Otter Tribe but the big, muscular side of it, "and headed toward part of this world that's all black. The ground, I mean."

"Which is where we were," Tito indicated himself, Brian, and Kevin. "It's all volcanic rock. And I mean all."

"And when we say black, we mean black, including all the foliage," Brian added. "Don't forget that. Different shades of black, but all black."

"As are most of the residents," Kevin added. He grinned. "I fit right in."

"Good to see everyone's keeping their senses of humor intact. We're a tad more stressed inside, just so you know."

"I'm a little more stressed than I seem," Brian said. "Where's Serene?"

"Safe."

Brian relaxed a bit and I took a closer look at the wolverines. Yep, they were all black, or black with white stripes, which wasn't common for Earth wolverines, but as we'd been noting for quite a while now, we weren't in Kansas anymore. The striped ones looked like Skunky, only a lot more muscular. They were all clearly warriors. Now probably wasn't the time to share that I was Wolverine With Boobs. They probably wouldn't get the reference and take offense at the same time.

"As Shealla has asked," Fancy said imperiously, "what were you doing sneaking into Haven?"

"Saving you," Tito said. He pointed through the open door behind the otters. It was still night outside, but the Snow Globe Beetles, or whatever they were really called here, were still providing soft, white, glowy light. Noted that there was blood and such on the ground.

Zipped outside to see five snakipedes dead on the ground. There was also a dead humanoid body with the snakipede bodies—and it looked like an Amazon. An Amazon with a lot of spear holes in her, but an Amazon nonetheless. I checked her eyes—they were all black.

I closed her eyelids. No idea why, just seemed like the

decent thing to do, despite the fact that she'd been trying to kill me and everyone else inside.

Took a look around. Saw no more snakipedes about. Also saw no signs of other Lecanora, other Amazonian Ancients, or anything else, really. Did see what looked like a large city off in the distance, with some impressive turrets and such. The lighting looked normal—torches and fires or something, but what I'd expect to see in a Bronze Age world, and unlike anything else I'd seen here so far. Figured this was the king's palace, aka where we'd be raiding shortly. But not right now.

As I looked up to check the air again, just in case some snakipedes were lurking about, waiting to smell prey, I spotted something very high in the sky—flickering lights. Possibly. It was hard to see clearly, but as my vision adjusted for what and where I was looking, realized that what I'd taken to be part of the night, so to speak, was in fact a huge mountain. Took a guess and figured I was looking at the All Seeing Mountain.

As I stared, I was sure that there were weird lights and colors flickering at the very top of the mountain. Really wanted to go find out what the hell was up there. However, it was dark, cold, and I wanted Jeff with me before we climbed every mountain or stormed the castle.

Chose discretion over valor and zipped right back inside and to the others. "Aha, so Fancy and Christopher, our worry was correct. There was another Amazonian Ancient trying to let the Horrors in. So, good job our team."

"Did I hear that right?" Reader asked. "Never mind, I'm sure I did. Care to tell us what's going on? Just so we're on the same page and all that."

"Sure, once we've okayed your entry into Fancy Corzine's domain and you've introduced us to your new friends."

"These are the Lecanora," Reader started.

Put up my hand. "We're extremely far ahead of you. There are Lecanora all over this continent—world, for them. They all resemble Earth mustelidae of all kinds, so don't think you're seeing the only three or four clan representatives here, we have them all—otters, beavers, skunks, woodchucks, ferrets, minks, weasels, and more." Looked at the wolverines. Decided not to call that one out just now.

"There are also those snakipedes which they call Horrors that you killed. We've already killed more of them, by the way, before you all get cocky. There are also a plethora of other sentient creatures here, some of whom are helping us. And this planet is extremely colorful and, for us, even more trippy."

"Okay," Tim said, "you catch us up and we'll fill in the blanks that relate to how we got here in time to save your butts."

"Trust me, butts have been being saved all over the place. You don't own the franchise on butt saving on Planet Colorful, Megalomaniac Lad, so don't get uppity."

"Look, we need to close this door and get back to the others," Christopher pointed out, sharing Patented Glare #3 with all of us. And just when I thought Planet Colorful was being good for him.

"If you would do so," Fancy said to him, with a huge amount of respect in her voice that hadn't been there before. I didn't get the impression she was more impressed with us than she'd been five minutes ago, meaning she was requesting this for a reason.

Christopher nodded, walked over, and pulled the door shut with one hand. The Black Wolverines all watched him do this and, to a furry face, they looked impressed. So, Fancy had wanted to show off that she had someone extremely strong—who didn't necessarily look extremely strong—on her side. Then Fancy secured the door just as she had with the other when we'd come into Haven.

All during this time, however, Fancy and the Lecanora I took to be in charge of the Black Wolverine Clan were eyeing each other. Wasn't sure if this was good or bad. He was definitely the biggest and most muscular of the bunch, and, based on where he was standing—in front of all the others, even though only just—had to figure he was the leader.

"Zanell," she said finally. "I see you're fit as ever."

"Corzine." He nodded somewhat stiffly. "You seem well."

There was something about how they were talking and acting. Something hugely familiar to anyone who'd ever had a romantic relationship that had experienced some kind of big fight and unhappy breakup.

"Oh wow, you two used to be an item? Super. Did you

break up because one of you is an evil madman or woman, or because one of you couldn't handle the fact that the other was just as strong a leader and warrior?"

They both stared at me, jaws open. "How . . . ?" Zanell started.

"She's Shealla," Christopher snapped. Clearly he was tired of pussyfooting around.

The Black Wolverines and their otter pals all snapped back, but to attention. Rigid attention. I received a group bow, which included Zanell.

"Thank you. This is Binalla." I indicated Christopher. Hoped like hell the other four guys would share their names with us sooner as opposed to later, and really and truly prayed those names didn't correspond to any we were already using.

"The Nihalani said we would find more of their number in the Dark Lands," one of the otters said. "And this was true."

"And the Nihalani then said we would find more of the Gods here," Zanell said solemnly. "And we see that this is true as well."

"Super. Leoalla and Alcalla are with a spy and possible though unlikely traitors. The Muses of Knowledge and the Winalla are still in a village with most of the Outcast clan, and some other sentient beings who are not Lecanora. So Brian, you can relax, Serene is with the other Muses, Claudia and Lorraine."

At the word "outcast," all the Black Wolverines jerked. "You have the castoffs here?" Zanell asked.

I moved deliberately and put myself between him and Fancy, and therefore him and the entrance into Haven. "Yes. And if you're here to hurt any of them, then I'm going to have to show you just how nasty the Gods can fight when we're protecting our people."

CHAPTER 52

ZANELL LOCKED EYES WITH ME. Then pointedly stepped back, cast his gaze down, knelt down on one knee, and put his spear at my feet.

"The Nihalani said that the other Gods were worthy. We have heard of Shealla's wrath, and we will never do anything to bring it upon ourselves."

"Wise choice," I said to Zanell. Looked over my shoulder. "I have a wrath reputation?" I asked Fancy.

Who shrugged. "Women of power should not be crossed lightly."

"Ah, so he had an issue sharing the dominance with you, check. Males can learn, by the way. Not all of them, but more than you'd think."

She grinned. "Nothing is hidden from Shealla."

"Not a damn thing, supposedly, anyway." Turned back to Zanell, who was still kneeling. "If you're not here to raid Haven or to try to harm the Outcast Clan, then you can stand up and take your weapon back. And if this is a test where I'm supposed to take it away from you, trust me, I can."

He looked up at me. "Normally for a boast such as that proof is required."

He reached for his spear. I picked it up at hyperspeed and put the point at his throat before his paw was even near the ground. He froze. Wisely.

"I hope for your sake that you're willing to call this proof, Zanell. 'Cause I think, if you really worked at the old 'I'm sorry I treated you as a lesser person than myself and didn't accept that you are a strong leader and an exceptional warrior' speech, Fancy might consider taking you back. And, so far, I'm quite fond of her, and not nearly as fond of you."

He stood up slowly. I kept the point of his spear at his throat the whole way. "The Nihalani did not lie."

"I'm happy to prove my Godhood, too," Christopher said. "Because this is a delay we really can't afford. Even Gods like to sleep."

True enough, and I hadn't had any. Had to assume no one in the village was sleeping anymore, and Jeff, Chuckie, and the others hadn't had enough rest, either. I pulled the spear back, then tossed it to Zanell.

He caught it and smiled at me. Then he spun it and slammed the butt of the spear onto the ground next to him. "You have our word, Shealla—we are here to assist you and the rest of the Gods, not to harm any others, let alone those who were wrongly cast out of their clans."

Nice to know he was on the side of Team Outcast. Really wanted to hear some music all of a sudden. OutKast's "Hey Ya!" would kind of fit with the mood. At least my mood. Figured now wasn't the time to not be paying full attention to everyone else, and chose instead to turn to Fancy. "Your thoughts?"

"Zanell keeps his word." She stood up even straighter. "And I keep mine." With that she spun and stalked off down the trail.

"Wow, dude, you really pissed her off, didn't you?"

Zanell sighed. "Yes, Shealla, I did."

"We need to move fast," Christopher said. "You grab Fancy and I'll have everyone else link up. Heading back to Jeff or the village?"

"You take them to the village, I'll go to Jeff. The Poofs should keep Usha under control."

"We can hope. If you're not back in the village within fifteen minutes, though, I'll come check on you guys."

"Sounds wise." I trotted off and caught up with Fancy. Took her paw in mine and we took off at my version of hyperspeed.

"This seems . . . slower," she said, as I felt people go by us. Normally you couldn't notice an A-C zipping around you. So either Christopher was tired, or there were just so many bodies he was dragging along so close to us that I sensed them. Figured it could very well be both.

"It is. Binalla goes a lot faster than any of the rest of us can. So, can we trust Zanell?"

"Yes. You were correct—he and I were . . . involved. But he could not accept that I would continue to rule and protect my clan, even if we were to join as mates."

"Think he's come around to a different way of thinking?"

"We'll find out, I suppose. But if you and Binalla were serious about wanting to put me on the throne, Zanell may object in a very strong manner."

"And then again, he may not. Guess we'll find out," I said as we turned down the path to get back to Jeff.

We hadn't been gone all that long, but we'd been gone long enough for Jeff and Chuckie to have started interrogating the prisoner. Had no idea if they'd managed to get anything out of her, but since Jeff could read her emotions, at least we had a hope of it.

And it was clear that they'd been trying. Jeff and Chuckie both were inside the Poof Circle, the Poofs were still Large and In Charge, and the five Lecanora potential traitors were still cowering between Bruno and Ginger and pleading with King Benny.

Got the distinct feeling that Chuckie had been using some of the nastier C.I.A. techniques, because the Lecanora were still crying and Usha looked a little worse for wear. Apparently the Ancients didn't regenerate like the rest of those I'd met from this solar system.

Wondered if any of the natives on this planet had faster regeneration. Hadn't really had time to see if they had more than one heart, or, in the case of the katyhoppers, if they even had a heart or if something else powered their internal engine. And thankfully we hadn't had anyone hurt that I knew of, so we hadn't had a live field test.

Jeff and Chuckie looked relieved to see us but also worried. "You help King Benny handle his people," I told Fancy. "See if you believe they're innocent, and, if so, try to calm them down."

"Calming them either way seems the right course," she said, as she left me and went to the other Lecanora. She gave Ginger a pet and stroked Bruno's head.

"Where's Christopher?" Jeff asked me by way of hello, as he left the Poof Circle to come over to me.

"Nice to see you, too. He's fine. Four of the doors were secure. We found the, ah, Nihalani at the last one we checked. They came with what I'm calling the Black Wolverine Clan and a couple of guys who look like they were at least originally part of King Benny's first clan. Christopher took James, Tim, Tito, Brian, and Kevin, along with all the Black Wolverines, back to the village. Fancy and I came here to get you all and get everyone back to the village, too."

"Good." Jeff now looked more relieved.

Pulled him away from the others, though not so far that we couldn't see them all clearly, and got a hug, which was nice. "Could you not feel me or Christopher when we were gone? We couldn't read each other's minds, so we think we are or were beyond the katyhopper's range."

"I've really had to concentrate on her," he jerked his head toward Usha. "She's not trained all that well, especially against a proficient C.I.A. operative and an empath, but she's got so many emotions roiling around in there it's honestly hard to differentiate. Chuck doesn't think it's a technique, by the way—he just thinks she's emotionally unstable, possibly from having to pretend to be a Lecanora male for so long."

"Is the Empire she's working with the Z'porrah like I guessed?"

"Yeah, we've done verification. There's more going on, though. We haven't gotten it out of her, but she sincerely believes she's one agent out of many and she also sincerely believes that there's a world of hurt coming. What exactly is coming, though, we haven't gotten. Chuck thinks she may not actually know, but we aren't sure yet."

"How *is* Chuckie?" Had to ask because he really looked seriously pissed.

"Ready to use her as a punching bag. And I'm half-tempted to let him."

Thought about this. Jeff didn't normally advocate allowing one of us to just attack a prisoner. However, he cared a lot more about Chuckie than he did Usha's well-being. "She isn't the right stand-in for Cliff. Trust me, if we need to allow him to let loose, I have a great target in mind."

"The so-called king, yeah." He sighed. "We all need sleep. Badly, by now. But I don't know what we can do with her here. I have no idea where you found those handcuffs, but she's spent the entire time you've been gone working to get loose from them. I can guarantee that she's going to succeed somewhere in the next few hours, if not sooner."

"We could just kill her. Or let the Poofs eat her. Same thing, really."

Jeff stared at me. "Chuck said the same thing."

"Mom's training, most likely. Not that my mother regularly advocates murdering people in cold blood or anything, but Usha's a dangerous liability. We have no way of containing her securely and we also have no one to negotiate her return with."

"Why don't we?" Jeff asked. "Someone put her in place. She firmly believes she has superiors—this is not someone acting alone."

Stared at him as he motioned for Chuckie to come over and join us. "Wow. You know, you're right. I keep on thinking it was LaRue who stationed her here, and even if it was, she might care about Usha." Hugged Chuckie as he reached us, then leaned back against Jeff.

Caught Chuckie up on who we'd found, what their God Name was, and everything else. Jeff reiterated that killing Usha might not be our best choice.

"LaRue might care about her, Kitty's right," Chuckie said when we finished. "And by the way, most of the Lecanora in the Blue part that Christopher and I saw were otters. Not all, but most."

"Good to know where King Benny's probably originally from. But back to the big elephant in our room. More than LaRue potentially knowing her—Usha is an Ancient but she's working for the Z'porrah. Meaning that LaRue's not the only traitor the Ancients have been blessed with over the years."

"Meaning the Ancients are still alive as a race," Chuckie said. "We've been working under the assumption that their race died out, but events are showing that not to be the case. The Z'porrah are direct enemies of the Ancients, and they're still going strong, as we learned all too well. That the Z'porrah are working in secret in this solar system indicates that their enemy—who is presumably on our side, in no small part because we're their 'creations'—is still very much alive and active."

"That's true. LaRue came to Earth after the other, for us original, Ancient ship had crash-landed. We now have proof that they have Faster Than Light travel, meaning she didn't leave hundreds of years earlier—she left long enough ago that communications between the Ancient home world and the ship that crash-landed on Earth crossed in transit, but otherwise, they're still around and kicking. Us, mostly."

Jeff shook his head. "The Ancients are at least helping both our solar systems, not trying to destroy them."

"But it explains why the Free Women look like they do," Chuckie said. "Their original strains mixed with Ancients, and clearly the Ancient blood is the strongest."

"Genetics rule. But the eyes are telling—I've never seen a Free Woman with all-black eyes, and since I've now seen two Amazonian Agents with them, I'm going to take a leap of faith and say that the Ancients have eyes like that." Meaning LaRue's eyes were all black in reality.

"Meaning LaRue's eyes are all black when she's not shapeshifted," Chuckie said, clearly reading my mind again.

Knew without asking that Christopher and a katyhopper were nearby. So I was unsurprised to see Christopher and Saffron round the corner. "I gave you fifteen minutes," Christopher said as they reached us. "Everything okay?"

While Jeff and Chuckie shared our latest thoughts with Christopher, I sidled over to Saffron. "Any chance you can mind read Usha over there and see what she knows?"

Saffron waved her antennae. Then she shuddered, and waved them again. Destruction was coming. Destruction for all of us, the planet, and possibly the entire solar system.

And it was coming soon.

CHAPTER 53

MOTIONED THE GUYS OVER. "Um, Saffron says that things are dire."

She waved her antennae again. Time was indeed of the essence, and she felt we needed to hurry up, because soon was going to come faster than we wanted. On the plus side, Saffron felt we had time to sleep, regroup, and possibly even raid the castle and visit the All Seeing Mountain. So soon was, apparently, a relative term.

"Ah. However, I guess, we still have time to do all the things we'd like to do here, like taking in the sights and taking over the castle." Managed not to ask why she felt this was helpful information, then reminded myself that it was her world and people who were in danger.

"I realize the katyhoppers, just like everyone else, are in danger, but how does this help us?" Chuckie asked, reading my mind again. Yep, we had a katyhopper nearby.

Saffron waved her antennae again. Got the impression she'd just heaved a huge katyhopper sigh.

"Ah, gotcha. I asked Saffron to read Usha's mind. She was confirming what you guys got out of Usha. But Usha doesn't know the whole plan. However, she's been activated—she was stationed in the castle, working as one of the King's Guard. And the king is who activated her to try to find and raid Haven."

"So that confirms that the king is a puppet for the Z'porrah, or whoever else is against the freedom of this planet," Chuckie said. "Honestly, the big question is why? Why is this planet important to anyone? Especially since no one else seems to have discovered the special abilities the katy-hoppers and strautruch possess. And since there's no min-ing, it seems unlikely that anyone's figured out that the core of this world is valuable, either."

"Which leads to my question—do we storm the castle first, or do we go to the top of the All Seeing Mountain as our next stop?"

"Mountain," Jeff said. "It's the one place none of us have been, even fleetingly. Unless James or the others have been."

Christopher shook his head. "They haven't. And they haven't seen Jamie or Paul, either. Or Abigail, Rahmi, or Rhee."

"So they're either in the Greenland area, on the top of the mountain, or they're not on this planet." Didn't know what I wanted to wish for, other than having Jamie back in our arms right this moment, which I knew wasn't going to happen.

Tried not to panic about her, but I was tired, and the panic started to come anyway. Jeff's hand was on the back of my neck, gently massaging, in a flash. "It'll be fine, baby," he said quietly. "We'll find her and she'll be fine."

"Jamie has ACE inside her," Chuckie reminded me. "ACE is allowed to protect himself, and therefore Jamie, and we all know he's not going to let anything happen to Paul, either."

"The best thing we can do for all of them is get some rest, get some food, and then get going," Christopher said. Rightly. "I realize we ate already, but I've expended a lot of energy and the guys, excuse me, *Nihalani* are starving, and the rest of you look like you could use another meal, too."

"Yes, but we're back to the issue of what we do with Usha, though," I pointed out. "Jeff seems to be against kill-ing her, and using her as a bargaining chip of some kind does make sense."

"They don't have prisons or anything like them here," Christopher said. "I asked when I took the others back to the village."

"This world is so unlike ours, or the others in this system. I don't get it. The moment you look closely, nothing seems normal. Oh, and Christopher, did you notice that the sound of water anywhere we went wasn't too loud?"

He nodded. "Yeah. I just sort of added it to the list of things that are strange about this planet, though."

Jeff looked around, and moved the five of us away from the others so there was no way they would hear us. "Saffron, I'm actually sure that your people already know or suspect this. But in case you don't, this is just a guess of mine. However, based on everything we're seeing, I think this world was specifically created, versus evolving like the rest of the populated planets we know about have."

Saffron waved her antennae. "She agrees. The Matriarchs suspect this, but haven't been able to prove it. The general belief, by the way, is that the Father of the Gods created this world in his image."

"So just like our creation stories on Earth," Chuckie said.

I nodded, but I was still thinking about what I'd said. I knew Algar had a vested interest in this planet. That he was the Father of the Gods was a safe bet, especially because he'd been hanging out on Alpha Four for millennia, cleaning the Royal Family's laundry and such and providing them with whatever their version of Coca-Cola was at the drop of a hat, which had to have gotten dull.

Really wanted a Coke badly now. Pushed the desire to ask my purse for one aside and went back to thinking.

So he sees a planet in the solar system. A planet with a core that's hugely valuable all over the galaxy, meaning a planet ripe for mining and destruction—which would be likely to destroy all the life on said planet.

And a planet whose entire core was made up of valuable elements that had no indigenous life on it that could fight back or plead their case was a planet that was probably going to end up a husk or destroyed. The results of which could negatively affect the entire solar system's orbits and such, not to mention giving whoever was mining the place all the destructive materials they'd ever need to wipe everyone else and themselves out of existence.

Just like Mephistopheles had.

Normally, though, valuable core or not, it's not a big deal—there's life on the planet, after all. In some instances that wouldn't be the case. But the beings in this solar system who are in charge are also being influenced by Algar, meaning they're likely to leave this planet and its people alone. *If* those people are showing clear signs of sentience.

Maybe the life-forms on this planet aren't progressing like the others, though. Maybe there's no progression that's possible for them or the planet in reality. Maybe the core of the world makes normal evolution impossible for some reason, or taints the soil in some way, so that the world would never be any place where sentient life could blossom and evolve up the brain food chain.

But Algar knows how to fix all that. Sure it's a risk, but there are so many populated planets in this system, who's going to notice one more? He's bored, he's not supposed to interfere—based on his own rules, versus the Black Hole Universe People's rules—but is it really interference? Not if he does it *fairly*. Plus, this could be how he's planning to make up for allowing Mephistopheles to destroy multiple worlds and billions of lives—by not allowing that to be repeated in this solar system.

Ergo to be *fair*, he uplifts every single creature on the planet, meaning all of them now will have free will. Some will evolve past this initial uplift and some won't, but that's okay because it's a fair fight at the start.

He creates a special continent for them, or alters the makeup of the continent they're on. He makes special places on that continent for them, too. For whatever reason, he wants the continent to be strangely set up, but he can swing that as well by making this planet conform and look just enough like some planets near the galactic core, at least superficially, that seeing one out here won't cause too much speculation from the various superconciousnesses and Black Hole Universe People who might notice. And he seeds each place with something special in some way. Some good things, some bad things, maybe. Areas better to live in—like Haven and the Purple Lands—along with others that aren't as well set up initially.

He has an underground area set up that powers the planet, so that all the special extras he's added in, like major climate control and muffling the sound of water, will run safely and effectively forever. Warp tunnels are added so that he, or his agents, can travel and survive in the world quickly and without necessarily being spotted. Or else they're there to help power the world or some such and the tunnel effect is just a happy benefit.

After all, Haven might not be the only underground

country here, or it might be. He can see how they do living underground versus how they do living on volcanic rock or literally on water.

He affects the world itself so that it gives off no obvious clues that it's different and valuable, in large part by affecting the world's gravity. Meaning the orbs are probably powering that as well, or the warp tunnels are, or both. Presumably the spiral worlds have different aspects to them than "normal" worlds, so he can do his thing and inquiring minds will ignore Beta Eight, seeing it as just another planet with intelligent life in an already crowded solar system.

And then Algar watches and waits to see what happens on the Free Will World.

That nothing untoward had really happened for a long time was indicated by the fact that no one in the Alpha Centauri solar system had paid attention to this planet beyond a cursory look. They'd decided the Lecanora were the dominant species, based on numbers and their uplift having taken them the Bipedal Way that the rest of the spacefaring planets had gone. Their Bronze Age level meant the planet would be left alone.

Only it wasn't being left alone now.

The Ancients and the Z'porrah couldn't resist meddling in the affairs of lesser beings, and Algar and the rest of the Black Hole Universe People were as far above the Ancients and Z'porrah as those were above us.

"I know that look," Chuckie said. "What are you thinking?"

Proof, as if I'd needed it, that Algar had my mind locked when I was thinking about him. But everyone was looking at me, meaning I had to say something. "I'm thinking that Jeff's right. I think the Father of the Gods is a real person, just as we are, and I think he's the one who truly made this world the way it is."

"You think he's who pulled all of us out here?" Jeff asked.

"No. I think he's the one who ensured that we all landed where we did. Specifically where we did." Meaning that, wherever Jamie and the others were, Algar had put them there on purpose. And I had to trust that Algar wasn't going to put my little girl in extreme danger any more than ACE would.

"So you agree with Jeff, that this world was far more created than ours?" Christopher asked.

"Yeah, I think Jeff's nailed it—this place is manmade, so to speak. There's too much that's unnatural for a planet. Sure, the girls think spirals like this exist elsewhere, but they have to be rare and I'd just bet that on those worlds it works far more randomly than here—no clear-cut divisions, more random borders, and so forth. This world is too . . . neat. Haven is too perfect—like it's climate and sound controlled. That doesn't happen in nature. But it can happen in an artificially created place."

Chuckie nodded. "Yes, it can. And this makes Jeff's choice even more correct—something's going on up at the top of that mountain, and we need to know what it is before we take on a ruling monarch."

"Right. But we have a dangerous prisoner. What are we going to do with her?"

Saffron waved her antennae. I raised my eyebrow. She waved some more. I gave in.

"Huh. Okay. Um, well, that's different."

CHAPTER 54

"WHAT'S DIFFERENT?" Chuckie asked.

"Saffron seems to think that if she covers Usha with her butt juices it'll work just like we've tied her up from head to toe and Usha won't be able to break free. And before you all ask, yes, Usha will still be able to breathe."

"Then let's do it," Jeff said. "I'll carry her if it works."

"Glad Saffron's on our side," Christopher said, speaking for all of us. Saffron gave him a gentle shove with her front legs, while explaining that this was the katyhopper version of a gentle punch to the arm between friends. Christopher grinned and nudged her back.

Then she trotted over to Usha, who started the whole rend and destroy stuff again. She reminded me a lot of Kyrellis but without the style. Clearly the Free Women had more going on in terms of trash talking than the Ancients. Go evolution.

I joined Saffron. "Usha, stop your blah, blah, blah. Trust me, right now, you want your mouth closed."

"Why?" she asked, as I hauled her to her feet.

"We're going to contain but not kill you. Consider yourself lucky."

"No prison can contain me—" she started. Right when Saffron started spraying. Had the feeling Saffron wanted to shut Usha up as much as the rest of us did.

I leaped out of the way, but Saffron had great aim, which was particularly impressive since she couldn't see where she was spraying. Usha slammed her mouth shut just in time, at least so far as I could tell.

Saffron walked around Usha, spraying as she went. She never missed and didn't hit anyone else. Noted that her spray was far more streamlined than when she and the others had been spraying out a protective wall back at the cavern.

"Amazing," Jeff said when she was done. "When will Usha, ah, be dry enough to pick up?"

Saffron waved antenna. She shared the drying time and the fact that this was something katyhopper youngsters did for fun—sprayed each other to learn how to better control their most important protective asset.

"Give it about a minute, Jeff. And Saffron says it was no big, though I'm still hella impressed over here."

Got the gentle shove from Saffron, which I returned. While we waited our requisite minute I had the Poofs go back to small and into my purse. Bruno flew over to Saffron and perched on her back, which she seemed amenable to.

Then Jeff heaved Usha over his shoulder. Her body wasn't able to bend, and I tapped on the outside. It was as if she was cocooned in fiberglass. Worked for me.

"Need help?" Chuckie asked.

Jeff nodded. "Only because it's awkward with her being rigid."

Chuckie took Frozen Usha's feet and Jeff had her head and shoulders, then they gave hyperspeed a try. It worked, and they zipped off, with an admonition for the rest of us to hurry it up. King Benny asked Binalla to help him handle the five other Lecanora, so Christopher had them link paws, grabbed them and Saffron, who still had Bruno with her, and followed after the others.

"What do you think, traitors or fools?" I asked Fancy as I picked Ginger up and held her with her front paws wrapped around my neck. Took hold of Fancy's paw and she and I brought up the rear at the slow version of hyperspeed. I didn't want to take an hour or more to get back to the village, but I did want to talk to her, woman to woman.

"Honestly, foolish more than fools. I think they were wooed with the idea that they would move up in the clan and Musgraff's regard if they brought in the so-called castouts. Usha has not impressed any of you, but she was convincing for those who do not have the Gods' wisdom."

"Or the wisdom that comes with leadership."

"Exactly." Fancy sighed. "If all goes as you plan, perhaps Musgraff should be who you put onto the throne."

"Are you saying that from a lack of desire to be a monarch, the worry about having to leave Haven or leave your people here in Haven without your immediate leadership, or are you worried that the people on this world won't listen to you because you're a female?"

She was quiet as we waited for her answer. "A little of all of those," she said finally.

"The katyhoppers come from a matriarchal society. They won't have an issue with a female on the Lecanora throne."

Fancy nodded. "I see how you counsel with them. You hold them in high regard. Perhaps one of them should rule."

I was impressed by the insight. "I would agree. However, the Lecanora have the highest population on the planet, meaning that they need to be ruled by someone they can relate to and respect."

She shook her head. "We are already ruled by someone we cannot relate to and whom most of us cannot respect. The katyhoppers are actually from our world."

"I think whoever does end up ruling, they're going to need to create alliances with the katyhoppers and the strautruch as well. And any other sentient groups we may not have met yet." After all, there were a variety of sections we hadn't hit—for all I knew there were brilliant lava monsters in the Black section and talking dolphins in the Blue one. At this point, had to figure that I wasn't going to be surprised by anything else Planet Colorful tossed at me.

"As you say, Shealla. I will do what the Gods advise."

"Only as long as you feel our counsel is wise and good. I don't care who it is, even us—no one should force you or your people to do something evil or wrong, not in the name of the Gods, nationality, or whatever."

"And it is because you say that, Shealla, that I know you are a true God." She squeezed my hand. "I thank you, you and the other Gods, for gracing us with your presence."

Felt embarrassed and more than a little like a charlatan. "Let's just get things taken care of first, before we go for the ticker tape parade."

"I don't understand you, Shealla."

"So few ever do, Fancy. So few ever do."

We reached the village to find everyone else having a

quick meal. The villagers were reeling from the news that their village leader had been murdered and that they'd been listening to an imposter for a good couple of years.

Fancy got things under control, and the presence of the Black Wolverines helped, too, though it was clear they made most of the villagers nervous. However, they were eating and socializing, particularly the otters with King Benny and the striped gang with Skunky. Got the strong impression that the otters in particular were King Benny's close relatives, and the striped ones seemed awfully close to Skunky, too.

While we ate, guarding arrangements were made, mostly by my assigning the Poofs, Bruno, Ginger, and Wilbur to guard Usha's body. The katyhoppers and strautruch offered to help guard as well, and there were enough of them that we felt they could sleep in shifts and also warn us if anyone else identified as an Amazonian Ancient Assassin. We left all of them in the group sleeping area we'd been assigned to by Usha when she was pretending to be Under-Clan Leader Karason.

The Black Wolverines were spread out within a variety of homes, just as the Gypsy Clan was. Hopefully this would mean they all made friends, rather than earn the enmity of everyone in this village.

Patrina was praised for her being the one to alert me that something was wrong. Her parents seemed dazed by all the kudos she and they were getting. Had the strong suspicion that Patrina's family were on the more destitute side of the outcast group. Made a mental note to request that everyone get an equal portion of whatever lands they were going to be assigned in Haven. But that was something for later, once we knew if we were going to actually overthrow a king successfully or not.

Since we now knew Karason was dead, and since he also had a large home to match his rank, as soon as our newest arrivals were brought up to speed on everything we'd done, learned, and guessed, we Gods split up into different rooms in order to get some sleep. The four couples each got a small room, with the rest of the guys in the next largest room in the home. Most of these rooms weren't sleeping rooms, but the other Lecanora brought in more of the comfy floor bedding and we all figured out how to make do.

It was nice to be alone with Jeff in a room, but the reality of this situation was that I'd never managed to be quiet when we were having sex, and as much as I wanted to do the deed, I didn't think it would help our God Images to have me howling like an ocellar in heat.

Jeff picked it up of course. He grinned and pulled me to him. "I think we can be quiet, baby."

"So far, my track record would indicate that you're a crazy optimist on that one. And trust me, there's no sound-proofing around here."

"Unless you're water. And while I'd love to suggest a romantic swim, these people use the river for far too many things for us to fool around there."

"The water's probably cold, too. Then again, since its sound is muffled, we should see if it's cold or not. But later. Like after we've had some sexless sleep later." Tried to keep the frustrated disappointment out of my tone, but I knew I didn't succeed because Jeff's grin got wider.

"We should have gone for it in those tunnels," he said with a laugh, as he nuzzled my neck. "We could make it a game . . . can you stay quiet and can I make you happy that you're staying quiet."

"Mmmm . . . ah . . . yeah . . ." Jeff's lips and tongue were on one of the areas in my neck that made me squirm in all the good ways.

He ran his mouth up to my ear. "I say we try it," he whispered. "And I also say you're going to obey me and do exactly what I say, when I say it." He bit my earlobe gently. "And the first rule is that you have to be quiet—not silent, but quiet. Or else I'll stop doing all the things you like."

He ran his tongue along part of my jaw and then back to my neck. I wanted to wail.

"You . . . are totally . . . evil," I managed to gasp out. But quietly.

Felt him smile against my neck. "You have no idea, baby. But you're about to find out."

CHAPTER 55

WE GOT OUT OF our clothes quickly and without fanfare. Sexy undressing was fun, but when you could be interrupted for any number of reasons—attack, small children coming in, and so on—you learned to save the time-consuming extras for when you were sure you had the time.

Decided a little ambiance wouldn't hurt, though, so I pulled out my iPod and speakers, selected one of my Sexy Times playlists, turned the volume down low, and hit play. Apparently Algar was all over us having sexy times right now, because the first song that came on was actually on the playlist, "Whole Lotta Love" by Smash Mouth.

Then Jeff pulled me down onto the bedding and we got laser focused.

He started by kissing me, though as he did so, he took my wrists in his hands and put them above my head, while his lower body pinned mine. I moaned into his mouth, and he deepened our kiss and ground against me. My hips started bucking and I was close to yowling already. Hey, not my fault the man was the God of Kissing.

However, he ended our kiss and nuzzled my ear again. "You have to stay quiet, or I'm going to stop doing whatever it is I'm doing to you."

"Mean thing."

He chuckled. "Just wait."

He moved my hands down to my hips, and his mouth down to my breasts. While he sucked my nipples and stroked them with his tongue, I closed my mouth tightly and did my best to keep the moaning in my chest.

"Mmmm," Jeff said between my breasts, as he moved from one to the other, "I like it when you purr."

Would have replied, but decided to focus on the purring instead. It was a little difficult to keep it all inside, so to speak, but it was kind of fun, too, especially because I could tell that Jeff really did like it.

From day one he'd been able to bring me to orgasm at second base, and as he sucked harder, moving at hyperspeed from one breast to the other, he did it again. I managed not to yell, shout, or yowl, but it took serious effort. He nipped me as my orgasm was slowing down and I gasped and made a little moan.

"Too loud," he said against my skin, as his mouth trailed down over my stomach, stopping so he could run his tongue around my bellybutton. "I have to move on."

"You . . . do what you . . . have to," I managed to gasp out quietly.

But as the music changed to Shaggy's "Luv Me, Luv Me," he didn't stay there long—he kept my hands locked against my hips and his mouth locked between my legs.

Now it was a lot harder to purr instead of yowl, and I clamped my jaws together while Jeff ran his tongue over and inside of me, with the standard excellent assists from his teeth and lips. When he took me between his teeth and gently tugged I did manage to stay quiet as another orgasm hit—if we define quiet to mean quiet groaning instead of screaming.

Apparently Jeff felt I'd been quiet enough, because as Fleetwood Mac's "You Make Loving Fun" came on, he continued to keep it fun, well, fun for me certainly, by running his tongue all over me again, this time at hyperspeed, meaning that another climax hit me, fast and hard.

This time I gasped too loudly apparently, because Jeff took his mouth away from my happy place and put it back over my mouth. Couldn't complain, in part because he also finally slid inside me. Everything else was always great, and I loved it, but truly nothing compared to when he was fully inside me.

My hands he still had held by my hips, but my legs were free and I wrapped them around his back immediately, as Robert Palmer's "Bad Case of Loving You" hit our quiet airwaves and Jeff ended our kiss. So that he could gently bite my neck.

"This is the real test, baby," he said against my skin. "Can you purr, only, while I do this?"

"Ahhhh . . ." Gave up trying to reply. Because right now, my answer was bordering on "no" and I definitely didn't want Jeff to stop his slow, deep thrusts inside me, or to have him stop nibbling on one of my main erogenous zones.

Decided two could play at this and, as "Bed of Roses" by Bon Jovi came on, bit him between neck and shoulder, while I pressed my feet against his perfect thrusters, aka his butt, and ensured he kept on going without any slowing down. He growled against my neck. "Naughty Kitty. I like that."

I didn't reply, in part because biting him kept my mouth occupied and therefore me still on the side of quiet. Jeff let go of my wrists and wrapped his arms around me, while I did the same to him. Have no idea how he managed it, but he moved us from a prone position to upright, with him on his knees.

"Crazy Little Thing Called Love" by Queen came on, and Jeff bounced me to the beat. Pretty soon I was as ready as Freddy, and I squeezed my legs tightly around him as he took me over the edge and came along with me.

I opened my mouth and drew in breath, but Jeff covered my mouth with his again, and instead of screaming out loud, I screamed into his kiss, while he erupted into me and I crashed against him.

As our bodies slowed down, and Jeff ended our kiss, I was able to take another deep breath and let it out silently, while Vanessa Carlton sang about the "Afterglow" and Jeff lay us down again.

"You were amazing," he murmured against my hair. "And I'm proud of you for staying so quiet, too."

"Hard as it was, you definitely made it worth my while." Rolled onto my side so I could nuzzle the hair on his chest. "And speaking of amazing, takes one to know one."

He chuckled. "Always nice to be appreciated."

We stayed like that for a little while, just enjoying being naked and satisfied together. But as "We Close Our Eyes" by Oingo Boingo came on, we got dressed. Even putting the clothes we'd been in for days back on didn't ruin the afterglow, which was nice.

"You need to sleep on top of me?" Jeff asked.

"Tempting as that is, probably not a good idea, and it would be uncomfortable for you, wouldn't it?"

"Nah." He rolled me on top of him. "You were such a good girl, I think you deserve to sleep on top of me, not the ground."

Put my face into his neck. "Whatever you say, Leoalla."

Jeff laughed softly. "I say that I'm going to make you purr more often."

I'd have told him that I had no argument with that, but I fell asleep before I could.

Had no idea how long I'd been asleep when I woke up, but I felt like I'd had some rest, so figured it had to have been a few hours.

Jeff's arms were wrapped around me, and he was still asleep but was stirring too, meaning it was either time to get up or we were being attacked.

"Knock, knock," a familiar voice said. Jeff and I separated and sat up as Reader came into our room. "Wanted to get a minute alone with you two before we start everything else."

"Sure, James," Jeff said, as Reader sat down on the floor with us. "What's up?"

"I think I got a message from Paul."

CHAPTER 56

"REALLY? Did he say anything about Jamie?" Remembered that we were talking about Reader's husband. "And is Paul okay?"

Reader gave me a shot of the cover boy smile. "Paul's a grown man and Jamie's a little girl—it's okay that you're more worried about her than him. I'm more worried about my goddaughter and namesake than my husband, too, though not by much. However, I'm a little less worried than I was before. But I'm not sure that I should be."

"Mind explaining that?" Jeff asked as he yawned.

"Yeah. I was asleep, so this might just have been a dream. But I saw Paul, and he was with Jamie. But they weren't alone. I couldn't tell who was with them, though. Or where they were. But . . . I don't think they're on this planet. What I could see looked much more . . . technological than this planet."

"Did it look familiar?" I asked. "Like a room or a ship or a city?"

Reader shook his head. "I didn't get a lot. What I saw was fast, and what I got was more of a feeling. I felt like . . . I guess as if Paul was trying to tell me to hurry up. But it wasn't to hurry up to rescue him and Jamie. I didn't get any feelings like they were in danger."

"That's it?" Jeff asked.

Reader sighed. "It's lame, I know. That's why I only wanted to talk to you two about it."

Jeff and I hadn't turned my iPod off, and I focused on the current music suddenly—"The Winning Side" by Oingo Bo-

ingo was on. That song definitely wasn't on any of my Sexy
Times playlists. Meaning Algar was warning me, because
the lyrics were about war.

Thought about everything we'd been hearing from King
Benny's Gypsy Clan, the katyhoppers, and Fancy. "We need
to get up to the All Seeing Mountain, and we need to get
there fast."

"What are you thinking?" Jeff asked me.

"Every being with us right now that's a native of this
planet has seen ships in their solar space somehow, or is
following orders of someone who has. Maybe someone's
figured out that this planet has far more value than previously believed."

"Then why aren't they on the planet yet?" Jeff asked.

"Maybe they're waiting to attack and that's why Paul
wants me to hurry up," Reader suggested.

The music switched to Motörhead's "Civil War." Wanted
to tell Algar that I was aware that we were about to start a
civil war on this planet. Then I thought about it. "Um, I've
got a really bad feeling about this, guys. We're forgetting
that we were dragged over here without a by your leave and
us landing on this planet probably wasn't anyone's plan. So,
that means we had a different destination. What if Paul and
Jamie actually arrived at that destination?"

"Then we'd better hope there really are ships in space
around this planet," Jeff said dryly. "Or we're not going to
be able to get off and find our daughter."

Decided we were wasting time Paul, and therefore ACE,
felt we didn't have. A mindset Algar clearly agreed with,
too. Besides, seeing always tended to be believing. "Get everyone up," I said to Reader. "Fast. Food can be eaten on
the run. And I mean that literally. I want us all linking with
Christopher and getting up to the top of the mountain as
soon as possible."

"Do we still want Fancy and King Benny with us?" Jeff
asked.

"Yes. James, can your Black Wolverines stay here?
Someone nasty needs to be guarding Usha in case she
breaks out of her butt candy shell."

"Zanell won't want to stay. He came in part to make sure
that Fancy, as you call her, was okay. Plus if he's left behind
he'll lose face with his warriors. The rest can stay, and I'm

sure a lot of them want to. Some of the others are close relatives of some of the outcast Lecanora."

"Yeah, I could take the leap that the otters and the skunks were looking for their family members. Hope they're glad King Benny's in charge and that Skunky's his right paw man."

Reader chuckled. "Yes. Everyone was relieved to find the outcasts here in Haven, by the way. That helped solidify our Godhoods to the, ah, Black Wolverines. Don't tell them you're Wolverine With Boobs, by the way, girlfriend. They won't get it."

"Miles ahead of you on that one. But let's get moving. Chop, chop, time's a wastin'. And I think Paul sent you the 'hurry it up, man' dream because we're running out of it."

Gathered up our stuff. Put my speakers back into my purse, but I didn't drop the iPod back in. Instead I pulled out my earbuds, clipped my iPod to my jeans, and put the earbuds in.

"Really?" Jeff asked.

"Really. I need the tunes right now." Like Jeff wouldn't believe, because I couldn't tell him. "I have the sound down low, I can hear everyone and everything, trust me." My iPod was playing "Civil War" on repeat, though it was on low in terms of volume. Algar really wanted me to get a message on this one. The worry that my suspicion was right grew.

Jeff didn't look happy, but he didn't argue. We joined the others, and said that we wanted to get a move on. Fancy had passed the "looking for a new homeland" idea around, so the Gypsy Clan didn't object too much to King Benny going with us.

True to expectations, Zanell insisted on coming along. We let him, because it was easier to bring him along, and him joining us made many of the Gypsy Clan, and all of the Black Wolverines, feel happier, so that was one small one for the win column.

Katyhoppers and strautruch were coming with us, which was fine. Ginger and Wilbur wanted to come, too. Had the feeling they were worried that I was going to leave them and not come back. Felt totally guilty, because, ultimately, that was what was probably going to happen. After all, I'd had to leave Stripes behind in the other universe.

Jeff picked it up. "Bring them," he said gently. "We may

need them and that way you'll have more time together. And they obey you, so they won't cause problems."

Hugged him tightly. "I love you so much."

He grinned. "Always good to know."

Fancy' Ferrets, Skunky assisted by Nanda, and the Black Wolverines were put in charge of protecting everyone and keeping Usha quiet. But at the last minute, Chuckie changed his mind. "We need to bring her with us."

"Why?" Christopher asked. "She's captive here."

"Yes, but if she gets loose, no one here is safe." Chuckie rubbed the back of his neck. "I can't tell you why I know she needs to come with us, but I know she does."

"Sounds like one of Kitty's explanations," Tim said. "Meaning we should probably do it."

Jeff nodded. "Alcalla has his reasons." He'd said this because we had a very interested audience in every Lecanora within audible distance.

So, once Fancy had given the exit code to Chuckie—who, of course, could both visualize and memorize it immediately—Jeff and Chuckie got Usha and carried her like they had a few hours prior. I tapped on her shell again. "Seems less dense now."

Saffron waved antennae. Yes, it would be lessening due to her not applying another coat. So Chuckie's decision was definitely the right one. I wondered if he'd come up on it on his own or if ACE or Algar had shoved the suggestion in. Figured it was even odds for either. Or both.

The rest of us did the linkup thing, but because the road out wasn't all that wide and because the strautruch and katyhoppers were more awkward to bring along at hyperspeed, we linked up in groups, each A-C taking a couple of humans or Planet Colorful beings with them. The strautruch were the hardest—Christopher and the katyhoppers were already practiced at hyperspeeding together—but that was solved by the Poofs. The five Poofs who belonged to the flyboys jumped onto the Big Bird backs and none too gently suggested their owners join them. Lorraine, Claudia, and Serene took King Benny and Kevin, Zanell and Tito, and Tim and Brian, respectively.

Bruno took the lead, then Jeff and Chuckie, then the girls, with the strautruch following.

Put Reader between me and Fancy, she carried Ginger,

and I hefted Wilbur up under my arm. We brought up the rear, and I was glad for both hyperspeed and enhanced strength, because chochos weren't exactly tiny, and Wilbur definitely weighed more than Ginger.

"Sure you don't want me to carry your pig-dog?" Reader asked as we started off.

"Nope, I have this. At least for now."

Turned out that for now was a relative term. I had to stop about halfway and put Wilbur down. It was that or drop him.

Reader picked him up. "Whoa, he's been eating well, hasn't he?"

"Normal for chochos as far as I've seen in the limited time we've been here. But yeah, Wilbur's a big boy." Gave him a pet, which he loved.

I moved between Reader and Fancy, and the five of us started off again.

We reached the door.

It was open.

And no one was there.

CHAPTER 57

"WELL, this is different."

"How's that?" Reader asked as he put Wilbur down, while Fancy did the same with Ginger. "I mean, I ask because I have to assume you're thinking what I'm thinking, which is that we're in trouble. Again."

"Oh, I am. But there've been people at the other doors, either trying to open them or coming in. This is a first for no one being at the special door."

"Perhaps they did not wait for us," Fancy suggested.

"Possibly not." Pulled out my Glock. Safety was off, go me, Most Careless Gun Handler in the Galaxy. "Civil War" was still playing. Not sure what that meant for this situation, but figured caution was always the better part of avoiding getting my head blown off. "However, I'm not betting that way."

Reader pulled his gun, too. "Kitty, make sure the animals stay behind you and stay quiet."

"Wilbur, Ginger, you two stay with Fancy and protect her. Only help if Kitty and James need it. James, I've got hyperspeed, Jeff, Chuckie, and Christopher aren't here, and I outrank you, so I'm leading."

He sighed. "Fine."

"And the ocellar, chocho, and I are coming, too," Fancy said. "In case you've forgotten, I'm a warrior, and a leader of warriors." Apparently they had sarcasm knobs on Planet Colorful just like everywhere else. Fancy was at a good seven on the scale.

"Yeah, yeah, sorry. Just follow James and let's all stay very, very quiet."

"I doubt we're hunting wabbits," Reader said.

"On this planet, dude, truly, who knows?"

We moved forward slowly. Hyperspeed meant I could go out and do a fast reconnaissance. However, for whatever reason, speedy just didn't feel like the way to go. My iPod switching to "Slow" by Fuel being a large part of why.

As we edged out, noted that there were no snakipede bodies around anymore. Maybe the Poofs had eaten them—it was possible and my Poofies had to be hungry. However, I didn't bet on that. There was also no blood around—the snow that never fell here was pristine.

The Amazonian Ancient's body was still there. This was weird. Maybe something had eaten up or cleaned up the snakipede bodies. But if so, why leave a different carcass around?

"Fancy," I whispered, "do the Snow Globe Beetles eat dead animal remains?"

"Yes, Shealla," she replied in kind. "It is my understanding that every region has insect carrion eaters who eat the remains of the dead. They would eat the blood, too, in case you're wondering why the area is again clean and clear."

"Yeah, I was so wondering."

"Then why is that body still here?" Reader asked. Wasn't sure if he was somehow in on the mind-reading plan, or if it was just such an obvious question, but since I saw no katyhoppers around, assumed it was the latter.

"No idea," Fancy replied. "At all, Leader of the Nihalani."

Interesting that Reader had the leader title for his warrior group. Made sense, but again, we were all slotting far too well into this world's Assigned God Roles.

However, we had other problems, and I focused on them. The others were literally nowhere to be seen.

I looked at the dead body again. The eyes were opened, and it had been moved. "James, Fancy, Wilbur, and Ginger—stay where we are, but focus on the body. Is there anything on or near it that could be considered to be a trap? I ask because everyone else is gone but last night the body was in a different spot, and I know that, because I closed her eyes."

"Why?" Fancy asked. "Why did you close her eyes, I mean?"

"It's a sign of respect for the dead where we come from."

"Ah. The Gods respect their enemies as well as their friends."

"I can't see anything out of the ordinary, girlfriend, but I'm the last one of our group to be able to, so . . ."

Wilbur was sniffing like mad, and he whined softly.

"Wilbur can't see anything, but he smells something wrong. He can lead us around the wrong so we don't touch it. So, everyone, single file behind Wilbur. Fancy, please carry Ginger, just in case."

Ginger made a soft growl-meow. She wasn't a kit, thank you very much.

"No, Ginger. I think we may have to launch you at someone or something. I'm having Fancy hold you so that she can use you as her weapon."

This earned a purr. Ginger was fine with being a commando.

Wilbur led us out slowly and he gave the body wide berth. I could see lots of footprints now. They reached spots near the body and then they just disappeared.

"The body's trapped in some way for sure." Nodded my head at the footsteps. "Meaning everyone else has been captured. They were moving fast enough that they'd have run or flown right into it."

"Why wouldn't Bruno or the Poofs, or the katyhoppers and strautruch have spotted it?" Reader asked.

"Too fast, too hidden, they don't have pig-dog noses, would be my guesses."

"Chochos have incredible senses of smell," Fancy confirmed, as we got around the body and we all relaxed a bit. "What do we do now?"

Considered our options. "We have no idea who took them or where they went. Our force is now down to five and however many Poofs are in my purse."

Checked. We had a lot of Poofs. Meaning the Poofs had been able to escape the trap. Or rather, the Poofs had been captured, and were now with the team who could perform the rescue. Only they were all snoozing. Pointedly. Meaning rescuing the team probably wasn't Job One. The song changed to "Band on the Run" by Paul McCartney and Wings. Rescuing the team clearly wasn't Job One.

"You want to go to the top of the mountain, don't you?" Reader asked.

I did, and not just because Algar and the Poofs were giving me such broad hints. "Yes, because ever since we've heard about it, something has been stopping all of us from getting there. I think we need to see what's there, and if that means it's just those of us here who see it, then so be it."

"The fastest way is quite steep, Shealla," Fancy said. "The chocho in particular will have a difficult time."

Wilbur whined. He didn't want to be left behind. Not ever, but especially when we were going on what appeared to be a dangerous mission. I didn't want to leave him anyway, plus we might need his chocho nose again.

"Then I'll carry him."

"He's heavy, Kitty," Reader reminded me.

Dropped my Glock back into my purse, hefted Wilbur up, and slung him over my shoulders like he was a chocho wrap. "He's not heavy, he's my pig-dog brother."

"Let's hope not." Reader flashed me the cover boy grin. "You going to be able to run us all up there?"

"Yep, not even tired. Per the girls this is an oxygen-rich planet. Fancy, you lead, I'll provide the speed."

"You're rhyming a lot, girlfriend. Oxygen-rich or just a poet and you don't know it?"

"I'll exchange grade school quips with you later, James. Right now, we're on a mission and I'm wearing the heaviest fur stole in the universe."

He laughed as Fancy shifted Ginger to her hip so she had a paw free. Then I grabbed his hand and her paw, and we took off.

CHAPTER 58

THE MOUNTAIN WASN'T all that wide or impressive — but what it lacked in pizazz it made up for in height. The terrain was interesting, in that this was the midpoint for the spiral, so I could see other lands pretty easily.

There was no way the snowy height of Iceland should be snugly up against the rocky yellow terrain. The Yellow Land also had a completely different kind of rocky setup — high peaks and lots of them, not a mesa to be seen. I could see the Purple Land in the not-too-distant distance, and it just started where the Yellow Land stopped, as if a line had been drawn. I was certain by now that a line was exactly what had been drawn for each border.

The Black Land, by contrast, was comfortably against Iceland but at a much lower elevation. However, there were the remains of volcanic eruption in evidence, which stopped dead at the Iceland border with absolutely no overlap of any kind. We were able to verify this close up, because the fastest way up to the top began where this color's spiral started. This part of the world smelled like licorice tasted, and also like coal looked. There were border guards, so to speak, but they were few, far between, and easily avoided at hyperspeed.

"Can we take a look all the way around the mountain before we go up?" Reader asked. "If it won't tire you out too much, Kitty."

My music changed to "Around the World" by The Red Hot Chili Peppers. Clearly Reader's plan was one Algar agreed with.

"I should be fine. We can always stop and rest if I have to. Is it safe for us to do that, though, Fancy?"

"I don't know why not," she replied. "This area is always kept open for any and all to approach the Mountain."

"Your king allows this?"

"If he did not, Shealla, then none would follow him. The All Seeing Mountain sits at the heart of our beliefs. No one who lives on our world can be denied access to it. That is our one inviolate law."

Interesting, but not necessarily surprising. Whoever had put this world in place—and my money was still all on Algar—they clearly wanted their uplifted races to have equal access to whatever was up there.

So we zipped along the road that encircled the mountain. It was nice and wide, and though there weren't a lot of people out and about, there were enough. I had to run us past a variety of the Lecanora, some of whom were clearly making their Up The Mountain Pilgrimage.

Other than confirming that the Blue Land was indeed all water with buildings of all kinds floating on it and a lot of otters, minks, and beavers representing for the Lecanora, it wasn't someplace I wanted to stay too long, mostly because I wasn't up to running fast enough to run us all on top of the water, and the jumping we had to do from floating bridge to floating bridge was disruptive enough that I wasn't sure we wouldn't dump some unsuspecting Lecanora into the water or be discovered, or both.

The Blue Waterway—really, once I'd seen it, calling it a Land seemed ridiculous—smelled like air, and sky, and water, but the wrong kind of water. Not that it smelled stagnant or anything like that, but it also didn't smell like ocean. Frankly, it didn't smell much at all, though scent was there—but the smell here was almost ethereal.

The next song up was Coldplay's "Glass of Water." Seemed like a hint to me. Risked stopping at the border, put Wilbur down for a moment, and put my hand into the water. Licked my fingers. "It's freshwater. Not salt."

"Of course it is," Fancy said, sounding confused. "What would we drink if the water was salty?"

"Rain water? Snow melt?"

She shook her head. "We have none of that."

"That's impossible." In a normal world. In the world of

Planet Colorful, though, it probably was possible. The power orbs might be controlling the weather, or lack thereof, too.

"Let's keep moving," Reader said. "You can discuss this with Reynolds when we find him and the others."

He was right, so I just hoisted Wilbur back up and we took off again.

Reaching Greenland was a relief, but only insofar as we could stop jumping and teetering and almost falling into the water. As with the Black Land, there were border guards but they were as easily evaded as the others had been. However, in addition to being the greenest place I'd ever seen, there was something different in the air here.

Like everywhere else, the scent here was green, combined with smelling like a tart apple tastes, while not actually smelling *like* apples. But that wasn't what felt wrong. There was a tenseness in the air, a tang, and it was fighting with the green scent.

"There's something really rotten in this particular Denmark."

"The king," Reader said. "But we have a different goal right now."

Reader was right again, so we zipped on, going faster through the Bronze and Purple Lands, simply because we'd been there before. I breathed their scents in deeply, though — they helped get the tang from Greenland out of my system.

Back to the Black Lands and the supposedly fastest trail to the top. The trail, if you could call it that, was steep, narrow, and treacherous. This was so par for our course that I didn't even comment. It was hard to hyperspeed with four others dependent upon my skills and I really missed Christopher.

"Do we need to go at regular speeds?" Reader asked as I ratcheted down to the slow version of hyperspeed.

"Not really. I'm just having issues with control and this is safer. It so figures that the fastest way up is also the most dangerous."

"It's the least dangerous," Fancy countered. "Each path has dangers on it, Shealla. This path is the steepest, so its dangers are less."

"Fantastic. Why is it a gauntlet in order to get up to look up into the sky?"

"Because every worthwhile goal requires sacrifice, courage, and perseverance to achieve."

"Cannot argue with that mindset."

"Good, because it is something you, Shealla, said to our forebears so very long ago."

"Go me and the pithy sayings, and I really can't argue with my wisdom. *Can* argue with the idea of running us what feels like straight up." Oxygen-rich planet or not, I was getting tired.

"It's not quite that, but close," Fancy said as "Eat Me, Drink Me" by Marilyn Manson came on my personal airwaves. I stopped.

"We could have run around the other obstacles," Reader pointed out. "And an easier path might have meant we got up to the top faster."

Fancy shook her head. "The obstacles are not avoidable. They are a requirement."

"Religion, James. That falls under the why ask why column."

Carefully took Wilbur—who'd been a total champ and not struggled or anything while I was carrying him—off and handed him to Reader. Rummaged around in my purse, found a waterfruit, and ate it. Selfishly didn't offer any to Reader or Fancy. Felt guilty. But not guilty enough to give them one. Presumed this meant that Pinky, Saffron, and Turkey were okay and possibly close by, or that the Matriarchs were able to extend their influence. Or that Jeff was wrong and I was actually addicted to these things. Really hoped for the former.

Selfish or not, I felt a ton better once I'd eaten the fruit. "Give me Wilbur back, I'm good now."

We took off again, and while I felt like I could have raced on, I kept us at the slow version of hyperspeed. It seemed wiser and a way for me to conserve my energy. Luckily, my track coaches in high school and college had all lived for the No Pain, No Gain mindset. I'd done hill charges for eight straight years. Sure, most of them weren't this bad, and I hadn't had a big pig-dog on my shoulders and two people and a hefty cat to drag along when running track. On the other hand, I wasn't running in 115-plus-degree heat, so it evened out.

There were a couple of times I thought we were going to

lose our footing and slide down or fall off. But each time Fancy or Reader managed to keep the rest of us steady. So, definitely not looking down, we forged on.

Hyperspeed, even the slow kind, meant that we made it up this hill in minutes versus hours or possibly days. As we crested the top, "I Have Friends in Holy Spaces" by Panic! At the Disco came on.

Couldn't really see much. There was a gigantic dome of iridescent material of some kind capping the mountain, but other than a railing that appeared to go around the perimeter, there was nothing special here. Though the iridescent cap flickered intermittently, but in a discernible pattern — it resembled the flickering of torches. Meaning this was what I'd managed to spot the night before.

However, looking like nothing much or not, we'd come a damn long way to get here, so I clambered over the metal railing — without issue, other than wearing the heaviest wrap in the universe and a minor tingling sensation — took said wrap, aka Wilbur, off my back, caught my breath, then really looked around. And then I looked up.

Had really only one thing to say. "Oh. My God."

CHAPTER 59

THE TOP OF THE All Seeing Mountain was obviously manmade, and not by any man native to this planet.

As with the mountains in Iceland, the mountain was a mesa with a completely flat top. There was a layer of what I was willing to bet was concrete—while I hadn't seen every inch of this world yet, I'd seen enough to be able to feel with some certainty that I hadn't seen anything like this yet anywhere on this planet. You know, something that looked like it came from Earth.

The metal railings were like those I'd seen at the Grand Canyon and any other tourist spot on Earth where the authorities didn't want people to fall over, in, or off—four thick metal rungs connecting to posts every few feet or so, with a thicker bar on top. Unlike Earth, though, this railing had no gaps to allow visitors easy access in or out. It was climb over the four-foot-high barrier or go home.

The mountaintop, while flat, was also round, far too round to have formed naturally. And it was the size of not just a football field, but the entire stadium and parking lot, too. One of the big ones, like we had in Pueblo Caliente.

The setup was interesting. The area was obviously made for tourists or pilgrims or whatever. The area on the immediate inside of the railings had benches, water troughs, and other niceties sprinkled throughout. There were trees in all the main land colors, including black, which gave off shade and scent. The trees were near the benches and water troughs, and they created a cacophony of smells up here. Not unpleasant, in no small part because the place was big enough that the different colored trees weren't that close to each other.

But it was the main area that really stood out, so to speak.

There were circles within circles—blue, then green, black, white, yellow, bronze, and purple—each one inside of and smaller than the ones before, leading in to the smallest circle in the exact middle. Well, small in a relative sense. The midpoint circle was easily twenty yards in diameter. It was also a shimmery, almost opalescent silver.

What had shocked me, though, other than circles instead of spirals up here, was what was hanging above the midpoint—couldn't swear to it, but it sure looked like a giant telescope. As we got closer, it was pretty easy to confirm that it was, indeed, a giant telescope. A very complex and advanced giant telescope. Which no Bronze Age culture could have invented.

A telescope that was just hanging there. Not sitting on anything, or being held up by anything. Just hanging there, hovering over the middle of this mountain. A telescope that resembled the spyglasses of olden days, only about a thousand times bigger. It hung at least ten feet above the concrete—meaning that it would be difficult to touch unless you could fly. Didn't exclude a good portion of the planet, but did indicate that No Touching was probably a given.

It was gigantic and there was no way anyone looking at this mountain could miss seeing it. And yet, Christopher and Chuckie, and Christopher and I, hadn't seen this when we were looking right at the top. And there was no way that anyone on the other Alpha Centauri planets had seen it, either, because this telescope didn't say "Bronze Age"—it said "Looking At The Heavens With Scientific Interest Age."

Felt certain there was another power orb somewhere close by keeping this thing running and, more importantly, floating. And, even more importantly, cloaked. Potentially several of them. But without the girls or Chuckie around to ask, just had to take that one on faith.

Realized that the railing wasn't here to keep people in or out or even make it hard to get into this area, though I was sure that the natives felt it was the Last Obstacle—it was what was powering or controlling or whatever the cloaking shield that hid the real top of the All Seeing Mountain and, more importantly, what people were all seeing through. Because that was clearly what the iridescent, shimmering thing we'd gone through was. Having this in place made sense—because there was no way that this planet would have been left alone if anyone else had noted that they were clearly spying on the neighbors.

Also had the strongest feeling of déjà vu that I'd possibly ever had in my life. I'd been here before, somehow.

"Do you feel like you've been here before?" Reader asked me quietly.

"Yeah, you too?"

He nodded. "It's incredibly strong."

"We'll worry about that later. Is that what everyone looks through?" I asked Fancy in a normal tone, pointing to the telescope.

"Yes, Shealla."

"One at a time, right?"

"It depends. If you have young ones, you go as a family. But never more than one family at a time. We go to look at the heavens, to see if we can see the Gods."

"And all of King Benny's people, they saw something other than stars and planets and such?"

"Yes. Just as I and all my people did."

"And, when you get to the railings, what do you see?" Maybe they saw things we didn't.

"We see everything that is here, Shealla." She sounded politely confused.

"You mean that when you're outside of the railing, you can see that?" Reader pointed to the telescope.

"Yes, Leader of the Nihalani. We can see it before we are on the top as well," she added politely, but in such a way I knew she was fearing for the Sanity of the Gods.

"Okey dokey, just checking. Hang tight, we'll be right back." Fancy nodded and remained outside the center circle, on the purple pavement. Wilbur and Ginger stayed with her. Took Reader's arm and headed us to the center. "That's why the cloak or whatever it is looks different from the ones we're used to. It's calibrated so that the natives on this planet can see it but no one else can."

"You, Reynolds, and Christopher all ate waterfruit. Why didn't any of you see it?"

"No idea, but my guess would be that we haven't been

on the planet long enough, or it's set to show for natives only. Which may mean that the king has never seen it."

"Possible," he said slowly. "Meaning that maybe LaRue hasn't seen it, either. But why ostracize all those Lecanora if they didn't know about it?"

"We'll find out, I'm sure."

We reached the center. "I wish Reynolds was here," Reader said quietly. "I'm pretty sure this is something from Earth. A few years ago a giant telescope disappeared. We kept it quiet, because the disappearance was inexplicable and we couldn't find the telescope or anyone who knew anything about its disappearance."

"I think we may now be able to explain it. Sort of. Was there anything special about that telescope?"

"Yeah, actually. It was designed for major amplification—the most powerful amplification we'd had to date. We've never matched it. Once you found ACE, I kind of figured he'd removed it so no one on Earth could see him, or see the Alpha Centauri system or something. This one looks like at least part of what disappeared."

Was positive ACE wasn't the Telescope Thief, but couldn't say that to Reader. "For all we know, the other part is 'buried' in the mountain right under us. But, why haven't we on Earth created another one of these?"

"Too expensive. And with the first one being stolen and remaining unrecovered, the consensus was that we'd already spent too much money on nothing so the plan to try again was squashed."

Tidy. Take the thing and thereby ensure no other thing like it will be created. And so like Algar. After all, the people who'd chosen not to make another telescope had the free will to choose otherwise.

There was one problem with this theory—the Planet Colorful natives had been looking through this telescope for thousands of years, not just a few.

Neither one of us had looked into the scope yet. "Ready to see whatever it is we're going to see?"

Reader took my hand in his. "Yeah."

Squeezed his hand and we both looked up. My iPod graced me with "Perfect Planet" by Smash Mouth. Wanted to tell Algar that I understood. And he'd been right—we'd needed to see this.

The clarity was shocking. The portion of the scope you looked through was large—easily three feet in diameter. The glass didn't need to be adjusted for eyesight limitations, either. Had no idea if this was just because the telescope had been made that way, or if Algar had had a hand in it. Gave it even odds for either or both.

It was easy to see why the people on this planet felt this was the high holy spot in the world, though—looking through this telescope was literally like gazing at the heavens.

If, you know, the heavens were filled with spaceships.

CHAPTER 60

THERE WERE SO MANY spaceships in Beta Eight's solar space that I literally couldn't count them all. It was difficult to see the other planets in the system, let alone all the other things out there in space, because they were blocked from view by the spaceships.

"I see at least seven kinds of ships out there," Reader said finally.

"I spy Alpha Four battle cruisers, the Reptilian Birds of Prey, Major Doggies Paws, and Cat People Heads, so the gang's all here."

"There are three other designs, too. Different enough that I think they represent other planets."

"Probably. Know what else I notice?"

"They're scattered and firing at each other?"

"Got it in one! We're not just talking about starting a civil war on this planet. I think there's a much bigger civil war going on. I think we have a civil war within this entire solar system."

"Looking at what's up there, it's easy to agree with you, babe. Based on Reynolds' theory about this planet's core, they could be fighting over who gets to rape this world."

"I'm sure that's part of it. But not all."

"Think this is going to be the end of the rule of Alpha Four in this system?"

"I think our enemies want it to be, yeah."

"Why are you assuming that Alpha Four's enemies are our enemies, too?"

"Because we're here. Because the others have disappeared. Because someone has Paul and Jamie, and therefore they have ACE. Because our luck never runs any other way. Because I put Alexander on the throne and Chuckie advised Councilor Leonidas. We made enemies when we overthrew Kitler. Those enemies are Alexander's enemies, too."

"And Alexander has blood ties with Earth."

"And he and some of those ships up there came to save us from the Z'porrah." As soon as the words left my mouth, I knew what was going on. That my iPod graced me with Motörhead's "War for War" was merely icing on my Megalomania Girl Cake. "I know what's going on."

"Care to actually explain it to me, or are you going to do what you always do and keep it all to yourself until the big reveal?"

"Wow, bitter much? You sound as whiny as Jeff, Chuckie, and Christopher normally manage to be."

"It's been a long few days, girlfriend."

"True. And it's you, so I'll be kind and share. This is a chess game."

He groaned. "It's always a chess game."

"Yes, but this one is the complex, three dimensional chess game. You know, like on *Star Trek*?"

"I've heard of it, yeah." Reader's sarcasm knob was heading toward eleven.

"So touchy. Anyway, there's the usual three plans going. I'd assume that each plan has three smaller plans within it, too." I waited. It was Reader, I kind of expected him to make the same leap I had.

"That's it? Three-dimensional chess and three plans and a bunch of mini plans going? That's what you're giving me?"

Okay, apparently not. "I thought you'd make the leap."

"No leaping here."

"Fine. You disappoint me and I'm worried about you, but fine."

"Leaping like you tend to do is, frankly, Tim's job, and he's not here. So, explain it for me, Megalomaniac Girl."

"Well, when you ask so nicely . . . Plan A is to get us the hell off of Earth, hopefully to be killed in a solar system far, far away, meaning Plan A involves Cliff and LaRue and probably Leventhal Reid." Controlled the shudder. The snakipedes were better than Reid. Anything was better than Reid.

Reader squeezed my hand and I got it together and forged on. "So, in order to achieve Plan A, there had to be interaction and connection with Plan B, which is to overthrow Alpha Four's leadership in the solar system, which also involves making this planet a sitting duck for takeover."

"You think they've figured out about anything other than the core?"

"No, but the core of this planet is more than enough reason for why all those ships are in this planet's solar space. But Plan B is why specific people were yanked out here. Mom and Richard were right—it's based on our wedding, because whoever was doing the yanking or being fooled into yanking us only had Operation Invasion to go on. I'm sure Cliff and LaRue didn't care about everyone who was tossed into this system, but Centaurion Division and American Centaurion's core team are off planet, and the Vice President has also disappeared."

"I really hope we get home soon. The longer Jeff's gone, the harder it's going to be to explain away his absence."

"The VP is usually a no big deal job. I'm sure Vince and Mom can shuck and jive it enough to cover. But that's not the real problem."

"Regardless of what's going on here, it's our real problem, babe."

"No, it's not. *Our* real problem is Plan C. Plan C is for the Z'porrah to overtake this solar system. Without Alpha Four's leadership, this system is going to fall into and stay in what we're watching on our Telescopic Vision Channel—civil war. But most of the planets are evenly matched, so it's going to be a long, drawn-out civil war. All the planets are going to fight each other, destroy each other, and so on. And then, when they're all worn and weary, the Z'porrah are going to sweep in here and destroy them."

And whichever conqueror got their hands, paws, claws, or talons on this planet was going to win. But at the cost of all the life on Beta Eight, and potentially all the life in the Alpha Centauri system, too, possibly before the Z'porrah armada even arrived. Mephistopheles all over again.

Reader was quiet for a few seconds. "And then they'll come and destroy Earth. We only survived before because Alpha Four and their allies intervened."

"And because of ACE. And Naomi and Abigail. Meaning Abigail's in danger—she wasn't taken because she was filling Michael's slot—she was taken because of her power. They must not know that she's not recovered from Operation Destruction. Or else they want to be sure she can't ever recover."

"And we have no idea where she is, any more than we know where Paul and Jamie are."

"Yeah, and Paul and Jamie are in danger, too. Wherever they are." My daughter needed me and I had no idea where she was. Or where her father was. Or where anyone else who mattered was. It was literally me and Reader and three Planet Colorful natives against the War of the Super Powerful Worlds right now. Felt the panic try to take over.

Reader put his arm around my shoulders and hugged me. "In my dream, Paul wasn't afraid. They're with friends, Kitty, I'm sure of it."

Took a deep breath, let it out, and leaned my head on his shoulder. As always, a nice place to be, and it helped me relax and focus. "They may be with friends, but that just means those friends are in danger. Not all the traitors from Operation Invasion are dead. And those who are dead had friends and relatives who were clearly not on the side of Alpha Four Right."

"Alpha Four all the way?"

"When in doubt, always back the guy who's had your back when it counted. Alexander's earned our loyalty. So, yeah, Alpha Four for the win. Besides, the Planetary Council told us that they need Alpha Four's leadership. To prevent all this." As Eminem's "Bad Meets Evil" came on my personal airwaves, I waved my hand at the telescopic images.

And triggered something. Because the picture changed.

CHAPTER 61

THE IMAGE EXPANDED, and we weren't seeing the ships anymore. At least, not the ships we'd been seeing. But they were certainly ships I recognized. Your typical saucer-shaped ships out of every movie and UFO sighting ever, with a little dome on top. And, as before, there were a thousand if there were ten.

"That's the Z'porrah fleet," Reader said, voice low. "Any guess for how far away they are?"

"No. Without Chuckie or the girls looking we have no idea if they're at the edge of the galaxy or at the edge of this solar system. But if they're moving already, then I think we can assume that this war has been going on a long time. It was probably starting when Queen Renata sent Rahmi and Rhee to us."

"Makes sense. That's over two years ago, though. Meaning this war's been going on long enough that at least one planet is probably looking for elements to replenish their supplies, or the edge that will give them the upper hand."

"Hence why they're all here shooting at each other over Beta Eight. I'm just hoping the Z'porrah are far enough away that we have time to fix this problem and get this system focused on the bigger threat, rather than merrily continuing their infighting."

"What's your plan for that? I ask because as far as I can see, we're pretty much the definition of being once again caught between a rock and a hard place."

Sadly, I didn't really have a plan. "Something's Gotta Give" by Royal Crown Revue came on my iPod. It was a good song, but I preferred the Aerosmith version. Totally different songs, music and lyrics both, of course. And while I liked RCR's version of the Sinatra classic, I'd rather hear my Bad Boys from Boston, especially when things were dire. And they were definitely dire.

Considered manually changing the tunes to something other than the Algar's Not All That Helpful Clues Playlist. But I didn't. Because I realized I was focusing on the music versus the clue, mostly because I was clear that something was going to have to give. I was just afraid that it was going to be our side.

Negative thinking wasn't going to help anything, though. Gave myself a mental shake and focused back on the situation at hand. "Okay. We have to foil Plan B in order to foil Plan C and Plan A. And not only because we're here, in the midst of Plan B, but because it's the crux of the entire three-dimensional chess game. Save the day here, save the day everywhere. Fail here, fail everywhere."

"I can agree with all of that." Reader sighed. "I know that, as Head of Field, I should be coming up with some great save-the-day plan. But I've got nothing right now. Our fighting force, if you can call it that, is captured. At least we think they're captured. So it's five of us and some Poofs against every ship in every fleet. And that's just this solar system."

Thought about what he'd said. "Actually . . . give me a minute to think." Might actually have the answers and I tried to get them into order.

"Ah, you're being quiet? Are you okay?" Reader sounded legitimately concerned.

"Other Me wasn't an out-loud thinker anymore."

"Yeah, dealt with that. She adapted, babe. I see that you did, too, but you're home and, frankly, I prefer to hear you talk out your thoughts."

"Really? I thought that drove everyone crazy."

Got another shot of the cover boy grin. "Not me, babe. I like hearing my girl's thought processes."

Heaved a dramatic sigh. "And yet, you still refuse to turn straight or even bi and take me away from all this."

Reader kissed my cheek. "True enough, but you're still and always my girl. So do what my girl does best and tell me what you're thinking."

"Okay. We have to think like our enemy is—in three dimensions, if you will. By that I mean that each plan is connected to the others in more than one way. So, if we can figure out how to counter even one part of one of the Big Plans, we can cause issues for all three Plans at the same time."

"Fine. So, what are we countering?"

"Frankly, it's what we're missing that's the key."

"Besides the rest of our people that we'd finally found, our people who we haven't found, and our allies on this planet, you mean?"

Turned and looked at Fancy, Ginger, and Wilbur, who all looked back at me rather expectantly. "But we haven't lost all our allies. The three most important are standing right there."

"Mind explaining that one?"

"Stop thinking like a Naked Ape and think like a Galactic Man About Town."

Reader groaned. "I'm channeling Christopher right now. That Kitty-ism I'm not getting, girlfriend."

"You're thinking that because Ginger and Wilbur seem like a cat and a dog that's it. But they're more than that—they're leading their particular clans, all of whom can fight and all of whom are also safely in Haven. You know, along with all of Fancy's Ferrets, all the Black Wolverines, and a host of other Albino Clan Lecanora. As in, we have a fighting force and then some. And we actually have the one being who can galvanize them all still with us."

"You mean Fancy. And yeah, I'm sure she can. But I don't know that she's ready to lead her people into battle with what's out there."

"The battle's coming, whether they're ready or not." Motioned for Fancy and the others to come to us, which they did. "Look up." They did. "What you're seeing are spaceships that belong to a race of aliens that hate all of us—those who live on your planet, my planet, and every other planet in this system—because we sort of belong to their most bitter enemies. They're coming here to destroy everything and everyone, wipe all our planets clean, and start over with people made in their own image."

"They are the enemies of the Gods?" Fancy asked.

Considered how to answer this. It was one thing to pretend to be Gods. But Gods had powers we didn't. And if I was going to ask Fancy to risk her people, I had to tell her the truth. "They're our enemies, yes. They're called the Z'porrah, and they hate us, deep in the bone."

"The enemy of my God is my enemy," Fancy said calmly.

"We appreciate that. But . . . we aren't Gods, Fancy. What we are is aliens, for you, at least. We come from a planet that's far away from yours, not even in the same solar system. There are a lot of inhabited planets in your solar system, but only one in ours. We've become friends with many of the planets in your system."

"The Gods come from far away, Shealla. This is not news."

"True, but this invasion is." Waved my hand again and, happy day, the closer view of a ton of spaceships that weren't Z'porrah ships appeared. "And here's more news. All of the planets in your solar system appear to be fighting now. And if they're fighting in your planet's solar space, and they are, then they're fighting over who gets to take over your planet."

"Why would they want our planet?"

"Your planet's core is valuable for weapons of mass destruction." Why bring up the katyhoppers and strautruch powers right now? I was still hoping we'd avoid anyone else learning about them, and even though Fancy knew by now, the less we talked about it, the better.

"But to reach the core, that would mean destruction of our world, wouldn't it?"

Wished Chuckie was here to bask in the glow of a really smart Bronze Age Like An Ancient Greek Lecanora. "Yes, it would. There are ways to drill safely, but no one's going to do that because this isn't their planet, it's just someplace they see as having resources they want."

"Why would they do this to us? Especially if they call you friends?"

"None of them know any of you down here—most of them aren't bad people, but they're at war with each other, and that means they'll do bad things in the name of winning. And they can tell themselves that it's okay because they haven't gotten to know you, any of you."

But we had. And now I realized why Algar had ensured we'd all land where and how we did. If I'd made it to wherever Gower and Jamie had, seen the Z'porrah fleet coming somehow, and been told this planet had all we'd need to defeat the Z'porrah, I might have said, oh well, just move the natives. Might have even said to kill them if they resisted, under the good of the many outweighs the good of the few mindset.

But I knew them now. And now I'd fight to protect them, we all would. Because they were ours somehow, just as they felt we were theirs. Their Gods, our people. Our responsibility. And yet, we still had the free will options to do whatever we wanted to. Algar worked in mysterious, sneaky, and really calculated ways.

"We're more like you than not. And so are they. Oh, they look different—some more like Ginger on her hind legs, some more like Wilbur on his." Well, that was stretching it. The Canus Majorians looked far more like our Egyptian dog statues than the pig-dogs the chochos were. But still, close enough for government work.

Forged on. "Some are walking and talking lizards. And some look like we do. But we all come from the same kind of origins. So, the moment most of the people in those ships up there realize that you're just like them, we'll be able to reason with them, and to explain that what they think they want to do is wrong." I sincerely hoped.

"We hope," Reader said under his breath. Wondered if we had a katyhopper nearby, but figured this wasn't mind reading so much as a clear understanding of human, and probably Alpha Centauri Populated Planets, nature.

"And they also need to know that we all need to band together to fight against the invader who hates us all. But to do that, we're going to need your help, and the help of your people."

"You are our Gods," Fancy said, still sounding calm. Wondered if she was grasping the situation properly. She pointed down. "Look."

We did. There were images underneath the opalescent paint. They were faint without being indistinct, and we'd been looking up at the telescope, which was why we'd missed these images. Images that looked a hell of a lot like all of those of us who'd been taken. And not just crude drawings, either—incredibly good carvings that looked amazingly like us. Just generalized enough that I could see how King Benny had believed that Jeff was a God Messenger, rather than Leoalla, for a little while, but accurate enough that I could point-blank tell which one of the Muses was Lorraine, which was Claudia, and which was Serene.

There was writing underneath each image. The Universal Translator Chip didn't provide a translation, but I was willing to bet that they were our God Names in Lecanora.

Looked carefully at the pictures. There was no image that looked like either Jamie or Gower. However, there were three female images that looked a lot like Abigail, Rahmi, and Rhee.

"What the hell?" Reader asked, speaking for both of us.

"These have been here for as long as we have been recounting our histories. They have been here since the Father of the Gods first came and gave us the All Seeing Mountain."

Meaning Algar had put our pictures here somehow. Thousands of years before we'd been born.

Would have been incredibly awed if I didn't know that he was a Black Hole Universe dude and that probably meant he was able to bend time, space, universes, and whatever else. So, he'd "gone back" and tossed our pictures up there. Probably easier to do than "go forward" and grab a ginormous telescope. Or maybe not. Presumably he'd put our pictures here so that we'd be listened to without a lot of argument.

"Who are they?" Pointed to the images of the three gals we were still missing.

"They are the Venida, the female warriors of the Gods. They are the counterpoint to the Muses—where the Muses of Knowledge bring creativity to the Gods, the Venida ensure that the Gods' laws are carried out. And they, like the Winalla and the Nihalani, are both the warriors and the protectors of the High Godhead."

"Are the Venida more or less powerful than the Winalla or the Nihalani?"

Fancy smiled. "Much more powerful. They are the special Gods of my clan, Shealla. We walk in the footsteps of the Venida."

"Nice. And who makes the cut for the High Godhead?"

"The Father of the Gods, Leoalla, Shealla, Alcalla, and Binalla," Fancy replied. "And the Guide of the Gods, who is not pictured here, because he can only be seen by the Gods themselves."

Figured the Guide to be Gower, because the role, like everything else going on around here, fit. No mention of Jamie, though. Didn't know if this boded or not. Hoped for not.

"Who's the Mother of the Gods?" Reader asked. The question made sense, even though I hadn't thought to ask, since a clan like Fancy's would indicate such a God existed.

"She is Ethereal and watches over all of us," Fancy said. "Even now, we know she is watching, guarding our hearts."

"Where is her picture, or a picture of the Father of the Gods?" It would be nice to be able to confirm my suspicions. "And why didn't you mention her in the High Godhead?"

"The Mother of the Gods remains hidden to us—we must find her in our hearts. She does not visit us in any other way. The Father of the Gods has visited us only once, when he bestowed the All Seeing Mountain upon us. Mother and Father both cannot be seen anymore, not even by the Gods themselves. To see them is to risk their destruction."

So the Father was indeed Algar and the Mother was Naomi. Sure, this was guessing on my part, but I'd seen her in the three-way mirrors in Bizarro World, so I knew she really *was* watching and guarding. And I also knew that no one in this universe—Chuckie, Abigail, and Gower especially—could know that she was here.

"Huh. Learn something new every single day, and sometimes every minute." Whoops. Had not meant to say that out loud. Darn Reader and his getting me back into my normal groove.

But Fancy took it in stride. "That the Gods might not remember themselves is a story passed down as well. But our Gods you are. Gods can die, we know this. Gods cannot do everything for us, we know this, too. But if our Gods say that we must fight, then let me assure our Gods that I have been training my warriors for battle, just as my mother, grandmother, great-grandmother, and all of our line before me have done. We are ready, Shealla, for whatever you need. And if that includes dying, then we will die protecting our world, and all those who live upon it."

"I think King Benny's going to make a great Chief Councilor. He's got a great presence, he's good under pressure, and he's a good thinker. You two are going to be a great team."

"You presume that I would be accepted as king, and that Musgraff would be accepted as less than me."

"It's all in how you spin it, babe. Trust me. King Benny's already been willing to be an Under-Clan Leader to you, and what I'm suggesting would make him your right-paw man, the guy you discuss policy and decisions with."

She nodded. "That would be acceptable, I'm sure."

"This is nice and all, but what, exactly, are we going to do, Kitty?" Reader was managing to only sound slightly stressed and a little impatient.

"We're going to go back and get Haven ready. I have hyperspeed and waterfruit, meaning that I can get to the Purple Land and talk to the Matriarchs there if needed. They can manage the rest."

"What is the rest?" Reader asked, patience now clearly forced.

"Doing what we planned to do in the first place after we visited the All Seeing Mountain—we're going to overthrow the so-called King of the Planet Colorful and take control of this planet."

CHAPTER 62

READER SHOOK HIS HEAD. "We're not going to be able to get all of Haven prepped and ready to go in five minutes, babe, you know that, right?"

"Yes, James, I'm clear. I want Fancy's Fighting Ferrets, the Black Wolverines, the ocellars, and the chochos. Everyone else needs to get ready and prep for siege or to come storm the castle *en masse*."

"Too large a force will not raid as effectively," Fancy said. "But I do agree with the Leader of the Nihalani—it will be difficult to gather our forces if you separate from us, Shealla, since the Nihalani do not move like the Higher Gods do."

"Call me James, would—" Reader looked up, stopped speaking, and I felt him stiffen. "I don't think we're going to have time for rallying the troops."

Fancy and I both looked up as well. She gasped. I didn't, but my stomach clenched. One of the ships—an unfamiliar shaped one—took a major hit and split apart. And parts exploded toward the planet.

Ran out of the circle area and to the railing and heard the others following. "Stay here," I said to Ginger and Wilbur. Grabbed Reader and Fancy and ran around the entire perimeter, but at the slow version of hyperspeed. I could see the edges of the continent from here, but only because I could see a ring of blue. If there were other lands on this planet, they weren't visible from this vantage point.

"What are you looking for?" Reader asked as I finally reached the point where I'd started. Good thing my track coaches had always made the sprinters run distance for training—hyperspeed or no, the distance traveled was the same, and I'd done a lot of running today, and had a lot more to do looming on the immediate horizon.

"Trying to see if the debris is going to land anywhere else with a population."

"Can't tell, but it's this population I'm worried about."

Wished ACE was here with us something fierce. ACE could create a shield over the continent and protect everyone.

But ACE wasn't here. And Reader was right—we were out of time.

Once part of a ship hit this planet, someone would be coming down to see if they had survivors. And in that case, they'd also be coming ready to bring the war directly onto this planet. Sure, we might have a few hours. Maybe even a few days, depending on how low or high the ship's orbit had been. Maybe minutes if the ships were in a low orbit and skimming the planet's atmosphere. The view from the telescope hadn't told me.

It probably would have told Chuckie or the girls. Wondered if the others had been captured to prevent them from looking through the telescope or if it had just been coincidental. Reminded myself that we rarely scored a coincidence. Whoever had captured them had wanted to get all of us, and undoubtedly had wanted to keep all of us from getting up here.

My brain nudged. If the king didn't know about the telescope, then why would he want to prevent us from going to the top of the mountain? So either he knew, wanted us for general reasons, or someone else had grabbed the others. Didn't have enough information to be able to tell yet, so tabled this discovery for later.

Also realized that my music had stopped. Considered taking my earbuds out and putting them and my iPod back into my purse. But on the off chance Algar was going to share his Semi-Helpful Hints again, figured I'd just keep things as they were for the moment.

Picked Wilbur up and handed him to Reader. Did the same with Ginger and handed her to Fancy. Dug out another waterfruit and ate it at hyperspeed. Noted that I still had a lot of Poofs on Board. Meaning, when push came to shove, I did have a fighting force.

Grabbed Reader and Fancy's free hands. "Fancy, what's the easiest, fastest, least obstacle-encroached path to the king?"

"None are 'easy,' Shealla, but the purple path is the most sedate in terms of its slope."

"I looked down while you were looking out," Reader said. "That path has switchbacks like you wouldn't believe, Kitty. Straight down the mountain would be preferable."

"There are traps and obstacles off the paths as well," Fancy said.

"The mountain's booby-trapped, James, think about it. Fancy, you're going to lead, I'm going to provide the speed. Pick the path that gets us to the king the fastest, and that includes factoring in obstacles and such."

She nodded, and we took off.

Getting down was both harder and easier than getting up. Easier because, thankfully, Fancy didn't choose to go down the way we'd come up, which was a relief to me and, I was sure, Reader, too, despite his saying straight down was a good plan. Unlike Fancy, Ginger, and Wilbur, we didn't have claws to dig into the mountainside.

It was harder though because Fancy hadn't been kidding—there were a lot of obstacles in the way. Hyperspeed handled most of them, of course, and they weren't dangerous so much as really annoying, but still, I could tell Algar had had some fun designing the Seven Paths to Pilgrimage. That, it turned out, was the real name given for the ways up to the top of the All Seeing Mountain. I refrained from comment. Barely.

Fancy stuck with her first choice and we zipped down on the Purple Path. She wasn't kidding about it being far less steep, and Reader hadn't underestimated the number of switchbacks, either. Naturally, it also had the most obstacles on it, but that was just the Way of Algar and I didn't complain about it. Too much.

The obstacles were really like what I'd seen in the movies about boot camp. Mud, water, climbing, sharp stakes and the like, all of which you had to get around "properly" in order to stay on the path. Fortunately, I was a God so I didn't care about pleasing anyone but myself, and myself wanted us moving as fast and smoothly as possible. Plus hyperspeed ensured that when I told the others to jump, I could drag them along with me. Missed White a lot, but he'd certainly taught me how to do this right—even though he'd be the first to claim that he wasn't a "real" Field agent.

Thinking about him meant that I, naturally, thought about Christopher. And then, of course, Jeff. I'd been avoiding thinking about Jeff and the others because I was as worried about them as I was about Jamie. If Reader was right, Jamie was safe somewhere. As long as she and Gower hadn't been on the ship that now had parts of it falling down, to land on us sometime in our near future.

But panic wasn't going to save my daughter, husband, and friends, so I shoved it aside and focused on getting us down as fast as possible.

The beauty of hyperspeed was that, tons of switchbacks and obstacles or not, we made good time and were down the hill in a matter of a couple minutes. Looked up. Saw nothing horrible falling out of the sky yet.

Stopped for a moment. "Not that I'm complaining, but why aren't the animals or Fancy tossing their cookies?" Reader asked me as I ate another waterfruit. Hey, I didn't want to run out of juice. Hoped that the juice was just juice and not "juice." Decided I'd worry about Just Saying No once we were out of this mess.

"The beings on this planet seem adaptable to hyperspeed."

"Huh. Interesting. Fancy, how many hearts to your people have?"

She cocked her head at Reader. "We have two, Leader of—"

"James. Please start calling me James."

"He means it," I added.

She nodded. "As you wish . . . James. I believe that all creatures on our planet have two hearts. Isn't that normal?"

"Depends on your planet," I replied. "Some of the beings in your solar system have three hearts, some two, some one. We only have one."

She looked shocked. "But, how do you do all the wonders that you can with so little internal power?"

Reader and I exchanged a glance. That wasn't really a Bronze Age Level question. "We're adaptable," was all I could come up with that wouldn't require an anatomy and physiology lecture. "And clearly so are you."

"Why didn't you all go as fast as we are going before now, then?" Reader asked.

Fancy shrugged. "I don't know that I could go as fast as Shealla on my own."

"We'll let the others do fun scientific experiments, James. We need to try to save the world and all that right now, if it's okay with you."

"Always nice to reverse roles with you, girlfriend."

"I'll hurt you later. Fancy, can we get into the palace without being detected if we're going really fast?"

"Perhaps, but there are traps. I don't know if you can go too fast for them or not."

"Well, lead on and we'll cross that exploding bridge when we come to it."

Fancy smiled. "That was humor. I think I begin to understand you, Shealla."

"Welcome to the Army of One, Fancy."

CHAPTER 63

WE TOOK OFF AGAIN, running around the path that encircled the bottom of the mountain, only in the opposite direction than before, in part because we were closer to Greenland from where we'd exited and in other part because I didn't feel like dealing with the Blue Waterway right now.

Greenland's wrong tang hit my nostrils the moment we stepped past the extremely precise Bronze Land border. Only now I could connect the smell to something specific — the wrongness smelled like decay looked. Not musty or dusty or old, but more like sadness for what once was.

"Has it always smelled like this here?" I asked Fancy quietly as we got onto the Green Grass Spiral Road and started off toward the castle in the near distance.

"No, as James said earlier, this area has changed since the king declared."

"The land isn't happy."

Reader shot me a sharp look. "You trying to say that the land can think?"

"This world is created, James. For all we know, the entire continent is actually a computer or a robot of some kind. And we know that there are robots and androids and such out there that can definitely think." The weather was too bizarre to be natural, after all — something had to be creating snow and water, fresh water, in a place where rain and snow didn't fall.

"Then why isn't the land helping us?" he asked.

"A good question. Maybe it is." But before we could continue this Fancy tugged at my hand.

"We're here."

"Here" wasn't a castle, however. It was a tree. A very large, very green tree.

"Um, seriously? Is this like the katyhoppers, where there's a whole city behind this tree that we can't see?"

"Ah, no, Shealla. This is a hidden entrance to tunnels that go under the castle."

"Well alrighty then."

"How many people know about this?" Reader asked.

"Just mine."

"Did your people build it?" he asked.

"No, the tunnels have been here as long as Haven."

"Then it's not just your people who know about it. Meaning that we could be ambushed the moment we enter."

"We raid via this path regularly, James," Fancy said. "And we have not ever faced any enemies on this path. Traps, yes. Enemies, no."

Reader didn't look convinced. "James, we can go in via Fancy's preferred path, or we can try a frontal assault on that heavy, ponderous, and most importantly not green castle sitting off in yonder distance. With, as you've pointed out, not a lot in the way of troops here and ready."

"Fine," he muttered. "I just hope I'm not going to say 'I told you so' in the next few minutes."

"Not as much as the rest of us." Looked up at the sky. It was definitely falling. "We need to get to cover before the spaceship's debris hits." Really hoped it wasn't going to hit the continent, and especially not the top of the All Seeing Mountain.

Fancy pushed at several spots on the tree that looked random but clearly weren't, and part of the tree's trunk slid inward to reveal a stairway going down.

I'd just done something like this in Bizarro World, and it had led to The Mastermind's Lair. Started to share Reader's apprehension. However, it was go down or risk getting hit with falling spaceship, and that was far too reminiscent of Operation Destruction for me. I'd take my chances with the Evil Overlord.

It was too narrow for us to safely use hyperspeed, so Fancy went first, with me following, then Wilbur, and Reader brought up the rear, gun out and ready. I dug my Glock out, too, but I also carried Ginger again, just in case we needed to launch her at someone or something.

Just as within Haven, it wasn't dark inside. There was a green glow all along the walls, floor, and ceiling. Not blinding, thankfully, but bright enough to be able to see clearly. "Green Glow Beetles?" I asked Fancy softly.

She nodded. "They are our friends."

"Let's hope," Reader muttered from behind me.

We trotted down the stairs at a good clip, reached the bottom, and trotted along a narrow corridor for a good few minutes. As Fancy had said, we ran into no one. Which was good because while it might be possible to pass someone going the other way, it would be tight at best.

There were places along the corridor that we had to avoid, and it was fairly easy to do so, even for Wilbur. The traps were ancient and pretty easy to spot. Most of them just required you to jump over, hug the wall, or duck down. These weren't *Raiders of the Lost Ark* traps—these were traps a little kid would think were hard and clever. Maybe.

Finally came to a door at the end of the corridor. Fancy listened at it for a few long seconds, then she nodded and shoved the door open just a crack, very carefully and very slowly.

She waited again a little longer this time, then pushed the door open a bit more. One more long listen, then she opened it wide enough for all of us to slip through. Once through, she let the door close as quietly as she'd opened it.

We were in a new corridor. This one was no wider than the one we'd just left, but it wasn't as well lit. The area around the door wasn't lit at all. In fact, when I looked back at the door I could only see it because I knew where it was. The Glow Beetles were definitely on Team Fancy.

This corridor was perpendicular to the one we'd just left, so we could go right or left. Either way, the path was intermittently lit, but it was darker toward the left. Unsurprisingly, that was the way Fancy went.

Another long corridor, another door, another corridor that was perpendicular to the corridor we'd just left, over and over again. If Chuckie had been with us, I wouldn't

have worried, because I knew he'd have memorized every
step we'd taken. Maybe Reader was doing that, but I wasn't
the greatest at mazes, and I was completely lost by the fifth
door.

"No traps here?" I asked her softly.

"Some of the doors do not lead to rooms or other hallways."

"What do they lead to?"

"Dead ends, flying spears, falling acid, a long drop with
spikes at the bottom, that sort of thing."

So this section had been created by someone far nastier
than whoever had set up the Secret Entrance. Interesting.

"The game gets harder the closer you get to the Boss,"
Reader said quietly to me. "Someone's having fun. Sick fun,
but fun."

"You think we're being watched?" My team and I had
been watched when we were in Bizarro World, after all.

He looked around. "Maybe."

Three more doors later we exited into a room. It wasn't
lit by the Green Glow Beetles but by a few weak, flickering
globules of light. Based on the barrels and such, it was a
large, rectangular storeroom. Based on the dust, it wasn't
used that often. Based on the crates in front of us, the door
we'd just come through couldn't easily be seen.

Of course, there was dust on the floor, too, and that
meant footsteps could be seen. Though the dust on the floor
was piled up more against barrels and the walls and such.

Which was explained by Fancy picking up a broom and
quickly sweeping the floor.

"Nice of you to perform maid services," Reader whispered, "but do we really have time for this?"

"She's hiding our tracks, so yes, we do have the time."

"If things go right, we won't need to have our tracks hidden."

This was a good point, however, Fancy was done. She put
the broom back and we headed off again.

"Is this where you take stores from?" I asked her as we
walked quickly down the path she'd cleaned toward a door
at the opposite end of the long room.

"No, there is nothing we need in this room. We raid
closer to the king."

Interesting again. Why have a storage room with things

in it no one wanted or needed? Reader's video game comparison seemed a bit more apt.

"What are those things giving us light?" I nodded toward one of the glowing globules.

"Naturally forming fungi. They're edible, at least some variations, and they only grow underground."

"Meet Beta Eight's mushrooms," Reader said.

We reached the far door and Fancy once again did her listen and open the door slowly thing. We exited onto another corridor, but this time there were many more doors. It reminded me of Guantanamo, when I'd been working with Gladys Gower during Operation Infiltration. Right before she died.

Got Reader's bad feeling going in my own gut now. But nothing happened.

We got to the end of this corridor and went up a long, curving staircase that clearly didn't see a lot of action. "I have to point out that this is an extremely empty castle," I said as we continued up the stairway, meeting absolutely no one and nothing. If this *was* a video game, it was set on the easy level. Or else it was lulling us into a false sense of security.

"It's a trap," Reader said. "Trust me, right now, we're walking into a trap."

CHAPTER 64

"I'M KIND OF WITH JAMES, Fancy. Do you consistently meet no resistance when you raid?" A fighting force that never had to fight wasn't necessarily a good fighting force. Practice, versus talking about or thinking about a skill, tended to make perfect.

"This is an old and unused wing."

"How can it be old if it's only been here two of your years?"

"The castle has been on our world for much longer, Shealla. The king took it over, he did not build it."

"Really? When was this castle built?" I examined the stone. It looked something like granite. I hadn't seen stone like this on the planet yet.

"It has been here since our world began," Fancy said. "The Father of the Gods created it. But it used to reside elsewhere."

"Where and how did it get moved?" Reader asked before I could.

"The castle used to be in what you are calling the Bronze Land. Zenoca put it here. Zenoca carries the Jewel of the Gods, and therefore he can make things appear or disappear."

Was pretty confident that the Jewel of the Gods was a Z'porrah power cube. The missing Z'porrah power cube to be exact. I hadn't realized they could move gigantic buildings but LaRue would definitely know how to work one better than any of us did.

Algar wanted that power cube found, too. He was really

getting at least a double, if not a triple or even a home run, on this particular excursion of ours.

"Didn't anyone question that?" Reader asked. "Especially when Zenoca shoved someone who's not from this planet into the ruling position?"

"They did not realize it was Zenoca. He appeared as a woman and convinced the others that a 'strong king' was what we needed. I know Musgraff believes that woman was Zenoca, and I do as well."

"Make it three, because I'm certain that was Zenoca."

"Yeah, it makes sense," Reader said. "Does anyone else think Zenoca put the king on the throne other than the outcasts and those in Haven?"

"Zanell does," Fancy replied. "And some others. But now to question the king is to be thrown out of your clan. Just as to contradict the king ensured that Musgraff and all those who now follow him would be outcast."

"What was their contradiction, exactly?" I asked.

"They said they had seen ships in the sky. The king said this was impossible, that we are alone here in space. When they insisted that they had seen wonders, the king called them liars. When they did not admit to a lie, the king cast them out."

"I didn't notice a lot of pilgrims on the way up or down the All Seeing Mountain. Is that normal?"

"No, Shealla. But right now, the king does not like us to go there. Only the most devout are traveling the Seven Paths to Pilgrimage right now."

Meaning the king knew there were so many ships in his solar space that all his people would soon know they were there, and therefore he'd either have to admit the ships' existence or banish every subject.

"So, here's a question. Why did Zenoca move the castle? Or, rather, what's more special about Greenland than the Bronze Lands?"

Fancy shook her head. "No reason was given. The people did ask—but we were told that the king could do as he pleased. And the display of power cowed most of the people."

"Understandably."

"Kitty, you said the Bronze Land dampened Jeff's powers," Reader pointed out. "Remember who we think is king here now. He's got troubadour and mind control powers, if it's really Ronaldo. Meaning he wouldn't want those constricted."

Things clicked. "That both makes sense and explains how they figured out that something in the Bronze Land region would dampen A-C talents. LaRue moves the castle to a more congenial location for Ronaldo and brings back Anti A-C Power Dust to Earth."

"Which begs an important question," Reader said. "Which is this—did Zenoca move the hidden tunnels as well?"

Fancy looked pensive. "I saw the magic and my people did as well. The entire castle glittered golden, disappeared from its original location then reappeared here. Zenoca was in the castle when it moved, but so were all clan leaders, myself included. Our people were outside and could confirm the miracle. Zenoca and the king had not visited the castle long before they insisted it be moved—they had spent their time prior explaining why we were in danger, and those talks took place in Zanell's land."

"Did they ever enter Haven?" Reader asked.

"No, I did not trust Zenoca in his female form or our new king, so I did not allow them entrance or even discuss where and how my people lived."

"Wise. The power cubes work on mental suggestion, James. Meaning that if LaRue wanted to move 'all' the castle, that would include underground and secret areas, too. She might have done so just to save time, and she also could have done it without being more specific." Especially if Algar was watching and offering a little "help."

"And you think Ronaldo hasn't examined the place since then?"

"I think that he might have, but if this area looked boring or confusing—or he almost lost his head due to a spear or something, that he might have stopped. He's not brave, remember. He's just a bastard, in every sense of the word."

The castle had clearly been created by Algar. Meaning that the traps were there both to keep interlopers out but, more importantly, to keep Ronaldo and his people away from the paths that let Fancy and hers in. A being who

could get our pictures and a ginormous telescope in place
thousands of years before we existed could certainly make
a castle that fooled Ronaldo and LaRue.

Fancy put up her paw. "We're approaching the end of
this stairway. Once we leave it, James, you will find more
people. Many more. The ocellar and the chocho must stay
quiet, and we must as well, or we will all die."

We nodded, and I whispered the Stay Silent instructions
to both Wilbur and Ginger, both of whom said they'd control themselves.

Fancy crept forward, looked around, motioned with her
paw, and scurried off. The rest of us followed.

Could hear the sound of people walking and talking,
though it was far off. Could also finally see daylight, meaning there were windows and we were again aboveground.
Looked up. The windows here were high up, just like the
ceilings, open, with nothing hanging over them. Clearly we
weren't in an area of this place where anyone lived.

We continued on, stopping, looking, scurrying, and, in
some cases, just avoiding someone. I was lost beyond belief
and stopped even trying to figure out where we were, where
we'd been, and how we could go back. The castle was even
more of a maze than the old secret tunnel area had been.

Smelled food of some kind cooking and my stomach
growled. Hoped it had growled quietly. Waterfruit were fine,
but they weren't real food, and it had been a long time since
we'd eaten.

Fancy heard my stomach and flashed me a smile. "We go
through part of the kitchens," she whispered in my ear. "We
can grab food along the way."

Sure enough, our next stop was what looked like a pan-
try. Long room with doors on either end and also in the
middle of each long wall. Shelves loaded with foodstuffs
everywhere else. We crept through here, but everything was
an ingredient—nothing was prepared.

However, our goal was the middle door on our left. Once
there, Fancy did the usual stop, listen, open a crack, listen,
lather, rinse, repeat thing. She finally opened the door and
we all trotted inside.

We were in the roasting room. Literally. There were different kinds of meats on spits, and the smell of roasting

meat, and it was as hot a Pueblo Caliente in the middle of summer.

"What kinds of animals are these?" I asked Fancy as she headed toward a spit near the back of the room.

"None you have met. Greenland in particular is filled with game animals. It and the Blue Waterway feed the majority of our planet."

"And there's another reason to move the castle here," I said to Reader as Fancy grabbed what looked like a bird of some kind and tore it apart. It was too small to be Bruno, for which I was extremely thankful. My Peregrine was here, and that meant he was in danger just like everyone else. And I knew without asking that Ronaldo would enjoy eating my pet if he could ensure I got to watch.

Reader nodded. "Control the food, control the people." He took a bite of the leg Fancy had handed him. "Tastes like chicken."

"It is chicken," she said. "The king brought chickens with him. They are the most remarkably stupid animals I have ever encountered."

"That's chickens." Ate my leg with relish. "But this confirms it's who we think it is. I doubt chickens show up all over the cosmos."

"And apparently they're Ronaldo's favorite food. Not sure how that helps us, other than getting us fed, but I'll take it."

All five of us devoured the chicken in record time. Fancy found a cloth that we all used to wipe hands and faces, while Ginger and Wilbur merely licked their chops. Then, sustenance managed, we headed off again.

"I still feel like we're in a video game," Reader muttered. "We earned our food and rest break, and now we get to go on, fortified for the next battle."

Fancy slipped us out through another door that led to the roasting room, and we were back in yet another corridor. Once more we crept and scurried along, and finally reached a small door.

Fancy listened at said door and did the usual rigmarole. We went inside. Small door, small room.

There was no apparent reason for this room, other than that there was another door on the opposite side.

"What's this?" Reader asked softly.

"Antechamber to the king's throne room."

Reader and I exchanged a look. "Get ready, girlfriend. It's about to stop being easy in three ... two ... one ..."

Fancy opened the door.

CHAPTER 65

"**W**OW, James, color me impressed with your pre-science."

The space in front of us was filled with what looked like Ancient Amazonians. But there were some regular Amazons from Beta Twelve in there, too. Nice to know where those who'd followed Lilith and Kyrellis had ended up.

Heard a click behind me. Raced to the door we'd come through. It was now locked. Sure, I could have used my extra A-C strength to pull it open, but why bother? It was a safe bet that there were just more soldiers of some kind out there.

"Do come in," a cheery voice called to us. It was a voice I recognized. "We've been waiting for you."

"Well, how can we refuse such a nice invitation?" Zipped back and stepped in front of Fancy, handing her Ginger as I did so. Decided Algar wasn't going to be offering much advice via my iPod in this circumstance so took all that off and dropped it into my purse. Then I walked through the threshold.

That it was Ronaldo Al Dejahl sitting on a really ostentatious and overwhelmingly gaudy throne wasn't a surprise. That there were a lot more Amazons and Ancients around than was probably healthy for us was also no surprise. That no one else we were looking for was in here with him was the big surprise.

Knew I looked shocked, and had to figure the others did, too. But, happily, Ronaldo wasn't the brightest bulb on the Hanukkah bush. "Surprised to see me and all my friends?" he asked gleefully.

"Um, yeah. Yeah we are." Not. Waited for a reaction—there was none. His power was mind control—at least the original Ronaldo had that trait, along with his troubadour talent—but not necessarily mind reading. But looking at the Ronaldo on The Chair of Ugly Chairs, had a distinct feeling that Chuckie's fears were groundless—as far as I could tell, this was indeed a clone.

Of course, I'd seen more of the clones than Chuckie had, so I could tell that there was just something slightly off about this Ronaldo. He didn't look quite right—something was subtly wrong. Couldn't put my finger on what or why, but I got the distinct feeling that he was a copy of the original.

As I remembered from the last time I'd seen him, he was typical A-C handsome. He was older than Serene but not by too much, about Jeff's size, with dark hair. When we'd met, he'd been mid-twenties. He didn't look much older than that now. But while he looked the way I remembered, there was something missing.

As he grinned at me, I realized one thing that was missing—recognition. He didn't look like he remembered meeting me—or threatening to make me brain-dead then rape me repeatedly so that I could birth all his children while in a coma. There was evil glee in his expression, but no real malice. The Original Ronaldo had come up with a lot of malice when he'd wanted to. Decided my gut, like Reader's, was rarely wrong and just went with it.

Sadly, the cloning process our enemies used meant that the clone had all the memories that the original had. At least, as long as the original or clone du jour had downloaded their brain into the cloning system.

Then again, the last time we'd seen the real original Ronaldo, Jeff had beaten him literally almost to death for a variety of reasons, threatening to make me brain-dead and then rape me being only two of them. And if this clone had been put in place prior to LaRue the First being killed, then that meant he'd been put in place prior to Ronaldo the Maybe Original returning to Earth, as well, and possibly also before Ronaldo the Maybe Original had taken his beatdown. But that would mean that he had a separate memory stream from that point on.

Thought about the Ronaldo Gladys had killed—he'd entered her mind so easily, so deeply, and yet, prior to Operation Infiltration, he'd never really tried. He'd controlled an entire facility full of A-Cs and humans, including Gladys, during Operation Confusion but he hadn't done more than just keep them acting like sheep. His mind control during Operation Infiltration was far more advanced. This could have been the Evildoer Society upping their game . . . or there could have been another reason.

"What are you doing here?" Reader asked, presumably because he'd made the leap, too, and realized that Ronaldo wasn't clear about why we were all shocked. This gave me time to keep on thinking. Yay, Bizarro World, for forcing me to try to think without speaking.

My mind was whirring at its own version of hyperspeed, helped, no doubt, by what I considered real food. What if the Original Ronaldo had been so close to dead after his beatdown that, even though Original LaRue took him off the planet, he couldn't be saved? That would mean she'd had to have cloned the original well before she'd found the Z'porrah, or, at least, before they all hit Earth again to try to destroy us.

If she hadn't cloned Ronaldo prior to the start of Operation Confusion, then the clones she'd made of him wouldn't necessarily have his memories. They'd know what she'd told them, and maybe she'd downloaded Ronaldo's brain in advance, but that download would be missing all the information that happened afterward. This would be the best-case scenario for us. Therefore, it was probably the most unlikely. Not impossible but, the way our luck ran, improbable. Of course, the man in the Butt Ugly Chair sort of said we were lucking out. Maybe.

So what if she'd cloned Ronaldo before Operation Confusion, and therefore even before Jamie was born? After all, they'd cloned Leventhal Reid, and his death predated Operation Confusion by a good year. The LaRue and Reid clones we'd met during Operation Infiltration had indicated they weren't cloning others beyond themselves and the Mastermind. But maybe that's because they already had, or felt that once the Ronaldo Clones were used up they wouldn't need any more? Or maybe Original LaRue hadn't shared with the others that she'd made Ronaldo Clones, and that would mean that LaRue 2.0 wouldn't share that, either.

Original LaRue had spent time on Alpha Four during Operation Confusion. A lot of time. And she had a power cube, meaning she could have easily left the planet and gone to this one and no one would have noticed. For all we knew, there was a cloning facility here. And my guess was that it was with the snakipede pens or cloning facility or whatever they were using to create those monsters. Who would even try to find something those things were protecting?

So, I could take as a working hypothesis that she'd made a couple of Ronaldo clones, just in case. When she'd made them was still iffy, but proof that at least one existed was sitting in front of me. LaRue was a long-term planner, after all.

Also safe to say that the real Ronaldo had been brain-dead or so badly damaged after Jeff's beatdown that, A-C or not, he wasn't worth it to fix or she couldn't fix him. So she installed her most ready Ronaldo Clone on this throne, and left him to keep her interests safe in this solar system.

Then it's off to the Z'porrah home world in her stolen hyperdrive spaceship with another Ronaldo clone in tow. This one, however, maybe they tinkered with. Increased his mind control powers, just in case. After all, the Z'porrah weren't going to stay on Earth. Earth was probably going to be the prize LaRue and Ronaldo got to keep. So, ensure that your man is able to use his mind control even better than before, because a few were able to avoid and ignore said powers in the past.

LaRue was accidentally shot by Esteban Cantu during Operation Infiltration. And it was likely that she hadn't had time to download her memories into her cloning facility on Earth, because they had no time to do so between landing impressively and her being shot. Maybe she'd had time to download before she'd taken off for galactic parts unknown, but she'd been off the planet when Operation Confusion went down, so it was unlikely that she'd done an upload.

Meaning that the Mastermind's team on Earth, the LaRue Clone included, might not know that a Ronaldo Clone was on this planet, running things, or that the guy who came back to Earth with LaRue was also a Ronaldo Clone. The LaRue Clone might not even know that there was a Ronaldo Clone on this planet. But that wasn't a sure enough bet to assume.

Clarence Valentino might have known, since he went to the Z'porrah home world with them, but he was dead now, and his loyalty would have been to LaRue and probably the Z'porrah. She was the one who'd saved him, after all. Even though Cliff had saved him after Operation Destruction, why give up your only ace in the hole? Even Clarence hadn't been that loyal or that stupid. Close, of course, but not quite. And if he'd told Cliff about a Ronaldo clone, then Clarence would have had no one to run to, and I knew for a fact that he hadn't been the kind of guy to go it alone, ever.

But would he have told the LaRue clone? When we "met" her she was about twelve in terms of maturity. Meaning that the chances were extremely slim that Clarence would have told a child about all the things he knew that she didn't. He'd probably planned to, but I'd killed him before she was old enough and he'd had the chance. The likelihood was high that LaRue 2.0 on Earth had no idea that this Ronaldo was on this planet or that the Ronaldo who was instrumental during Operation Infiltration wasn't the real deal.

On Bizarro World, LaRue hadn't told Cliff she was an alien. We'd never seen any indication of her shapeshifting on Earth, so maybe the Cliff in this universe also didn't know. Meaning the Cliff in this universe also might not know that there was a Ronaldo Clone, let alone that he was sitting on the throne of Beta Eight.

"I'm ruling my world," Ronaldo 2.0 said, still cheerfully. "What are you doing sneaking in here?"

"Taking your world away from you." Hey, why waste time with verbal gymnastics? Things were falling from the sky and meant that, in short order, others would be here to do the same. Only I was prepared to defend this world and its inhabitants and I knew without asking that The Clone King was not. He was prepared to welcome the Z'porrah, and that meant he was also willing to let every other creature on this world die. Louie the Lizard and his kind and the snakipedes might have a shot with the Z'porrah, but everyone else on the planet was going to be Dino Chow unless we prevented it.

Ronaldo smirked. "Just how are all of three of you and a couple of pets going to do that?"

Took a look around the room. We were easily outnumbered five to one. Had to assume anyone here was an Ancient traitor—of which they either had an amazing amount or most of them were clones—or a Beta Twelve traitor, because there was no way Queen Renata was in on this.

But it always paid to be sure. Looked at one of the Amazons. "Your queen has allowed you to follow a man's rule?"

She smirked. "Our queen is unfit to rule."

"Ah, that old wheeze again. You all believe that?" I asked the room in general.

Ronaldo's grin went wider as all the female heads nodded. In far too much unison for the Amazonian Ancients. They were clones for sure. Usha's clones, maybe. But while there were a lot of similarities, they didn't really look like exact copies of her.

"Where's Usha?" I knew where the one I'd met was, and I also knew where the one Reader and the others had killed was.

All the Ancient Amazonians smirked. The exact same smirk at the exact same time. Smirking was the thing in this room, apparently. "Around," the spokesclone said.

"Around where? I ask because you all look a lot like her." Actually, now that I'd examined them some more, they didn't. They looked like the dead one. But I didn't know her name.

Group shrug. This was freaky. The whole Multiple Man thing was great, but all the clones I'd met so far were independent thinkers. With these, I didn't get that impression. The Free Women who were here didn't look freaked out. But, thankfully, they also didn't look like carbon copies of each other, either.

"Nearby," the spokesclone said with another smirk that was duplicated by all the others.

"Yeah? Because at least two of you aren't nearby. One's dead and one's captured."

All the eyes narrowed. "What do you mean?" the spokesclone asked.

"Where are my warriors?" Had to figure someone we were looking for was here, and warriors was a nice word that covered everyone.

"Who wants to know?" one of the other smirkers asked.

Was shocked as hell until I realized it was a Free Woman, not an Ancient Amazonian.

"The person who's going to end all of you and save them." No time like the present to see if I had the backup I thought I did or not.

They all laughed and assumed fighting stances. The Ancient Amazonians' stances were exactly the same, the Free Women's were similar but slightly different from each other.

"I think you're going to have to prove that," Ronaldo said with a happy laugh. Had the strong suspicion that he'd been brought along too fast because he sounded like he'd been eating at the Cray-Cray Buffet for a long time. Didn't know if that was going to help us or not, but until proven otherwise, my working hypothesis was that Ronaldo 2.0 was as mad as a bag full of hatters.

"Happy to. Poofs assemble!"

CHAPTER 66

SENT THANKS OUT TO ALGAR, ACE, Naomi, Sandy, and any other superconciousnesses that might be hanging about, because Poofs poured out of my purse. Many more Poofs than I'd been prepared for. I had all of those who'd definitely made this trip with us from Earth—but there were more than those assembled around the five of us.

Ronaldo, the Free Women, and the Amazonian Ancients all laughed. The Poofs were still small and adorable. And the extra Poofs were not Poofs that I recognized at all.

"This is what you think will defeat us?" the spokesclone asked. "You are truly pathetic, and these even more pathetic creatures prove it."

"Poofies? Feel free to be insulted, and also feel free to have a nice snack. Kitty's sure you're all very hungry."

Harlie turned, looked at me, purred, then turned back, gave a growl and went large. Then Harlie growled again, only this growl thundered. It was answered by two other Poofs, one of whom I realized with a shock was Tenley, who was Queen Victoria's Poof. The other Poof I also recognized—it was the Poof that Alexander had kept with him after Operation Invasion. Meaning the Alpha Four Royal Poofs were here. And presumably the two that were left on the planet had gotten as busy as our Poofs.

All the Poofs went large and in charge. There were screams from the Free Women and the Amazonian Ancients as well, though they didn't scream too long. Hey, my Poofs were really hungry and they didn't stop to play with their food.

"I think there are some more of these in the hallway or close by," I said helpfully. A few Poofs zipped out. I heard more screams. And a lot of crunching.

In short order, the Poofs all rejoined us, went to small, and burped as discreetly as they could manage.

"Good Poofies!" Looked at Ronaldo, who hadn't moved from his throne. His expression was an interesting combination of horror and terror. It was a great look on him as far as I was concerned. "Ronnie, thanks so much for letting my adorable weapons of mass destruction have a great meal. They were really hungry. They might be full now, but, you know, I have an ocellar and a chocho who haven't had much food, and I'm sure the Poofs would be willing to share and let them eat you."

"Who *are* you?" He sounded shocked. "They never said you could do anything like that."

Mentally gave myself a high five and sent up another round of thanks—he wasn't a Clone in the Know. The likelihood that he'd been put in place before Ronaldo the Original's embarrassing loss to Jeff and had never had an upload or an update since rose up to the top position.

"We're people on a schedule, Ronnie. And we hate being late. Right now, there's a gigantic civil war brewing, both at home and abroad. And you're at the center of all of it. Aren't you *lucky?*"

Ronaldo 2.0 didn't look like he felt lucky. So he did have a brain in there. Could feel him trying to control my mind. Looked at Reader and Fancy—they looked annoyed but not controlled. Same with Wilbur and Ginger. Looked back to 2.0.

"Ronnie, babe, seriously, we aren't really the mind controllable sort, so stop straining yourself. Or I'll seriously let my cool Beta Eight dog and cat eat you. Right now. In front of me. While I cheer them on."

Felt him stop. "Fine," he snapped. "What is it you want?"

"You off the throne. The civil war on this planet to be fast and bloodless. The civil war going on within this solar system to be over with no more bloodshed. The snakipede factory shut down. Any prisoners you might have or think you have returned to us. For starters. I'm sure I'll have more in a moment." Hey, it paid to ask for what you wanted.

"I have powerful friends."

"Actually, you don't. LaRue or Zenoca or whatever she told you to call her is dead. As is the original version of you and all your clone bros. Clearly we have ways of dealing with your cloned Amazonian Assassins and the Free Women who are going against their Queen. And there's a lot of firepower up there in space that will look at you as the only impediment to their claiming this world for their very own. And then mining the living hell out of it."

He looked smug. "There's more out in space than those."

"Yes, you're right, there is. The Z'porrah fleet is on the way." He looked shocked that I knew this. Always nice to impress your host. "However, I'll kill you before they can ever contact you, let alone land, so I wouldn't be counting on them. They aren't going to help *you*. Sure, they might be able to hurt *us*, but *you'll* be long dead."

2.0's eyes narrowed. "Fine. Which of your many demands should we deal with first?"

"Let's go with prisoners. I'd like to see everyone you have captive, and that includes natives and non-natives, in case you weren't clear."

He stood, nodded curtly, then headed toward a door at the back of the throne room, opposite from the doorway we'd come through.

Reader stepped up behind me. "It's too easy," he murmured. "Assume something bad is coming, in some way."

Fancy was on my other side. "I agree," she said in the same low tone. "Impressive fighting force or no."

"Agreed. If we get separated, figure I'm heading toward the snakipede pits."

"Why would we get—"

Fancy was interrupted by 2.0 reaching the door and kicking up the hyperspeed. I'd been expecting it, and not only due to Reader's warning. So I took off as well. Figured Fancy would catch onto the whole "getting separated" idea rather quickly.

Had to give it to 2.0—he wasn't lacking in the hyperspeed. Of course, neither was I. And him running off had done me a solid—I was angry.

Followed him down a corridor, up a set of stairs, down another corridor, into a room, out the door on the opposite side of this room, up another set of stairs, down yet another corridor, and outside onto a walled walkway. Didn't get a chance to admire the view since we ran across the walkway, down another set of stairs, into another room, out of that room, down a really long corridor, and to a big metal door. Waited for over the river and through the woods, but it wasn't to Grandmother's House we were going.

This was easier to follow than the path Fancy had taken us on to get inside the castle, but I still wasn't confident that I'd have a hope of finding my way back on my own. And I hadn't had a lot of time to note landmarks along the way— one room or corridor in this castle looked pretty much like the rest. Exciting architectural and design elements were not what whoever had built this thing was going for. Stolid, boring, repetition that meant it was easy to get lost apparently was.

On the other hand, it hardly mattered. I'd probably have to check every room of this place anyway to ensure that we'd found everyone we were looking for and to verify that more of our enemies weren't lurking about.

If, you know, I got the chance. Because 2.0 opened the big metal door and ran in, and I ran in right behind him.

Nice to know that Reader had been right. It had definitely been far too easy.

CHAPTER 67

NICE TO KNOW that I'd been right, too. We were in the snakipede pens. And I was really glad I was already angry.

In 2.0's defense, he'd actually brought me to some of his prisoners. Not the ones I was expecting, but I was glad to see them anyway. And, under the circumstances, they were totally living up to their God Names. Really hoped Wilbur would be able to follow me and bring the others—Fancy should get to see her religious idols in action, after all.

The pen was gigantic, built like the biggest scientific hothouse and elephant pen combination you could imagine. There weren't really stalls, but the walls were lined with things I recognized—cloning water chambers. These were different from the ones I'd seen when we'd destroyed the cloning lab under Gaultier Research during Operation Infiltration. However, that was because these were much cruder.

Crude didn't mean ineffective, though. There were a lot of, for want of a better term, snakipede larvae in the vats, and there were a lot of vats as well.

There were also a lot of snakipedes of various sizes slithering and flying about. It was basically the most horrific snake pit in the history of snake pits. And I had to run right damn into it, because 2.0 was in there—and so were my friends.

Rahmi and Rhee had their battle staffs out and activated. How they always had them defied logic, because they had them whether I saw them on their persons or not. It was probably spatial and quantum and deeply mathematical. Decided not to argue when the advanced science that would sound like magic worked in our favor.

The girls were backed up against the far wall, which had gigantic metal barn doors. This was, after all, a barn, albeit an incredibly creepy one. Couldn't tell if the girls were trying to keep the snakipedes in or just wanted something solid against their backs, but the doors were closed and appeared locked.

The princesses were holding off the snakipedes with some truly impressive staff work. Abigail was holding them off as well with some truly impressive glaring. Hoped this meant that the oxygen-rich atmosphere had helped her get all her powers back, versus her just trying to grimace the snakipedes to death. Didn't have time to ask, however.

This Ronaldo might not be doing all that well with mind controlling me and the others with me, but he was spot on with the snakipedes. I could tell because they stopped attacking Abigail, Rahmi, and Rhee and turned all their attention toward me.

"Kill her!" he shouted, as if I couldn't have guessed what he was going for.

When in doubt, go for the classics, that was my motto. Put my hand in my purse. "Self-contained nukes, self-contained nukes, how I'd love to have as many self-contained nukes as there are snakipedes."

Touched something that felt like a softball, only hard and kind of tingly. Pulled it out. Looked familiar, like Christopher had pitched it to Jeff, who'd batted it into Mephistopheles' mouth what seemed like so long ago now. Felt a pang of nostalgia for Operation Fugly—there had only been two terrifying snakes I'd had to deal with back then.

Of course, having the nukes was only part of the battle. I had to pitch them all into the snakipedes' mouths. And I had no bat. And while I was good at throwing, I wasn't sure that I was up to Nolan Ryan standards.

Tossed the nuke at the nearest snakipede. And, this being my luck, missed. The nuke went sailing toward the girls and I cringed. Blowing up my friends hadn't been my plan.

The snakipedes turned to follow the path of the nuke. An animal reaction to something flying by them, presumably. Though this shouldn't have been the case if they were still mind controlled. Meaning maybe they weren't anymore, or else 2.0's mind control wasn't all that strong. But, independent thinkers or not now, that put them facing the girls again. Also not my plan. So far, I wasn't doing so well on the save.

Decided I was better off next to the girls, if only so I could catch the nuke and toss it again, so I took off. Realized I wasn't going to reach the girls before the nuke did and I winced. But Rahmi and Rhee had the equivalent of bats, and they'd spent a lot of time on Earth and they worshipped Tito, who, like me and Tim, was a baseball fan.

Rahmi jumped out and swung her staff at the nuke. She hit, and the nuke sailed back just as I reached them and spun around. The trajectory wasn't destined to hit a snakipede. At first. But then it moved and sailed right into a nearby, gaping snakipede maw.

"Great to see you three. How's this plan sound? We are all going to run like our lives depend up on it—because they do—and we are going to run for the door I came through."

Of course, as I said this, the door closed with a bang and a really loud click. Wasn't sure, but I thought I heard Ronaldo 2.0 laughing.

"Or not," Abigail said. "Any other ideas?"

Reached into my purse and pulled out a nuke. Tossed it at a snakipede, badly, but Abigail sent it into an open mouth anyway.

"Do you have more of those?" Abigail asked. "Because I don't think two is going to be enough."

"I do indeed. And by the way, batter up!"

I tossed nukes up in the air in front of the three of them. The princesses batted the nukes and Abigail aimed them. This was great in that we were all doing this at hyperspeed so every giant snakipede was getting a nuke treat. The problems were plentiful, though—there were plenty of smaller snakipedes to cover for those who had Nuke Treats, Ronaldo 2.0 had disappeared and locked us inside the literal House of Horrors, and when the nukes exploded, we didn't want to be here. If, you know, the nukes exploded before the snakipedes ate us.

"Girls, after we toss these next few nukes, we need another plan."

"Sounds good," Abigail said. "Do you happen to have one?"

The snakipedes were within arm's reach. And we all had hyperspeed and they didn't. And Claudia and Lorraine had done similar during Operation Fugly, after all. Besides, it would be the most horrible option for me, so naturally it was the only option we had.

"Yeah. Run fast, grab hold, get on their backs right behind their heads, and ride 'em, cowgirls."

Ducked and ran under the snakipede in front of me. Kept on running and went for the door, just in case. Naturally it was locked.

Not a problem, I was using hyperspeed and I headed for the nearest one—which was this moment's definition of "spoilt for choice"—and leaped up. Grabbed a scale and hoisted myself up. Reached a wing and grabbed it.

This wasn't so wise, as the snakipede felt and didn't like my doing this. It turned and struck at me, but I'd managed to get up on its back and ran forward as fast as I could, which was pretty fast, since my adrenaline rush was off the charts. Controlling myself from screaming at the top of my lungs indefinitely was really helping fuel my other abilities.

Reached the back of its head as its fangs slammed onto its own tail. Didn't stop to wait and see what was going to happen, just leaped for the next nearest snakipede.

The other girls were on the snakipedes, doing similar. Riding them was kind of out, but jumping onto them and making them crazy was definitely in. We were causing chaos, which was great, but I didn't figure we had long before the nukes went off.

The smaller snakipedes were getting into the act and starting to head for us, either because 2.0 was telling them to or they'd realized what was going on. There were a lot of them and only four of us, and all it was going to take was one snakipede biting each one of us to ensure we all died, fast and ugly.

The princesses were using their battle staffs to keep the smaller snakipedes away and it was possible that Abigail had a shield around herself, but I didn't, and none of us were going to hold out long in any case. It was really time for another new plan. I just didn't have one.

Looked into my purse. "Help. Is there anything that kills

these snakipedes fast that won't kill me and the other gals at the same time? Or just, you know, any possibility that someone else could perform the miraculous save?"

The snakipedes all thudded to the ground. Was really happy the girls and I were on top of some of them when this happened because if we'd been on the floor we'd have all been crushed.

The monsters weren't moving. Chose to take this as a really good sign.

"What the hell?" Abigail called.

"No clue. Time to get off them and open a door."

"We can't open the big ones," Rahmi said, pointing to the barn doors as we all ran for the door I'd come in through. "They're reinforced with iron bars and more. This entire room is designed to keep those things inside until someone wants to let them out."

"We haven't been able to open this door, either," Rhee said. "Believe me, we've tried."

Heard the first explosion. "We need to get out of here, immediately if not sooner." Reached the door, grabbed the handle, and pulled with all my might.

CHAPTER 68

LUCKILY FOR ME, Rahmi was behind me, because the door flew open and I flew back. She caught me as we all saw a happy sight—Reader was there. "Get out!"

Didn't have to tell us twice. We ran and he slammed the door behind us, as more explosions went off.

"How did you get explosives in there?" he asked me, as Wilbur put his paws on my shoulders and licked my face.

"Long story. I can guess how you found us—good boy, Wilbur—but how did you get the snakipedes to stop and drop?"

"That took a different kind of persuasion." Reader pointed and I looked to see Ronaldo 2.0 on his knees, with Fancy's very long claws at his throat and face, with particular emphasis on his eyes. Meanwhile, Ginger was growling right at his groin.

The explosions continued. The whole place shook, but nothing came down. "How'd you catch him?"

"Wilbur tracked you, and as Ronaldo there ran out and closed the door he laughed, meaning Ginger could hear him and she attacked. He's clawed up a lot on his backside. Fancy joined in and we suggested that he call off whatever was attacking you or we'd slice him up slowly and let him watch us feed him to the Poofs."

"I love it when you're nasty." The explosions finally stopped. Heaved a sigh. "Girls, you were awesome. How long were you in there?"

"Days," Abigail said. "We landed in the throne room. We were outnumbered and they captured us."

"We took down twenty before they did so," Rhee said. "I counted."

"Good job. How did you survive in there for minutes, let alone days?"

"We were in a cage," Rahmi replied. "The cage dumped us out about a minute or so before you arrived. We used it to hold them off for a while, but then when it got knocked aside, we went back to our normal fighting styles."

"Good call. I wonder why they captured you, though. Everyone else has treated us all like Gods or at least strangers to help."

"He knew who we were." Abigail went over to 2.0. "And I know who you are." Her voice was low and icy and more dangerous than I'd ever heard. "You're why my brother and my aunt are dead, and because of that, why my sister is dead."

Went to her and put my hand on her shoulder. "No, he's not. He's not the real Ronaldo Al Dejahl. He's a clone. The one who caused us all so much trouble during Operation Infiltration was a clone, too. There are a lot of clones around, and not just the snakipedes." Pulled Abigail gently away from 2.0. Now wasn't necessarily the time to kill him.

"The what?" Rahmi asked.

"The things we were just fighting."

"Oh, them. They told us they were called the Horrors. That name seemed apt."

"It is apt but, um, well, you know . . ."

"Shealla is the Giver of Names," Fancy said, as she nodded solemnly to the three girls, while never letting her claws waver from 2.0's face and throat. "You are the Venida. You know the Queen of the Gods will rename as she sees fit."

The girls stared at me. "Long story. They all, um, know we're Gods here, okay? So don't try to fool them."

"No," Abigail said dryly, "we surely wouldn't want to do that."

"We need to verify that all the snakipedes and the snakipede cloning equipment is destroyed," I said quickly.

"I'm not willing to die from radiation poisoning," Reader said. "So I vote that we take it on faith and send in a hazmat team later."

"We need to find the others," Fancy added.

"Speaking of whom, Ronnie, where are your other prisoners?"

"I don't have any." He sounded strained, not snippy, meaning he was very aware of the claws and fangs hovering nearby. "I'm injured."

"I care. Deeply. But until I have every single solitary prisoner of yours in my custody, you're just going to keep on bleeding. And potentially keep on getting clawed up. Hard to say at this precise time."

"Where are the other warriors under your command?" Rahmi asked him.

"Her creatures ate them," 2.0 said.

The girls all looked at me. "All of them?" Rhee asked.

"Think so. Not sure. Ah, Poofies? Where are you? Come to Kitty."

Waited. No Poofs appeared. Oh great—we now had this moment's new definition of "not good." Lucky us.

"Who else is missing?" Abigail asked while I tried not to fret. Failed.

"Everyone. We were all together and only missing you three, but there was a trap set around a dead body—one of the Amazonian Ancient Clones—and the others ran into it. We five didn't."

Abigail turned back to Ronaldo 2.0. "So where are they?" she snarled. "You took them and put them somewhere. Tell us, and I might let them stop me from doing to you what I wanted to do to your clone brother."

"I have no idea. You three were the only ones who landed here."

Wished Jeff was here, for multiple reasons. Right now, though, I wished that I could tell if 2.0 was lying.

"You obviously knew there were others," Reader said, picking up the slack. "Otherwise you'd have chosen your words differently."

"You all just told me there were others here," 2.0 snapped. "I had three aliens land in my throne room, obviously attempting an assassination. They failed. Clearly the rest of you are doing a better job eliminating me."

"Why would you think we were here to assassinate you?" Rhee asked. "When you pulled us here?"

"Wasn't me pulling anyone here. We don't have the technology to do that on this planet."

This wasn't true. But none of the natives had known about the power sphere and 2.0 didn't sound like he was lying.

"So you thought someone beamed some assassins in here?" I asked him.

"Why not? Every other planet has higher tech than we do. They wouldn't be the first to try."

Oh really? "Why would someone want to assassinate you?"

"You mean besides them and her?" He waggled his eyebrows toward Fancy.

"I am containing a dangerous prisoner," Fancy said haughtily. "If I wanted you dead, you would already be dead."

"She has a good point, Ronnie. I'm still back on how you would think two Free Women would be here to assassinate you, when you had a room full of them at your beck and call."

"I figured they were with her." Now the brows waggled toward Abigail.

"So, you did know what your clone brother did to my family?" Abigail asked, voice silky with menace. I'd never seen her like this, but then again, I could understand her mindset.

"No," 2.0 said with clearly forced patience. "I was warned about all of you before I took the throne. And I was also warned about my enemies in this solar system."

Realization dawned. "Who are they?" Pointed to Rahmi and Rhee.

"The bloodline of the Royal Family of Beta Twelve, and the sworn enemies of those who protect me. Is this some sort of stupid test?"

"Yes. Why would you think they were coming to assassinate you?"

He rolled his eyes, which was an interesting look considering Fancy's claws were still in front of them. "Because I know there are a lot of other inhabited planets in this system and they all want my world. Beta Twelve, in particular, wants it."

They did? "They do? Why?"

"Because what we have will give them the spaceflight ability they want more than anything else."

CHAPTER 69

"**QUEEN RENATA IS** aware of why her people aren't being allowed spaceflight."

Ronaldo 2.0 shrugged. He was ballsy, I had to give him that. But then, that was a Ronaldo Trait. As was being an asshat, a jerk, and a murderous psychopath, so I didn't allow myself to get too impressed. "Maybe when you last saw her she was good with it. Now? Not as much."

"What changed?" Reader asked, of Rahmi and Rhee as much as Ronaldo.

Rahmi shook her head. "When we were sent to Earth, things were exactly as Kitty has said. My mother was in close agreement with the Planetary Council and the King of Alpha Four about most, if not all, things." Rhee nodded.

"So how do you know this?" Fancy snarled at 2.0.

"I have spies on the other planets," he replied, as if this was obvious. "Just like they have spies here. I think your pets ate some of them."

"Bummer. Maybe." Thought about this. "You know ... why would the Snow Globe Beetles have eaten all the snaki-pede corpses, but not have eaten the Usha clone corpse?" Got a sick feeling in my stomach. "Do you think the Usha and other Amazonian Ancient clones are deadly in some way if ingested?" Because, if so, I'd just killed all my Poofs.

Felt ill. Then felt something soft at my neck.

Reached up and found Poofikins in my hand. The Poof purred at me, mewled a bit, and I snuggled it to my face. "Kitty is *so* glad you and the others are okay."

"Poofs are okay?" Reader asked, sounding tense. He had

a Poof he loved, too. We all did, and they were all on this planet with us.

"Yeah. Per Poofikins they've been searching the castle. Amazingly enough, Ronnie here isn't lying—none of the rest of our people are in here. In fact, there are no other living souls in here, since we apparently wiped out the snakipedes, go team."

"They checked the area that had just been nuked?" Abigail sounded worried.

Poofikins mewled at her, purred, then went into my purse. "Yes, they were fast." And protected. Being Black Hole Universe creatures, they had protections the rest of us didn't and probably never would. Being Algar's pets meant they could do what they wanted, when they wanted, so I was personally relieved that they'd all searched for the others. Attached Poofs were *attached*, so that made sense.

"There were other Poofs," Reader said. "More than I thought had come with us."

"Good point. Ah, Poofikins or Harlie, if it's convenient, could you come to Kitty?"

Poofikins popped out of my purse with a sleepy grumble. The Poofs believed in napping at any and all times when they weren't needed. Wasn't sure if they'd picked this up from the A-C's or vice versa, but it was a trait I was very familiar with by this time. Poofikins mewled, purred, grumbled, and mewled again. Then back into my purse. Apparently the Poofs were tired out from their activities, because, as I looked in, I had a lot of them in there now.

"Yes, those are local solar system Poofs. Here to help us, regardless of their owners' views."

"Are you saying Alexander or Victoria are against us?" Reader sounded worried. Couldn't blame him.

"No, but there are a lot more Poofs now, and therefore, a variety of different owners. Alexander has allowed the Poofs to go to other planets."

"Why?" Abigail asked flatly. "That seems remarkably stupid or generous. Or both."

Looked at 2.0 and thought about it. "Because not all spies have to look like us."

The Poofs were attached to me, but they were also attached to the Alpha Four Royal Family, and had been attached to them first and for far longer than they'd been with me. For millennia, really. And the same was definitely true of Algar. And my husband and therefore our daughter were also part of that Royal Family.

So, the Poofs were going to be on Alexander's side, and, by extension, ours. Perhaps he had a talent for Poof Chatting like I did, or else the Poofs got their points across to him. But I was pretty sure he was utilizing the Poofs as a spy and defense network. Which was hella impressive, when you thought about it.

And it begged a question—had the Alpha Centauri Poofs come to help us on their own, because of a request from Harlie, or because Alexander had asked them to?

"So, where are the others, then, if they're not in this castle?" Reader asked, pulling me back to the most relevant conundrum.

"No idea," 2.0 said. "I only knew you were coming because you came through the tunnel."

"You're saying you know of the tunnels?" Fancy asked with a little growl.

"Yes. I let you raid. Because I'm a nice king that way."

"Dude, seriously, no one here likes you. Stop baiting everyone, or someone's going to end your life, and, news flash, there is no way for you to make another Ronnie. And even if there was, *you'll* be gone."

"Tell her why you supposedly allowed her to raid," Reader added. "Or I'll be happy to agree to let the ocellar and chocho eat you. Because as far as I'm concerned your original murdered my in-laws and I'm really not above taking all our rage and grief out on you. Sure, it's not fair, but then neither is life, right?"

"James, seriously, I *love* it when you're nasty! Now, Ronnie, let's try this again. Answer the questions."

"You people . . . you think in such straight lines. Look, can everyone stop threatening me? I'm aware that half of you can catch me and all of you want to kill me. This position isn't comfortable. Can I at least sit?"

Figured Fancy and Ginger could be getting tired. "Sure. Wilbur, you sit behind the nasty man, Ginger, stay in front, and the rest of us will surround all of you. All campfire cozy."

Fancy and Ginger backed off a bit, Wilbur got into position, and 2.0 sat on his butt. "Finally. Thank you."

"So, you were trying to insult us, I think. So do go on."

"Not an insult. You all just tend to think in straight lines. 'If I wasn't caught when I raided, then they don't know I was here.' And so on."

"How is that thinking in a straight line?" Abigail asked. "It makes sense."

Reader nudged me. "You don't think in straight lines," he said quietly. "It's one of the reasons you always figure out what's going on."

He was right and I decided to take the hint and once again toss on my Megalomaniac Girl cape. "I get why you'd let them think they weren't seen if you were trying to trap them. But you don't appear to be trying to trap them . . . Oh. Duh."

"What?" Rhee asked.

"He let Fancy's Ferrets raid so that he could follow them back. They're good, and they were cautious, so it took time. Get a little farther each time. Soon enough, you know where Haven is. Then you sneak your spy into Haven and wait."

"I didn't have a spy in Haven," 2.0 said. I shot him a look that said I knew he was a liar. He shook his head. "Seriously. You're right, I had them followed. And yes, we were ready to attack tonight. That got foiled." He made the Ate A Lemon Face. "I presume by all of you."

"Pretty much. But I still don't buy it. Usha was in Haven and she was trying to open the door to let snakipedes in. If she wasn't working for you, who the hell was she working for?"

"You mentioned that name before. I don't know an Usha."

"Pull the other one, it has bells on."

He shrugged. "I just thought you were using a common Free Woman name. I didn't have a spy in Haven. Frankly, if you hadn't shown up, I wouldn't have needed one. Open the doors, let in my Horrors, no more Haven."

"Fancy, you said the Horrors had been here forever, right?"

"Yes, Shealla."

"Have we, by any chance, destroyed all the Horrors by blowing up the giant pen they were in?"

"No, Shealla. Because where you and the Venida were is

not their nesting place. The Horrors nest out of doors, at the far side of the castle. We have never entered the room you and the Venida were in."

"Huh. So, Ronnie, why were you making Horror Clones? Just not enough bad in the world or something?"

"You actually have to ask? Because I can control them and they are the best fighting force anyone could have."

"Not quite, apparently. What about the naturally born ones? Can you control them, too?" As the words left my mouth, I knew the answer. Of course he could. And, point of fact, of course he *was*. Contemplated all my options. Decided to go for the best one. Stood up. "Ginger, please come to Kitty."

She backed away from 2.0 and came to me. Picked her up and gave her to Reader. Then stepped closer to 2.0 and gave him a nice roundhouse to the head. He went down.

The others stared at me.

"Not that I object," Rahmi said finally, "but may I ask why?"

"The why is that he was spending his time 'being helpful' so that he could call the other snakipedes here. I'd imagine we have a bunch of them really close by, and if they can get inside this castle in some way, assume that they have done and are doing so."

Sure enough, heard a far-off hissing and what sounded like scales scraping against rock.

"Oh, good," Reader groaned. "So, we're once again caught between a rock and a hard place."

"Figures," Abigail said, as she and the other girls stood up. "Or, as we call it, routine."

CHAPTER 70

"**F**ANCY, how well do you know the castle?"

"Not well enough to ensure escape, Shealla, but well enough that we may have hope."

"Good enough for government work. Rahmi, please carry Ronnie there and be sure to knock him out again if he starts to wake up. Rhee, take the last position and keep Rahmi in front of you, so you can cover the rear and help keep Ronnie unconscious."

"Yes, Kitty," the princesses said in unison.

"James, carry Ginger—she's an attack cat and is trained to fly through the air, land on snakipedes, and do them serious bodily harm. I don't want us throwing Ginger unless we have to, but since we may have to, you get the honors."

"Why me?"

"Because I want Fancy focused on tracking and leading us out, Wilbur focused on smelling for danger and sniffing for a way out, and, frankly, I don't think I can actually force myself to toss Ginger at a snakipede."

Ginger purred at me, leaned out of Reader's arms, and gently head butted me. I snuggled her back.

Reader pulled her gently away. "Got it. I'll only toss her if it's life or death, or she has the best shot of killing one of those things."

"Thanks."

"So, what are you going to be doing? Tossing nukes?"

"No idea what you're talking about. Fancy, Wilbur, let's get going, because I could just be jumpy, but I'd swear the hissing and scaly slithering sounds are getting louder, and I also think I hear something that sounds like hundreds of horrible wings flapping at hummingbird speeds. In other words, we need to get moving."

Fancy and Wilbur took the lead, him sniffing, her slinking cautiously. Next came me and Abigail, then Reader and Ginger, with the princesses at the end.

"How good is their hearing?" Abigail asked.

"No idea."

"Not as good as ours," Fancy replied quietly. "But if we choose to make noise and make it easy for them . . ."

We all took the hint and shut up. The long corridor that I'd followed 2.0 down to reach the metal door seemed clear, but Fancy didn't take us that way. There was another hallway that went to the right, if you were facing the door, and we went down that instead.

The reason for this became clear—the hallway led to a narrow staircase, a staircase too narrow for a full-grown snakipede to fit into. Of course, there were smaller snakipedes, too. However, I hadn't seen any of them hunting, and hopefully that mean that 2.0 hadn't called the youngsters over, too.

We could go up or down, and we went down. We'd been on ground level, at least I thought so, when we'd been at the snakipede pens. Meaning we were going underground again now.

But only for a short while. We reached another landing and, though the stairs continued down, we didn't. Down another dark corridor and into a room that looked a lot like a dungeon. The door wasn't locked, though, and there were no prisoners in evidence. Rhee stayed at the door, on guard, while the rest of us went in and did a thorough search.

"He may have been telling the truth," Fancy said quietly as we finished perusing this room. "I felt it was best to verify that the others were not here."

"No argument here." Nothing in this area looked too old, meaning that it had probably been furnished once 2.0 was on the throne. "Where to from here, though?"

"Through the torturer's chambers." She opened a small door that was behind something that looked very much like an iron maiden, though not the cool band, and trotted through.

Motioned to Rhee to join us, then we followed Fancy through into a rather cheery looking room that was set up for comfort. Nice to know that the torturers were treated well, presumably under the idea that everyone should be happy in their work. Hoped Ronnie would wake up so I could punch him and knock him out again, but then again, had to figure that the person who'd actually set this all up was LaRue.

The cozy torturer's chambers led to another corridor. This one had a lot of hallways crisscrossing each other. Wilbur sniffed a lot down here and took the lead. Once again we were in Maze Central but since I hoped to never have to come back this way, chose not to care.

After a few twists and turns, I realized we were in the underground working area of the castle. That no one was here was beyond strange. One didn't reign as a monarch with no servants, no workpeople, and no one hanging about trying to curry favor.

"How has this place been functioning if there are no people in it?"

Fancy shook her head. "There have always been many Lecanora working here when we have raided."

"In the torture chambers, too?"

She shook her head. "I have only seen those used to hold prisoners, and not too many. He may not be a good king, but he hasn't stooped to that."

"Then why are they there?" Abigail asked.

"Maybe because others planned to use them and never made it back or got around to it. At any rate, if Ronnie's had a full staff before, where are they now? I find it hard to believe that he sent them all away to protect them, and since there are no bodies or evidence of people being murdered, where are all those who work here? We had to avoid people when we came in."

"They were all the ones you call Amazons," Fancy said.

"Curiouser and curiouser. James, any thoughts?"

"Many, but the main one is that a lot of people appear to have disappeared. More than we were expecting and more than makes sense. If we think in straight lines."

"You think Ronnie's staff were spirited away like our people were?"

"I think that if he's telling the truth and he didn't take Jeff and the others, then someone else did. And if that someone else is working against Beta Eight, they might have taken the king's staff with the idea of making said king more vulnerable to attack."

"He wasn't joking about thinking we were assassins," Abigail said. "When we appeared in front of him he freaked out, screamed for guards, and basically acted like the biggest baby in the galaxy. He put us into a cage in with the Horrors because he said he thought we could escape anything else."

"So, our question is—is the enemy of our enemy our friend, or a worse enemy?"

"Figure we'll find out the hard way, girlfriend. You know, like we always do."

"Ain't it the truth?"

We forged on. Wilbur found stairs up so up we went. We were much more quiet and cautious again, because we could hear things above us. They sounded slithery. And big.

Reached a landing and Fancy motioned us to stop while Wilbur backpedaled as quickly and softly as possible. Didn't take genius to guess that we'd come up around snakipedes.

"Do we go back down and try the other route?" I asked her as quietly as possible.

She shook her head. "We avoided the exterior walkway this way, which we want to continue to do. We need to reach the tunnels we used to enter. They will be our only safe passage out."

"How many are out there?"

"Two. But the room is small."

"Safe to take a peek?"

She nodded, so I slunk over and checked the situation out. There were indeed only two snakipedes in the room, but they weren't flying. Meaning they were blocking the door we clearly had to get to which was, naturally, on the opposite side of the room. Hadn't thought these things could be more horrifying but, strangely enough, being on the ground and looking the most snakelike that they had so far made them much, much worse.

We all backed down the stairs a ways. On the positive side, the stairway was too narrow for the snakipedes to get through. Shared the situation with the others.

"Go back and risk it or try to get through this and probably die?" Reader shook his head. "I pick going back and taking our chances."

Heard a noise and realized 2.0 was coming around. Managed to stop Rhee before she could club him. "I have a plan," I said to her surprised look.

We sat him upright and sort of gently slapped him awake. He glared at me. "I hate you."

"Feeling is beyond mutual, Ronnie. But here's the thing—we're going to get out of your creepy abandoned castle full of snakipedes and—"

"Wait, what? What do you mean, 'abandoned'? I have a large staff. They might be hiding because of the Horrors, but they're here."

"There's no one here but us and the snakipedes, dude. We've checked, as have the Poofs. And before you suggest it, the Poofs didn't eat everyone else." Looked in my purse. "Did you?" Harlie looked up and gave me a hurt mewl. Petted the Poof. "Sorry, just had to check." Turned back. "No, the Poofs didn't eat anyone. And there was no one else here when they searched."

2.0 went pale. "Could the Horrors have killed them all?" He sounded genuinely upset. "I didn't want that. My people who work here are good people."

Reader and I exchanged a look. "I hate it when they show humanity," he said.

"Dude, it's like you read my mind." Wondered if that meant a katyhopper was nearby. Kind of hoped so, but on the other hand, didn't want any katyhoppers to become Snakipede Chow, so better that it was just us being on the same wavelength. "Ronnie, the people were gone before you called the Horrors from outside to come in and kill us."

This didn't reassure—his face drained of more color. "You have to protect me."

CHAPTER 71

"EXCUSE ME?" Abigail asked, speaking for all of us.

"If they've taken my retainers, it's to get to me."

"You're amazingly paranoid for a guy on a planet that appears to be pretty darned peaceful. Who is out to get you? Aside from us, I mean."

He shook his head. "I don't know. I never see them. But over the past few months, I know I've been watched."

"That's it? You think you've been watched? For this you're all freaked out? You, the guy speaking to snaki-pedes? Speaking of which, we'll deal with your paranoia along the way—we need to get past your pets. In an extremely unscathed manner. So you're going to call them off or put them into a stupor or whatever you did when James threatened your life before. And we are all going to walk out of here together. Or we'll kill *you* before they can kill us. You follow?"

He nodded. "I'll do that if . . ."

"You don't have a lot of bargaining power with us," Reader pointed out.

"If you protect me from whoever's trying to kill me. Being deposed, okay, I suppose. But I don't want to die. Yes, I'm a clone, but . . . I'm still a person, I'm still real, still me. And I don't want to stop being me."

"You aren't exactly someone worth keeping around," Abigail snarled.

"Oh, let's not sell Mister Mind Control short, okay? He's not effective on any of us, for which he should be grateful because I'd have already broken his neck, but he's going to work some magic on our terrible predators out there. I'd call that a modicum of worth."

"Promise me," 2.0 said. "Promise me you'll protect me. Or else there's no reason for me to help you, if I'm just going to die anyway. How you'll kill me will be better."

"Why would you say that, if you don't know who's actually trying to kill you?" Fancy asked.

"I don't know who they are—they're invisible to me. But . . . we hear things. Footsteps where none are, low laughter, quiet banging in an empty room, small things missing, things rearranged with no explanation, food gone, and not due to her raids." He nodded toward Fancy.

"That sounds like a haunting," Reader said. "And let me just share that I don't believe in ghosts."

"Yes, but . . . it also sounds like something else." During Operation Destruction Clarence Valentino had "hidden" like this in the Bahraini Embassy, freaking everyone out. He'd done so on purpose. "I think we may have a superfast being or beings around who are potentially up to no good." And they'd have to be Surcenthumain-enhanced fast in order to not be seen by 2.0, who was an A-C clone, or the Free Women, who all had hyperspeed.

"It could be something else," Rahmi said.

"Yeah? What?"

"A superconsciousness, like those who visited us on Earth."

Let that sit on the air for a bit. "Okay," I said slowly. "Could be. But that seems a little too . . . capricious for the ones we've met. Let's assume a corporeal being for now—versus a ghost or superconsciousness—and go back to focusing on getting out of this castle in one, living piece. So, yes, Ronnie, we'll do our best to protect you as long as you return the favor and do your best to protect us. Start with putting your snakipedes in the next room to sleep or sending them home. Your choice, but make it snappy."

He nodded and closed his eyes for about a minute. "They're asleep," he said as he opened his eyes. "It's simpler than sending them home. They came expecting to feed. If I can't send them to food source, then letting them sleep is better."

"Who goes first?" Reader asked. "Putting him in the center doesn't protect us."

"I will go first," Rahmi said. "And Rhee will go last. Our staffs will keep the Horrors at bay better than any other weapon."

"Bullets work really well, but it takes a lot of them, and it's noisy, so I'm okay with that plan. Ronnie, should anything hurt either one of the princesses, you, and you alone, will be directly responsible for whatever kind of horrible war thing happens. And while you might want that, trust me when I say that we'll make you pay for it in a really nasty way. Nastier than anything we've suggested so far, I might add."

"I suggest we stay close together," 2.0 said. "And move swiftly. I can't keep them asleep forever."

Rahmi took the lead, Wilbur with her, then Reader and Ginger followed, with me and Fancy holding onto 2.0 tightly and Abigail right behind him, with Rhee at the rear. We were all close together and stayed that way as we entered the room.

There wasn't a lot of sneaking room in between the two giant snakipedes, but we managed it, in a slow and winding way. Couldn't speak for the others, but I had to control my screaming impulse the entire time. However, terrifying though it was, the snakipedes didn't wake up.

Resisted the urge to kill them where they slept. They were animals—horrible animals, created animals, but animals nonetheless. They were doing things that were in their nature. And while they'd have eaten us if they'd found us asleep, we weren't them.

Got out of the room and moved faster down the hallway, though there were a couple of snakipedes here, too. Also snoozing, for which I thanked anyone and everyone who might be paying attention.

Clustered together and staying very quiet we wended our way through the castle, past more sleeping snakipedes than I cared to count.

Maybe it was because 2.0 had mentioned it, but after a short while I truly felt like I was being watched. We reached a room miraculously devoid of giant flying snakes, and we all took a little breather. "I wish you hadn't said you felt like you were being watched," Reader said to 2.0.

"You felt it, too?" Rhee asked.

"I'm sure we all did," 2.0 said. "Because we are being watched."

"Or else you can affect us and make us think so, power of suggestion assisted by mind influence and all that."

He rolled his eyes. "Look, the concentration it takes to keep hungry animals asleep while we're trying to get out takes me to my limit. I don't have the energy to try to affect people I've already had no effect on. Some of us know when to stop banging our heads on a wooden door."

"Blah, blah, blah. And some of us don't trust you at all. But anyway, we're all agreed we felt the creepy?"

All the heads nodded. "But I don't feel it here," Fancy said.

Group consensus—no one felt like they were being watched in this room. Looked around. Just another room in the castle, a room whose purpose I couldn't figure out. "So, what's special about this room? As in, why couldn't someone see us or follow us or whatever in here?"

"It's an oratory," Reader said. "The private chapel for the lord of the manor."

"James, your hidden depths never cease to amaze me. Ronnie, are you the prayerful type?"

"Not really."

"So, whoever's watching us either can't see into this room because it's protected, or they want us to think that they can't see us when we're here, so we'll get superstitiously freaked out."

"Who would do that?" Rhee asked.

"Someone who's testing us." Considered the options. Could be the Sandy and the Superconsciousness Seven, but I doubted it. They liked to show up, be all impressive, and boss beings around. Definitely wasn't ACE's style. Was Algar's, but I knew this wasn't him. Couldn't be Naomi, since she wasn't allowed to be near us, in the cosmic sense. This also wasn't the Z'porrah's style. Had no idea what style the other planets around here were fond of, nor if this could be an Ancient spy, but it didn't feel right. This *was* totally Siler's style, but he wasn't here.

Had to stop thinking in a straight line. The question wasn't who was watching us or not. The question was—who had something to gain by making Ronaldo 2.0, aka the King of Beta Eight, think he was being watched and turning him paranoid? And the corollary question was, who could do it all while being invisible?

The answer wasn't anyone native to this planet. We'd met all the sentient races, at least as far as anyone had mentioned. Siler wasn't here, and his blending ability seemed incredibly rare, and was probably due to experimentation more than natural genetics. And no one had been playing these games with me and my team here until 2.0 had mentioned being watched. Meaning whoever it was could hear us, too.

Glanced around the room again. It was by far the smallest room we'd been in so far. Thought about when we'd felt like we were being watched. It was never in an area where we were really cramped in with snakipedes. Every place we'd mentioned was one where we had a lot more space around us, snakipedes or no.

As Sherlock Holmes and my "uncle" the top assassin in the business both said, once you eliminated the impossible, whatever remained, however improbable, was the truth. We lived in a universe where impossible didn't seem to exist, however. Even so, there were a lot of improbables I could eliminate for a variety of reasons, such as ghosts and Siler. Meaning the obvious answer was, despite what logic would want to tell you, the right one.

Looked at Wilbur, bent down and gave him a pet. "I know there are a lot of smells here," I said softly, as I ruffled his neck and head bristles. "But can Wilbur find someone who doesn't belong? Not a snakipede, and not those with Kitty, but someone who's hiding from us? He's probably moving very fast, too, but we might not feel him. His smell will be all over, because he's been here for some time. It could be in this room, too, but he's not in the room right now. Search quietly, though. Kitty's bet is that he's in the hall, but we need to be sure."

Wilbur gave a very quiet honk and began to snuffle the air in a different way than he had before. Before he'd been looking for the safe way out, so his nose had been focused on finding our scents again and avoiding snakipede scent. The castle was loaded with smells, so he had to be selective.

Continued petting him and looked back to the others. "Let's take a few moments in here to relax and figure out what we're going to do next where there are no snakipedes or something creeping us out. I think we've earned the rest."

The others stared at me. Reader recovered the quickest. "Ah, okay?"

Had to give a clue, at least to Reader, but not tip off the person I was sure was close by and definitely listening. "Yeah. It's kind of Old Home Week with Ronnie here. Always shocking to come face-to-face with someone you thought was dead, after all. Kind of haven't had time to collect from that. And doesn't this all kind of remind you of Operation Destruction? You know, when we met Mona, Khalid, Oren, and Jakob?"

Reader opened his mouth—to tell me he didn't see the connection I was pretty sure—then I saw him catch on. "Oh! Right. Yeah. Let's rest, you're right. We could make a mistake if we go rushing off like we're fighting ghosts."

Mercifully, the girls had learned not to ask questions when we were being strange, and Fancy's expression told me she knew Reader and I were passing code. 2.0, on the other hand, wasn't as tuned in to the program.

"What are you blathering about? We need to get the hell out of here before I tire out and lose control."

"Oh, we will, we will. Patience, Ronnie. Patience. It's a virtue, so I hear."

2.0 opened his mouth, to be snide, I was sure, but before he could say anything else, Wilbur lunged at the doorway. Reader let go of Ginger at the same time, and she bounded over just in time to slam into the man's chest as Wilbur latched onto his leg.

The screams weren't all that I'd hoped for, seeing as I knew they were going to wake the snakipedes up, but we'd deal with that later.

Wilbur dragged the screaming man back into the room, Ginger still on his chest with her claws still *in* his chest, and I closed and locked the hallway door, while Fancy did the same with the other door that we'd originally been planning to go through.

Put my foot right on his throat. Wisely, he shut up.

Took a good look at him. Always nice to be right. "Clarence Valentino, how *do* you do?"

CHAPTER 72

CLARENCE STARED AT ME. Though I knew it wasn't
the real Clarence. Him, I'd killed. As with Ronaldo 2.0,
this Clarence didn't look totally right. Clearly the cloning
equipment on this planet was much less refined than what
they had going on back home. Go Earth Evil Geniuses.

This also indicated that whatever cloning process they
used on the Ancient and/or Z'porrah home world that
LaRue had used to make the Ronaldo who'd come back to
Earth with her was exceptionally good, because that man
had never looked off, as 2.0 and this version of Clarence did,
and he'd been more powerful than his original.

"How did you catch me?" The Clarence Clone asked.

"I'm smarter than you. Who are you working for and
when was the last time you checked in with them?"

He shot me a derisive look that I remembered. Hadn't
missed it. "As if I'd tell you anything."

"Ronnie, time to go to work, dude."

"If I focus on him I can't stop the Horrors."

Listened. "I hear slithering and such. Assume Clarence
here woke them up screaming. We need his intel more, anyway. We can toss him to them as a snack once we're done."

"Why would I tell you anything if you're just going to kill
me?" The Clarence Clone sounded legitimately shocked.

"Because spies who don't answer questions are just dead
weight. How long have you been on this planet?"

He looked confused. "What do you mean?"

"I mean how many days, nights, weeks, months, or years

have you been on Beta Eight? Or do you think you're on Earth?"

"No, I know I'm not on Earth. It's just a stupid question. I've been here forever."

"Ronnie, seriously, some mind control on him, right now. I want him giving me the truth, and trust me, I will know if he's lying."

"Then why do you need me?" 2.0 muttered.

Clarence's expression changed and became much more amiable. "What do you want to know?" he asked in a friendly tone. Either he and 2.0 had practiced this to lull us into some bizarre form of false security, or the mind control was working.

"How long have you been on this planet?" I asked nicely.

"Oh, forever. This is my home."

"Where do you live?"

"In the little room way downstairs."

Thought about it. "Do you mean the torturers' room, right off the dungeons?"

"Yes. No one goes there and I've made it very comfy."

Well, good to know that 2.0 really wasn't torturing prisoners and such. Score one for us not killing him. So far.

"Do you have a wife?"

His brow crinkled. "I . . . think so? Maybe I don't. I don't know." He gave a little laugh. "She's not here, is she?"

"No. How about kids? Remember having children?"

"Maybe? Not here, though, are they? I'm alone," he added plaintively. "Ronaldo isn't allowed to be my friend."

"Is that why you were playing games with him?"

The Clarence Clone nodded. "Can the animals stop hurting me?"

"Uh, sure. Ginger, Wilbur, let him up. Rahmi, Rhee, be ready to club him in case this is a ploy." The animals and the princesses moved into guard positions.

The Clarence Clone sat up. "Thanks. I hurt."

"Get used to them not caring," 2.0 muttered.

"Ronnie, be a good boy and we'll care."

"Who's she?" Reader asked, pointing to me.

The Clarence Clone squinted at me. Then he looked shocked. "Shealla?"

"Wow. Yes, that's right." Maybe he was faking. But the Clarence I'd known hadn't ever been smooth enough to pretend to like me and he'd never, ever pretended to be impressed by me, either. "Clarence, have you been to the top of the All Seeing Mountain?"

"Yes. Everyone goes there. I like it there. I can see forever there."

"Why does he sound so . . . young?" Abigail asked softly.

"I've told him we're his friends," 2.0 replied in kind. "So he's not trying to sound tough."

The timeline had been rushed due to our successfully surviving Operation Confusion. LaRue had to grab the almost dead Ronaldo and captured Clarence from Earth, go back to the Alpha Centauri system and activate the clones, then take off for the Z'porrah home world in a very short period of time.

Ronaldo's clone had clearly been farther along than Clarence's. Clarence had probably "earned" a clone somewhere during Operation Confusion, whereas Ronaldo was intimately involved in things earlier. But LaRue was out of time, so she'd activated him before the brain was advanced or downloaded or whatever. But it did pay to check.

"Clarence, do I have another name you know?"

"They call you Kitty," he said, pointing to the others. "So that's your other name."

"Yes, it is. Have we met before?"

"I . . . don't know. I want to say yes, but I think I just know you from the Mountain." He looked at the others. "The Venida! I didn't realize it was you. And, the Leader of the Nihalani, too!" He sounded excited. As if he was meeting the Gods. Not as if he was chatting it up with family members he didn't care for. Not as if he was talking to people he knew. A-Cs in general couldn't lie to save their or anyone else's lives and in particular there was no way the Clarence we all knew could fake anything this well.

"Clarence, why are you here?" Abigail asked.

"To protect our interests."

"Whose interests?" Abigail kept her voice relaxed.

"Ours."

"Who is part of that? Part of 'ours'?"

"I . . ." He took a deep breath. "Mine, Ronaldo's, and . . . hers."

"Is she LaRue or Zenoca?" I asked.

"When is she coming home?" He sounded lost and hopeful.

"Not sure. What's her name?"

"She . . . said I don't get to know it yet. I'll get to know her name when she comes home."

Interesting, in the typical bizarre bad guy way. "Okay. Why, if you're supposed to protect Ronaldo's interests, couldn't you tell him you were here?"

"She doesn't want us to corrupt." He said this as if it was something he'd been told, not something he actually understood.

"Did you make anyone disappear?" Reader asked.

"No. When the others laid the traps I avoided them. I'm only supposed to make sure that Ronaldo behaves, I don't have to do anything with the others who are here."

2.0 looked shocked. "Behave? What do you mean by that?"

"You're not allowed to make alliances, to let the other sentient creatures have a voice, to consult the Gods, or to let anyone else have this planet." This was definitely said as if it were rote memorization.

"Why *not?*" 2.0 sounded outraged.

"Your role is not to lead but to be a figurehead, to hold the planet until she returns." Again, rote memorization.

"Ah, Ronaldo is talking to the Gods right now," Fancy pointed out, before 2.0 could say anything else.

The Clarence Clone nodded. "I don't know how to stop the Gods."

"Well, that's a relief," Reader said under his breath. "Clarence, who laid the traps?" he asked in a normal, friendly tone.

"I don't know them."

"Can you describe them?" Fancy asked. "Tell us what they looked like?"

"Yes. They looked like —"

But before he could finish the sentence, we were rocked by an explosion that knocked everyone to the ground.

And then the building started to crumble.

Always the way.

CHAPTER 73

"EVERYONE, link up!" Abigail shouted as we scrambled to our feet, which wasn't as easy as it sounded, since the building was still shaking like we were in a major earthquake. "Grab the animals, too!"

Reader was closest to Wilbur so he grabbed the chocho and I picked up Ginger. The princesses each grabbed one of The Clarence Clone's arms, and Fancy grabbed 2.0. Abigail held onto 2.0's other arm while the rest of us hooked up. Then she concentrated.

Before and especially during Operation Destruction, Abigail and Naomi had learned to use their talents to provide shields. They were the reason Washington, D.C. still had all the monuments and museums in the National Mall, as well as all the people who'd been able to take cover inside them.

But that effort had burned the power out of both sisters. Naomi had taken a terrifying amount of pure Surcenthumain in order to protect Chuckie and Jamie from the Mastermind, which was why and how she'd first gotten her talents back and then, about five minutes later, become so powerful that she became her own superconsciousness.

Abigail had been working to get her talent back, but it had been slow going, in part because she refused to try the drug and no one would have let her near it anyway. That is, before we were on Beta Eight it had been slow going.

On this oxygen-rich planet, however, apparently all the bells and whistles and a whole lot of other special luxury extras had been added onto Abigail's abilities.

A shimmering field went around us and, as stones started to crumble and fall, they bounced off. I'd been in a shield like this before, only it had taken both of the Gower Girls to create it. Wasn't in any mood to complain that Abigail seemed to be fine handling this on her own, however. I knew when not to look at a gift horse's butt.

"I need a destination!" She had to shout, the rumbling, creaking, crashing, and hysterical hissing was so loud. Apparently the snakipedes were getting crushed and, no surprise, not enjoying the experience. "We've only seen this castle since we got here, and not much of it."

"Ronnie, have you seen more of this world than your castle?"

"Of course I have, I'm the king."

"Super. Choose a safe location somewhere else in the world, preferably in Iceland, the white section, if you can manage it, or the Purple Land."

"Ah, I haven't seen *all* of the world."

"Fine, whatever. Choose someplace. Anyplace. Anywhere but here. Find the place, and show it to Abigail in her mind."

"I can't mind control her."

"No, you can't. But you can show her a picture." The Ronaldo who'd come back to Earth had done that to Gladys—shown her places he wanted her to go. Time to see if this one had those skills, too.

"But—"

"Do it," Abigail said. "I can't hold this shield forever."

He nodded and closed his eyes. Abigail looked thoughtful, nodded, and then, suddenly, a sort of bubble went around us and we did the thing that I could only describe as time-warping.

We raced through the castle at hyperspeed, but without actually moving ourselves and as if the walls weren't there. Well, a lot of the walls *weren't* there anymore, but for those that were, we went through them like they were mist. Sailed over a part of Greenland, then up and up, until, there we were, at the top of the All Seeing Mountain.

The landing felt as if we'd always been standing right where we were now, which was inside the railings.

"Abby, nice to see you got your powers back and then some."

She grinned. "I figured out how Sis did things and I've been working to learn how to do them myself." Her smile faded. "I miss her every day, but I'm never not going to do my best to make her proud of me and carry on our work." She looked at 2.0. "You did well. Thank you."

He shook his head. "Thank *you*. What happened? What was that?"

"That was Abigail using her talents, like you use yours. What happened, however, was an attack. And, seriously, Ronnie, I ask you to get us out of danger and you take us to the point where we're closest to the attackers?"

Looked up and around. Sure enough, we had spaceships in the air. They weren't like any of the four kinds I recognized, meaning they were from a planet that had a high probability of being anti-Earth, or at least anti-Alpha Four, which, under the circumstances, was likely to be the same thing.

As was typical for this solar system, the spacecraft weren't bullet shaped. There were three, two hovering higher up and the one shooting up Beta Eight. They did have aerodynamic bodies that were elongated ovals. They also had what could only be described as wings, though they didn't resemble bird wings all that much, but were more rigid-looking and seemed like they could expand out or contract in, sort of like an accordion.

The ones floating higher up had their wings mostly contracted. The third, however, had its wings fully expanded. The craft fired out of the wings as well as out of the front of the oval, which ended in what I assumed was a command center bubble, looking like a crude head.

There were only these three crafts I could see, and only the one appeared to be firing on the castle. However, we were far enough from the Greenland area that I couldn't be sure, even though the height we were at should have given us a better vantage point. It would have, but buildings and such being blown up made a lot of smoke and dust and such and we were hella high up, meaning everything down below looked extremely tiny. Our location probably also made us really great targets, but no one was shooting at us at the moment. Didn't expect that to last.

"You wanted someplace safe. I didn't have a lot of choices—the area I know the best is the Horrors' Nesting Area. I just took a guess and figured you wouldn't want to go there." 2.0 definitely had a sarcasm knob, and it was headed for eleven.

"No, you're right. I just wanted to get somewhere where we might have a hope of mustering up reinforcements or even fighting back. Not where we'd be the definition of sitting ducks." Wondered if there were ducks in the ships, and if so, if Howard the Duck was amongst their number. I'd have a shot of getting Howard on our side, which was more than I expected for whoever was really up there raining fire down on a defenseless planet.

"Why not fight back from up here?" Rahmi asked. "We are much closer to the ship."

Chose not to discuss the merits of a handful of humanoid beings attacking a big, nasty spaceship without a major weapon among them. Felt I deserved some kind of medal for my restraint.

"Think those are Alpha Five or Six spacecraft?" Reader asked, effectively changing the subject, for which I was grateful, and which I was sure he knew. "They didn't have the means when you and Jeff got married."

"No bet. I mean, I think it's a safe bet that Alexander or the other spacefaring planets gave the others who wanted it spaceflight capabilities and help, because that's the sort of thing you do if you're trying to be a kind winner. And I'm also sure that we have Alphas Five and Six represented in the fight, I just don't know if things that look kind of like giant bats would represent either of those planets."

"It is not the same as the ship that fell," Fancy said. "That ship was more triangular."

"Yeah, it was sort of stealth bomber-ish, now that you mention it. In a really geometric way."

"Does that mean this ship is trying to kill any survivors of the crash?" Rahmi asked.

"Did any survivors fall onto the castle?" Wasn't sure if Rhee was being sarcastic to her older sister, but based on her tone and expression, she wasn't. The princesses didn't do sarcasm as a rule.

"I think all the parts fell into the ocean," I said, lest I be wrong and a sister catfight was about to start. "But if they hit the land, they didn't hit the castle."

Reader nodded. "We'd have felt them before this—the debris was hitting when we went underground."

"So, we have possibly Alpha Five or Six down and also possibly Alpha Five or Six shooting at whoever is down. Think that either Alpha Seven and/or Beta Sixteen have joined the space race and they could be one of the two down here?"

"Considering we saw three distinct ship designs that we couldn't identify, it's a good bet, babe," Reader replied. "But like you, I don't have any idea which planet has just destroyed the seat of power on this one, but we're out of time—the war's arrived."

CHAPTER 74

"WHAT DO WE DO to stop them?" Fancy asked. "We don't have the means to fight them while they're in the air."

"We do if any of the Horrors are still alive," 2.0 said. "They can take on something like that."

"I sincerely doubt it, Ronnie, but it would be worth trying. If we knew for certain that whoever is blowing up the castle is actually our enemy."

"Well, it was my castle, so they're my enemy."

"Can't really argue with that one, girlfriend." Reader shook his head. "I'm kind of with Ronaldo here—why would you even wonder if they were friendlies?"

"Because someone removed every, single, living Lecanora from that castle before it was bombed. Said removers might be siding with those whose ship was shot down, those who are currently shooting up the Capital of Greenland, or someone else."

"They didn't remove any of his honor guard," Fancy pointed out.

"Said honor guard was eaten by the Poofs. I think that means we can't judge if whoever's snatching people out of thin air are pro Free Women extremists and Amazonian Ancients or not."

"They didn't remove *us*," Abigail said dryly, indicating herself and the princesses.

"Well, they tried to remove me, James, Fancy, Wilbur, and Ginger. They got everyone else."

"We're assuming those who took the others were the same as those who took the servants in the castle?" Rhee asked.

"Good point." Heaved a sigh. "Honestly? I don't know. We have so many planets involved, and a lot of them have hyperspeed and most of them have advanced tech. It could be any of them. It could be beings we're not even aware are involved."

"And we don't know if they've taken people from other areas or not," Fancy said. "Do we have the time to verify if Haven is still secure?"

"No." Reader had a Commander Voice and it was on High right now. "If they're taking people off this planet it's either to save them or enslave them. Period. But us knowing how many are gone tells us nothing, so it doesn't matter at this time. We need a plan of action, but since we don't know what we're up against, it's harder to devise. But spending time verifying who is or isn't here is just a time waster."

"It would help if we knew who took the Lecanora out of the castle," I said. "It's either someone with hyperspeed—meaning, to our knowledge, it can't be someone from Alphas Five or Six, but it could be someone from Alpha Four, a Free Woman, an Iguanodon, a Major Doggie, or a Cat Person—or it's someone with Snatch You Out Of Thin Air Tech, meaning it could be anyone on any of the inhabited planets. But otherwise, I agree with you, James. I just have no idea what actions to plan."

"He was about to describe them when the attack began." Rahmi pointed at The Clarence Clone. "Those who had taken the servants out of the castle."

"Yes, I was." He looked rather proud. "They looked like flightless waterfowl."

We all stared at him. "Excuse me?" I asked finally.

"Flightless waterfowl."

"Like . . . penguins?" Reader asked.

Clarence brightened up. "Yes! That's the name. Penguins. Black and white, with wide and thick webbed feet, big flippers instead of wings, sort of rotund bodies, and bird-like heads with pointed beaks. They're very pretty. At least, I think they are."

The rest of us, 2.0 included, all looked at each other.

"How does he know what penguins are but couldn't remember their name and can't remember his family?" Abigail asked.

"I'd imagine there's a basic knowledge base they have for all the clones—all basic living functions like how to eat, how to breathe, how to blink, and so forth. Then you'd overlay a standard knowledge base. For all we know, Clarence and Ronnie can both speak multiple Earth languages."

2.0 nodded. "I can. I can understand, speak, read, and write in at least twenty languages. Maybe more. I haven't really tried." Noted that he seemed far more on our side than an adversary right now. Possibly because the devil you knew that wasn't trying to blow you up was better than the devil you didn't who was.

"Right, so a generalized knowledge base would be Earth-centric, because that's the planet that our clones are technically 'from.' So, our Clarence Clone pulled up the description before the name—memory is funny and I can buy it working that way." Turned to said Clone. "How big were these Penguin People?" Without an Earth A-C here, didn't have a guess for which planet the Penguin People were from, but it had to be either Alpha Seven or Beta Sixteen because we'd never seen them, and if faded memory served, the races on those planets were avian-ish.

"Big. Our size. And they weren't all black and white. There are some that are a pretty blue with white, and some that are a deep brown with white. That I've seen so far."

"All working together?" Reader asked.

The Clarence Clone nodded. "Yes." He cleared his throat. "Can I be on your side?"

We all stared at him, 2.0 included. "Excuse me?" Apparently I was the designated WTF asker at this time.

"I'm alone, and I don't like being alone, and I've been alone *forever*. You're the Gods and Ronaldo is the king. And I . . . ," he looked down. "I'd like to have some friends."

2.0's eyes narrowed for a few seconds—was pretty sure he was in The Clarence Clone's head. "He means it," he said quietly, as his expression relaxed. "He doesn't want to wait for 'her' anymore. You haven't hurt him, too much, and he feels needed right now." 2.0's turn to clear his throat. "And, frankly, I feel the same way. I was set up by someone I thought cared about me, and the people who saved me are my supposed enemies. I'd also like to switch sides."

"He could be lying," Abigail said quickly. "About both of them."

Studied 2.0 and The Clarence Clone. They looked a lot like I felt—out of their element, lost, and mostly alone. Only they were far more alone than I was. "Could be. But we have to remember—they aren't the originals, they aren't the people who are our enemies. They're similar but different." In the case of The Clarence Clone, very different.

"Look, on behalf of both of us, clearly we were created to fill roles, do jobs, but not be *real* people. But we are real, at least I am, and I'm pretty sure he is, too." 2.0 indicated The Clarence Clone with his head. "I don't want to be exterminated when she gets back, or when the Z'porrah arrive. Deposed kings can have decent lives. Assassinated kings cannot."

"What's the name of the one who put you onto the throne?"

"She has a lot of different names. On your world, it's LaRue. Here it's Zenoca. I don't know if either one of those are her original given name. I don't know that it matters, either."

Fancy hissed. "Our world has been ruled by Zenoca for these past years!"

"Fancy, that's not necessarily news. Ronnie, any guess for why she didn't tell Clarence her name?"

He shrugged. "Not a confirmed guess, but my bet would be that she didn't want him giving her away. She knew I wouldn't." He sounded quite bitter, not that I could blame him. "Basically, she had two patsies here, just at different knowledge levels."

"It's always hard when you discover the person you thought had your back is instead the one shoving in the knife. We tend not to backstab, but we get the knife far more than we like." Tried not to think about what I wanted to do to Cliff Goodman for what he'd done to us. Failed. But I figured the anger would probably give me an assist:

"In the short time I've known you, you've threatened me, beaten me, and saved me, but as far as I can tell, you haven't lied to me. I'd like to try working with people who actually tell me what the hell's really going on."

"The love on the mountaintop is great and all," Reader said, "but we have bigger problems than the two of you realizing you've been used and wanting to come over to the side of right. War. On this planet. Right now. With technology so advanced there's nothing here that can protect everyone."

Thought about this. "Well, actually, that's not true."

CHAPTER 75

GOT SEVERAL WTF LOOKS. Ignored them. "We have a power source we know about in Iceland. More scattered throughout this continent. And there's likely one somewhere under us, right under us, because that gigantic telescope isn't hanging up here simply because it wants to."

"You guys told us about that last night," Reader said. "And while Serene insisted she could rig things so that she could handle and control the orb, Chuck also made the point that it was extremely dangerous and that only he, Serene, Lorraine, or Claudia were even close to being qualified to do so."

"I think we're going to need to try." Pointed to the two ships that were hovering—they were moving slowly down toward us.

"You think we can turn the telescope into a weapon?" 2.0 asked. "Because I thought of that, a while ago. I can't touch it. As far as I've been able to tell, no one can touch it, because I've been up here a few times and I've seen youngsters try to reach it, and even if they're on each other's shoulders, they can't. I think it moves away from them, though it doesn't appear to."

The Clarence Clone nodded. "No one can touch the All Seeing Eye."

"Is that what you call it, or what everyone calls it?" As I asked this I took a better look around. There were other beings up here with us. Far away, because this was a big area, but still, here. And I was pretty sure that they were katyhoppers. Based on the coloration that I could just make out, they were Matriarchs. Meaning they weren't up here by accident, because per our katyhoppers, the Matriarchs never came up here all as one.

"It's what it's called." The Clone sounded stubborn, but like a child would be. He looked down. "I know the Gods know all the names."

Looked to Fancy, who shrugged. "Different regions refer to things differently. I have heard it called that before, Shealla—by you, for example."

She had a point. "Fine, fine, works for me, then. And, Clarence, you're right about the name. I'm sorry I doubted you."

He looked up at me and smiled. "It's okay, Shealla. Everyone says the Gods like to test you. I guess that means I passed?" The Clarence Clone wasn't very much like his original other than in looks and expressions. I preferred the Clone.

"Yes," I said gently. "You passed." Cleared my throat. "So, Clarence, Ronnie, have either of you ever seen a big glowing orb or something like it, most likely in a cave?"

The Clarence Clone shook his head. "No. But I don't go into any of the caves."

"Why not?" I asked him.

"They scare me. Everyone is afraid of the caves."

Fancy nodded. "This is true for my people. Haven is not the same as the caverns."

Knew this to be true from what we'd seen of the planet so far, so I didn't argue with it. 2.0, on the other hand, didn't look afraid—he looked pissed off. "So she put some sort of power source here and never told me about it?" He sounded pissed off, too.

"No, actually, I'm pretty sure she didn't know about it. Frankly, she might not even know about the All Seeing Mountain and the All Seeing Eye. We think the power orbs have been here a really long time. Like, beginning of the world long time."

2.0 shook his head. "That should be impossible."

"You're both clones of dead guys, which should also be impossible. Welcome to the New Realms of Possibilities."

2.0 shocked the hell out of me by laughing. "Okay, good

point. So, what do we do? Even if we can find the orb you think is up here, I don't have a scientific background."

"What background *do* you have?" Reader asked.

"Business. I know why I'm supposed to dislike all of you, I have all of the original Ronaldo's memories. But the father you killed isn't someone I knew or know. And I'm smart enough to know the difference between someone else's memories—even someone who was and is technically me—and my own. And I didn't know Ronald Yates. He didn't raise *me*. And, as you pointed out earlier, I'm not the person who conspired against you, either."

"Other than here," Abigail pointed out.

"Yes, but I've seen the error of my ways. I'm willing to not care about the past wrongs I'm supposed to be all worked up over, and far more willing to do what I can to ensure that we all have a future. Not that I can offer any help at all here, because, again, science is not my area."

We had scientists with us and a certified genius, too. Only they weren't actually with us right now. Which was frustrating on so many levels I lost count. "Can anyone actually reach Chuckie telepathically?" Hey, it was a long shot, but I liked to live by the cat motto that it never hurt to ask for what you wanted.

Abigail cocked her head. "You know . . . I think if Ronaldo and I work together, we just might be able to." She looked at me. "But can I trust him? Really?"

Took her hand in mine. "I don't know. But I'm willing to take the leap of faith. However, the decision has to be yours, because it's your head he'll be in." I could ask the Matriarchs if we needed to, but with Abigail's powers seemingly fully back and then some, it would be better not to let everyone know that the katyhoppers were mind readers, 2.0 and The Clarence Clone in particular.

"My world is going to be destroyed," Fancy said quietly. "If our now-deposed king could enter my mind and help me to save it, then I would take that risk."

Abigail got a funny smile on her face. "The good of the many outweighs the needs of the few. Sis and I risked similar before, when our world was under attack. This world deserves the same help." She reached her hand to 2.0. "Prove that Kitty's right to trust you."

He took her hand in his. "I'll do my best. And not only because I know the rest of you are all ready to kill me if you even think something's going wrong."

"I think LaRue enhanced your brain from your original's. You seem a lot smarter than Ronaldo Number One."

This earned me a grin. "He was in love with her. I'm not. That probably helps."

"I'm sure it does. Was she in love with him, do you think?"

"I don't know, but I doubt it. She's been alive a long time, much longer than she looks. When you're that old, you probably have a fondness for someone, but love?" 2.0 shrugged. "I think she loves her mission."

"What *is* her mission?" Reader asked.

2.0 looked mildly surprised by this question. "To take over the galaxy."

I sighed. "Or, as we call it, James, routine."

Abigail laughed. "Nice to know nothing ever changes. Okay, Ronnie, let's see if we can reach the smartest guy on any planet and figure out how to save this one."

Abigail and 2.0 faced each other, held both hands, and concentrated. Couldn't speak for anyone else, but I was ready to knock him to the ground if she appeared to be in any kind of distress.

She knew it, too. "It's okay, Kitty. Remember, if you guys are stressed, it makes me stressed, if you're angry it makes me angry, and so on. So relax—I'll let you know if something's wrong." True enough, that was how part of her talent worked, she was sort of a reverse empath.

2.0 grunted. "This is harder than it looks. I've never tried this before, so can you all stop sending threatening thoughts about me out? I can feel them through Abby's mind and not only is all the distrust unsettling, understandable or not, but it's making it really hard for the two of us to link up."

"Why are you calling her Abby?" Reader asked suspiciously.

2.0 heaved a sigh. "Because that's the nickname she prefers. I'm *in* her mind, remember? There are some things that are fairly easy to spot."

"Let's let them work, gang." I took a giant step back and the others followed suit.

Before we had any time to fret, Abigail jerked. "Kitty, I've reached Chuck!"

"That's awesome, go team."

She and 2.0 opened their eyes. They both looked terrified.

"No," he said, voice shaking. "It's not."

CHAPTER 76

"COME AGAIN, RONNIE?"

"All the rest of your people are captured." 2.0 sounded as freaked out as he and Abigail both looked. "They're in one of the ships above us."

"Chuck said we need to run and hide, Kitty." Abigail matched 2.0's terror. "He said to tell you that we're up against people who are like Thanagarians. Complete with the attitudes."

"Oh. That's not good." Looked around. We could run down, but the katyhopper Matriarchs were up here, and I wasn't going to allow them to be destroyed. "Follow me!"

I ran toward the katyhoppers, everyone else running after me. Reached them pretty quickly, and I'd been right, they were the multicolored Matriarchs. Heard Reader explaining who they were to those we'd found in the castle. Unsurprisingly, 2.0 and The Clarence Clone had no idea what the katyhoppers were.

"We're under attack," I said without a lot of preamble. "We all need to get off the top of the mountain."

The Matriarchs all waved their antennae calmly. They knew what was coming, better than I did. And they were not leaving, thank you very much. Because they felt I'd need them. Well, nice to have more backup.

"What are Thanagarians?" Abigail asked. "Chuck didn't give us a picture, he knocked us out of his mind fast."

"That might mean the Thanagarians have mind-reading capabilities or similar." Fantastic. That meant the Matriarchs weren't going to have the edge. "And Thanagarians are hawk people. Like Hawkgirl and Hawkman."

"And that means absolutely nothing to me," 2.0 said. Could tell Fancy felt the same, and the princesses probably didn't have a full grasp, either.

"They are comic book characters," Rahmi said, proving me totally wrong.

"Humanoids with wings, so very birdlike humanoids," Rhee added, showing that both of them had been boning up on things I cared about.

"In the comics the Thanagarians are warlike," Reader said. "So that certainly fits."

"And that means those who captured the other Gods are not the same as those who saved Lecanora from the castle," Fancy concluded. "How do we fight these Thanagarians?"

"Having Superman around helps." But they'd captured Superman, in the form of Jeff. And Batman and the Flash, aka Chuckie and Christopher, too. Plus all our other potential Justice League and Avengers stand-ins.

Sure, I'd been Wonder Woman in Bizarro World, but here I was Wolverine With Boobs. Normally that was enough, but right now, wished I had Wolverine's adamantium claws, because I wasn't sure if my skills were going to be up to the task.

"We have Megalomaniac Girl with us." Reader flashed me the cover boy grin. "That's usually all we need."

"You're a liar, but I love you for it, James." Before I could say anything else, Fancy gasped and pointed up.

Sure enough, the hull of one of the ships opened up and bird people flew out. They weren't as human as Hawkgirl or Hawkman. They were humanoid, and they had giant wings, but Hawkgirl and her comics compatriots had human faces and bodies and they wore raptor masks as their helmets and such, along with attractive, skimpy outfits to show off impressive abs and other muscles.

These didn't look or dress that way. Though they had the same giant wings as Hawkgirl, their heads were bird heads, complete with beaks and eyes that indicated they were not now, nor would they ever be, mammals. Their arms were muscular, but ended in bird claws, not hands, and while they weren't wearing clothing on their upper bodies, it was impossible to tell if they were ripped or not, because they were covered with feathers.

Their lower bodies were far more humanoid. Unlike the tight track pants that Hawkgirl favored, they were all in what looked a lot like Roman togas or tunics, but only the skirt part, which went down to mid-thigh on all of them. Their legs had no feathers, but appeared to be covered in down. Their feet were a combo of human feet and bird claws that any number of horror movie makeup artists would love to imitate.

The only guess I had for which were males and females was size—the females might have had breasts, but since they all appeared to be quite muscular, the feathers did a good job of hiding gender. Took a wild one and figured the smaller and slighter ones were the females.

Even though they appeared to be weapons all on their own, they were carrying weapons as well. Completing the Hawkgirl comparisons, most of them were carrying maces or flails. On the plus side, I saw no projectile weapons, but then again, their ships had those in spades.

As they flew nearer, Ginger backed up against me, growling and hissing, and Wilbur shoved next to me, growling and snarling. Clearly they weren't fans of the hawk people.

"Stay with Kitty," I said quietly. "Kitty doesn't want Ginger or Wilbur attacking or getting hurt."

Considered calling for the Poofs, but diplomacy should be tried first. Not that I was going to try it for long, but I knew without asking that the attempt had to be made.

Some of the hawk people landed. The rest stayed in the air, wings flapping lazily. Now that they were closer, noted that each one of them wore a circlet with a shiny jewel that sat right over their foreheads, as if it was a third eye.

One who I felt was a male stepped forward. "You will surrender."

"Or what?"

He blinked at me. One of those very birdlike blinks. Other than the Peregrines—and Bellie the parrot, on rare occasion—I wasn't much of a girl for birds. This group wasn't doing anything to change my mind. "We claim this world in the name of Beta Sixteen."

"Nice to see you've joined the solar community with gusto. This world already belongs to the people of Beta Eight, sorry."

"We have destroyed their king," the spokesbird said. "Therefore, we now rule this planet."

"Not how this works. But let's be polite. I'd like to know what you call yourselves, as a race, I mean."

"Why would that matter?"

"To me? Honestly it doesn't matter all that much. I'm going to call you Hawkpeople no matter what. Well, I might call you Thanagarians, too. It'll depend on my mood and if we are ever, at any time, friends. However, if you'd like the others to use your preferred designations of choice, I'd spit it out right now."

A smaller specimen, so probably a female, stepped up. "We are the Rapacians. And we demand your complete surrender." She sounded female. Sort of. Their voices had a cawing tone to them, as if they were about to screech or squawk, not talk. Maybe they did screech or squawk and the universal translator turned it into something we could understand. Decided now wasn't the time to care.

"Or, I ask again, what?"

"Or we will destroy you," the male said.

"Okay, good to know. Why is it that you think you have the right to destroy this planet and all the people on it?"

They stared at me, big bird eyes unblinking. "Because we want it," the female said finally.

"Doesn't everyone else want it, too?"

They nodded. "But we are here first," the male said.

"Oh, the old 'I saw her first' rule. Yeah, I can confirm that that one doesn't really hold up over time, here or in a court of law."

"Why not?" the female asked.

"Because we were here first. And I say that the people who live on the planet get to keep it, because it's theirs, and they were really here first."

"We have captured your people," the male said derisively. "Easily."

"Using subterfuge, sure. Not in a straight-out fight."

"Are you suggesting we fight?" the female asked. Was pretty sure she was trying to sound cagey. She didn't do it well.

"Oh, no, not at all, at least, not at this precise time. But why use a dead body as a trap? Just curious and all."

"We are no friends to those from Beta Twelve," the female said haughtily. "They have lost the Way and want harmony. We have not lost the Way and we want domination."

"Huh, interesting, especially for people who didn't have space travel until those nice other planets gave it to them."

"They have shown that they are not strong," the male said. "Therefore, we no longer will follow their rule."

Interesting. Apparently they were mistaking kindness for weakness. At least, I hoped. But we needed information and I also needed to come up with some kind of plan for what to do. Meaning it was back to my most favorite go-to move—keep 'em talking.

"We tend to like to know the names of the people we're talking to, by the way. One of my names is Kitty. What are your names?"

They were quiet again.

"Sorry, but was that a hard question?" Reader asked. "Because if you're so primitive that you don't have names for each other, I don't see how you can hope to claim another planet. I don't see how you can keep your own, frankly. One of my names is James, by the way. I mention it because we're not primitives."

That worked. "I am Otari," the guy I was going to call Hawkman said. "And this is Kares," he indicated the female, aka Hawkgirl. "I am the leader of our forces involved in this battle, and she is my second in command."

Nice to know I'd guessed genders right.

"What are those with you?" Kares pointed to the katy-hoppers. Which had to be her being cagey again, because I knew they had Saffron, Pinky, and Turkey up there along with King Benny and Zanell, as well as the five strautruch. And all my people. Wondered if they had my daughter, too. Decided getting really, seriously pissed was probably in my best interests, so assumed they did.

"The actual highest sentient lifeform on this planet. And they don't want to let you destroy their home or their people, either. Oh, and I don't think you've destroyed the king as much as you think you have."

Otari glared at me. At least it looked like a glare. Wasn't sure, but probably best to assume glaring unless or until this was proven to be his Pleasant Expression Face. "We understand we have captured the Gods of this planet. That makes the planet ours."

"Oh, you haven't captured all of the Gods, not by a long shot."

Kares sniffed, which I wouldn't have thought possible with a beak for a nose and mouth, but she proved me wrong. "Your Gods are weak."

"What did you do to those you captured?" Abigail asked softly. Was pretty damn sure she was getting seriously pissed, too.

"Subdued them. Easily." Otari was big into giving us the impression that the rest of our team had just rolled over and played Throwing the Fight. I didn't buy it. But I knew he had them, because Chuckie had told Abigail and 2.0 to run.

But we hadn't run. And Chuckie knew Abigail was with me, and he'd point-blank told her to pass along information to me. Chuckie also knew exactly what I would do when he suggested I run away while he and Jeff and the others were in danger. And he'd shoved the two of them out of his mind fast, faster than you'd think he would if he wanted to pass along warnings and information. If all we had to do was run, then why lose the mind link?

The only reason to lose said link was because someone else had been in Chuckie's mind and the only reason to shove our people out of his mind was to protect all of us—or to ensure that neither Abigail nor 2.0 gave away the fact that we weren't going to play dead. He'd also passed along a clue for me.

So the Rapacians had some form of mind reading going on. Meaning also that the Matriarchs were probably up here to block our thoughts from the Rapacians. At least I sincerely hoped so. Especially because Otari and Kares were really ugly and their mothers dressed them funny.

No reactions from the Rapacians, though I saw a couple of the Matriarchs wave their antennae in a way I knew meant they were laughing. Good, our side was working together. Time to take it to the next level.

Pity I didn't have any idea what that was going to be.

Heard gasps from the princesses. They sounded overly loud and kind of fake. But everyone turned to see where they were looking. So that worked. Rahmi and Rhee had really learned a lot while they were on Earth.

"Oh, wow. Ronnie, well done, dude. Yo, Otari and Kares? Some of our cavalry has arrived."

A giant swarm of snakipedes were heading our way.

CHAPTER 77

I'D NEVER THOUGHT I'd be happy to see a snakipede again, let alone a host of them, but I was wrong.

"What are those?" Otari asked, voice shaking just a tiny bit.

"Those are what we Gods call our Special Pets who love to eat chicken. Everyone else calls them the Horrors. We've found that to be a really fitting name for them."

"What is chicken?" Kares asked. Her voice wasn't shaking, but she didn't sound all that confident, either.

"A tasty bird we eat on our planet." They turned and looked at me. "Yeah, where I come from you're dinner. Let that settle in your minds for a second or two."

"Our ships will blast those creatures before they can reach us," Otari said, managing to sound in charge again.

"Yeah? Maybe. They're pretty tough. And they're also coming right for you. Meaning that your ships are going to have to shoot right at you. Oh, and they're not going to attack any of us." I sincerely hoped. "They're here because we asked them to come." Well, 2.0 had done so, and right now he was part of the Royal God We.

The snakipedes were above the Rapacian ship that was still firing at the castle. Right above it, as in they were flying up while still remaining above the ship, which meant that the two other Rapacian ships were at great risk of hitting their own ship if they fired on the snakipedes. Clearly they'd realized this, because they were not firing. The only ship shooting was shooting at an empty castle.

There was something really stupid about them doing that, because they'd already turned the place to rubble, I was sure. Wondered if one of the katyhoppers onboard was affecting the Rapacian minds. Sincerely hoped so.

"So, I guess you all had better get going and engage the enemy. And all that. We'll wait here and see how you do with it."

"We are not done with you," Otari snapped. Very literally, with his beak. Got the distinct impression he didn't like me. Found the will to go on somehow. Then he cawed an order, and this time it was a real caw. Couldn't really understand it, but it was clear the Rapacians were going to engage.

Which they did. It might have been impressive, but their maces and flails weren't charged like Hawkgirl's was. They were just nasty weapons, but not magical nasty weapons. And from personal experience, the snakipedes were damned tough to kill.

They were also hungry, a fact proven as a couple of them grabbed Rapacians out of the air and ate them. There were a lot of bird screams, and more Rapacians poured out of the two ships above us. In less than a minute the air was thick with wings and battle. Couldn't tell who was going to win, but now was definitely the time for my team to take some action.

Decided I'd been working cluelessly for a while. Not as in having no idea what was going on—that was kind of standard operating procedure these days. But as in not having any audio hints from Algar. Plus I was about to go into battle, and I always preferred to do so with my own soundtrack. Dug my iPod out of my purse and put my earbuds in. It was time to rock and roll.

"Is now really the time for tunes, girlfriend?"

"James, you wound me. Is there ever *not* a time for tunes?"

"As I think of it, particularly in respect to you, no. Go for it. What's our plan, aside from congratulating Ronaldo here on some really quick thinking?"

"It seemed like the obvious move," 2.0 said. "I think the Rapacians have mind-reading abilities, by the way, though they don't appear to be reading us."

"I agree. And they're not reading us because of our good friends here." Indicated the Matriarchs as I hit play to hear "Fly" by Sugar Ray. Nice to know that I was on the same wavelength as Algar. "Ladies, I have a request. May we ride on your backs in order to get into one or both of those Rapacian spaceships?"

The Matriarchs waved antennae to indicate they were wondering if we'd ever ask.

"Mount up, gang. Please be aware that these are some of the most important beings on this planet, so let's not kick or grab and such if at all possible. Rahmi, you're probably the strongest—can you carry Wilbur?"

She nodded. "I should be able to wield my staff even with the pig-dog along."

"He's a chocho on this world, but I can't argue with your description. Rhee, you able to take Ginger?"

She nodded. "But the cat does not want to leave you, Kitty. And the chocho does not, either."

"Ginger's an ocellar here, and I don't want the animals to leave me, either. I really don't want to drop either one of them, though. Besides, I plan on having you two lead the charge, meaning that Ginger and Wilbur will be on the front lines."

Both animals perked up and trotted to their assigned princess. The princesses got onto their Matriarchs and Reader handed Wilbur up to Rahmi while Ginger leaped gracefully onto Rhee's Matriarch's back. The rest of us mounted up as well.

The Clarence Clone was really excited, but 2.0 looked apprehensive. "Are you sure it's going to be safe?"

"Safer than standing around waiting for our enemies to attack us," Abigail pointed out.

"Ronnie, you're not saying you're scared, are you?"

"I'm scared as hell, actually, Kitty. But I think I'm better off sticking with all of you than going it alone, so, fine, fine, I'm set. Please don't drop me," he said to his Matriarch. Who waved her antennae.

"She's laughing at you, Ronnie. You're safe on the Katy-hopper Express, okay?"

"Enough stalling," Reader called. "The rest of us are ready. I'd mention that I'm the Head of Field, babe, but I think I learned first that you never follow orders or the chain of command."

"Just proves you're always on top of things, James. Now, everyone, let's go get our people and teach these nasty neighbors how we handle a property dispute in this part the 'hood."

CHAPTER 78

HAVING TAKEN THE Katyhopper Express already, I was prepared for the flight. The others adapted quickly, which was good, since it was a long way down if anyone fell off. Oh, sure, Rahmi and Rhee both had to hold onto Ginger and Wilbur a little tighter than expected when both animals almost fell off, but otherwise, we were pros by the time we were halfway to the nearest spaceship.

Not counting Ginger and Wilbur, there were eight of us riding, but there were more Matriarchs than that here. They all came with, which I was relieved about. We needed the protection from the Rapacians' mind reading.

"Her Diamonds" by Rob Thomas came on my iPod now. Which made no sense, really, because it was a song about his wife's illness, which didn't seem really relevant to our current situation.

The song skipped, which was an extremely rare occurrence, and the next song started. Elton John's version of "Lucy in the Sky with Diamonds." So Algar wanted me to focus on diamonds? Treasure hunting right now seemed like bad timing.

The song skipped again. Didn't think it was my iPod dying. Clearly Algar knew I wasn't catching on. This time, "Free Your Mind" by En Vogue came on. And I got it.

But before I could share my revelation with the others, we reached the ship. Sadly, it was still manned, which was proven by the fact that several Rapacians flew out to engage us.

The princesses had taken the lead, and they were able to

use their battle staffs while riding a katyhopper and holding a large animal. I was impressed. They were also the only ones with blunt weapons. The rest of us had nothing or guns, which weren't necessarily the best choice when flying around very high up in the air with a lot of your friends involved in the fight.

Fancy, however, was hella impressive. She stood up on the back of her Matriarch and whipped out a knife from somewhere—had to figure out where everyone from this solar system stashed their weapons and how—and engaged the Rapacian nearest to her.

Reached into my purse. "Need weapons that will work against Rapacians." And pulled out a Beta Twelve battle staff. "Abby!" Tossed it to her and she caught it just in time to block an attack.

Reached in again and this time came out with a baseball bat. "James!" Tossed it to him, reached in, and pulled out three more bats. Tossed them to 2.0 and The Clarence Clone, and kept the last for myself. "I can use a battle staff, too, you know," I said to my purse.

But then a Rapacian was attacking me and I had to focus. Kept a good grip on the bat and swung for the head, not just to brain this bird, but to break the jewel on its forehead.

Missed, naturally. But because I did, my body slipped to the side, meaning that the Rapacian's mace missed me.

Tried to send a message to the Matriarchs that we all wanted to get into the spaceship more than fight outside of it. Figured they already knew, but it couldn't hurt to try to share that info again.

Meanwhile, had to deal with the Rapacian flying around me. Was pretty sure it was a male. It was also above me in just the right way, so I aimed for what my mother, father, Chuckie, and every martial arts instructor I'd ever had always said to—the groin.

Slammed the bat upward, ensuring that I hit all of whatever was between this birdman's legs.

The scream was indicative of a good hit. He dropped his mace, which I just managed to grab before it hit me or my Matriarch. He'd dropped the mace to curl up into a fetal position. He also plummeted downward, since flapping his wings wasn't the first thought on his mind.

"So far so good. Gang!" I shouted, hoping the Matriarchs would assist with broadcast. "The males are just like ours. Go for the family jewels!"

Had a moment to look around. Interestingly enough, none of the Rapacians were attacking the Matriarchs. Hoped that would continue. The Rapacians were also, for the most part, doing a one-on-one combat style. The few that weren't were after Fancy and Abigail, who were now both standing on the backs of their Matriarchs. Those appeared to all be females, meaning my attack strategy was unlikely to work.

Wasn't sure at all where Abigail had learned to fight, but experience reminded me that the battle staffs responded to women and definitely gave their user an assist. Even so, though, clearly someone had been making sure that Abigail could fight. Probably Chuckie, but maybe not—she wasn't fighting in a style he used.

The others all listened, even the princesses, and shortly another five Rapacians were screaming and falling out of the sky.

The rest of us went to help Abigail and Fancy. But they were doing amazingly well all on their own—in fact, their Matriarchs were flying close together and the women were jumping back and forth on their backs, fighting as if they'd done so together for years, slicing and dicing on Fancy's part, slamming and sticking on Abigail's.

But Fancy's knife wasn't nearly as long as the battle staffs, or the maces and flails she was facing. Waited for her to have a break in her fight. "Fancy!" Tossed her the mace, which she caught. She shot me the same toothy smile King Benny had done, stashed her knife, then swung the mace two-handed into the nearest Rapacian. Said birdwoman went flying, and not from her own power.

"Thank you, Shealla!" she called as she slammed the mace into the back of a birdwoman attacking Abigail.

My music switched to Queen's "Fight from the Inside" and I figured it was time to divide the attack. Flew over to the princesses, grabbed Wilbur, and flung him over my mount in front of me. Ginger took the hint and leaped over, landing behind me. Both animals managed to stay on and not struggle. "Rahmi, Rhee, help Abby and Fancy! Try to hit the jewels on the birds' heads. The rest of you, come with me!"

The princesses leapt into the melee—literally. Their Matriarchs flew behind the other two, creating a sort of living platform for the four fighters. Decided watching wasn't going to do anything but make my stomach create a lot of acid due to worry about all eight of them.

2.0 took the lead into the spaceship. "Get away from my world, you feathered bastards!" he screamed as he slammed his baseball bat around like he was trying out for the Yankees. He hit heads, and The Clarence Clone followed up and hit groins. They worked well together as a team and more Rapacians fell. Either we weren't facing the good fighters, or the Rapacians rarely engaged in hand-to-hand combat.

Reader and I, meanwhile, were able to fly around them and into the ship. As soon as we were inside, Wilbur and Ginger jumped off and led their own kind of charge. Reader and I dismounted too. "We're looking for the command center, where they fly this thing."

"I'd guess it's the area that looks like a head, though that could be wrong," Reader said. "But that's where your cat and dog are going, I think." The animals were indeed racing off somewhere. Decided we should follow them.

"I think the jewels on their heads give them the mind reading or control or whatever power," I said as we ran after the animals, Matriarchs right behind us. "We need to destroy those."

Reader shook his head as we stopped to assist Wilbur and Ginger with three Rapacians. "We need to destroy whatever it is that powers them," he said as he slammed his bat into a Rapacian head.

"Wouldn't that be on their home planet? Or their minds, or something?" Did some cool kung fu moves on one Rapacian while Wilbur chomped on the birdman's leg.

"Ronaldo carries his power with him, but he doesn't power anyone else. Same with the katyhoppers, right?" Reader slammed his bat onto the head of the Rapacian Ginger was clawing up.

"Right."

2.0 and The Clarence Clone rejoined us, ran past us, and attacked the third Rapacian. Apparently they were enjoying themselves. Grabbed the circlet off the third Rapacian right before 2.0 smashed his head in.

"None of them use something else to power their abilities," Reader pointed out, as the animals took off again, with 2.0 and The Clarence Clone in gleeful pursuit. "I could be wrong, but I'm betting on a device that sends amplification through the jewels, or the circlets, or whatever. And I'm also betting that it's on each ship, or the command ship, since I wouldn't want to risk losing my mind-reading abilities merely because I left my power source back home."

"Works for me." Third Eye Blind's "Faster" came on my personal airwaves. Chose to take the hint. Grabbed Reader's hand and kicked it up to hyperspeed. I agreed with Algar—it was time to get where we needed to go. We passed several Rapacians who literally had no idea of what hit them. Caught up to 2.0 and The Clarence Clone. "Ronnie, grab Ginger. Clarence, grab Wilbur. Then follow us at hyperspeed."

Reader and I zipped off. It was a lot easier to get through the ship this way and we were in the command center shortly, even though we made a ton of wrong turns.

"Never thought you'd find it," Reader said as we slammed bird heads together.

"It gave us an opportunity to knock out every enemy in this portion of the ship."

"Whatever answer lets you sleep at night, girlfriend. Now what?"

Found the chair that was obviously the one that the pilot used and shoved Reader into it. "Now you fly this thing."

"What? I've never seen this ship before, let alone have any idea of how to fly it."

"James, you're the best pilot we have. Just channel Will Smith from *Independence Day* and do it." My iPod chose now to share "Put a Lid on It" by the Squirrel Nut Zippers. Grabbed an available circlet from a nearby unconscious Rapacian and put it onto his head. "Maybe this will help."

He concentrated. "Actually . . . yeah, I think it does help." He started flipping switches and such. "I need a copilot."

Grabbed 2.0, flung him into the chair Reader indicated, and put another circlet onto his head. "Help James fly this thing. Resist any urges you might have to take over."

He nodded. "Interesting. I . . . understand how the ship works."

Put the other circlet I had on my own head because why not?

Why not was expressed in one word. "Whoa!"

CHAPTER 79

TO CALL THE EXPERIENCE mind-expanding was an understatement. I could see everything going on in the solar system, could feel all the billions of minds, could feel all the emotions. The music stopped mid-note. Wasn't sure if Algar was doing me a solid or if my mind had short-circuited my iPod. I'd find out later if my head didn't explode.

"Kitty, are you okay?" Reader called.

"How can you fly? How can you concentrate? How can you focus?" With this on my head it was as if I was spinning out of control. Felt someone hold and steady me, and realized it was The Clarence Clone. It didn't help much, but it helped a bit.

Right before I thought I was going to pass out, I felt something soothing, and the barrage of everything stopped.

Kitty needs to relax.

Recognized the voice in my mind. ACE? ACE is that you?

Yes, Kitty, ACE is here.

What's going on? What was that? How is it that the Rapacians can deal with that, let alone James and Ronnie?

ACE apologizes. This was the only way ACE could speak with Kitty. Kitty saw things as ACE sees them.

I'd seen things as ACE saw them before, but not like this. This had been far more than I'd experienced before. Maybe I was more ready to handle it now than before.

Yes. Kitty has seen and done many things Kitty had not before.

Right. ACE could "hear" the lower mind thoughts as easily as the upper ones.

The others do not and cannot see in this way, not even Ronaldo. ACE could not reach Kitty until Kitty put on the Rapacians' Mind Melder.

That's what this is called?

By the Rapacians, yes. It allows them to communicate with each other.

There was something in how ACE's voice sounded—I recognized a leading hint from him by now.

Have they always had this capability?

No. ACE sounded pleased. This ability is new. Very new.

Huh. So, were they always this bloodthirsty?

No. That comes with the Mind Melder.

ACE was constrained by what he could or should say to me. Meaning I had to ask the right questions. That was fine, I had several.

Is whoever created the Mind Melder making the Rapacians more savage than normal?

Yes. They must be stopped.

No argument. Does Jamie see things like this, through you?

No. Only if Jamie needs to. As Kitty experienced it can be . . . too much, even for a mind as advanced as Jamie's.

Well, that's good. Can the Rapacians talk to all their people at the same time?

No. The Rapacians have to choose the mind they wish to join with. Only a very powerful mind could do what Kitty just described.

Even better. Is one of those powerful minds controlling the Melder Prime right now?

In a way. Now this was the evasive tone ACE used when I had to figure things out on my own. Decided not to push it.

So, how do we use this Mind Melder?

As Kitty would think.

I think I'm not sure how to use it, but I'll take this to mean we'll all figure it out. Is Jamie okay? You haven't talked to me much since you joined with her unless she was asleep.

Jamie is in a controlled sleep. So is Paul.

James saw them in a dream.

James saw a dream that was sent to James to reassure James, and Kitty, that Jamie and Paul were well. But Jamie and Paul will not be well unless Kitty can come to the rescue. ACE needs Kitty to hurry.

This again. And so much for me asking ACE for help. If ACE wanted me to hurry, it indicated things were bad for him, Jamie, and Paul. Pushed the panic aside, there was no time for it now. What do I need to do? Where are you and Jamie and Paul?

We are where we should not be. But Kitty has to save everyone else before she can save Jamie, Paul, and ACE.

It figured. Who has all of you, ACE? Is it the Rapacians?

No. It is someone who wishes to rule the solar system. And wishes to make ACE their slave.

I won't allow that, ACE, I *promise*. Who is it? The Z'porrah?

No, they are not here. Yet.

I know they're coming ACE. And we *will* stop them. But if not them, who? Do I have to guess?

It is someone Kitty knows. Someone Kitty has forgotten about, because Kitty barely met them before. But it is the one who was behind all before.

Interesting. ACE could be referring to the other superconciousnesses out there, but I doubted it. And he wasn't talking about the Z'porrah. Meaning that the "before" he was referring to was probably someone we met during Operation Invasion.

Gregory is dead, Uma is dead, King Adolphus is dead, and Lilith is scattered.

Many think Kitty is the one in charge, always. And yet, Kitty answers to someone else.

Jeff. Or Richard. Or Paul. Or the President. A long list sometimes. It's not Alexander, is it? Or Councilor Leonidas? Alexander's mother, Victoria? Queen Renata?

No. Kitty's friends are still Kitty's friends. But they will not be for much longer.

Because they're going to switch sides?

Because they are going to be killed.

And with that, felt ACE leave my mind.

CHAPTER 80

HAD TO HAND IT TO HIM, ACE knew how to make both an entrance and an exit.

The Clarence Clone was still holding me up, which was good, because the ship rocked.

"The other ship is attacking," Reader said, reasonably calmly. "But I don't think we can blow it out of the air because I'm pretty sure that's the ship that has the others on it."

Okay, we had these Mind Melder things. Time to meld minds. Focused and—while the ship tossed and flipped and The Clarence Clone kept us both upright—tried to find Jeff. It was fairly easy, but that was because I could feel that he was being tortured. This was a technique that our enemies liked to use to bring Jamie to them. Maybe it was a good thing our other enemies had her in some sort of Sleeping Beauty trance. This moment's definition of choosing the lesser of two evils.

Jeff needed adrenaline, and that meant I needed to get to him. But I had no idea where he was. However, unhappy as this made me, we had more pressing matters.

"Clarence and I are going to search this ship and hopefully get the girls inside before you have to take a lot of evasive maneuvers."

Reader steadied the spaceship. "Do that at hyperspeed, because I don't know how long our shields are going to hold. Ensure we have control of the ship, and then get the others in here, fast," he barked.

"Sounds good." Took The Clone's hand in mine. "Go as

fast as you safely can, we need to search every inch of this ship and get the others inside if we're able to." We took off.

As we ran through the ship, I stopped focusing on Jeff and went for Chuckie. Got him on the first try. Realized why—they had him in a circlet, but I could see through his eyes, and he was definitely a prisoner. The horror of what was going on dawned on me. They were using Chuckie's brain to power the Mind Melders.

In fact, it was a good bet that they were torturing Jeff, and maybe the others, too, in order to *get* Chuckie to let all of the Rapacians mind meld at the same time. ACE had said the mind would have to be exceptional. That's why Abigail and 2.0 had reached him so quickly and why he'd tossed them out of his mind even faster.

I could tell the strain was wearing on him. Every mind, even the biggest and strongest, had a breaking point. And if Chuckie was seeing what I'd seen when ACE was with me, that would be a tremendous barrage that he probably wasn't prepared for.

Of course, the Rapacians wouldn't care. If they burned Chuckie out, no worries—they had my little girl and ACE trapped somewhere. All they wanted was to take this world that didn't belong to them and destroy it.

The rage came and it was, as it always was when the people I loved were threatened, massive. But I controlled it, because the last thing either Jeff or Chuckie would need was feeling my rage emotionally or mentally. However it did mean I was an expert at braining birdbrains, and I was moving as fast as The Clarence Clone with ease.

Chuckie didn't toss me out—either I'd snuck in well or ACE was giving me some kind of mental invisibility cloak. Meaning I could see that the prisoners weren't all together. The human and A-C men were all in the room with Jeff and Chuckie, but the Beta Eight natives and the A-C women were missing.

The Clarence Clone and I not only searched the ship, but we gathered up all the Mind Melders. Kept my connection with Chuckie and destroyed one of the jewels by smashing it with my baseball bat. Felt him smile in his mind. Good, he knew I was there and he was encouraging what I'd done.

We didn't find any of our people, but by the time we'd

searched the ship and gotten all the Mind Melders in hand—
or rather in arms, since we had them slung onto both our arms
and both of our baseball bats like bracelets, there were so
many—Fancy and the Venida had managed to get inside with
their Matriarchs. And all in under three minutes, go team.

Truly, the princesses and Abigail had earned their God
Names, because when I leaned out to take a look, I saw
several snakipedes going for the low-hanging fruit and
snapping at a large number of falling winged bodies that
were not fighting back.

The Clarence Clone pulled me back before I got too en-
raptured with the view and fell out or dropped the Mind
Melders, and closed the hull door.

"You guys were awesome! You're totally the Venida!"

"Couldn't have done it without Fancy," Abigail said with
a grin. "She was amazing."

Fancy bowed. "I have lived my life in the ways of the
Venida."

"It shows," Rahmi said. "We are proud to call you Warrior Sister."

Rhee nodded. "There is a ceremony, but it will have to
wait until this battle is over."

Fancy looked like every dream she'd had as a little ferret
had come true. "I . . . am honored."

"Back to fighting first, though."

"Why are you wearing all those?" Abigail asked.

"Oh, these are Mind Melders, they're what's allowing
the Rapacians to talk to each other. We need to destroy all
of them."

"But you're wearing one," Rhee pointed out.

"Right. I am. And so are James and Ronnie. Um, okay,
everyone take one, and then we destroy the rest."

"Shouldn't we save some for the others?" Rahmi asked,
as she took a Mind Melder and put it on. The others did
likewise. Didn't make much of a dent in what The Clarence
Clone and I were carrying.

"No. We'll get more when we raid the next ship. The
Earth males are together. They're torturing Jeff and they're
doing something equally horrible to Chuckie. No idea
what's happening to the other guys. The Beta Eight natives
and the Earth women I haven't found yet. But none of the
prisoners are on this ship."

"Do we toss all of these," Fancy indicated the unconscious Rapacians lying on the floor nearby, "to the Horrors, or do we merely kill them here?"

"How you do handle normal prisoners?" This was a test question, because the wrong answer would mean that Fancy wasn't actually the Ferret for the Job of Planetary Ruler.

"We imprison them," she replied. "But none of us have ever waged this level of war against another clan. If these awaken, we will be fighting again."

"Good answer and good point. Which is why we're going with imprison them. There's a large room clearly made for prisoner containment. Clarence can lead you to it. Everyone needs to move these bodies in there and get them locked in as fast as possible."

"I can do most of it, Shealla," The Clarence Clone said respectfully.

"Okay, then, um, give me the Mind Melders you have."

"I will carry them," Fancy offered. The Clarence Clone gave the tonnage on his arms to her, gave her the baseball bat and all the Melders on it, put one onto his head, then he disappeared. Along with all the bodies in the hallway we were in.

"The Venida will assist," Abigail said with a grim smile. Then she, Rahmi, and Rhee zipped off.

"Works for me. Let's get back to the command center and let James know he can rock and roll."

CHAPTER 81

I RAN BACK, jangling like the Queen of the Gypsies, Fancy rode her Matriarch, jangling like the Gypsy Caravan, and the other Matriarchs flew behind. I was too revved up on rage to ride right now.

Dumped the Mind Melders onto the ground and started grinding them under my heel while Fancy smashed hers with her baseball bat. Her mace was resting on her Matriarch's back.

"What in God's name are you two doing?" 2.0 asked.

"Getting rid of things that are detrimental to our cause." Despite looking like diamonds, whatever the jewels were made of crumbled pretty easily. Good. I was still mentally tethered to Chuckie and could tell this was helping him in some way.

"Thank God I chose to switch sides."

Chose not to grace this with a response. "James," I said while I crushed at hyperspeed but talked at human, "do whatever you need to from an evasive standpoint. We're all inside. However, you're right—at least some of our people are on that other ship. Possibly on both of the ships. The girls and natives aren't with the guys."

"Fantastic."

"I think we should land," 2.0 said.

Let that sit on the air for a bit. "Um, why?" I asked finally.

"To draw them down. In the air they have an advantage. On the ground, well, this is a world they're unfamiliar with."

Fancy nodded. "This is true. And we do have a fighting force inside Haven. And elsewhere, I'm sure. Not all will have run and hidden when they saw the ships and the Horrors in the sky."

"Only the sane ones."

"That's a great plan," Reader said, ignoring me, as the others joined us in the command center, "but you're forgetting that they're cool with just staying in the air and shooting at targets on the ground. That would work if we could really draw them down, but I'm not betting that we can."

"That means we need to get into the other ships." Always the way. And I knew who had to do it, too. Oh well, Fancy and I had finished destroying all the Mind Melders. Someone else could do the cleanup. "Fancy, you up for another exciting ride?"

"Absolutely, Shealla."

"What about the rest of us?" Abigail asked.

"James needs backup. In case the prisoners know how to escape from their holding cell, someone has to cover him and Ronnie while they fly this thing. Draw straws for who gets to clean up the mess we just made."

This earned me some dirty looks, but the girls all nodded. "Sensible," Rahmi said, disappointment clear. But she stationed herself between Reader and 2.0.

Rhee went and stood by the door, while Abigail took a point in between the two. "You guys get to have all the fun," Abigail said with a grin.

"I know, we just hog it all, don't we?" Turned to the Matriarchs. "You guys in?"

Many antennae waved. A few indicated they were staying on this ship in order to assist Reader and ensure that 2.0 didn't try anything funny. The rest were in it to win it.

"James, we'll be back, I hope, or else we'll be trying to fly the other ships. Ronnie, don't try anything funny. Clarence, I think we're going to need the speedy skills, so are you up for coming along?"

"Yes, Shealla, of course."

Ginger and Wilbur both whined. "No, you two have to stay here and help James," I said as I gave them both big hugs. "Kitty won't be able to fight if she thinks Ginger and Wilbur are in danger." Plus with the flying we were going to have to do, while the animals could be a huge help once we were inside a ship, outside of it there was just too much risk they'd get hurt, fall off, or limit one of us from fighting.

They heaved dog and cat sighs, but Ginger settled herself next to Rahmi and Wilbur did the same with Rhee.

"Girlfriend, you're going to have to time when you leave the ship, because the other ships *are* firing at us, both of them now, and I'm not sure that I can evade that and keep you from getting hit at the same time."

"I have faith in you, James."

"I'm touched. I'm also going to run. They'll probably chase us, but it'll give us the advantage for a little while and possibly mean that you're left alone. By the ships. Remember there are still plenty of Horrors out there as well as Rapacians."

"I'll try to tell the Horrors to avoid all of you," 2.0 said. "Not sure how effective I'll be right now, though. They're in full bloodlust."

"We'll deal with it. How long do you figure you'll be gone, James?"

"Not sure, but I want to go around this world at least once, more if they're actually following us. On the plus side, we'll be able to see if there are other continents we need to be worried about being invaded. And everyone should be able to stay standing, at least for a while."

"Okay, just come back for us."

He turned and flashed me the cover boy grin. "Always babe. Can't leave my girl out here fighting Thanagarians without the rest of the Justice League, now can I?"

"Thank you, Green Lantern."

He laughed and turned back to the controls and the three of us, accompanied by most of the Matriarchs, left the cockpit and headed again to the hull door.

Abigail followed us. "You're supposed to stay here," I told her.

She shrugged. "Someone has to open and close the door."

"Oh. Ah. Good point. Carry on."

Knew where I wanted to go first. But reality said that the place with the most guards on it would be where Chuckie and Jeff were. Ergo, needed to see where the others were first.

Focused on Serene, because I knew she'd be pissed off, freaked out about Brian, and probably a little scared, and therefore broadcasting. Also, she was the head of the A-C

C.I.A., meaning that even though she might be losing most of her head, so to speak, she'd be keeping part of it occupied with figuring out how to get free.

Sure enough, managed to find her. Interestingly and somewhat unsurprisingly, she was focusing on me. It was a Meeting of the Mind Melders.

Because neither one of us was practiced with this form of communication, I only got a flash of information before I lost my mental grip on Serene's mind. But that flash was enough.

"I know where the gals are. We're going to get them first."

"Why?" Fancy asked.

"Because the Rapacians seem to think that Earth girls are easy."

CHAPTER 82

OF COURSE, no one got the reference, not even Abigail. As surprises went on the scale of one to ten, this shock rated at about a negative two. But I soldiered on.

"Are they in danger?" Fancy asked, sounding politely confused.

"Yes, though right now not quite as much as we are. They're captured, and their guard is light. They haven't been roughed up too much because the Rapacians seem to be looking to test out interspecies breeding." And they'd chosen three hottie A-C women as test subjects. This meant the Rapacians' had good taste, but not my friends and not on my watch.

"That's horrible." Fancy sounded appalled.

"Yeah, well, the girls will fight them if they have to. But they felt laying low and pretending to be helpless was the right way to go under the circumstances."

"Will they do that with our females, too?" Fancy asked.

"We won't let them," Abigail said strongly.

Considered my reply as we mounted up. "I honestly don't know." Seemed like the safest answer. Besides, it was true.

"Then let's stop them now and not have to find out," Fancy said as she leaped onto her Matriarch.

"Here." Abigail handed me her battle staff and took my baseball bat. Fancy handed her bat over, too, wisely choosing to hold onto her mace. "I think you're going to need the staff more than the bat. Where did you get those from anyway?"

"Oh, you'd be amazed at what I can come up with." Speaking of which. Looked into my purse. "If we need goggles or some such right now, I'd just love to reach in and grab them," I murmured. Reached into my purse and, sure enough, pulled out aviator's goggles. "Hey, look what I found." Put a pair on, tossed another to Fancy, and the third to The Clarence Clone. "Good thing I pack for any and all occasions."

"Yeah." Abigail sounded slightly suspicious, not that I could blame her. Now wasn't the time to cough up the "I asked the Elves to make my purse a portal" story. Later. If she remembered to ask.

The Clarence Clone put his goggles on, mounted up, and took the other bat from Abigail. "I think I can use both."

She laughed. "Go for it." Then Abigail opened the hatch.

After we weathered the first big gust of wind, we all took off. Waved to Abigail as we cleared the ship and she closed the door. Meaning we were officially on our own now, and there wasn't much anyone inside this ship was going to be able to do for us.

Or, as we called it, routine.

Of course, there was nothing routine about what we had to do, which was get the hell away from the spaceship before Reader hit the gas.

Conveniently, we wanted to go low—the girls were in the ship that had been firing on the castle.

"Dive!"

The Matriarchs didn't need telling twice. To a katyhopper, they nosedived.

I'd had no idea how fast a katyhopper could go. When I'd been riding on Pinky and the others, sure, we'd gone fast, but not hyperspeed fast. Now, either the Matriarchs had figured out how to turn it up to eleven on the speed factor, or else they were using gravity to help them reach escape velocity, only going down, not up.

I'd have bragged about my brilliance in asking my purse for goggles, but I was too busy holding on and not screaming. "Wheeeeeeee!" Okay, maybe a little screaming. But in a positive way.

The Clarence Clone was having the time of his life next to me. Fancy, on the other hand, was showing that she was a ferret who preferred to do her flying more sedately, if you could call fighting and jumping around on the backs of the katyhoppers sedate. But her expression shared she wasn't a fan of the kamikaze style of flight.

On the other hand, this method meant we were going so fast that we zoomed around Rapacians and snakipedes both without much issue. Sometimes we were close enough to slam our weapons into a Rapacian and sometimes we weren't. Holding onto the weapons was hard, at least for me. Fancy and The Clarence Clone didn't seem to be having any issues.

In this manner, we zoomed past the main part of the aerial fight and reached the lower spaceship rather quickly. Of course, now the issue was how to get inside.

The Matriarchs whizzed us around the ship several times. Couldn't spot an easy entrance and neither could the others. Which meant we were going to have to blast our way in. Only we had no blasting capabilities.

Was about to suggest we beat on the command center's windshield when my iPod, which I hadn't put back into my purse, came back to life, playing Sir Mix-A-Lot's time-honored "Baby Got Back."

"Head for the rear, let's see if we can get in via this ship's butt."

My Matriarch waved her antennae to share that this was both a good idea and a description she didn't recommend I use again.

"This from a people who spray butt juices out for any and all occasions and needs?"

My Matriarch admitted this was so and gave me a pass on my ship's butt description.

We reached the rear and took a look. As we searched I risked a look up. Some of the Rapacians who were flying around had spotted us and were coming. But that wasn't the real issue.

No, the real issue was that the ship Reader was flying was finally taking off, and the ship above the aerial fight was following. Got the proverbial bad feeling as I watched the ships gun it, because flames shot out of the rear of both.

"Gang, we need to find a way in, faster than fast. My fine Katyhopper Steeds, a little mind reading right now would not be taken as overstepping your self-imposed bounds. It's hard for the cavalry to do the save if they're burned to a crisp. So, wave those antennae in the air like you just don't care and find someone who knows how we get in from back here."

The Matriarchs moved forward quickly. There was a flap that looked like it was between and under the rocket exhaust pipes. Two of the riderless katyhoppers lifted it up, and the rest flew inside.

"What a wonderful smell we've discovered. I just want to say that us going in via a garbage shaft is exactly what I expect out of a mission."

"Shealla, I believe our voices can echo in here," Fancy said, proving who was the stealthiest, not that this was a shocker moment for me.

The Matriarchs flew quickly through the shaft, which was just wide enough for them to turn a full 360, but not really wide enough for us to fly side-by-side. The shaft was long and, even going fast, I didn't see an exit coming up.

I wasn't in the lead, a riderless Matriarch was. So when she spun and started spraying I got a good view of why. Apparently whoever captained this ship liked to dump his garbage before he slammed the pedal to the metal.

Always the way.

CHAPTER 83

AT THE SAME TIME as the Matriarch's butt juices created both a shield and began to flow over and around
the rest of us, I heard the sound of angry Rapacian voices.
They were coming from behind us, which was serendipitous.

The other Matriarchs moved up so they were all nose to
butt, antennae straight up, legs extended out. This enabled
the shield to flow around us but not on us, as it had when
Saffron was covering and containing Usha. Wondered
where Saffron and the other Beta Eight natives were and if
they were okay. Also wondered where Usha was, and if she
was helping the Rapacians or not. But not for long—the
shield really demanded my attention.

Butt Juice Shield completed, miraculously without covering us like icky plastic wrap, the Matriarch in the lead flew
backward, while the rest of us continued on facing front,
still going hella fast, like the weirdest NASCAR lap ever.
Garbage of all kinds flowed past us. Chose not to look as
much as possible. But still, the Rapacians behind us were
going to get hit with a lot of crap. Literally.

Sure enough, heard the screams and shouts of disgust as
we flew on. In this bizarre fashion we sailed along, while
"Bicycle Race" from Queen played in my ears, the sounds
of Rapacian disgust getting weaker and farther away as we
went. Apparently our shield was working like a drain plug,
in that what got past us was going through in a supercharged
kind of way.

Felt the ship start to move while we were still in the garbage shaft. This coincided with the flow of garbage stopping. Always nice to be right, in that sense.

Our lead Matriarch spun around and broke through the shield. She sailed through the opening but the shield stopped moving with her. The rest of the Matriarchs flew a little lower as the shield sank, and all of them flew a bit faster, too.

We reached the exit in time to surprise a couple of Rapacians. Despite the screaming in the shaft we'd caught them unawares. I readied my battle staff but before I could do anything my music switched to "Up in Arms" by the Foo Fighters and the lead Matriarch stood up on her back legs and proceeded to do some incredibly impressive kung fulike moves on both Rapacians at the same time.

They went down and I jumped off, grabbed the circlets on their heads, then went to the shaft door. "That was amazing! Can all of you do that?"

The Matriarchs in the area shared that, yes, they could. It was something a katyhopper learned over time, and therefore the eldest were the most adept and dangerous.

"It's like you're the Teenaged Mutant Ninja Turtles! Only you'd need to be called the Ancient Katyhopper Kung Fu Masters."

Antennae waves shared that they felt this was an appropriate and pleasing title.

The moment our last Ancient Katyhopper Kung Fu Master was in the room I slammed and locked the garbage chute's door. The last Matriarch through sprayed it with butt juices for good measure.

"Awesome. We need to split to cover as much ground as possible. Clarence, I want you finding whatever and wherever this ship's holding cell is. Figure it's in the same place as the one from the ship we just left. Once you find it, knock out all the Rapacians you find, take the circlets off their heads, and lock them in there. Then destroy the circlets."

"Just like last time, yes, Shealla."

"Super. If you find the prisoners—pretty much anyone who isn't a Rapacian or isn't obviously working with them like a loose Free Woman or an Amazonian Ancient, like those who were protecting Ronaldo—find me immediately and let me know."

"Should I stop anyone trying to hurt them?"

"Absolutely. Just realize that they won't know that you're not the Original Clarence and probably won't trust you."

He nodded and zipped off.

"What about me, Shealla?" Fancy asked, as one of my favorite songs to fight to—Clutch's "Electric Worry" —came on.

"You're sticking with me. Clarence is the fastest and, of the three of us, strongest, and he's used to sneaking around without being seen. So are you. I'm not as smooth at it, but it won't matter because what I want us doing is busting heads, both literally and figuratively. It's the Matriarchs who have the tough job because they don't have hyperspeed."

Antennae waved. They weren't sure they should leave us, for our protection, not theirs.

"Yeah, I know you can help, but I don't think most of this crew left their ship, meaning we have a lot more Rapacians on board than we did with the ship James and the others are on. We appear to be in hot pursuit—and that means that someone has to ensure that this ship doesn't blow the ship we captured out of the air. And other someones need to help us get captured and hopefully unconscious Rapacians into the holding cell. Plus, let's face it—you guys are going to kick more Rapacian butt than the three of us have any hope of doing, hyperspeed or no hyperspeed."

More antennae waves. They'd do what needed to be done. Then they all stood on their back legs and did a kick and hit in unison, much like a form in martial arts. Antennae waved again, then the Ancient Katyhopper Kung Fu Masters took off and scattered.

"Ninja katyhoppers. I'd say that now I've seen everything, but I know that will be proven incorrect in less time than it takes to drink a Coke, so I won't."

Really wanted a Coke. Resisted the desire to ask my purse for a nice can of delicious refreshment—there would be time for that later, after I'd saved my family, friends, the solar system, and the galaxy. But no pressure.

Instead, dug around in my purse for a waterfruit, pulled one out, and ate it. Felt refreshed and better and really worried that these were addictive. Well, probably no more addictive than Coke, right?

Finished up, took Fancy's paw in mine and, "Electric

Worry" on repeat, for which I sent a thank you to Algar, we headed off.

I missed my baseball bat almost immediately. It was a lot easier to maneuver than the battle staff. Probably why Algar had given it to me. However, this just meant I had to let go of Fancy—who seemed, to the clutch of Rapacians we'd found, to appear out of nowhere—and spend my time knocking them out without them being able to see me, due to the speed I was going.

This actually worked far better than I'd expected, and we ended up doing it all through the ship as we worked our way forward toward the command center. This time, though, we destroyed the circlets as we found them, just as I'd told Clarence to do, in part because there were going to be so many and in other part because they'd make noise and alert the Rapacians to our presence.

Hyperspeed being what it was, between us and The Clarence Clone—who'd found the holding cell that was not holding anyone we were looking for—it only took us about ten minutes to clear the back half of the ship.

"We are out of room in that cell, Shealla," The Clarence Clone informed me as we met up and took a short breather. "I haven't searched the forward part of the ship, though."

"Let's move forward, then. We'll have to leave the bodies where they fall, at least for a little while."

We moved on as a group, which was convenient because we didn't find any Rapacians for a little while, and that way when we came upon the room the Matriarchs were using for their prisoner holding—the mess hall—we were together.

They'd moved all the heavy equipment to block all exits but one, and then sprayed the butt juices over them, on both sides, to ensure they remained closed.

"That can't hold forever," I pointed out to the Matriarch I'd been riding, who I decided to call Boz for no reason other than it was a cool name and the only other Boz I knew of was Scaggs. All the Ancient Katyhopper Kung Fu Masters needed cool rock star names. I didn't have time to assign them all yet, but that was definitely on my To Do List, right after all the Save The Husband, Save the Daughter, Save the Besties, Save the Worlds stuff.

Boz shared that she liked the nickname and also that the

older a katyhopper got, the stronger the shields. So this would hold long enough. Plus two of the Ancient Katyhopper Kung Fu Masters were staying outside the room, to keep a mental eye on the prisoners.

Thusly reassured, we all headed off again. Most of the Matriarchs scattered again, but Boz stayed with me, Fancy, and The Clarence Clone.

Boz led the way, but not toward the command area. Instead, we went into the bowels of the ship. Clarence had already done half of this area since this was the section the prison hold was in. But he hadn't finished the front half, and clearly Boz felt this was an oversight that needed immediate rectification.

Found out why pretty quickly. This front area wasn't loaded with Rapacians but it was indeed holding something else in addition to food stores.

"Katyhoppers, strautruch, and Lecanora, oh my."

CHAPTER 84

SURE ENOUGH, the missing Beta Eight natives were here. Did a fast headcount—five strautruch, three katy-hoppers, and two Lecanora. No partridge in a pear tree, but that was probably somewhere else on the ship.

No Peregrine either. Really wondered where Bruno was, because I hadn't seen him when I'd seen the Earth males and he wasn't with the other "animals." Hoped he was okay, just like everyone else we were trying to rescue.

The prisoners all looked uninjured, but there was a weird glow around them.

Boz used three of her legs to hold the three of us back. All the natives seemed frozen in a kind of stasis, but I could see their eyes and they were awake and aware, because they all blinked when they saw us.

"Got it. That's some kind of energy cage, isn't it?"

King Benny, sans antlers, blinked his eyes three times. Wondered what had happened to his antlers, but figured that was low on the Worry Totem Pole.

"Three times for yes, got it. Is anyone hurt in this group?"
He blinked twice.

"Twice for no and thank goodness. Okay, hang on, King Benny and Friends. We'll figure this out." I hoped. Turned to Boz. "I think it's time to use the impressive mind-reading skills again."

She bowed her head and we all waited. It took a good minute, then Boz raised her head again and waved antenna.

"Always the way. Of course there's a remote that controls this and of course it's on the person of a Rapacian who's on the command deck."

"Shall I fetch it, Shealla?" The Clarence Clone asked.

"No. I'll do it, Clarence, thanks." Boz had shared that she'd link with my mind and help me. "Everyone, this is a clone of someone we knew on our home planet. Some of the Gods will think he's an enemy but he is *not*. Also, the king, who is also a clone of someone we know, is now also working with us. And, as with this clone, some of the Gods will think he's an enemy and, so far, he's not. Okay?"

King Benny, and anyone else whose eyes I could see, blinked three times.

"Good. The Leader of the Nihalani and the king are flying one of the Rapacian's spaceships. We're going to try to free you and take over this one. So, um, sit tight. Clarence, you guard Boz and everyone else here and make sure there are no Rapacians on this level at all. Fancy, it's time for you and me to kick it again."

The two of us took off, Boz giving me directions in my mind. It was different than speaking to ACE or Algar, or when Serene and I had mind-melded with the brief flashes of information as opposed to a conversation. This was a conversation but we didn't talk. I just knew what she, or the other katyhoppers, were thinking and they knew what I was thinking. But in a conversational way.

Different or not, it worked, which was a particular relief because the ship was like a maze. The other had been, too, but I'd been following others to get to the command deck area, had had enough time to get lost and search everywhere, and had then just gone back the way we'd come. Here I was actually having to navigate with purpose and I knew we were running out of time.

Reached the command area and made a pleasant discovery—my missing Dazzlers were here. And, surprises of surprises, Usha was with them.

They were all also in an energy cage, of course, all four of them. Meaning that I should be able to kill two big, nasty birds with one remote control. If I could identify the Rapacian holding it and make it work right.

I kept Fancy and myself at hyperspeed and ran around the room, checking out everyone here. We had a dozen Rapacians to deal with, ten of whom were armed to the hilt.

The pilot and copilot were armed, but lightly. But I didn't spot anyone holding a remote control, or anything I could sort of guess was a remote control. They were holding maces and flails and, lucky me, staffs and clubs, but not remotes.

Could tell all the trapped women could see me and Fancy, though, by the way their eyes were following us. Fortunately, none of the Rapacians seemed to be paying any attention to them. Probably because they were paying attention to chasing the ship Reader and the others were in.

They were also angrily demanding information from stations that were utterly silent. If they'd been humans, every one of them would be suggesting anything from alien monsters to psychopathic killers as to why no one outside of this room was responding. If they were A-Cs they'd have deployed a couple people to zip around looking for what superbeing had just manifested where.

But these Rapacians seemed unaware of these options. They just kept on demanding to hear from people who weren't responding.

Wondered if Chuckie and/or the Matriarchs were somehow affecting this, then realized that if they were, time was of the essence. It was just a pity that I had no clear plan of action because I was hesitant to knock someone out in case the remote had a kill switch. Then again, saw nothing in anyone's claws that indicated such.

Boz finally did me a solid and shared that it was the big Rapacian in charge who had the remote. Which was great news and all, only they were all big in here. In fact, there were no female Rapacians that I could identify. And if they had ways of showing rank, they weren't ways I could identify.

Oh well, when in doubt, go with the classics, that was my motto.

Let go of Fancy near the pilot and, still at hyperspeed, started slamming the staff up into everyone's groins.

Apparently no one here had gotten the memo that Earth girls fought dirty, because, to a birdman, they crumpled, screaming or gasping and, in some cases, crying. Ah, I loved my work sometimes.

Took the opportunity to remove their circlets, though these I kept. Had a feeling we were going to want our people mentally able to chat.

Meanwhile, Fancy had the mace at the copilot's head and her knife at the pilot's throat. "Give us the means to safely release our friends, or you both die." She was speaking in a growl that shared that she was a hungry carnivore and they were, claws and weapons and spaceship or not, food. "I won't ask again."

"Trust me," I said as I slowed to human speeds, "she's kind of itchy on the trigger finger, so to speak." Removed the circlets from both pilot and copilot. "And, really, we only need one of you to point out who has the controls for the electric cages."

"I don't have it," the pilot said stiffly. "If you kill me we'll crash."

"Oh, blah, blah, blah. We'll just fly the ship instead of you. Duh."

"I don't have it, either," the copilot said. "I'm not even sure why we're here."

Interesting. *If* he wasn't faking this. ACE had indicated the Rapacians were being controlled. Felt a tiny bit sorry for all the ones we'd made dead, but war was hell, after all. And there was no proof that they'd resisted or were even against this particular invasion. True, ACE had said the circlets had made them more bloodthirsty, but he hadn't said they were unwilling participants. Moral dilemma over.

"We'll worry about the existential questions later. I'm impatient, but not as impatient as Fancy is, so, geez dudes, who does have the thing which we wish to possess?"

"The Sergeant at Arms," they said in unison.

"As if we can determine your ranks based on plumage or something? Show me which writhing ball of pain has what I want or join them in the writhing. If you're lucky."

"They won't be lucky," Fancy growled.

Went to the copilot and hauled him out of his seat. "Point out the right Hawkman."

"I don't understand you."

Slammed my battle staff up into his groin. "So few ever do," I shared as he collapsed, gasping. "I didn't hit you as hard as I hit them. I *can*, and will, but I'm the nice one of the two of us, so you get one more chance. Crawl over to the dude who has the controls for the electric cages."

Had to hand it to this one, he wasn't that stupid. He crawled to a Rapacian that, if I had had time to really line them up and do a body mass comparison, was probably the biggest.

"Thanks."

Beta Twelve battle staffs glowed and could be quite deadly, like javelin-lightsabers, basically. During one of the many skills workout sessions I'd done with Christopher, the princesses had shown me how to turn the glowing side on and off. I'd kept mine off since I didn't want to hit anyone on my side with it. But this wasn't someone on my side.

Turned on the lightsaber side and put it at the Sargent Sergeant at Arms' groin. "I can hurt you a whole lot more than I already did. Give me the things that control the electronic cages and I may not hurt you more."

The Sergeant at Arms stared at me beadily for a few moments. Then he nodded and reached into a pouch he had hanging around his waist. He tossed a rectangular box toward the doorway.

"Cute." Spun the staff and slammed the non-glowing end into his stomach. He went back into a fetal position. "That's the last mercy either one of us show anyone in this room. We'll see how birds like you fly without your wings next."

Heard the pilot gasp and the copilot draw his breath in sharply. Apparently the wings were even more important than the family jewels. Well, they were avians, that made sense.

I knew The Sergeant at Arms had tossed the remote so that I'd have to go get it and therefore be distracted so one or more of his compatriots could attack me and Fancy. Pity the Rapacians didn't seem clear on hyperspeed and how it worked. Well, pity for them.

Zipped over and grabbed the remote, then slammed my staff onto the backs of the heads of the three Rapacians who'd worked through their personal pain and planned on catching me off guard. They went facedown with satisfying thuds. Then I cracked the heads of all the rest besides the Sergeant at Arms, pilot, and copilot, just for insurance.

Was back exactly where I'd been standing next to the Sergeant at Arms within two seconds. "You're lucky," I said conversationally, as I hauled the copilot to his feet and shoved him back into his chair. Fancy put her mace right back at his head. "I haven't cracked you across your head yet, but that's only because I may have a question about how to work this device."

"I won't help you," the Sergeant at Arms said. "You're our enemy."

Went to him and put the glowing side of the battle staff against his head. "You have no idea." My turn to growl. "Your people have my family and friends, and you're hurting some of them. Know what I do to people who hurt the people I care about? I hurt them back, worse. A beak for a beak, a wing for a wing. And if you push me even a little bit more, delay me from finding my family and friends, cause someone I love to suffer longer because you made me later, then you're going to get to truly find out what it's like to be a Rapacian with no wings."

"She means it," Fancy snarled. "And I'll help her strip the wings from all of you."

Apparently there was something in my expression that convinced the Sergeant at Arms that cooperating was in his best interests. "The white button turns the cage on, the blue one turns the cage off."

Took a look at the remote—there were three sets of buttons. There were also buttons of another color—red.

"What's the red button for?"

"That's the destruction button. Hit that and kill everyone in the cage."

Boz confirmed that the rest of the Rapacians were captured, their circlets destroyed, and half the Matriarchs were guarding prisoners while the rest were with her and the Beta Eight captives. She also confirmed that the Earth men weren't on this ship and, as far as she could tell, the Sergeant at Arms was telling the truth.

"What's the third set for?" Didn't figure I'd be lucky enough for it to be for the cage that the Earth guys were in. The third cage might have nothing in it, so hitting the blue button might mean nothing. Or it might make something explode.

"The cage I'm going to put you in when this is over."

I'd have given a snarky comeback or kicked him in the balls again, but the ship took a hit that rocked it. Just managed to keep my balance, but only because I slammed the staff into the floor. It made a hole, undoubtedly lessening the spaceship's trade-in value, but those were the breaks.

Did have the satisfaction of seeing the Sergeant at Arms look a lot less cocky, you know, while he was rolling around on the floor.

Fancy had stayed upright by holding onto the pilot. This meant that her mace was across his chest and the copilot was uncovered. Not that it mattered, because he wasn't trying to attack or escape.

"Lakin," the copilot cried, "Trevik's ship is firing on Otari's and ours!"

CHAPTER 85

DECIDED WE WERE in enough trouble already and hit all the blue buttons. Thankfully, Boz was right—Lakin, who I assumed was the name of the Sergeant at Arms, had been telling the truth.

The electric cage disappeared and the women were able to move again. The Dazzlers all shook themselves. Usha, of course, started attacking. However, she wasn't attacking me or Fancy. She went straight for Lakin. Not that I could blame her. He was a world-class jerk.

It didn't take a gigantic mental leap for me to figure that Trevik was the guy in charge of the ship Jeff, Chuckie, and the others were in. And Trevik or someone on his ship had figured out that the other two ships had been commandeered. Wasn't sure how, but figured our pilot or copilot had shared their situation with the other ships, and since the ship Reader was piloting was running away from the others, anyone with half a brain could have guessed that something was wrong over there.

"Take evasive action, and that's an order. Then tell Trevik that this ship and Otari's are in the hands of those protecting Beta Eight. And also tell him that both ships are loaded with Rapacian prisoners. As in, if he blows us up, he's going to kill every Rapacian that's inside."

"I can't communicate with him," the pilot said, while he and the copilot took evasive action, forcing us all to keep holding on to stay on our feet.

"Bullpookey. You told him you'd been boarded. Why else would he be firing at us?"

"Yes, but I mean I can't communicate with him now. He's locked everyone else out of his mind."

Or else he'd taken off his circlet, so no one could affect him one way or the other. Meaning this Trevik might be smarter than the average bear, or bird.

Took a look out the windshield again. There weren't any Rapacians in the air anymore. Meaning they were all dead or that Trevik's ship might have been the one the survivors were able to run to. And this meant that Trevik's ship might have also rescued Otari and Kares.

"Don't you communicate in normal fashion via radio or something? I mean when you're not getting to use fancy mind-reading headwear."

"Yes, and he's closed the channels."

"What's the chain of command? Who's in charge if Otari and Kares are incapacitated or killed?"

"Lakin, then Trevik," the pilot replied.

This move made a lot of sense if Otari and/or Kares had survived. They were in charge, and their number two man's ship had confirmed that they were commandeered.

"These are your command ships?"

"These are our only ships."

Fancy and I exchanged a look. "Three ships seems like . . . not very many," she said finally.

"It's not," Claudia said, as she kicked a nearby Rapacian in the groin. Lakin and Usha were still fighting.

"They're working with another planet," Lorraine said. "We could hear through that horrible cage, but we couldn't determine which planet has armed them."

"Gather these Rapacians in here together. Oh, Usha, stop. I think we need Lakin. Use your strength to get the rest of them in a nice clutch so I can put them into their own cage."

She punched Lakin, then stared at me. "You believe we are on the same side?"

"Hardly. However, right now, there are so many enemies of my enemy running around that I think we all need to work together before we all start fighting again."

"When we were captured, the trap was around Clea's dead body. How were you not captured?"

"First off, it was around one of her cloned bodies, I think." Now wasn't the time to mention that the Poofs had eaten all her other clones and, potentially, Clea herself. "But we weren't caught because the body was moved from where I'd seen it the night before, and her eyes were open."

"The eyes of the dead normally stare up into space."

"Yes, but on my planet we close the eyes of the dead as a sign of respect. I'd closed hers the night before, they were open when we left Haven, meaning something was off."

Usha stared at me some more. "You gave respect to our dead?"

"Yes. Why is this so surprising?"

"We have been told that none on your planets know respect of any kind."

"We don't respect the Z'porrah, I'll tell you that. However, we have plenty of respect to go around. But since this solar system is under internal attack, I'd really like to get back to stopping this civil war. So, are you in or out?"

She stood slowly. "In." She lifted Lakin and dumped his body at my feet. Then she and the Dazzlers gathered the rest of the Rapacians and stood them where they'd been held a short while ago.

Serene took the remote from me. "May I?" I nodded and she aimed the box at them and hit one of the white buttons. Sure enough, the electronic cage went around them. "See how you like it," she snarled at the prisoners.

The rest of our team arrived now, other than the Matriarchs on guard duty. The command center was kind of full.

"Happy reunion hugs later. Has anyone seen Bruno, my Peregrine?"

"Not since we were all captured, Shealla," King Benny said. "Thank you for rescuing us."

"It's all in a God Day's Work." Turned back to Lakin, who was coming around again. "Dude, you have exactly one chance to not be imprisoned like the rest of your people or to be dead, like a lot of your people. Figure out a way to tell Trevik's ship that if he blows us up he's destroying a third of your fighting force. And if he blows the other ship up, he'll be destroying another third." Give or take, depending on how many had died already and how many were in Trevik's ship now. Decided Lakin didn't need this exact an explanation, however.

Lakin shook his head. "To die in battle is to die with honor. Trevik will not listen."

"To slaughter half of your fighting force *yourself* is to kill like a moron. You have so many people on your planet that you can afford to lose all those who are imprisoned in this ship and Otari's?"

"No," he said slowly. "We do not."

"Then figure out how to keep everyone alive, because either Trevik, Otari, or Kares are trying to destroy the ships we've taken over, and both of those ships are loaded with your own people who are all prisoners."

"Lakin, all communications are blocked," the pilot said.

"What about communications to the other commandeered ship?" Lakin asked. I was impressed and embarrassed that I hadn't thought of this myself.

The pilot fiddled. "I told them we were under their rule and they are responding, Lakin."

"Good." Lakin looked at me. "The longer the Jewel of Power," he pointed to the circlets I was holding, "is not on my head, the clearer I can think. I cannot remember why we are at war with anyone."

"Does anyone on my team wearing these circlets feel angrier or more controlled by an outside influence than normal?" Everyone shook their heads.

"No, Shealla," Fancy said. "Perhaps they were not made to work on us as they work on these Rapacians."

"Brain waves could be different, yeah." Meaning they were using Chuckie as a battery and Jeff as the spark to keep that battery operating. Meaning I really needed to get into Trevik's ship.

I'd be willing to go in as a "prisoner exchange" or something, but there was no way to do this if they weren't hearing anything we said. Thought about what 2.0 had suggested. "What if we land on the planet? Will they come down to talk?"

Lakin shook his head. "No. They will shoot us from the air."

So Reader had called that one right. "How do we get them to talk versus shoot?"

"I have no—" He stopped himself and cocked his head, which looked very Regular Bird. As with King Benny and his antlers, I controlled the Inner Hyena. "There is one way. If my ship and Otari's ship were to fly back into the fight outside of this planet's solar space, Trevik might follow."

"They are my ships now, but we'll argue semantics later. You're suggesting we engage again with the rest of the fleet, or rather, fleets that are out there?"

"It's risky, but yes. Trevik would need to open communications channels to speak to our allies."

"And, before we do this, just who are your allies?"

He looked a little shocked. "You don't know?"

"If I knew, would I ask?"

"Maybe. You are strange creatures."

"We're seriously pissed creatures on a deadline, too, let's not forget that. Your allies, who are they?"

"We support the Planet's Rights Faction. There are beings from all the inhabited worlds who fight with us against the Imperial Monarchists."

"Wow, I'm on the side of the Imperial Army this time? That kind of makes you think of *Star Wars* in a whole new way, doesn't it?" Looked around at the room of blank faces, including those in the electronic cage. "Or it could just be me. So, who was in the triangular ship that you guys blew up that fell into the oceans of this planet?"

"That was a noncombat ship from Alpha Seven, coming to provide humanitarian aid."

Figured the universal translator had really had to knock itself out translating whatever Lakin had actually said into "humanitarian."

"So, you guys shot an unarmed, noncombatant, nonthreatening ship out of space? Any reason why?"

"No one is allowed to be neutral."

"Got it. Officially, you guys suck. What do the Alpha Seven beings look like?"

He shrugged. "War isn't pleasant. One of their other ships arrived on the planet without incident. And they claim to be avian in their makeup, but they are nothing like us. No feathers, no wings, no claws, just smooth skins, flippers, and wide, flat feet."

Confirmation that those who'd saved the Lecanora in the castle were from Alpha Seven. Their first ship must have landed out of sight of the continent, and they clearly had super-duper hyperspeed, which, under the circumstances, was good. They seemed like they were on the side of the people on the planet, so leaving them down here wasn't going to be a terrible choice.

"Okay, I want the communications channels open between us and Otari's ship, and I want them open now."

The copilot nodded. "On speaker."

"James, you guys okay?"

"So far, but not if I have to keep on flying around the planet. There are only so many ways to go, despite what math and science would tell you. There's no other continent, by the way, just ocean, ocean, and more ocean. Oh, and one fully intact giant triangle, which is a spaceship that's floating, somehow, just out of view of the continent."

Brought him up to speed fast on what was going on. "So, we're going to leave the Alpha Seven Penguins here, because they're clearly here to help."

"And we're going to head up into the battle in ships that all our allies know to be their enemies'? Manned in your case by people you can't trust and in my case with someone we only sort of trust?"

"I'm in the room," 2.0 said.

"And we're going to just hope that the ship that has everyone else in it, including people we know are being tortured, is going to follow us up there?"

"Got it in one. Or, I guess, two or three. But anyway, yes. Off we go into the wild blue yonder. And all that."

Reader sighed. "I knew I should have stayed in bed instead of going to that meeting."

CHAPTER 86

THE SHIPS READIED to leap up into space. This was great in the overall scheme of things, but not great in the areas that mattered most to me. But I had no way to get near, let alone into, the third Rapacian ship.

My iPod, which had been playing "Electric Worry" on low and repeat, suddenly changed songs to "Sparkle" by No Doubt.

"Thanks," I said quietly. Pulled The Clarence Clone aside. "I'm going to be leaving this part of the ship. I need you to keep an eye on Usha and Lakin both. If they try anything against anyone else, you need to stop them."

"You don't want me to come with you?" He sounded disappointed.

"No, I need someone here who can back up Fancy and the others. You're the strongest and the fastest, so I need you to stay here and protect all our friends."

He brightened up. "They're my friends, too, now?"

Patted his arm. "Yes, I believe they are." Trotted over to the Dazzlers. "Serene, need you for a minute. Girls, make sure that the pilot and copilot are doing what we want, and give Fancy a break if possible. The Clarence Clone will help you, as the others will, I'm sure."

Lorraine gave me a suspicious look. "What are you up to?"

"Tell you if it works." Grabbed Serene and headed for the door. Boz came with us. Decided telling her not to was silly. Headed for the prisoner containment areas and reached the mess hall one first. "Serene, can you make one of the cages cover everyone in here?"

"I think so. But I'll need to be in there." She fiddled with it for a moment, while the Matriarchs on guard readied to open the door. Serene nodded, they opened, then she stepped in and hit one of the white buttons, but not the button she'd used in the command area.

Sure enough, the glowing cage went around everyone in the room other than her. She backed out and the Matriarchs locked the door in their own special way.

We headed for the other prisoner containment area and once again the cage worked. Boz shared that all the prisoners remained contained in all areas. We headed back, but I stopped halfway between the prisoner containment room and the mess hall.

"Kitty, if we have to put anyone else in a cage I'll have to let one of these go."

"I'm hoping we won't have to. I'm going to try to get over to the other ship, the one Jeff and the others are on. I don't think they have time to wait for us to fight and negotiate a peace treaty."

"How are you going to do that? This ship doesn't have that kind of tech on it."

"I'm hoping I have the right kind of tech on me." Looked into my purse. "Poofies, Kitty would like a word."

Several Poofs looked up at me sleepily. None of these were Poofs I knew. Had no idea where "my" Poofs were, but hoped they were trying to protect my family and friends. Wasn't positive, but it seemed likely that these were the Alpha Four Poofs taking a breather.

"Kitty needs to go save Jeff, and Chuckie, and everyone else. But in order to do that, Kitty needs a Z'porrah power cube. I know they're being kept far away for safekeeping, but I think many people are going to die if Kitty can't get a hold of a cube."

Lots of cute looks, some embarrassed mewling, no power cubes.

"Um, can you ask one of the Earth Poofs for an assist? It's kind of dire."

More cute looks, more embarrassed mewls, still no power cubes. They didn't know where the cubes were, or what they were. These were definitely Alpha Four Poofs. Why they'd been kept in the dark I couldn't fathom, but my guess was one word and that word was Algar.

I couldn't tell them to ask Algar for a cube, not only because I literally couldn't, but because now wasn't the time to have the "Our Elves are one dude who's from a really wacked-out universe" chat with anyone. My iPod switched to "Try" by Pink. Clearly it was time to pull out what I hoped was the Big Gun.

"I can't save Jamie without one, I don't think."

Mous-Mous appeared, mewing angrily, but the Poof wasn't angry with me. Had the feeling the other Poofs were getting an Anti-Free Will lecture but couldn't be sure. Then the Poof jumped out of my purse, went large, hacked up a power cube, and went back to small.

Picked up the cube and the Poof. The cube was glittering but not sparkling, as nonsensical as that seemed. However, there *was* a difference, and I knew the thing had to sparkle to work. "Thanks." Nuzzled Mous-Mous. "Is Jamie alright?"

The Poof mewed. She was okay for now. Mous-Mous gave me another nuzzle then disappeared. So much for any additional help with the power cube.

"Do you want me to go with you?" Serene asked.

"No. You and James are in charge, which is nice since you're each on different ships. But I need you here, running things as the Head of Imageering and making sure our tentative alliances and new friends all remain intact. Besides, if this doesn't work, then it's only one more of us captured, not two."

Boz waved her antennae. She wasn't sure how far her range was for mind reading, and it was about to be severely tested. Not only due to distances about to be traveled, and the sheer number of minds the Matriarchs were about to experience, but because she had no idea how well their powers would work once they were far enough removed from their homeland. She was, therefore, offering to go along with me.

"Thank you, but no. As with Serene, I need you here. Serene, Boz and the other katyhopper Matriarchs are awesome, so let them help you, too."

"You want us doing our best to negotiate a cease-fire, right?" Serene asked.

"Right. Good luck with that."

She smiled. "I've been reading up on a variety of Earth methods for this. Is it okay if we make a stop on the planet before we leave it, though?"

"Um, the impression everyone has is that those in Trevik's ship will blast you if you do."

Boz waved her antennae and asked me to give Serene a waterfruit. I complied. Without feeling too regretful about it.

"Eat this. I think Boz is going to do some mind-melding with you, which will be helpful."

Serene nodded. "You okay with me rolling with the plan I have?"

"Sure. I know as much about your plan as you do about mine, though."

"You're going to use the power cube to get to where the guys are. I'm going to try to extract one of the backup power spheres from the planet so that we can rig that giant telescope into a weapon."

"You can see the telescope?"

"Yes, but only because when we were taken they took us to the top of the All Seeing Mountain and then brought us up to the ship from there."

"How? I thought they didn't have beaming tech."

"They don't. They do have a smaller ship that they use for raids. It came down and didn't make a lot of noise."

"It must have cloaking on it, because we never saw it, and we went up to the top of the Mountain pretty much right after you were taken." Though we'd toured the world first. Decided I'd kick myself about that later. "And it must dock in Trevik's ship because I've been all over this one and the other one, and so has The Clarence Clone, and no smaller ships were seen or mentioned."

"Probably, since the trap they used was cloaked. They took us up to the top of the Mountain using a powered platform. By the way, everyone had a severe déjà vu reaction when we were up there, at least all of us from Earth. But then they knocked us all out and when we woke up, we were separated."

"Good to know. We did, too. Didn't ask Abigail and the princesses about it, but if you have a spare moment, feel free. Now, get back to the command area. If I get over there alive and in one piece I'll do my best to keep them too busy to shoot at you."

Serene hugged me. "Go get our husbands, family, and friends back. I'll go get our weapon." She and Boz headed forward to the command area and I chose an empty room.

Power cubes worked via telepathy, just like half the things and beings in this solar system, apparently. You had to visualize where you wanted to go, set the cube up to "send" and then you touched the cube and, voila, you were there. Only I didn't have a clear idea of where I wanted to go.

No worries. I still had the circlet on. Focused on Chuckie and realized we still had our link together. But it felt tenuous, meaning he was draining and that I needed to get there fast. I couldn't really see where he was, though, and I didn't want to land right on or, worse, in him. Sure, the cubes weren't supposed to allow that, but I hadn't used them enough to feel confident.

The song changed to Pink's "True Love" and one of the Alpha Four Poofs hopped out of my purse and onto my shoulder. It mewled and Poofikins appeared on the power cube. The Poof did something to it and all of a sudden it was sparkling. Then Poofikins jumped onto my other shoulder.

"Thanks, I needed that."

Took a deep breath and focused on Jeff. I could see him, feel him, and it was clear that he needed me. I could see the area around him and realized that Chuckie was helping me by looking at Jeff. Focused on my husband, tucked my battle staff under my arm, and sent out a prayer to ACE, Algar, and all the other Powers That Be.

Then, Poofs on my shoulders, I put my hand onto the now-flashing part of the power cube.

CHAPTER 87

FRANKLY, I'd been expecting nothing to happen. But the cosmos did me a solid and transferred me right to where I'd been thinking. I almost didn't react, I was so shocked.

However, self-preservation kicked in fast. Dropped the cube into my purse and readied my battle staff at hyperspeed because, naturally, the room where Jeff, Chuckie, and, thankfully, the other guys were wasn't devoid of Rapacians. In fact the room was rather large and there was easily a full platoon if not a battalion of Rapacians in here.

I'd been seen but I started running around the room and that meant I disappeared, at least per the Rapacians' shouts. Kicked it up to the higher gear my total rage at seeing what they were doing to my men gave me and ran up to and on the ceiling, making sure I avoided the glowing square that indicated where I could utilize the cube's Free Return Trip option. If I hit that, I'd go back to the ship I'd left, and that wasn't happening until I'd saved my men.

Jeff was on his knees, our enemies' fave position for him, and as per usual, he was stripped to the waist. They had his hands tied and had him holding them behind his head. Great view, since even in pain and close to death the man was drop-dead gorgeous. But I was here to avoid the drop-dead part.

Interestingly, the torture the Rapacians were doing was physical. The A-C fast regeneration meant that Jeff was healing quickly whenever they lashed him with something that looked like a nasty cat-o'-nine-tails.

Chuckie, meanwhile, was in a contraption that looked a

lot like what they'd put plain old Steve Rogers into so that
he could walk out as Captain America. He also had a gigantic version of the jewel in the circlets clamped to his forehead. However, if Chuckie was going to walk out as
anything, it seemed like the Rapacians were shooting for
Vegetable Man. He was still all there mentally—I could tell
due to our connection—but he wasn't going to hold out for
too much longer.

My music had stopped the moment we'd gotten into the
room, presumably because Chuckie couldn't take anything
more barraging his mind, and/or because the Rapacians
would be able to hear it somehow. Gave it even odds for
either. Or both.

The other guys were shackled to the walls in shackles
that looked like they really hurt if the prisoner was just
standing there, let alone if they tried to move. Clearly only
Lakin had the "kind and gentle" containment setup on his
ship.

The room was a basic rectangle, but there was a little
alcove. Went over there to discover that they did indeed
have Lakin's energy cage—they were just using it to control
Christopher. The Rapacian standing there was constantly
pushing blue buttons. Realized that Christopher was using
his speed to try to break through, and that meant they had
three of the cages around him—as he broke through one,
they reactivated it.

Had no idea of who to try to rescue first. This wasn't
based on love or anything, but on reasonable chance of success. The Rapacians knew I was in the room, and while I was
mad enough to hit all of them possibly before one of them
got a lucky hit on me, that wasn't guaranteed.

My music changed to "Built for Speed" by the Stray
Cats. Decided not to argue.

Dropped down from the ceiling onto the Rapacian with
the remote. The remote dropped out of his hand and skit-
tered toward the energy cage. What would happen if it hit
the cage I didn't want to find out, but my imagination shared
a lot of options with me, all of them horrifyingly bad.

However, I had a Rapacian to overpower first, because
my landing on him hadn't knocked him out, just down.
Leaped up, brained him, hard, then leaped for the remote.
Caught it just before it hit the cage.

Leaped back and ripped the circlet off of the now-unconscious Rapacian's head, destroyed it, tossed him to the side but out of sight of anyone who wasn't looking directly into the alcove, then took a look at the remote. Had the same number and color of buttons as the one Serene now was controlling and in the same order. Hit all the blue buttons.

The cage disappeared and Christopher collapsed. Fortunately I was still going at the super speeds he usually used, so I was able to grab him before he hit the floor. Dug around in my purse and pulled out a couple of waterfruit. His Poof, Toby, came out with the fruit. "Eat these," I said softly, as Toby jumped onto his shoulder and nuzzled him.

Somehow, no one had heard us. Possibly because they were still busy shouting at each other and searching for me. Well, at least that meant they weren't hurting Jeff for the moment.

Christopher ate at hyperspeed so he was done quickly. "Thanks, for the save and the waterfruit. I feel a lot better."

The shouting sounded far less chaotic. We peeked around the corner. There were a lot of angry Rapacians all doing the same thing—swinging their weapons around themselves. They were placed so that each one was just at the edge of the other's weapon range, so they were covering all the available space. There were two Rapacians guarding the door in the same fashion. The likelihood of one of them hitting us, fastest hyperspeed around or not, went up dramatically. The likelihood that one of them would ask where the guy guarding their special prisoner was went off the charts.

"What we need is a distraction," I said softly to Christopher. "Something to focus them while we take them out." But Fancy wasn't on this ship, and neither was anyone else, and, frankly, I didn't want either one of us to be the distraction because the likelihood of us getting hurt was high and getting higher. Basically, I was at a loss unless I asked the Poofs to do something. However, them eating the Rapacians was out, at least for the moment, and if they couldn't devour, then they'd just be big targets for people already in a killing mood.

"I'm out of ideas," he whispered back. "All I want to do is kill everyone in this room that isn't from Earth."

"I feel your pain, believe me. But we have to do something, and fast. Not only do we need to get them all under control but we need to also destroy all the circlets on their heads. We've kept a few, but the majority need to go sooner than soon." Before they drained Chuckie's brain.

"Ah. I see everything you just went through and what you and Serene are trying to do. And, God, is that really what they're doing to Chuck? I thought what they were doing to Jeff was bad enough. Yeah, we need to get the others free and take over this ship."

"Nice to see our mind-reading abilities remain intact up here. And, I guess I could see if I have another self-contained nuke in my purse."

"I don't even want to know. That will just kill Jeff and the others, so no, even if you have one."

"I could try the *Return of the Jedi* gambit."

"Good grief. I can see what you're thinking, and no, that won't work in this situation. No one's going to believe you're willing to blow yourself and everyone else up."

"I'm seriously open to ideas. My husband and best friend are both about to die, and in ugly ways I am not willing to allow. We need a distraction and we need it now."

And, proving that sometimes you really did get what you asked for, a distraction presented itself. Loudly.

CHAPTER 88

HEARD A CACOPHONOUS shrieking I recognized—
Bruno was here and on the case.

"That's our distraction."

Christopher nodded, grabbed the mace from the Rapacian I'd knocked out, and ran into the main room at his Flash level. I was right behind him.

Bruno was flying at the top of the ceiling, shrieking very nasty things in Peregrine. Realized they'd missed him because he'd gone chameleon when they'd all been captured. He'd been waiting for someone to come so he could help effect the rescue.

However, the men in this room all had wings, so Bruno being up high wasn't going to keep him safe for long. Meaning Christopher and I had to work fast. Not a problem.

Decided I could live with killing anyone in this room since this was the Torture and Force Them To Do Terrible Things Against Their Will room. Activated the battle staff, got in between several of the Rapacians who were trying to get Bruno, stuck the staff out, holding it with both hands, and spun.

The less said about the screams the better. Most of these had been up in the air, but the staff was scary effective and it sliced through their legs. On the plus side, it cauterized the wounds at the same time, so there was minimal bloodshed. Made sure I killed all of them as they fell to the ground, some out of anger, mostly out of necessity, and some out of kindness, since I wasn't going to do anything to help them or relieve their pain.

Christopher, meanwhile was braining everyone near him, and he was an A-C and, like me, enraged. He was killing them with one blow.

Now that we were engaged, Bruno stopped being the distraction and flew into the faces of the nearest Rapacians, clawed, and went on to the next, all at hyperspeed. It wasn't as effective as when he did this to beings without beaks on half their faces, but the screams shared that he'd hurt and probably blinded most of them. I followed behind him and delivered the death blows.

Working this way, we had the room cut down by half, literally, within two minutes.

Some of the Rapacians caught on that, despite their greater numbers, they were on the losing side. These tossed their weapons down and flung themselves on their knees, hands out, wings widespread.

But not all of the remaining Rapacians did this. Meaning Christopher and I, and the Rapacians, too, had to jump over the prostrate Hawkpeople in order to fight. Fortunately we were both athletic because the leaping was a lot easier to do if you had wings. I'd been a hurdler all through high school and college, though, and my sadistic track coaches had always wanted everyone on the team to be able to do every sport, so I was decent with both high and long jump.

Shockingly, none of the prostrate Rapacians were faking it, or used us jumping over them as a way of catching us off guard. Apparently surrender meant surrender if you were a Rapacian.

Took a moment out of the mayhem to grab the circlets off of every head I could—dead, prostrate, and even those still up and fighting. Destroyed them all, which wasn't me taking time out from the fight in that sense, since stopping the mental drain on Chuckie's mind was part of our overall goal.

Spotted a big Rapacian who was still fighting and who also had a large set of what certainly looked like keys. "Bruno, my bird, we need to unlock the prisoners!"

Bruno headed right for the Keymaster, with me in hot pursuit. The Keymaster heard me, of course, and he tried to block the Peregrine, but that just left him open for me to slam my battle staff into his stomach. I didn't shove the glowing end through him, though, in case we needed his help with the keys.

Bruno had to fly off so he wouldn't take a hit, leaving me to fight the Keymaster alone. Well, sort of. Unlike how it had been in the air, these Rapacians weren't following the polite one-on-one method. I was surrounded shortly.

Meaning Christopher had some sitting ducks, pun totally intended, which he rather gleefully brained by running around them with the mace at head height. Some of them were taller than he was, but he seemed to enjoy the jumping he had to do in order to knock these out, so I didn't comment.

However, the remaining Rapacians came up with a new strategy—threatening the other prisoners. Christopher was a good fighter and the fastest man alive, but there were still plenty of them and enough of our guys trapped that Christopher was being kept busy defending as opposed to attacking. Bruno went to help the person who was totally outnumbered. Meaning I was on my own with the Keymaster.

The Keymaster was a good fighter, better than most of the Rapacians I'd faced so far. He'd forced me to slow down and I wasn't even sure how he'd done it. Which made me question why he wasn't in charge of more than prisoner containment and torture.

"You can surrender and we won't kill you," I shared as he and I slammed our weapons into each other.

"Thank you for the offer, but no. I cannot offer the same in return. All of you must die." He tried to sweep my legs.

I jumped. "How bloodthirsty of you."

"War is what it is. In order for my people to survive in the new world that is coming, we must win here, and that means all who are not like us must perish." He slammed his mace at my head.

Took the leap—literally to get out of the way, and figuratively by assuming the Z'porrah had infiltrated Beta Sixteen. Probably some time ago, maybe during Operation Destruction when they were on their way out to Earth to try to destroy our planet. Everyone in this solar system had been watching the fleet—if the Z'porrah had sent in a small ship that was sneaky in how it arrived, it would have been fairly simple to drop in spies, dissidents, and instigators.

"Sorry." Managed to slam the battle staff down on his arm and pull it back before he could grab it or parry. "Many of the people on my planet are considered to be pretty damn bloodthirsty land stealers, but most of us frown on total genocide."

"And we and our benefactors do not." He tossed his mace to his other hand and swung at me.

I ducked and rolled. "Your benefactors aren't who gave you space travel."

He shrugged as he advanced. "True. But they gave with restrictions. Our new allies do not."

Who he was dawned on me. Just because Lakin had been hanging out on his command deck didn't mean that's what the other ship's commanders did. Lakin had had the hot women up there, so maybe he was trying to impress them. After all, Otari and Kares had flown out to engage us because they'd thought we were easy prey. We hadn't been. Meaning this ship's commander had decided to hang with his most valuable cargo—the prisoners his enemies would want back.

"You're Trevik, aren't you?" I was backed up against a wall.

This surprised him. "You know my name?"

"Oh yeah. Your unwillingness to respond to the others ships in your tiny fleet ensured I learned your name."

He shrugged again as he stepped closer and raised his mace up. "A larger fleet is coming."

"Longer boats are coming to win us. Yeah, I've heard it before. I'm not going to let that happen." I crouched down.

He laughed, one of those nasty bad guy laughs, and I realized that he wasn't wearing a mind control circlet. This was the real him, no outside influence one way or the other. "You're going to die, little female so-called God."

"Probably. No one gets out of here alive, you know. But you're going to die first."

Trevik brought the mace down, his feet nicely spread, just like every other Rapacian male. At the same time I slammed the glowing end of my battle staff up between his legs as hard as I possibly could.

The staff hit and Trevik screamed what I was pretty sure was going to be his last scream. But I wasn't in a good position to block the mace. I winced and put my hand up.

But before the mace could hit me, someone else slammed it away.

CHAPTER 89

JEFF, HANDS STILL TIED, used both of them to knock the mace aside. Due to the combined force and trajectory changes, the mace slammed back into Trevik's face.

Then Jeff collapsed on the ground.

Pulled my staff out of Trevik and slammed it right back into his middle. He hit the floor and, if he was alive, he needed to stop this war business and get a job in the movies immediately.

Pulled the staff out again and deactivated it so it couldn't hurt Jeff, then dropped to the floor next to him. I already knew that my purse had been equipped with a lot of adrenaline and I dug it out.

"Hang on, Jeff." Had to get the adrenaline in him before I had to defend against an attack. And before he died. I'd seen him close to death—far too many times, really—and I could tell this was one of those times.

"I . . . love you . . . baby," he gasped out. "Help . . . Chuck. He's going . . . to . . . go . . ."

"You first." Found the case, pulled out the needle, and then did my ritual. I kissed his forehead. "I love you, Jeff." Then I slammed the needle into his hearts.

Normally he'd bellow and start thrashing. Not this time. He looked a little better, but that was now the current Damning With Faint Praise Champion. Well, Algar had given me a lot of adrenaline. Pulled out another needle and did the ritual all over again.

A little better, but not enough. Another needle, another

ritual, another slam. His chest was one big bruise in the area of his hearts.

"Kitty," Tito called. "Stop! You have to stop the emotional onslaught!"

Duh. That was what Jeff had been trying to tell me. Chuckie was headed for whatever mind explosion they were doing to him, and that meant Jeff was feeling all of it. That much agony in someone he cared about would be impossible for him to block against, even if he felt perfectly fine.

Kissed his forehead. "Don't die." Grabbed my staff, Trevik's mace, and all of the keys on his ring, and ran to the metal sarcophagus Chuckie was trapped inside.

Yeah, he looked awful, but we were still connected. When Jeff was massively close to death during Operation Fugly I'd sent him loving emotions and they'd helped him to hold on. Emotion wasn't what Chuckie needed, though. He needed a mental shield.

It dawned on me what the real reason was for how ACE had spoken to me. I could access ACE, but I'd have to open my mind like his was, and Chuckie's was, in order to do so. Meaning my mind could be destroyed. And if that happened, the bad guys were probably going to win. What was one man compared to billions?

I didn't hesitate.

Leaned my head against the window portion of Chuckie's chamber, closed my eyes, and opened my mind.

The result was immediate, but it wasn't the same shock it had been. The massive number of minds was overwhelming, but I could feel someone helping me sort through them. Make that many someones.

The Ancient Katyhopper Kung Fu Masters were working as one, sending their minds to join with mine, because of the link I had with Boz. And they were channeling my mind toward its goal—the mind that was currently at the center of everything.

The Matriarchs were helping me to see the minds as energy fields, not just a wild blur of thoughts and feelings. Energy fields were somehow far easier to focus on and ignore at the same time. Decided now was not the time to ask why.

Chuckie's energy field was a brilliant green, but it was flickering. I knew without asking that a flickering field wasn't good.

Felt another mind, a familiar one. Jamie's.

She might have been in a forced slumber, but that just meant that her mind was free to wander. And it had wandered to her Uncle Charles' mind, the man who was her father in a variety of alternate universes. One of the men in this universe that she knew would die to protect her. The widower of the woman who *had* died to protect her. One of the people she loved best in the world.

There was a shield around the energy source that was Chuckie's mind. Jamie's shield. Hers was golden and it was strong and bright, but there were little flickers here and there. She was holding on, but she was a little girl, and the onslaught was tremendous. And ACE had said that even a mind as advanced as hers couldn't hold out forever.

I moved faster, sending my mind to both of them. I had an energy field, too. Mine was bright white, and I sent it around theirs, blocking the onslaught, letting it hit me instead. Concentrated and fended off the other energy fields that were coming at us. Realized that the jewel they'd stuck onto Chuckie's head was an attractor and was pulling all the minds into itself.

Saw everything and nothing at the same time. Billions of lives, billions of years. Saw a flash of something that seemed to be all of us from Earth who'd been dragged out here, other than Gower and Jamie, standing around under the giant telescope on the All Seeing Mountain, talking to a bunch of Beta Eight natives I'd never seen before. But before I could tell what was going on and if that was something that had happened before or would happen later, the general onslaught slammed into my energy field, because I'd lost my concentration.

Had no idea how to stop the onslaught, stop everyone's mind from trying to get into Chuckie's, and therefore get through my shield and Jamie's. I just knew I couldn't let anyone else get past me, or else they'd kill my daughter and my best friend, and those deaths would kill my husband.

My kung fu instructors had always wanted me to meditate, under the idea that clearing my mind would be helpful. I'd never managed it because I couldn't settle my mind in that way and it seemed like a waste of relaxation time to just go "Ommmm" or similar over and over again when I could, instead, think about all the things.

However, the idea behind it was sound—only let one thing in, and you can shove everything else out. But what one thing?

Love, maybe. But I loved a lot of people, all differently, but still, all loved. Love alone wasn't going to be enough, because I didn't know what love to focus on.

Heard the sound of something, something that didn't fit. But I recognized it. The sounds of The Black Eyed Peas singing "Just Can't Get Enough" swirled into my ears.

This wouldn't have been the song I'd have thought would be anybody's idea of a great song to meditate to or focus on, but as it played I found it relaxing me in a positive way for the situation. Felt stronger and calm at the same time. Noted that my energy shield was also kind of ebbing and flowing to the beat.

This was also a great song for mega repeat, which it was definitely on, because, as with "Electric Worry," the ending led nicely into the start so the repetition felt seamless.

Hoped Jamie wasn't hearing this, because this was definitely a song that made me think about Jeff in the total sexy times way. But apparently what was going to keep the rest of the solar system at bay was my sex drive and a tempo-changing rocking beat.

One of the positives was that when my energy field bobbed out to the beat it literally expanded, pushing the other energy fields away. Started singing along, both the Fergie and the will.i.am parts, because why not?

Had no idea how long this went on, or how many times the song played. I just relaxed and enjoyed my cosmic pop concert of one song.

And then, suddenly, it was all over.

CHAPTER 90

THE MUSIC WAS still playing, and I was still singing along, only I realized I wasn't seeing the entire solar system's minds and energy fields. I was seeing Tito's face. Said face was trying really hard not to laugh.

"You can stop now, Kitty," he said, as he turned off my iPod and pulled the earbuds out of my ears. "Everything's okay."

"By everything do you mean that the war is over, we've won, and we've also repelled the Z'porrah invasion fleet that's on its way?"

"Ah, no. I mean that Jeff's okay, Chuck's okay, and the rest of us are okay, Bruno included."

"Ah. Okay. I'll take it." Realized I was lying down and sat up. "Whoa. Head rush."

"I'm not surprised," Chuckie said. He was on my left, sitting and looking reasonably good, all things considered. "I can't believe the song you picked to listen to over and over again." He laughed, then his expression turned serious. "Thank you."

Took his hand in mine and squeezed. "You're welcome." Decided I'd worry about what Jamie had heard later. Like after we rescued her, Gower, and ACE later. Looked to my right, expecting to see Jeff there. Only he wasn't. Looked around the room. No Jeff. No Christopher, either. "Um, where are my husband and his cousin?"

"I had to give Christopher adrenaline," Tito said. "Chuck, too." Realized Chuckie was shaking a bit, which made sense. "Glad you had plenty in your purse. Once you went into your trance, we got you lying down, and Tim and Kevin figured out how to unlock the metal box they had Chuck in. Once we got him out of it, we destroyed that thing they'd stuck on his head."

"That's all great, but not explaining where Jeff and Christopher are." Bruno came over and settled himself in my lap. Gave him lots of pets and scritchy-scratches between his wings.

"Once Chuck was out and in control of himself again, the emotional onslaught he was unintentionally and uncontrollably sending at Jeff stopped. You gave Jeff three giant doses of adrenaline. Christopher's not used to the adrenaline and that was a hell of a lot even for Jeff. They're both so wound up that they couldn't stay in this room."

"So they went off to knock Rapacian heads and take over the ship," Tim said. "Which means that Airborne needs to head to the cockpit of this thing and take over the controls. Probably in about two minutes, give or take."

"Go team. You're sure Jeff's okay?"

"I think he'll be a lot better after he kicks some alien bird ass," Brian said. "Those bastards said they wanted to mate with Serene, Lorraine, and Claudia, pardon my French."

As I concentrated, did think I heard the sounds of someone roaring. Yep, that was Jeff's Lion Takes Over the Veldt roar. He was fine and probably even enjoying himself a little.

"No worries, the girls are in charge of one of the Rapacian ships and James is in charge of the other. No forced interspecies matings will be happening. But seriously, should Jeff be fighting right now?"

Tito nodded. "He needs it, emotionally and psychologically as well as physically. They were hard on him, and I want to get him to isolation, but since the only option for that in this solar system is Alpha Four, we'll wait until we're home. You had enough adrenaline in your purse that I think we can keep him going without hurting him."

"Where do you want to go, Kitty?" Kevin asked me. "We know the other ships have left the planet's airspace."

"We need to follow them. If Chuckie and I can walk, I'll fill you guys in on all the excitement while we go to the command section."

Kevin and Tim helped Chuckie up, Hughes and Walker helped me. Bruno stayed right by me. "What do we do with the prisoners?" Joe asked.

"Where are they?"

"We put them where they'd had Christopher," Randy said, walking over to the alcove. Sure enough, all the Rapacians who'd surrendered were standing there, looking confused and apprehensive.

The remote was on the ground. Indicated it should be picked up, which Jerry did. "Point it at them and push a white button. Just be sure you remember which white button you push."

Jerry stared at the remote then handed it to me. "I have no idea which way is front."

Looked at it. I didn't really, either. Remembered the remote Serene had had. This one looked turned around from that. It hadn't mattered when I'd rescued Christopher because turning things off wasn't nearly as worrisome as turning them on.

"If I imprison myself, it's the blue buttons that turn the electric cage off. Don't hit the red button because that's the Fry Everyone Inside The Cage Button." Turned the remote around, aimed it, and pushed the button down.

Successfully didn't entrap myself and did trap all the prisoners. Handed the remote back to Jerry. "The buttons are a little closer to the front than the back."

"Got it." He grinned. "Nice to have the band back together again, Fergie."

"You're hilarious." We left and made our way to the command deck. This room had been at the very back, somewhat ironically right next to the ship's garbage chute. We had to step around a lot of Rapacian bodies. Because everyone with me was human, decided we'd just leave them there and hope that they didn't all wake up soon. I did have the guys destroy every circlet as we came to them, an action Chuckie wholeheartedly supported. While we did this I filled them in on everything that had happened since they'd been captured, the situations with 2.0 and The Clarence Clone included.

We finally reached the command area. Jeff had this ship's pilot's and copilot's heads in his hands. They were still alive and flying the ship, but it was clear he was going to squeeze really hard if they didn't obey. It was also clear they'd had a demonstration of said head squeezing, because there was a Rapacian body lying close by that had been the example. Was fairly sure it was Otari. Had no complaints.

Looked around. "Where is Kares?"

"She was killed in battle," the pilot said.

"Works for me." This meant the only Rapacian in charge was on Serene's ship, and already adjusting to a more intelligent viewpoint. Took the circlets off the pilot and copilot and put them onto Hughes and Walker. "You should be able to figure out how to fly this. And before you whine, as I told James, just channel Will Smith and do it."

"*Independence Day* for the win," Hughes said with a grin as he took the pilot's seat.

"I *got* to get me one of these!" Walker said as he took the copilot's spot.

Gave Christopher the remote. "You need to get the circlets off all the Rapacians you knocked out, then group them together. There are two more electric cages in this." Pointed to the buttons I hadn't used. "They can hold a lot. Let's get them all contained."

He nodded. "Jeff, kiss your wife and then come with me. This is a two-man job."

Jeff knocked the pilot and copilot's head together, dropped them on the ground, and stepped over to me. He still didn't have a shirt on. I found this totally acceptable.

He gathered me up into his arms and lifted me up as he kissed me. Wrapped my legs around his waist as his tongue twined around my tongue strongly and his lips owned mine. Managed not to grind against him, but only because we had a huge audience.

Jeff finally ended our kiss and let me slide back down. Was ready to forego saving the world to have sex in one of the empty rooms in the ship, but knew someone would tell us not to.

He grinned as I managed to only nuzzle the hair between his pecs a little bit. "Later, baby. But not too much later." He nodded to Christopher and they zipped off.

"No one needs to strap in, apparently," Hughes said. "James found the gravity controls so we're all set. You might want to hang on, though, just in case."

We took off. The velocity made those of us who were

standing stagger a little, but we all kept our feet and the ride was smooth. "This is my first trip into space in an actual spaceship."

"Mine, too," Kevin said.

"This is a lot better than however we got dragged over here," Tim agreed.

"Not my first time, but I have to say this thing can move." Brian sighed. "I miss Michael a lot right now. He'd be loving this."

"I miss him, too. Speaking of whom, though, we need to find his older brother and my daughter. I don't know where they are, but they're somewhere that's not good for them, I think."

We reached escape velocity and broke through the planet's atmosphere. Everyone gasped. Some because of the splendor and amazement that was the experience of space.

But mostly it was because we were in what looked like a spaceship parking lot. And the lot was full.

CHAPTER 91

THE LOT WAS ALSO circular. There were a lot of ships inside the circle, the two other Rapacian vessels included. We reduced power and headed for this group.

"I'm just going to point out that the ships on the perimeter are all focused in."

"And all the ships in the middle are facing out," Tim said quietly.

"Yeah. I have a feeling that the ships we're joining are on the side that's presumed to be losing." There were a lot of ships I recognized in this group. But there were the same in the perimeter group. This was truly a civil war, on the planets and in the system. And we were now right in the center of it. Then again, we'd been in the center since we'd gotten here.

"Hailing frequencies open," Hughes said, with no sign of humor. "This is the third commandeered Rapacian vessel, formerly under the control of Commander Trevik, now under the control of Commander Martini, representing Earth and Beta Eight."

The sound system crackled. "Former Rapacian Vessel, this is the command ship for Alpha Five. You are broadcasting to all ships in this solar space. We have only been waiting for you."

Well, we now knew which side was winning. Naturally it wasn't ours. Frankly, wouldn't have known how to handle it if our side was actually winning at this time. Perhaps by going home. Pulled myself back into the now.

Walker looked at me over his shoulder. "Kitty, you should take this," he said softly.

Stepped up to stand between Walker and Hughes. "Waiting to call for the official cease-fire, Alpha Five Command?"

There was a pause. "Ah, no. We are awaiting the surrender of the Imperial Monarchists and then will claim Beta Eight as an Alpha Five colony." This voice was different than the first one; this voice was female. Like us, the Alpha Five command ship had put their leader or mouthpiece on the com. The voice was also vaguely familiar. Very vaguely, though. Needed to pull it up from the memory banks, though, and quickly.

My memory did me a solid and shared what little I knew about Alpha Five. "Interesting. If memory serves, Alpha Five claimed only a few years ago to not want to leave their planet. What changed?"

"Circumstances. Who is speaking?" Who did I know from Alpha Five? Only one person. Hadn't heard her talk a lot, even when she'd been on Earth. If this was who I thought it was—and ACE had certainly insinuated that was the case—then we'd ignored her because she'd been mousy and quiet. Uma had appeared to be the leader of those Planetary Council members who were traitors. But she was also the only traitor who'd survived Operation Invasion.

"Commander Martini. To whom do I have the pleasure of speaking?"

Another pause. "Was that a joke?" She didn't sound mousy, but if what ACE had said was true, and I had no reason to doubt him, then the mousy part had been an act. We'd figured she'd used some sort of emotional blocker to keep Jeff from reading her way back when, so what she was really like had been a mystery none of us had thought to consider solving. Because she wasn't in our solar system and we'd thought Alexander and the Planetary Council would have solved that mystery.

"Nope, that was me being overly polite since we're in what looks like a really bizarre Mexican Standoff to the Stars. *This* is a joke. Knock, knock."

"Excuse me?"

"Earth protocol says that you're required to say 'who's there' when an Earthling says 'knock, knock.' And then you repeat whatever the Earthling says but add the word 'who' to the end, so it's a question. So, we begin again. Knock, knock."

"Ah. Er . . . who's there?"

"Screw."

"Er . . . screw who?"

"Screw you if you think you're taking over Beta Eight or any other part of this solar system, Lenore."

Despite the situation, all the men with me cracked up. Which was audible to whoever was on the other line, which, per the Alpha Five command ship, was everyone else in every other ship out here. Oh well, it was always nice to have a large, captive audience.

"How dare you! I am the Leader of the Resistance!"

"You're the leader of the Z'porrah Invasion Fleet is what you are."

"True enough." This was a voice I knew well—Queen Renata. "You told us you had reformed, Lenore. And we chose to believe the best about you. Then you played a double game, pretending to be a positive part of the Planetary Council and the Imperial Monarchy when you were actually leading the rebellion. You are a liar and a traitor both."

Heard a slap. "You will not speak to me that way again. You are conquered. By your own people." And now I knew where Renata was, too. Hoped Rahmi and Rhee were keeping it together.

"Only by those who listened to your lies," Renata replied. "And you can hit me all you want. You hit like a man." From a Free Woman this was a cutting insult.

"So you found some Free Women who were disgruntled and turned them," I said, to distract Lenore from hitting Renata again. "That's the old playbook, isn't it? You've also managed to convince the Rapacians to be your muscle and your patsies. You started a civil war so this solar system would be in chaos when the Z'porrah fleet arrived. The dino-birds sweep in, kill off everyone who hasn't kowtowed to them, give the planets to their loyal supporters, then they come take over Earth. Have I missed any part of the new playbook?"

"The part where I give your child to the Z'porrah," Lenore said nastily.

Well, ACE had said they weren't where they should be. Shoved the fear and rage to the side. Needed a clear head right now.

Felt a nudging in my mind. Boz had a suggestion. Liked

it and told her so. "There's a gigantic telescope on Beta Eight. No one knows how it got there. But it's huge, and amazingly powerful. You can see what feels like forever through it. I'd like to have everyone take a look at what the telescope is picking up."

"How can we do that?" This wasn't Lenore, it was Alexander.

"King Alexander, how are you, my friend?"

"I've been better, Commander Martini."

"I'm sure. And I'm glad you asked. Since, ha ha ha, we can't all go down to Beta Eight and take a gander, can we? Based on the number of ships out here, that would take us an easy Beta Eight year. However, we have some amazingly smart people with us. They've rigged the telescope so that the images it's seeing can be beamed into your viewing screens or whatever you're all looking at. Commander Dwyer, to you." Sincerely hoped I'd understood Boz correctly, or else I was handing off to someone completely unprepared.

"Thank you, Commander Martini." Serene's voice was cool, calm, and totally in charge. I could feel her troubadour talent radiating out through the airwaves, telling everyone that what she was showing them was of vital importance. "Please observe your screens, beaming live data to you in three ... two ... one ..."

The windshield of our ship turned into a TV screen. And we saw the fleet in all its Space Standoff glory.

"As you can see, the telescope is clearly live and aimed at all of us," Serene said. "Enlarging view, now. Please be prepared, the view will be expanding past this solar system, aimed for the galactic core."

Sure enough, just as Reader and I had seen it do, the ship's screen showed the far reaches of the Alpha Centauri solar system, then it enlarged three more times. To show the Z'porrah fleet. It contained easily ten times the number of ships we were hanging out with.

There were a lot of gasps on the com.

"I'm sure many of you fought with King Alexander and Earth Forces when the Z'porrah tried to claim Earth a few years ago," I said. "The Z'porrah weren't happy about that defeat. And despite this system showing them mercy, they've littered it with spies and instigators, sowing the seeds of hatred and rebellion."

"But," Serene said, "as you know, the Z'porrah want no creatures they didn't create in their own image."

"They will support the Reptilians," someone said.

"Hardly," another voice said. This voice I definitely recognized. "My husband and I keep on telling you that Alpha Four and Earth are our allies. Anyone who's ever dealt in a positive way with those planets will be destroyed by the Z'porrah, be they Reptilian, Rapacian, or any other. And denouncing them now won't be good enough. The Z'porrah's bitterest enemies helped all of our planets' evolutions—to the Z'porrah we're all tainted. Even those on Alpha Five."

"Jareen, it's good to hear your voice. You're insightful as always. And what she said is true. The fleet we're all looking at could come in here and kill everyone." Waited a few moments. "But that same fleet was defeated, by fewer ships than are massed here, let alone all the ships in your fleets that are fighting throughout the solar system."

"You have a choice," Serene said. "Continue to fight and make yourselves easy to conquer and destroy, or live free and reject the death and tyranny the Z'porrah will offer you and all your offspring."

"All ships in the interior have already chosen to live free," Alexander said.

"They are not free if they answer to the Imperial Monarchy," Lenore snapped.

"Oh, I think they are. You all had enough freedom to get space-ready really fast. That came with a lot of help from Alpha Four and the other spacefaring planets. You had enough freedom to instigate rebellion to serve your own ends, not the people of this system."

A new voice spoke. "We have made our decision."

CHAPTER 92

THIS NEW VOICE was sort of squeaky. Definitely not someone who'd spoken before.

"And that is?" Alexander asked formally.

"Choose wisely," Lenore said snidely.

"We will remain neutral no longer." Aha, so this was a representative for Alpha Seven. I hadn't seen one of their ships up here, though. "I am Rohini and, as you know, I speak for all of my planet. We have seen what the Earthers are showing you with our own eyes. We have also seen the viciousness that the Planet's Rights Faction has perpetrated. They cannot be acting with goodwill toward anyone. We of Alpha Seven side with the Imperial Monarchy."

There was a lot of background noise. Apparently this decision was big news. Heard several arguments going on, but it was hard to tell who was saying what.

"Then you get to die, too," Lenore said with a distinct sneer in her voice. This increased the background discussions and arguments.

"That's not a shocking statement, seeing as you had the Rapacians try to shoot the Alpha Seven humanitarian ships out of the sky. One of those ships was destroyed and crashed on Beta Eight. And none of you came to help the survivors."

"Oh, we will not die," Alpha Seven's spokespenguin said calmly. "And Commander Martini, they didn't come to help us because they fear us. Rightly so. What you fail to understand, Commander of the PRF, is that we have stayed apart and stayed neutral for a reason. But we realize that if Beta

Eight is conquered, Z'porrah fleet or no, our planet will be next. And that we will not allow."

"How will you, a planet with no weapons, achieve that?" Lenore asked.

"Simply put, we are on a planet right now that has many weapons. One of which is aimed right for the Alpha Five command ship."

Lenore laughed. "What weapon is that?"

"I mentioned the giant telescope?" Serene asked sweetly. "It's amazing how simple it is to alter the light refraction to make the most powerful telescope in two solar systems into the most powerful laser gun in two solar systems. It helped that Beta Eight has far more defenses than you're aware of."

"Mind explaining that?" Jeff asked me quietly, as he put his arm around me. Hadn't realized he and Christopher were back. He'd found and put his clothes back on. Bummer.

"No idea," I said softly. "We left Serene in charge of one of the Rapacian ships. She said she was going to go down to the planet first. Apparently she did."

"We have created an alliance with both Beta Eight and Alpha Seven," Serene said. "Both of those planets are under Earth's protection."

"Fire away, then," Lenore said. "You'll kill hundreds of people. Including the deposed Queen of Beta Twelve and the Planetary Representatives from Betas Thirteen, Fourteen, and Fifteen."

In other words, the Reptilians, Canus Majorians, and Feliniads. Meaning, most likely, Jareen and Neeraj, Wrolph, Wahoa, and Willem, and Felicia and Arup. Or, as I called them, my friends.

"And," Lenore added, "the religious leader of the Earthers, along with Commander Martini's daughter. But, feel free to fire at will."

"Only cowards threaten children," someone in what I assumed was another ship said.

"Or bullies." Recognized the voice—this was 2.0. He sounded as angry as the rest of us.

"Only cowards and bullies threaten those who lead their people's souls," another added, sounding horrified.

"Cowards, bullies . . . and terrorists," I added, as Jeff's arm tightened around me. "We have a lot of experience with these kinds of people on Earth. And Lenore appears to be all three."

The image on our screens went away. Noted that some of the ships that had been on the perimeter had moved into the center.

"The Earthers speak the truth. I am Usha. I have been a traitor to my race, the ones you call the Ancients, working as a spy for the Z'porrah for many years. The Z'porrah will show no mercy when they arrive. They consider this entire solar system to be tainted, even worse than they consider Earth's solar system to be tainted. Because my people mingled their blood with many of the planets here."

"Beta Twelve in particular," I pointed out.

"Yes, but others, too. Though they cannot change their shapes, Alpha Seven has Ancient blood in it. Every planet here has Ancient influence, if not blood. And that makes every living being here something the Z'porrah wish to destroy. They wanted to destroy Earth to make destroying this solar system easier."

"Why do you speak out now?" someone asked. "Are you being coerced?"

"No. Those who captured the Earthers treated my sister with disrespect. The Earthers, on the other hand, treated her with respect."

"That's it?" Lenore asked. "That's why you've switched sides?"

"No. I've seen what the weapon can do. I've seen what those from Alpha Seven can do. I respect might. Alpha Seven is far mightier than you realize."

A few more ships moved from the outer circle to the inner one.

"They're barely space competent," Lenore said. "Alpha Four had to give them spaceships."

"Just like they did for you," I pointed out.

"Space travel is not the be-all, end-all for advancement," Alpha Seven's spokespenguin said. "As with Beta Eight, our world has vast water resources. Our world is large, and our waters are deep."

Took the leap. "How many sentient races do you have who live underwater, Rohini, if I may ask?"

"Many." Heard laughter in Rohini's tone. "What we have focused on is allowing our water brothers and sisters the ability to breathe outside of the seas. We can do both, and we wished for them to be able to do both as well. We have succeeded. Trust me when I say that the Horrors on Beta Eight look like fledgling's toys compared to our allies within our own oceans. Allies who are, as we speak, heading here to support us."

"In what spaceship?" Lenore sneered.

"In no spaceship," Rohini said calmly. "The same apparatus that allows them to live in the air and on land if they wish also allows them to fly through space without danger. They will be here quite soon—they left our planet when our ship was destroyed."

More background talking. A few more ships moved into the center. Pulled Jeff aside. Chuckie and Christopher came with us. "We need to get over to the command ship and get Jamie, Paul, and everyone else that bitch Lenore has captive. Then we can blow her up or let Alpha Seven's Space Sea Monsters eat her ship or whatever. But while she has hostages, every single ship other than hers can join Alexander's side and we'll still lose."

"Can you do whatever you did to get to us?" Christopher asked.

"I used a Z'porrah power cube. And if I knew where I was going, then yes, I could. However, I have to visually see where I want to go in my mind, and I have no idea. I can see the outside of Lenore's ship, where we don't want to go. But inside? We haven't seen it."

Chuckie spun and went to stand where I'd been. "I'd like proof that Lenore has the hostages she's claiming she possesses. Right now, all of that could be subterfuge. Alpha Five has certainly set that precedent."

More voices talking, many agreeing with Chuckie.

"Really? That's what you want? Fine." The windshield turned into a screen again and there was Lenore, big as boring life. She still looked average in all ways—height, weight, coloring. Only her smirk was above average. She was quite good at smirking, it turned out.

Behind her were some of those I'd expected to see—Neeraj, Wrolph, Felicia, and Queen Renata. Jareen, Wahoa, Willem, and Arup weren't there. Needed to find out if they were elsewhere, or if they'd wisely remained on their own ships. Jamie and Gower weren't in evidence, either, but I hadn't expected them to be. Lenore would have them off in a room somewhere under heavy guard.

Had a feeling Lenore was holding onto Gower because she thought ACE was still inside him. Had no idea how this might help us, but figured I needed to be aware of the possibility, just in case.

However, my friends from the Planetary Council weren't alone. There were a couple of human-looking people, a man and a woman, who also appeared to be hostages. Presumably they represented the pro-Imperial factions on Alphas Five and Six. There were Rapacians there, but they were all pointing weapons toward the hostages, so they were on the side of the Planet's Rights Faction, not that this came as some sort of a shock.

That there were no Alpha Seven Penguin People didn't surprise me all that much. And I saw no Alpha Four A-Cs, meaning no one with Lenore was drop-dead gorgeous by human standards.

Stepped up next to Chuckie. "Where are my daughter and our religious leader?"

"Safe," Lenore snapped.

"Prove it," Chuckie snarled. "Or else you'll be showing those who are following you what a liar you are." More background talking. Hoped the Imperial side was smart enough to realize that peer pressure was going to work for us. Chuckie waited about thirty seconds. "So, you don't have them. Meaning you're a liar. And if you're lying about this, what else are you lying about?" The background noise continued.

"I have them," she said. She turned to one of the Rapacians. "Get the special prisoners."

CHAPTER 93

THE RAPACIAN SEEMED to have an issue with this, but he was speaking quietly and his back was to whatever camera they had in there, so couldn't tell what he was saying.

However, Lenore seemed disgusted. "Please wait a moment," she said with false sweetness. "We'll be right back. Talk amongst yourselves about who's going to surrender first." She and the Rapacian left their command area.

Took a step backward. Reached into my purse, pulled out my iPod, clipped it back onto the waist of my jeans, and put in my earbuds. Then reached in again and got the cube into my hand. "Need Poofy assistance, please and thank you," I said softly, moving my lips as little as possible.

Heard a soft mew and looked down. Poofikins had the cube all ready to go, sparkle on full.

"Earth Poofs are ready?"

Received a confirmation mewl. Whatever the Poofs were planning to roll, it was going to be rolling when I rolled our plan.

Jeff took my free hand in his. Pulled my hand away. "I'm coming, too," he said quietly but sternly.

"Yes, fine, but I need both hands. Hold something else."

He grinned and slid his arm around my waist. "That's different."

Christopher handed Jerry the electronic cage remote, stepped up next to Jeff, and put his hand on Jeff's shoulder. We basically looked like a worried family.

"Music again?" Christopher snarked quietly. "Really? Now?"

"I don't complain about how you work, dude."

Chuckie noted what we were doing and he stepped back, too.

"You should stay," I told him.

"No." He put his hand on my shoulder. "I don't need to tell you why."

"No, you don't."

Bruno flew up onto Chuckie's shoulder. Wanted to tell him to stay here, but didn't feel like arguing with a Peregrine—and losing—in front of everyone.

Chuckie cleared his throat. "Are there any other prisoners on board, Queen Renata?" he asked in a normal tone of voice.

"No, just those you see here and the two that are being fetched." She was looking around at our ship. Knew what, or rather who, she was looking for.

"Kitty, Renata's right," Jareen said. "Only one representative from each planet went to the command ship." Hadn't heard her since my wedding, but I could tell she was angry, stressed, and scared. Not that I could blame her—her husband was the Reptilians' representative after all.

"Alpha Four was smart enough to stay home," Felicia said with a rueful cat-smirk.

"You know, you guys should stand closer together. So we can take a good picture."

Got a lot of blank looks from the prisoners. Knew Jareen would have already figured out what I wanted them to do—she was my Reptilian Soul Sister after all. But she was on her ship, so no luck there.

Renata might have figured it out, too, but she was still looking at everyone she could see on my ship. Hoped no one on the enemy side had caught on to the order I was trying to impart. Time to give up on subterfuge and innuendo with this crowd and change the subject.

"Renata, they're fine. Not going to say where they are, just in case, but they're doing great." Queen Renata visibly relaxed. "But while we're waiting, how deep is Alpha Six in with Alpha Five's plan?" Might as well get some intel while we waited.

"Deep, just as they were when we first met. Though there are still loyalists on both planets. Just as there are loyalists on Beta Twelve."

"Usha, any idea of how much of Beta Twelve's dissent is being caused by more of your friends or relatives?"

"All of it," she replied. "I assume my fellow agents are on some of the ships that are aligned with the Planet's Rights Faction. Some are probably on ships that are loyal. Hear me, brothers and sisters — Clea is dead because she opposed the Earthers. And we have been lied to — the beings here are no better or worse than we are. They deserve to live as much as we do."

Wondered if Serene had a gun to Usha's head or something. Apparently I wasn't the only one. "Your heart and mind has changed so suddenly after so long, Usha?" someone asked. Presumed this was an Ancient traitor, aka a Z'porrah spy. Either they were on a Planet's Rights Faction ship or they were an idiot. Didn't hear the sounds of someone getting a beating, so assumed they were on a PRF ship.

"Yes. I have lived on Beta Eight for a long time. In this solar system for even longer. They are no better or worse than we are. Younger, yes. So much younger. And young children deserve to grow up, even if they are not our children, or are the children of our enemies."

"Usha, you are a traitor to our cause," the same someone said.

She laughed. "No, fool. We are all already traitors. To our own people. And all we have done is poison the minds of all these others, these younger races who deserved guidance, not deceit. I see now what our people, our real people, have always tried to do. And I will return to those ways, even if my life ends today and my return is brief. Better to die a decent person than live as a vile one."

Had no idea how she'd made the switch so fast and so believably. Either she was the greatest actress the Ancients had ever produced or we were just rolling hella lucky. Doubted that either one was the right answer.

Felt a gentle laugh in my mind. Aha. Boz had broken the Katyhopper Prime Directive. She'd shown Usha what was really in Lenore's mind, and what was in others' minds as well. She'd given Usha the clarity to see how her actions looked over time. And she'd shown her the Day of the

Gods, which was what all of Beta Eight considered the official dawn of their time—when the Father of the Gods had bestowed the Gods upon them.

Wasn't sure this would have convinced me, but apparently Usha was very impressed and flipped sides instantly. Decided not to argue and just thanked Boz for taking a gigantic one for the team.

More background chat had been going on while I'd been talking with Boz in my head. Time to toss out some more hard-learned diplomacy lest the com go silent. In most cases, silence was golden, but not when you were trying to sway a lot of various beings into not killing each other.

"It's also better to die on your feet rather than live on your knees, or your species' equivalent. Bowing to terrorists, no matter who they are, isn't freedom. And while Alpha Four's hand can be heavy at times, they've never made you crawl." I sincerely hoped.

Background noises indicated I was right. "Every person on Alpha Five and Six isn't evil. Every Rapacian isn't a bad bird. Every human isn't good, trust me on that one. I'm sure there are some Alpha Seven folks who don't like helping others." Scored some chuckles, go me.

"But overall, as a general group? We're all just people trying to do the best we can with what we have. And fighting each other just means we live and die on our knees, because the enemies of the Ancients are our enemies, now and forever. That's their decision, not ours, but since that *is* their decision, let's stop making it easy for them and remind them that this solar system cannot be taken in any kind of a fair fight."

Lenore chose this moment to return, carrying Jamie in her arms. Jamie didn't look happy, most likely because Gower had a spear being shoved into his back. Gower and Jamie both looked groggy, too. Had a feeling the enforced sleep had been achieved with drugs. The rage someone drugging my little girl gave me was really well timed, so I just let it build.

"Well?" Lenore said. "Here they are. Now are you ready to surrender?"

My iPod came to life playing Corey Hart's "Never Surrender." I laughed. Then I caught our reflection in some glass that was behind her, so reflected back onto our viewing screen.

We were grouped like the Justice League—Superman, the Flash, Batman, and, for now, Wonder Woman, complete with our requisite kickbutt animal companion. We also all looked relaxed but ready for action. I laughed again.

"What are you laughing at?" Lenore asked. "Your defeat?"

"No. The picture I'm going to take when this is all over. Smile for the birdie." Then I pulled out the cube and slammed my other hand onto it.

CHAPTER 94

THIS WAS BY FAR the easiest cube transfer I'd ever done, because I was looking right at where I wanted to go. The five of us moved from the Rapacian ship to Lenore's command ship in less than a second. We landed right in front of her, because that's what I'd focused on.

Lenore gaped. And we moved.

Bruno flew off of Chuckie's shoulder screaming the nastiest things in Peregrine at Lenore and hit her in the face with all his claws.

I dropped the cube back into my purse, pulled out of Jeff's hold, and wrenched Jamie away from Lenore. I had to pull hard. Lenore screamed, possibly because I'd broken her arm while getting my innocent child away from her. She could take that complaint up with the Planetary Council later.

Jeff slammed the Rapacian who had Gower to the ground, broke the spear over his thigh, and slammed the pointy half into the floor. It went in deep. Then he grabbed Gower and held him up.

Christopher zoomed around and moved all the hostages into a tight group.

And Chuckie walked around behind Lenore's back. He nodded to Bruno, who flew off and onto my shoulder. Then Chuckie took her head in his hands and broke her neck, looking right into the camera all the time.

"This is how Earth deals with our enemies," he said in the Smooth Criminal way the C.I.A. seemed to love. "Beta Eight and Alpha Seven are under Earth's protection. Earth is an ally of the Imperial Monarchy in general and Alpha Four in particular. Choose your side carefully."

He let Lenore's body fall, pulled the spear Jeff had slammed into the floor out, rammed it through her heart, pinning her dead body to the ground, then nodded to me. Apparently I wasn't the only one channeling my rage.

"Link up, team, right now!" Grabbed Chuckie with one hand and Jeff with the other. I didn't need the cube to go back home, but whoever touched the cube was the only one who could see the reentry point glittering in the air.

"Set!" Christopher called.

I walked into the glitter. And we walked out right back on the command deck of our Rapacian ship before Corey Hart's second and only other hit was even halfway done.

"Now," I said calmly as I cuddled Jamie, "who wants to fight us, and who wants to play nicely, live in harmony, and repel the Z'porrah fleet?"

"Commander Martini, the weapon is aimed and ready," Serene said, right on cue. "We'll fire on your order."

"Awesome, Commander Dwyer, thank you. First off, if there are any Rapacians, or anyone else, wearing a circlet with a jewel in it given to them by Lenore or someone working for the Planet's Right Faction, those need to be removed and destroyed. If you see someone wearing one, please remove it for them if they're slow about it. We'll wait. Check in when all circlets are removed."

"How will you know if they're removed?" yet another voice asked. There were a lot of people out there.

"We're using the honor system, but trust me, we'll know."

There was a scream from another ship. "There are giant monsters here!" The voice sounded like the one who'd first spoken from the Planet's Rights Faction command ship. Heard familiar growling.

"Are they fluffy with lots and lots of terrifying teeth?"

"Yes!" This came from several ships.

"Shoot them and die," I said calmly. Nice to know the Poofs were taking part. "Give them the circlets. I'd also assume they're sort of herding some people into a group or a corner?"

"Yes." Also coming from a lot of ships.

"Those are your traitors, or your Z'porrah spies. I'd put them into some form of restraint. Or else the Poofs will probably eat them."

Lots of background noise indicated that many circlets were being tossed. Other ships also shared that once the prisoners were rounded up, they and the Poofs had disappeared from whichever ship they were on. There was a corresponding response from the PRF command ship that all those people were now over there. Amazingly enough, there was also a group of Rapacians and others the Poofs brought over to Reader's ship who were apparently on the side of good.

"Us too?" Hughes asked quietly.

Considered our options. "Yeah, us too. Send that order to our three ships, will you, Matt? And tell everyone to check and see if their Rapacian prisoners are still there or not." Took my circlet off while Hughes shared the news. Christopher zipped off to check our ship, while Jeff trotted around and gathered up the circlets. Then he handed them to Chuckie. Who destroyed them with extreme prejudice.

The ships called off their version of No More Mind Melders or Traitors Roll Call. Received confirmation from Christopher, Reader, and Serene that most of the Rapacians were still on board, but many were gone. Lakin, in particular, was still with Serene.

"I will speak for the remainder of the Rapacians," he said. "We renounce our actions and apologize for them as well. While we were under a form of duress, there is still no excuse, and we will accept our punishment from our solar community once this war is officially over. Until then, all Rapacians who have been shown to be loyal will fight for the Imperial Monarchy."

"Super, glad that's out of the way. So here's the deal, kids. Like Lakin and Beta Sixteen, you get to choose your side now, free from outside influences. To make it easy, here are your choices. All those who want to continue fighting against the Imperial Monarchy I will consider to be on the side of the Z'porrah and pro this solar system's annihilation. All those who want to say sorry, kiss and make up, and remain a fractious but ultimately cohesive solar system family I will consider to be on Earth's side and pro this system's longevity."

A throat cleared somewhere out there. "How, ah, do we show you which side we've chosen?"

"Oh, let's make it easy. Does every ship have some kind of exterior lights?" Lots of voices spoke at once. "New plan!" I shouted. The voices stopped. Looked at the former hostages. "Are there any ships that don't have lights of some kind?"

"No, Commander," Neeraj said. He was a giant, walking lizard, but it was great to see him. He gave me the Reptilian smile which was a lot like the Lecanora smile—toothy. "Every ship can turn exterior lights on."

"Excellent. So, everyone who wants to play nicely with Alpha Four and maintain the Imperial Monarchy, turn on your running lights, or whatever you call them."

The view on my screen switched and we were looking out at all the ships floating here in space. All of them had their lights on. Even the Planet's Rights Faction command ship.

"Just making sure, but ship where we just killed your commander and where all the traitors have been sent, are you sure you want your lights on?"

"Yes, Commander," a shaky voice replied. "We took a vote. We'd like to live. And, ah, we'd like the fluffy monsters to stop growling at us. And drooling. We'd really like them to stop drooling."

"Not really up to me what those fluffy monsters do. They have free will and all, just like you all do. And did, when you chose to become rebels against a regime that wasn't doing anything other than helping you."

"Commander Martini, if I may make a request?" This was Alexander.

"Of course, King Alexander. Request away."

"I would prefer that we accept that the dissidents have had a change of heart and allow them to remain with us. They are still part of our system, still our people, even though they've opposed our rule. We have encouraged and will continue to encourage positive discussion. Any rule can be improved with the support of the people."

"And yet those people wanted to oust you and let Lenore or whoever else rule. Why show them mercy?"

"Because that's what good rulers do."

It was like we'd scripted this exchange. Wondered if the Matriarchs were affecting me and Alexander at all, but it didn't feel like it. Alexander had learned a lot since we'd first met.

"That works for me, King Alexander. Especially because this system is going to need every ship to fight off the Z'porrah attack."

"Actually," Serene said. "Maybe not."

CHAPTER 95

"**THIS ISN'T GOING** to work," Jeff said quietly. "We're talking about people who want to wipe every one of us out of existence."

"They also don't want to die, and they were defeated before. By the people in this solar system. Plus, we have a lot of help."

What Jeff was worried about working was a plan Serene, the Matriarchs, and the Alpha Seven Penguins, who called themselves the Shantanu, had come up with.

All the spaceships were still in space around Beta Eight, but no one was firing at each other anymore. Instead, ships were getting into position for the plan we were going to roll, the one Jeff was stressed about.

We'd been back and forth to the planet, though not using the power cube. Jeff and Christopher had found the Rapacian shuttle in the late and unlamented Trevik's ship, and we'd used that to ferry people between, up to, and down from the Rapacian spaceships. And of course the other ships had shuttles, too, and moving people had been relatively smooth once everyone stopped shooting.

The other fighting forces throughout the system had been advised that the Planet's Rights Faction had been pretty much destroyed. Without the core leadership, and with the Alpha Four Poofs being helpful and going to snatch circlets from anyone wearing one, reports were coming back to Alexander that the cease-fire was going smoothly. Ships were now being moved into position to defend the system.

With things in motion planetside and our defenses being shored up, we were having a planning session on the Rapacian ship that Serene was commanding. As with most of our planning sessions, we had a big group. But since we'd moved all the untrustworthy prisoners to another location, we used the mess hall. Sadly, no snacks were available. Rapacians and Earthlings did *not* eat alike.

All Earthers were in attendance besides Airborne, who had maintained flight control of the three Rapacian ships. But we had Airborne on the com system, so it was like they were in the room with us. Alpha Four military had taken over the flying of the former PRF command ship as well as security on the planet, at least for now.

We also had all of our Beta Eight allies in the room, which included 2.0, who was back from being planetside, and The Clarence Clone, who'd pretty much stuck as close to me as he could. There had been a lot of arguments about this but Jamie had gone and hugged both of them, which shut up the main arguer, who happened to be her father.

The Planetary Council members who were our friends were here, too. It had been great to get to hug them all, even if we didn't have time yet for a real reunion. Queen Renata and the princesses had a far more emotional moment than I'd have expected—was pretty sure I saw some tears, but they were quickly hidden—and the princesses were flanking their mother.

Alexander was sitting near us, between Jeff and Christopher. Gower and Chuckie were next to me, because Jamie didn't want them far from her, and no one was going to argue with that.

"I'm just glad no one called Serene's bluff." Jeff heaved a sigh and cuddled Jamie—who had Mous-Mous on her shoulder and Bruno in her lap, with her feet resting on Wilbur's head and Ginger settled next to her—with an extremely possessive and protective expression. Not that I could blame him. "I have no idea what we would have done if that hadn't worked."

"Frankly, we'd have done just what we're talking about doing now."

It had turned out that what Serene had done when she'd taken her Rapacian ship down to the planet was find the Shantanu ship and ask Rohini for his support, which he'd given gladly. She'd wanted to do just what they'd said—convert the telescope into a weapon. But there hadn't been time, and Rohini and the Matriarchs were worried that removing the power spheres could cause Beta Eight's infrastructure and ecosystem to collapse.

Rohini, however, felt that bluffing was a reasonable option, especially since he did have gigantic sea monster allies on their way and, essentially, I and my team were providing the distraction needed to make the bluff work. Rohini was my kind of Space Penguin.

"And the rest of the solar fleet is ready to fight if needed, or will be." Jeff sounded like he felt our Plan B was going to be a lot more effective than our Plan A. Which was why he wasn't going to be too involved in Plan A.

"And, once they're clear that the new world order is the old world order, massing at the galaxy core side of the system, yes. Now stop nattering at me."

"So," Serene was finishing up her scientific explanation for the logistics of the plan, which was why I'd allowed Jeff to distract me, "we have the ability to project any image, including filmed images, utilizing the telescope's capabilities. We can absolutely reach the Z'porrah fleet, thanks to Usha."

Usha, who had somehow moved from Murdering Terrorist to Helpful Side Switcher Who'd Be Punished Later, nodded. "They will accept the transmission, and if you can truly show them what you have described, they will retreat."

"That's the big if, though, isn't it?" Reader asked.

"I will do my part," Lakin said. "They will believe."

"You know I'll do mine right," 2.0 said with a grin.

"Ah, Kitty?" Jerry asked on the com. He sounded like he was freaked out but controlling it. "If you have a second, could you run, and I do mean run, up to your vessel's command deck and take a look at what's coming?"

"Ah, I believe our allies have arrived," Rohini said. "Please, any who would like to see them, come with me and Commander Martini."

I wasn't the only person who trotted out of the room to take a gander. We reached the command deck and took a look. There were three Shantanu Triangles arriving. But they weren't alone. And I was pretty sure I spoke for everyone.

"Oh. My God."

The Space Sea Monsters had arrived. And, as advertised, they were gigantic and terrifying. They truly looked like Kraken and all other leviathan nightmares, only with a lot more teeth and tentacles. And a whole lot bigger. Apparently Alpha Seven was a giant planet.

There were snakelike ones, and dragonlike ones, and sluglike ones, and a whole lot of What The Hell Is That ones, and even more Oh God Make It Go Away ones. They went from beyond huge to gigantic to Makes Godzilla Look Tiny size. Myriad colors as well as sizes, too, though deep purple, dark blue, and iridescent green seemed to be the common accent shades.

They all seemed to have a lot of teeth—more teeth per head than the Poofs or snakipedes, potentially combined. Some had legs and arms or things that looked leg- and arm-like, and some didn't. Some had tails that looked prehensile, looked like weapons, or looked like both, and some had no tails. It was hard to call them a "race" but apparently they were all related somehow. Chose not to argue.

"You're all seeing Cthulhu and his family, right?" Tim, who was copiloting Reader's ship with Jerry, asked. "Tell me you're seeing this, and we're not just hallucinating up here. This is not what I want to see in any kind of dream or vision."

"Yes, Tim, we're all seeing them. In all their terrifying glory. Rohini, are they cuddly when you get to know them?"

"In their own way." Rohini was trying not to laugh. "And as long as you're their friend."

"Chip and I want to share that we want to be their *best* friends," Hughes said.

Joe and Randy were piloting the ship hosting the pow-wow. For possibly the first time since I'd known them, they were both silent. "You two okay?" I asked them quietly.

Randy shook his head. "We're not in Kansas anymore."

Joe nodded. "I think the plan's going to work."

"They're sentient beings who are our allies," Lorraine said, giving Joe a look that said he was a baby.

"They're not even as scary as a superbeing," Claudia added. "And you didn't freak out when you rescued us from one of those, Randy."

A throat on the com cleared. "Ladies, before you disparage your husbands anymore," Walker said, "understand that objects in the mirror appear smaller than they are in real life. You're seeing them via magnification. They're not actually with the fleet yet. They're just coming into Beta Eight's solar space."

Everyone looked again. "Ah," Queen Renata said. "I agree with Captain Billings' husband—the plan is quite sound."

"We need to be sure they can do what we're talking about without getting hurt," I pointed out. "I mean, looking at them, they seem invincible, but since they're using special equipment to be able to be safely out in space without ships, that equipment can get damaged and then they could be harmed. Or worse." Hey, I was against any ally of mine dying, regardless of how scary they looked.

"Your concern for their well-being has warmed their hearts," Rohini said approvingly.

"Um, how would they know? They're not mind readers are they?" Maybe everyone in this system had special teletalents of some kind and just hadn't taken over the entire galaxy out of restraint and a massive case of goodwill.

Rohini chuckled. "Oh no. I have a specialized comlink that connects me to them. It's not a weapon, but we find that it's quite helpful." Rohini had a sarcasm knob, too, apparently. "So when the link is open, which it is right now, the Cleophese hear what I hear and what I say."

"Well, that's convenient."

"Yes, since we will be using that technology to reach the Z'porrah. I and the Cleophese wish to reassure you that they will not be harmed by anything they will need to do. Their armor is thin but far stronger than any metal. It can withstand the pressure at the bottom of the ocean, the coldness of space, and the dangers of battle."

"In other words, these are people no one in their right mind should want to make mad. Or, as we call them, perfect."

Rohini gazed at me for a long few moments. "You refer to everyone here as a person."

"Well, you are. I mean, 'people' isn't necessarily a designation for humans only. At least not as I see it."

He nodded. "The Cleophese wish me to tell you that they are pleased to fight alongside one such as you, Commander Martini."

"I'm honored. But honestly, don't sell me too hard. I also refer to everyone as Giant Lizards, Major Doggies, Cat People, and Amazons. And those are my closest friends in the system." All of whom grinned or laughed.

He laughed as well. "What do you call the rest of us?"

Figured someone would tell him if I didn't. "Ah, you're the Penguin People, the Cleophese are the Space Sea Monsters, and the Rapacians are Hawkpeople. The Lecanora clans are diverse and they resemble Earth species, so I kind of think of them as their Earth equivalents. Like Fancy is a ferret and King Benny is an otter and Zanell is a wolverine."

King Benny had found his antlers somewhere, but he wasn't wearing them right now. Wasn't sure if that was good, bad, or indifferent, but figured I'd find out after we defeated the Z'porrah. Or after we were dead. But chose to focus on the positive.

"Why is this important?" the Alpha Five hostage, whose name I hadn't bothered to get, asked. Decided that, hostage or no, I didn't care for her or the Alpha Six dude. Figured I needed to learn their names so I'd know who was in charge of formulating the next rebellion. But, as with the antlers situation, something for later.

"I call Alpha Five and Alpha Six the Potential Traitor Worlds. If that helps." Wondered why the nasty seemed to come from them. Then remembered they were essentially humanoid with single hearts. Humans—we remained the nastiest things out there. Good. Because we needed to be extremely nasty to the Z'porrah.

Rohini's eyes twinkled. "Indeed it does. And it is important because Commander Martini speaks for Earth, and Earth has placed Beta Eight and Alpha Seven under its protection."

"Oh, everyone calls us Naked Apes. By the way. That probably includes everyone on Alpha Four, too, though as a human I'd designate them as the Hottie Naked Apes. Just in case you're keeping a record or something."

Rohini laughed. "I am pleased for the Penguin People and the Space Sea Monsters to join with the Naked Apes of all hotness levels in protecting our worlds and solar systems. And we will be keeping a watchful eye on those people you have designated as not Naked Apes."

The Alpha Five and Six representatives had the grace to look embarrassed, worried, and contrite. They also tossed in a little truculence and resentment in there. Definitely needed to have eyes kept on them and their planets.

"Excuse me, King Alexander," a voice from what I assumed was one of the Alpha Four battle cruisers interrupted, "but we have an incoming message from sentries at the edges of the system."

"Go ahead," Alexander said.

"The Z'porrah fleet has been spotted. They're almost to our solar system, sire."

CHAPTER 96

WE ALL LOOKED at each other. "The time for planning's over. It's showtime, kids. But, happily, our headliners have arrived just in time to put on a great show for their audience."

"With no dress rehearsal," Reader pointed out.

"Or, as we call it, James, routine. Time for everyone to scatter to their assigned positions."

We were sacrificing four ships to Plan A—the PRF command ship and the three Rapacian vessels. So those were put on autopilot and left floating in space. Well, make that five ships, really, if we counted the already-destroyed Shantanu ship, which we did.

Part of the on-planet activities had involved the Shantanu on Beta Eight retrieving the wreckage with assistance from the strautruch, who had come out in force to help. These pieces had been dragged out of the planet's atmosphere and were now floating nicely in Beta Eight's solar space, near the PRF command ship.

The Cleophese were positioning themselves around the wreckage and the four intact ships while the rest of us used shuttles to get to other ships or, in the case of a few, down onto the planet. Some of the other ships were already in position—the ones that weren't were waiting for passengers from the Ships About To Be Sacrificed.

Jeff and I were not going to be on the same ship because, as previously noted from the first day we'd met and every day thereafter, he was unable to lie. Serene, on the other hand, was heading down to the planet with Rohini because she was definitely the Troubadour For The Job in this case. Brian was going with her because they needed his skills, too.

The argument for which one of us Jamie was going to stay with had been won earlier. Needless to say, we both wanted to keep her within arm's reach, if not right in said arms. Other than seeming extremely tired and a little clingy with Gower, Chuckie, and all the animals, Jamie seemed okay.

This didn't matter at all to Jeff or me, of course. They'd taken our little girl and drugged her and we basically wanted to hunker down and hide her. Of course, events were not going to allow us to ever be regular parents, and this particular excursion was definitely Exhibit A.

That Lenore had drugged Jamie and Gower was certain. With what was the question that, so far, no one had had time to determine. Lakin and the other Rapacians had no idea, and neither did Usha. Since there were plenty of beings around who could tell if they were lying or not, we could believe them, not that it helped. I'd talk to ACE if I could reach him when Jamie was asleep, but right now wasn't the right time, for a variety of reasons, Jamie being awake being the biggest.

However, because I had the largest role in the theater we were about to perpetrate, Jamie was going with her father, meaning all the animals were going with them, as were Tito and most of the Matriarchs. From what Boz had told me, the Matriarchs were doing their best to determine what drug had been used on Jamie and Gower, but they were more concerned with Chuckie, who was having migraines and mood swings. So Gower and Chuckie were on Team Imperial Cruiser.

Tim, Kevin, Abigail, the flyboys, Rahmi, and Rhee were spread out and with the Reptilian, Canus Majorian, and Feliniad command ships, in part to show solidarity and in other part to keep their eyes open in case a traitor on those ships had been missed somehow.

There was risk in this, of course, because if the Z'porrah didn't withdraw, then they'd be doing their best to get here and take out Alexander's ship. But we'd have a little time if that happened, and Jeff was faster and stronger than me, so again Jamie being with him was logical.

At any rate, it was time for us to say goodbye, in that

sense. Hugged Jamie tightly. "You be good for Daddy and be sure all the animals behave. Mommy loves you *so* much."

She hugged me back. "I will, Mommy, I promise. And I love you so much, too."

Jeff took her from me then hugged me tightly with his free arm. "I don't like the idea of Jamie and me being separated from you, baby. Again, I might add."

Leaned up and kissed him. "We have jobs to do. This is yet another part of the three-tiered chess game where we have to allow our pieces to be on different boards. We'll be separated, Jeff, but never separate."

He grinned and kissed me. "Good." Then he and those going with him to Alexander's battle cruiser got onto their shuttle.

The Planetary Council Members were going to their respective ships, other than Queen Renata, who'd come into the system on the battle cruiser but was also on Team Kitty, so she was with me.

Jeff and Christopher had found the Rapacian's shuttle in the late and unlamented Trevik's ship, and that was what my team was using. Able to lie or not—and with him it was definitely "not"—Christopher was with me, because we were going to be using his speed for scene changes, in that sense.

"So, Renata," I asked while we loaded our team into our shuttle, "do you know who pulled us into this system and how?"

She nodded. "I did. We were under cease-fire to see if we could come to a compromise. I was on the Planet's Rights Faction ship for this negotiation and realized they were about to double-cross everyone. I'd seen that they had an advanced teleportation system on board—it's something Alpha Five has had for years, and they constantly work to make refinements. I used it to try to bring help."

"Why did you bring Jamie? And Abigail?"

Renata shook her head. "I didn't. I also didn't bring Paul—though he had been a warrior when we first met, I am aware that he is now your people's religious leader. I chose all the others who had been involved during the invasion attempt, plus my daughters. But I did not bring those three. I apologize for how the transfer worked—clearly I made an error. Plus there was quite a fight when I was caught."

"Some hitting of the Stop and Go buttons?"

"Yes. Quite the melee, honestly. I'm thankful you all arrived safely."

"Me too." Considered this as we started off. Sure, Renata would have been using tech that she wasn't totally familiar with, but clearly it was easy enough to use that she could select us individually and make the transfer happen. "So, does the transfer allow you to see the people being moved?"

"Yes. It's quite advanced, similar technology to what we're using to repel the enemy fleet. Alpha Four has had the technology to watch all of us, Earth included, for decades."

"Yeah, knew that for sure. So . . . you found us how?"

"Simple Galactic Positioning. I had a good idea of where to look for you. You identify the area where the target is, magnify the image until you can see them clearly, select the target or targets, 'catch' them, and then activate the pull. Or the send. That's doable also. Normally there are no issues, this technology has been available for many years, after all, it's just that Alpha Five has been perfecting it to make farther distances more attainable."

2.0 nudged me. "I don't buy it."

"Buy what?"

"That Renata did something wrong and somehow, despite a tech that works accurately and has been working for years, randomly grabbed not one, not two, but three people she didn't intend to. Is it possible to target an individual regardless of where they are? By using their DNA signature or similar? Or to do a 'group grab' that would override individual selection?"

"I honestly don't know."

"I'll bet there is, Ronnie, and I like where your head's at. Something to follow up with later. Renata, we'd originally thought Jamie was taken because she is a legitimate heir to the Alpha Four throne."

"But Jeff refused on behalf of himself and all his heirs. Therefore, she cannot ever accept."

2.0 jerked. "She can't in *this* government. However, if you stole a little girl, drugged her, brainwashed her, and then a few years later said, 'she is the rightful heir,' you could indeed put her right onto that throne."

"Especially if you killed off all of the former rulers," Usha added. "That plan makes sense."

"And then you can claim that you were respecting the wishes of those who wanted to go back to the Imperial Monarchy, even though you'd have her brainwashed to do your bidding. Whatever that bidding might be." Was seeing red at this point.

Christopher put his hand on my shoulder. "Kitty, I agree that what Ronaldo has come up with seems the most likely plan, now that we know more. But either the people who put that plan in place are already dead, or we're about to do our best to get them the hell out of our part of the galaxy. You being ready to kill right now isn't what we need."

Took my now familiar deep breath, let it out slowly, and forced myself to bank the anger. "I suppose you're right."

"What benefit would be gained?" King Benny asked politely. "I'm sorry, Shealla, but I don't understand. If the invaders are coming to take over, why would your daughter matter to them? Would we not all be dead or enslaved?"

2.0 and I looked at each other. "Yes," he said slowly. "That makes sense. The plan sounds like LaRue, or Zenoca, take your pick. But taking your daughter doesn't make sense."

"Especially because LaRue is dead, and I don't know if her clone on Earth actually knows anything about this system. My bet is that she doesn't."

"The Z'porrah wanted Jamie before," Christopher said. "They wanted her for her power."

2.0 scrunched up his face. "I'm trying to see if I remember anything about this. Give me a minute, but keep on talking."

"Okay. The Z'porrah would still want Jamie for her power. But, King Benny's right. If the Z'porrah take this solar system, then they would take Earth, because they'd have their might and the might of the Alpha Centauri system. They could get Jamie then, if they wanted her."

"I wouldn't want the Gods to be here if I was invading," Fancy said. "You are why the plans have failed."

This time it was Christopher and I who exchanged the meaningful look. "She's right," he said. "But that fits with Renata being the one who pulled us here. She wanted us, they didn't."

"Why does this matter now?" Zanell asked. "We are about to find out if our ruse works or fails. Shouldn't you focus on that?"

Lakin cocked his head at me. "You wish to be sure that you defeat all the enemies, not just the obvious ones."

"Wow, Lakin, welcome to Team Megalomaniac. Yes."

2.0 sighed. "I get nothing other than that I'm supposed to hate all of you for things that happened to someone else. I don't have anything specific about your daughter, Kitty. Nothing at all about her, really."

"Because your clone was made before they made their first bid for her. You were made right before she was born, I think. Clarence, what do you think?"

The Clone looked surprised. "Me, Shealla? You want my opinion?"

"Yes, I do."

Now he looked incredibly proud. And as if he was thinking very hard. "I guess the question is this — who would benefit the most from Jamie being brought to the system, right? And Paul and Abigail? Who benefitted from them coming?"

Opened my mouth to answer and slammed it shut. Because I knew the answer.

The person who'd benefitted by Abigail being here was Abigail. The person who'd benefitted by Gower being here was Jamie. And the person who'd benefitted, truly benefitted, from Jamie being here was Chuckie.

CHAPTER 97

"**WE'RE HERE**," Reader, who was flying our shuttle, said over the com. "Docking, so hold on in case it's not my perfect three-point landing."

Everyone looked at me. "You were going to say something, Shealla?" Fancy asked politely.

"Just was going to say that Clarence has a great point." The Clone beamed at the praise. It was official—I liked The Clarence Clone about a million times more than the original. "I just don't know who benefitted the most."

"We did," King Benny said simply. "All of us on Beta Eight, as you all call it. Perhaps the Daughter of the Gods made the choice to come herself."

"Perhaps she did." She might have, at that. But I had a better guess for who'd gotten involved. After all, Algar and ACE didn't hold the patents on rule breaking. She'd brought her brother along to protect Jamie, because Gower was the ruse, the person our enemies thought was housing ACE. And her sister had gained all her powers back and then some while on Beta Eight.

Wanted to get angry, but I couldn't. Naomi was out there, doing her best to protect her family. Maybe she hadn't realized Jamie and Gower would get drugged. Maybe she knew they would, but chose that as the lesser evil because she knew they could recover from the drug, but that Chuckie's mind would never recover if it had broken.

But this meant that the bad guys outside of Earth hadn't actually wanted our daughter here. None of them had added Jamie, Gower, and Abigail on as last minute additions to the group pull. Sure, they'd used Jamie when she appeared in their laps. Which she and Gower had. They were the only ones who'd made the original target—and Renata hadn't actually grabbed them. Meaning Naomi and Algar might have come to an accord. Or else they'd enjoyed the serendipity of each of them helping the other achieve mutually beneficial goals.

Abigail being with the princesses also made sense, since the goal there was to give her all her powers back and all of Naomi's powers, too. No one would question if she was kicking butt with our own Amazonian Butt Kickers and the oxygen-rich atmosphere was a great cover.

All of this made a hell of a lot more sense than someone in this system wanting Jamie here, let alone Gower and Abigail. With all of us off the planet—and instantly turned into hostages or killed by Lenore and her cronies—that left Jamie open for Cliff to snatch her. He didn't know we'd figured out he was the Mastermind, after all. And that made the Earth portion of this chess game much more logical.

That Renata had been "allowed" to pull us here made sense. Perhaps the failure was that she'd managed to hit the On button more times our enemies had hit the Off button. After all, if the pull hadn't reactivated when we were in the middle of nowhere in space, we'd all have been dead in seconds.

Maybe we were never supposed to have made it to any planet. Which would have solved every problem on all three chessboards and ensured a fast checkmate for all three parts of the overall plan.

So Jamie had been taken here for her own protection as well as Chuckie's. And probably ours, too. If she'd been on Earth, ACE would have been conflicted about the "rightness" of saving us. But she was out there with us, giving ACE the easiest of outs for protecting all of us when we were exposed and helpless in space. The final proof, as if I'd needed it, as to who'd engineered the "accidental grab."

I was used to thinking quickly, and I'd done so now. We bumped gently up against the Shantanu command vessel that had arrived with the Cleophese.

"But Christopher's right. We need to focus on what's going on here, make sure we do it right. We can figure out all the other stuff later."

This seemed to appease everyone other than Christopher himself and 2.0, both of whom looked like they suspected I wasn't telling them everything. I'd worry about what to tell them later. It was truly show time.

We were met by a variety of Penguin People. It turned out there was more coloration in them than The Clarence Clone had seen. Rohini, for example, was a beautiful blue with gold. In addition to the colorations The Clone had told us about, there were also some that were deep red and gold, deep brown and gold, and even some blue with red tummies, and red with blue tummies. The Clone was right—they were very pretty.

We hustled to their ship's command deck. Along the way Reader took my elbow and pulled me to the back. "I heard what you were all talking about," he said in a low voice. "You think ACE engineered everything, don't you?"

I didn't, but I couldn't tell him who I really thought was involved. Time to lie. "Yeah, I do."

He nodded. "Okay, we'll just move the conversation off the topic if it comes up again. We can tell Christopher when we're alone with him, but no one else outside of our inner circle needs to know."

Hugged him. "Thanks, James." That was the outcome that was best for everyone, after all.

We hurried up and rejoined the rest of the group. We had a long way to walk, so we really hadn't missed anything, and caught up right as we entered the command deck, which had the nice, large windshield that was also a viewing screen.

Everyone got into position—Lakin and Usha were on their knees, Renata was "controlling" the prisoners, Christopher was "off screen" so he couldn't be seen by anyone, and Reader and I were up with the Beta Eight natives, this ship's captain, who was of the brown and gold variety, The Clarence Clone, and 2.0.

Looked into my purse. "I need something that looks enough like a small laser to fool dino-birds." Reached in and came up with a snazzy penlight. Not Algar's finest hour, but it was something that could believably be in my purse, so I didn't argue.

The go sign was sent over from other ships. Our ship's captain, who was named Bettini, also had a comlink to the

Cleophese, and they were ready. Our fleet was all connected, too. The entire fleet—all planetary ships, regardless of where they were located within the solar system—was on the group com. It was a nice setup, and one that ensured that if the Z'porrah tried something, we'd know about it immediately.

"Hailing Z'porrah fleet," the Group Operator who was on Alexander's ship shared. Usha had given us a variety of channel codes, so one of them was definitely going to work.

The first one, apparently. "Usha, you have news for us?"

"Go live onscreen," she said.

"As you wish." Our windshield went live and there they were, the dino-birds in all their humanoid-ish Mini Tyrannosaurus Rex With Wings And Feathers glory. Apparently their weird Space Toga Muumuu look was their everyday garb, as were their design-painted talons that stuck out from the bottom of the Space Toga. The Space Togas hid their small wings and little T-Rex arms, so I figured the feathers that stuck out of the Space Toga sleeves were decorative, like the talon paint.

There were three Dino-Birds onscreen. They looked like every other Dino-Bird I'd seen. Happily, I hadn't seen enough Z'porrah to know if I'd met this set or not. They literally all looked alike to me.

"Usha, what is the meaning of this?"

The beauty of having flipped a spy was that she'd given us a lot of intel. "Hey there! You must be K'tano. And that's Ast'ria and Riol flanking you, am I right?"

K'tano gaped at me. "How do you know us?"

"Well, here's the thing—we have your spy. Spies, really. The ones that are still alive, that is, which isn't nearly as many as you had here only a day ago. And we have ways of making spies talk. Like Usha, here. Made her sing, really. She's explained that you three are really hella old, at least by Earth standards. Three hundred years if you're a day, Earth years-wise. And you three have been in charge of many things in those many years."

"What of it? You are a lesser race. You have no business—"

"Oh, shut it. We know what you're doing. Or at least what you think you're doing. But here's the thing—we don't plan on allowing it. Your underlings tried to invade and conquer Earth three years ago. They failed. Utterly. In no small part because the Alpha Centauri system came to help us. They're who you wanted, anyway. So, even though they showed you mercy, you formulated a new plan."

"You have no right to speak to K'tano in that way," the one I was pretty sure was Ast'ria snapped. Literally. She snapped when she spoke. It was charming in that totally not at all way.

"I have every right, Bird Bitch. I am speaking for the combined Earth and Alpha Centauri leadership. All of whom are still very much alive and kicking."

That was the cue for more pictures to be shown. We got to see them, too, as they popped up and stayed up. Everyone in Alexander's picture looked pissed. Same for those in the Reptilian, Canus Majorian, and Feliniad command ships. Wahoa and Felicia, in particular, looked like they were the last dog and cat in the galaxy you'd want to cross.

Even the Alpha Six command ship people looked angry, as did the Alpha Five representatives who were with them.

"Note, if you will, that the only Rapacian you see is kneeling at my feet on the Alpha Seven command ship. Also note that you don't see a visual from an Alpha Five command ship. Let's show you why."

Jeff picked up Lenore's dead body, which had been moved to Alexander's ship, and held it up. Then he threw it, hard, onto the floor. The body thumped in that sack-of-potatoes way a dead body will.

The Dino-Birds looked a tad concerned. "What did you do to her?" the one called Riol asked. He sounded just mildly upset.

"I killed her," Chuckie snarled. "With my bare hands."

He looked impressively dangerous and deranged. There was only one problem—this was not on script.

CHAPTER 98

"**A**ND I CAN'T WAIT to kill all of you in the same way," Chuckie went on. "Every last one of you."

Got the distinct impression that he meant this, in a very real and very personal way. Also had the impression that the Z'porrah were standing in for Cliff right now in his mind. Couldn't argue with that, really.

"And right after we enjoyed that particular hand-to-hand combat," I said quickly, before he could go on, or Jeff had to obviously restrain him, "we took over her ship. What you fail to realize is that this system has far more protections than you're aware of. One of those is on Beta Eight. Beta Eight has more protections than this one, as well, but what I'm talking about for this scenario is a giant laser cannon. We'd like to show you what it will do to an attacking ship. Lenore's command ship, for example. Commander Dwyer, go ahead."

"On your order, Commander Martini. Firing in three ... two ... one ..."

This was our biggest special effect, and the one everyone was most worried about working. Serene and Rohini had altered the telescope to reflect the sunlight. We had several ships in the fleet stationed at points both within the planet's atmosphere and at different distances in space, all leading toward the wreckage of the Shantanu ship.

The picture shifted to the ship nearest the telescope, which was a Feliniad vessel. Happily, the telescope "fired" right after Serene said "one" and the ship caught it well. The view onscreen instantly shifted to the next ships in line, some of whom were catching the light, and some of whom were making their own and enhancing the light coming up from the planet.

Because everyone involved in this portion had hyperspeed—the crew member handling the view switches in particular—it went well, with no discernible breaks in coverage.

The picture switched for the last time, to show a gigantic burst of light. This had been filmed earlier, by having every ship in the fleet shine their lights toward where our action was taking place, and then splicing them together to create the huge light show. Serene was the current Head of Imageering and Christopher was the former, meaning that this was done well and easily.

As the light died down, remains of the Shantanu ship we'd brought up from the planet were floating there. The Cleophese had broken it up into smaller pieces for us, so that it would be difficult to tell that the remains were from an allied ship.

"That wreckage was from one shot. A wide lens shot. We can make the shots more pinpoint, but when you're destroying something you really want to obliterate, wide lens is the way to go. And lest you think we're faking it, I have a handheld version with me. Please watch your live demonstration."

Pointed my "laser" penlight at Usha, who screamed. "No! Please! I helped you! I cooperated!"

"Sorry. You work for the Z'porrah, so you get to die." Turned the light on her.

This was Christopher's cue and he didn't disappoint. He zipped in at full Flash Level, grabbed Usha, and took her off-screen, while Reader surreptitiously took pictures with his phone camera aimed right at our ship's internal camera—with the flash on high. To everyone watching it looked like Usha was here one moment and completely obliterated by the laser flash the next.

Turned the penlight off and looked back at the screen. "So, one more Z'porrah spy down."

"We will destroy you," K'tano said. He sounded angry and, happily, just a little scared.

I snorted. Loudly. "Oh, you can try. I mean, I know what you're thinking. 'Oh, they have a laser cannon and some spaceships and lots of people who are seriously angry with us. But we don't care because we think we have more ships and we know that we still have allies in that system. Plus we have a giant Dino-Bird army. And now we're here to say that we don't just have one Hulk. We have a plethora. Dino-Guys and Gals, meet the Cleophese."

Another cue, this time for the cameras to beam what was going on outside, a little ways away from the site of the laser destruction, to the Z'porrah, and for the Cleophese to do their Hulk Smash thing.

There were only four ships and a lot of Cleophese. So it took them almost no time to rip the four ships apart. Then they ate all the remains. Nice to know the Cleophese could do that without harming themselves. Had no idea how they could do that and not explode in space, either, but since they were not exploding, figured they had their ways. Maybe dwelling at the bottom of deep seas gave them special advantages in the airless vacuum of space. Maybe I'd ask Rohini about it later. Much, much later.

I let the silence build as the Space Sea Monsters did their thing. Then they sort of swam over to the ships in our part of the fleet, being careful not to block any key ships' windshields. They dwarfed most of the ships—only the gigantic Alpha Four battle cruisers looked normal next to the Cleophese.

"Now," I said sweetly, "you've met some of our other allies. They happen to live in this solar system and they happen to dislike you Z'porrah on general principle. Which shows how highly intelligent they are. Your allies here are conquered. Speaking of which . . ." Pointed the laser at Lakin.

Who cringed and put his claw hands up. "No! Please! I beg for mercy! The remaining Rapacians give full fealty to Earth and Alpha Four. We will fight for the Imperial Monarchy forever if you will spare us."

He was acting, but he did actually mean this—that had been agreed to during our planning session. And since he was now the leader of the Rapacians—us having killed off the other leaders—Lakin's word was Rapacian law.

"But King Alexander showed mercy to the Z'porrah, and they returned that kindness by sending more of their spies and insurgents into this solar system. They repaid the magnanimous gesture by coming here to destroy everyone. You're a bird-race, too. Why should we trust you?"

Lakin shook his head and stood up slowly. "We are avian, yes. But we are not of the Z'porrah. We are of Ancient blood and design, and we will always be. The Ancient's enemies are our enemies, just as enemies of the Earth's and the Imperial Monarchy's are our enemies. I vow this for all Rapacians, from here forward."

I appeared to study him for a few long seconds. "Fine. We'll be keeping an eye on you—just as we're keeping an eye on Alpha Five and Alpha Six. But for now your life and your planet are spared."

Looked back at the Dino-Birds. "So, despite all this, I know you still think you have an ace up your flowing, feathered sleeves, and that's the fact that you have a puppet as the king of Beta Eight."

2.0 stepped up next to me and waved. "Hey there, K'tano, is it? And Ast'ria and Riol, too, right? How's it going? Look, apparently I was supposed to be some useless figurehead, just holding a planet for you until you came to destroy it. But, well, I got a better offer. I'm happily with Earth and the Imperial Monarchy, where they don't just use you and then throw you away. So, there is no planet in this system that is open or sympathetic to your cause."

"Thanks, Ronnie. Keep an eye on Lakin for me, would you?" Handed him the penlight, which he then aimed at Lakin. Those two moved back, so that I was once again in the foreground. "I realize this has been a lot for your birdbrains to take in. So, let me lay out your options for you.

"Option A is that you can turn your nasty Dino-Bird asses around and leave, and by leave I mean never darken Alpha Centauri or Earth solar systems again. And by never darken I include that to mean that you will stop sending spies and insurgents into our systems.

"Or, as Option B, you can try to fight us. Keeping in mind that there are more Cleophese on their way to guard every planet and support all of the fleet—which conveniently enough your actions mobilized, so everyone's all fired up and ready and, now that the civil war is over, just itching to shoot at the people who made them start fighting in the first place. You know how it is when you get your fancy ships up into space—you just want to blow stuff up all over the place. Something I realize you're all itching to do, too."

"If you do choose to fight," Chuckie said, once again not on script, "then know that we know where you are. I saw all of you in your ships, coming here. I saw where you came from. I can find your home planet now, with ease. And if you attack I'm going to ensure that everyone in this system knows where your home planet is, too."

"Meaning we'll bring this war to you next," I said. Off script or not, had a feeling Chuckie was definitely scaring the Z'porrah. "We're going to make sure that everyone in both solar systems has a map to your house. And then we're going to use that map and we're going to turn your planet into rubble. Because if that's what it takes to make you leave us all the hell alone, then that's what we'll do."

I made and held eye contact with K'tano. Not as hard to do as it sounded—the audiovisual in this solar system was top-of-the-line.

"If it were me, I'd choose Option A. But I've never felt you were as smart as me. So, if you go with the same plan that failed before and choose Option B, I have just one thing to say to you. Bring it."

CHAPTER 99

AND NOW WE SHUT UP. This was what I'd stressed the most in the planning session—that once I made this final offer, no one else, on any ship in the fleet, was to speak.

Everyone—even Chuckie, which, today, seemed like a miracle—managed to keep their traps shut. The silence spread out. And still we waited. And while we waited, I tested my staredown skills on K'tano.

He was tough, I had to give him that. But in the end, maybe because of the oxygen-rich atmosphere I'd been in for days, he wasn't Mom or Chuckie. I won—he looked away.

Then he turned away from the cameras, as did Ast'ria and Riol. And their screen went blank.

"Audio as well as visual cut to Z'porrah fleet," the fleet announcer shared.

"All ships, stand by," Alexander said.

We waited.

"Sire, this is Battalion Ship Twenty-Seven-Twelve, on sentry at the Z'porrah point of entry into our system."

Felt everyone on every ship hold their breath.

"Go on," Alexander said.

"Sire, the Z'porrah fleet is in full retreat. Repeat, enemy ships are in full retreat at warp. And have just made a hyperleap through their traveling wormhole. They are now nowhere near our solar system."

As we cheered, other sentries reported no signs of the Z'porrah fleet popping out anywhere we didn't want them, Earth solar system included.

Christopher and Usha rejoined us. "I'm honestly shocked they fell for it," he said.

Usha shook her head. "They aren't used to being lied to. They're used to frantic begging and a variety of offers and bribes, but someone risking everything by staging a fake show like this? I don't believe it's ever happened to them."

"You'd think a people who'd been around for longer than humans can contemplate, let alone individuals who've been around for three or four hundred years, would figure out that liars and fakes exist. But I'm perfectly happy with the outcome, so let's keep them naïvely in the dark."

"I'm all for that," 2.0 said. "So, now what?"

"Now we all go home." Of course, I knew it wasn't as simple as that. No one leaves a war, even one that's over, all that quickly. Especially when there were innocents who still needed protecting.

"By home, do you mean Earth or Beta Eight?" 2.0 asked. "For me, I mean."

"Honestly, Ronnie, I'm not sure. I think discussion needs to happen. About a variety of things."

"I have no home," Usha said. "Though I assume a prison will be where I reside for the foreseeable future."

"Perhaps," Fancy said. "You have committed grievous crimes against my people. But you have also done much to save them."

"Like I said, we have a lot of discussion topics."

"As long as we're discussing when we go back to Earth," Reader said, "I'm good with that."

"Let's regroup on Beta Eight," Bettini suggested. "I would like to have Rohini involved in discussions."

This plan was agreed to by all. So, all the Earthers and Beta Eight natives, along with the leadership from the other planets, went on down to the spiral world.

The first order of business was advising Earth of our whereabouts and the situation that had just happened. Who to tell was the question.

"I'd let Vince know, and Kitty would tell her mother," Jeff said, accurately.

"But I'd tell Cliff." Chuckie wasn't on the angry side of his latest mood swing—he was on the depressed side.

"So tell him," Tim said. "Just do it in a way where you don't sound like you want to kill him."

"What if they've already caught him? What if he's on the run?" Chuckie sounded ready to cry. This was so unlike him that I could honestly say I was more worried about him than Jamie, who was in Jeff's arms and asleep, her head on his shoulder.

Time to solve this dilemma. "We'll send the communication to Hacker International. Chernobog can decipher anything, and Stryker will disseminate as needed."

Everyone stared at me. "Good one," Reader said finally. "I don't know why the rest of us didn't think of that."

"Um, just finished a gigantic civil war? Anyway, that's the easy decision. The rest are going to take a little more thought."

"I agree," Rohini said. "And I believe everyone should rest, relax, and eat before those discussions begin."

No one argued because we were all coming down from the adrenaline rush of the last day.

Where everyone was going to bed down and such was decided quickly. While the strautruch and the Lecanora offered to let us all stay with them, everyone other than a select few actually ended up in a Shantanu Emergency City, which was something they carried with them. It wasn't really a city, though it was big. But it provided shelter and set up quickly. It was put on the site of the now-demolished castle.

The Matriarchs insisted that several of us needed to stay in the Purple Land. So Jeff, Jamie, Gower, and Chuckie were required. Jeff had been near death, Jamie and Gower were still showing signs of sluggishness, and no one needed convincing that Chuckie wasn't himself. There was no way I wasn't staying with them, and Reader and Christopher said the same. Tito insisted on coming along, too, since we were all his patients.

The Medical Family Group was taken to Boz's nesting city, which happened to be the one closest to the All Seeing Mountain, meaning those of us in the Purple Land were relatively close to those sleeping above the former castle, especially with hyperspeed, and vice versa.

We were given our own large family nest. Saffron, Turkey, and Pinky weren't katyhoppers from Boz's clan, but they'd requested to stay with us and Boz and their Matriarch had agreed. Surprising no one, Wilbur and Ginger had insisted on being with us, too, and of course we had Bruno as well.

So we were one big cuddled-up family. Proving how worried Jeff was about Chuckie, he'd suggested I sleep between the two of them. However, Jamie had insisted on sleeping between me and her Uncle Charles, and no one had argued, especially when the two of them curled up together, with Gower's back up against Chuckie's with Reader next to him. Wilbur and Ginger settled themselves between me and Jamie, too, Ginger at our heads, Wilbur snuggled from the waist down. Bruno went to Chuckie's head and nested down. And a variety of Poofs, both our attached ones and some unattached, snuggled around them, too.

"I feel special," Jeff said dryly.

"I could put you into isolation, if you'd like," Tito said. "The Matriarchs can make something that would work similarly."

"I'll shut up and go to sleep," Jeff said with a laugh, as I snuggled into his chest.

Christopher was next to Jeff and Tito was sleeping at everyone's heads, with Saffron next to Christopher, Pinky at our feet, Turkey next to Reader, and more Poofs scattered in between everyone.

As everyone fell asleep, I spoke in my mind. ACE, are you there?

Yes, Kitty, ACE is here.

Is it really over? Silence. Sorry. Is our battle with the Z'porrah really over? At least for now?

Yes, Kitty. Kitty has done well.

Will Jamie, Paul, and Chuckie recover?

Yes. Jamie and Paul will recover faster than Chuckie, but Kitty saved Chuckie in time.

Jamie saved him. Or was that you?

ACE helped. Jamie would have made ACE help if ACE was unwilling.

Is that a bad thing?

He didn't reply for a few moments. No. Not in this case.

Decided now wasn't the time to ask about other cases. How long should we stay on Beta Eight? Or, to put it another way, where will Jamie, Paul, and Chuckie recover fastest?

On Beta Eight, though Kitty should only stay a few more days. Once things are settled Kitty and the others can go home. Jamie and Paul will be well by then.

What about Chuckie? When will he be well?

ACE . . . does not know.

CHAPTER 100

MY STOMACH FELL. Will he ever be himself again?
Chuckie has been harmed. The Matriarchs are do-ing good things for Chuckie, and the Matriarchs will repair Chuckie's mind.

It's his emotions and psyche that are really hurt, aren't they?

Yes. To discover that one you felt was your close friend is actually your betrayer? That is a terrible thing. And then to suffer as Chuckie did, right after? That makes all the rest worse. Chuckie will need Kitty, but Chuckie will need Jeff, and Christopher, and Paul, and all the others just as much.

He needs to know, really know, that they're his friends, right?

Yes, but Chuckie needs to know more that the others will not betray Chuckie. Chuckie will know this in time, but Kitty must be patient with Chuckie. Kitty must also not let Chuckie do what Chuckie wants to do.

Murder Cliff Goodman.

Yes. If Chuckie does this, no matter what the reason, unless it is in self-defense or the true defense of others, Chuckie will never recover.

But he's killed people before. We all have. Not that I'm condoning it, but we've all done what we had to do at one point or another.

Yes, but all those times Kitty and the others were killing in self-defense or in the true defense of others. Killing in cold blood, no matter the motivation, alters the killer in ways that Kitty cannot see. But ACE can see those changes, and ACE does not want those changes for Chuckie, or Kitty, or anyone else ACE watches over. Anyone else ACE loves.

I can understand that. Thank you, again, for your part in helping us survive all of this.

ACE felt evasive in my mind and he didn't say anything.

When Sandy or, more likely, the Superconsciousness Seven, or whoever else might come, tries to make anyone involved pay for it, I will fight for you. For all of you. I promise.

Kitty keeps her promises. ACE is not afraid for ACE.

I know. I know who you fear for. But we'll cross that bridge when it falls down on us.

Kitty will prevail. Kitty thinks right.

Then I felt the warm, loved feeling that was ACE hugging me in my mind. Heaved a sigh, snuggled closer to Jeff, and went to sleep. Mercifully dreamless.

The next days were busy, and though Chuckie was involved in all the discussions, he went nowhere without a katyhopper escort. Usually it was Turkey, Saffron, and Pinky, but sometimes it was Boz or another Matriarch.

Jamie went everywhere with us, too, simply because Jeff and I weren't going to leave her alone anywhere. Within a day she and Gower were looking normal, and Boz assured me that the drug was out of their systems with no side effects. The Power of the Purple Land apparently. Though Tito, of course, was planning many tests for the moment we got home.

We did get to have a proper reunion with our old friends from this system. It was fun to show off Jamie, take them around the planet, and have the Beta Eight natives get to meet their solar system neighbors.

Haven and the All Seeing Mountain were the biggest hits, but the Blue Land's floating buildings were a draw, too. Everyone only got a cursory look at the Purple Land, but the strautruch rides through the Yellow Land were a highlight for everyone, other than those afraid of heights.

I had to focus on diplomacy in a big way, however, because setting up the political system on Beta Eight was of high importance, and Beta Eight wanted the Gods speaking for them. And my first suggestion raised a lot of controversy.

"I can't believe you want to leave a clone of Ronaldo Al Dejahl in power," Tim said for, by my count, the tenth time.

"I want him as part of the government, not all of it. But there are at least three highly sentient races here in the katyhoppers, the strautruch, and the Lecanora, plus the ocellars, the bosthoon, the chochos, and all the other life-forms, including the snakipedes. Ronnie can actually control those, and no one else can."

"Why not get rid of them completely?" Reader asked. "Why leave that dangerous a predator on the world?"

"They're our best protection," 2.0 said. "I can train them to protect, not kill, the other people on this planet. It'll take some time, but not as much as it could. And they were here before we came. They're native to this planet."

"We've been told that Zenoca created the Horrors," Fancy said.

"I'm sure she took credit for them. And she did make them bigger. I believe they started out as small pest control. Most of the giants are dead now anyway—they died protecting us during the Rapacian attack. As far as I can tell, there are only babies alive right now, and I can train them and their offspring. But they were here first."

He had a point, and we'd spent some time determining that I'd destroyed the only cloning facility on the planet. And maybe 2.0 really could make a monster into a useful part of the ecosystem. Precedent had certainly been set, with him as Example A. 2.0 and The Clarence Clone both gave me hope that if we could possibly find Earth clones before they were completely twisted, maybe we could redeem them as well.

"Then they belong here," Rohini said. Rohini was definitely the deciding voice for all of the system, though he was careful to let it appear that Alexander's word was law. "If Ronaldo will train them and control them, we agree that they should not be exterminated. And before anyone complains, please remember that the Cleophese are frightening beings capable of much mass destruction, too. But they evolved on our world before we did. It is their world, too."

Alexander nodded. "We agree." He was working well with Rohini, probably because he'd spent a lot of years working with Councilor Leonidas.

"Great, then we move on. I think we keep Ronnie as part

of the government because, frankly, while he wasn't the greatest king, the Lecanora know who he is, and calm transition would be nice. Add on a katyhopper representative, a Strautruch representative, and a Lecanora from the white, green, black, and blue sections of the world, and you have seven representatives with equal voice, meaning there can never be a tie in terms of voting."

"Who chooses them?" Jeff asked.

Everyone looked at me. "Fine. I was going to push my agenda anyway." This earned a laugh from the humans and 2.0 and polite looks of confusion from everyone else. Forged on. "In addition to Ronnie, Fancy Corzine should represent Iceland, Zanell will represent the Black Land, and King Benny will represent the Blue and Bronze Lands."

King Benny raised his paw. "Shealla, I feel that my appointment will be argued. Plus, why are you giving me two parts of the world to represent?"

"Don't care about the arguments or arguers. You've proved your leadership ability constantly since we've met. They haven't. You're representing your land of birth and the land you led your people through. You're the Lecanora who will think of the disenfranchised first, and therefore you are vital to the world government."

"I agree," Fancy said strongly. "I will not accept my position if Musgraff does not accept his. I will only lead if he leads also."

This earned a shocked and very pleased look from King Benny, some applause from the group, and King Benny a really dirty, jealous look from Zanell. Noted 2.0 noting it, and he nodded at me and winked. Okay, he'd keep an eye on that potential love triangle.

"The strautruch can and should elect their own representative. The Matriarchs should as well, or, if they prefer to have a rotation in and out of the position, that's up to them."

Antennae waves indicated the katyhoppers were good with this and would be doing the rotation plan. The strautruch were also pleased and shared that they'd choose their representative shortly.

"And the last Lecanora slot should be chosen via random lottery out of those who live in Greenland." This earned me a variety of raised eyebrows and shocked looks.

"Random means the winner may or may not want the position. We come from a world where political power is far too coveted. I'd suggest making all the Lecanora slots random within the sections of the world, as leaders pass on or wish to retire."

"What Shealla says we will do," King Benny said. The others nodded and, after a little more discussion, my plan was agreed to. Go me.

Rohini and his people were going to leave the Emergency City in place. The populace could build a new seat of government wherever they chose, but this way they had a building to house refugees and the government at the same time. I really liked that juxtaposition.

"What of the Rapacians?" Lakin asked. "What will become of my people?"

"You'll be sent home, and Alpha Four will install some of the Royal Guard on your planet," Alexander said. "As we will do with Alpha Five and Alpha Six."

"As you wish," Misorek said.

I'd finally learned their names. Misorek was the dude from Alpha Six and Haliya the chick from Alpha Five. They were both ordinary looking to me, which, so far as my limited experience showed, was typical for both planets. They accepted Alexander's decision without question or argument. I'd already told Rohini that I didn't trust them, and I'd passed along the same to 2.0 and the Matriarchs.

"What will happen with me?" Usha asked.

"You will come back to Beta Twelve with me and my daughters," Renata said. "We are best equipped to deal with you if you try to go to the bad. You will be imprisoned, but not as harshly as we might want—the Lecanora have pleaded on your behalf and mercy will be granted."

Usha looked shocked. "Thank you," she said to the Lecanora with us. "I realize this will feel hollow to you, but I actually enjoyed living amongst you. Perhaps, one day, I can return and live here again."

"Perhaps," Fancy said. "Time will tell."

Rahmi and Rhee, however looked unhappy. And also like they weren't going to argue even though they wanted to. Rahmi, in particular, looked ready to cry. She was also looking at Tito. A lot. And he was doing his best not to look at her, but he looked more than a little down.

Put two and two together. Hero worship and mutual respect had apparently worked their romantic magic. "Ah, Renata? Not to create familial disharmony or make you think your daughters haven't missed you, because they have, but I'd like to see if they want to remain on Earth."

Renata looked confused, then she took a good look at the princesses. "Ah," she said sadly. "And this is the true loss the war has given me. My daughters love another planet more than their own."

Cleared my throat. "Maybe not the planet, so much as, ah, people *on* the planet."

Tito heaved a sigh, stood up, and squared his shoulders. "I'd really wanted to do this more privately, but Queen Renata, while I'm not royalty, I do love one of your daughters with all my heart. I would like to ask your permission to see if Princess Rahmi would have me as her husband. Which I also realize is somewhat shocking for your culture."

Renata might have been surprised, but she hid it well. She looked sharply at Rahmi, who was trying not to look pleadingly at her mother and failing utterly.

"I view marriage as a partnership," Tito went on. "Not with one subservient to the other. And I believe Rahmi feels the same, even if it is marriage to a man, not a woman."

"Since when?" Christopher whispered to me.

"For a while," Abigail, who was next to him, whispered back. "He's been working with me, Rahmi, and Rhee on fighting and fighting styles since Sis died. Those two hide it well, but they've been a thing for quite a while. And I totally approve."

Renata nodded. "I have never demanded that my children blindly follow. I raised them to think for themselves. If Rahmi wishes it, you have my permission."

"I do!" Rahmi jumped up and ran to Tito at hyperspeed. They hugged, then did a family hug with Renata, and Rhee joined in.

"She's taller than him by a lot," Jeff pointed out.

"And he's definitely someone who's secure enough in his manhood to handle it. Wow, that's your objection?"

Jeff laughed. "No objection at all, really. I've known for a while."

"I'm sure you have. How'd you manage to keep it a secret?"

He grinned. "Easy. No one ever asked."

While this was going on, The Clarence Clone came over to me, Wilbur and Ginger trailing him. "Shealla, what will I do?" He looked lost and afraid. But he needn't have worried.

"Clarence, you're coming home to Earth with us." Felt and saw jaws drop. "You're the good version of your original, and I think your family will be overjoyed to have you returned to them."

The Clone beamed. "Thank you, Shealla! Will Wilbur and Ginger be coming, too?"

The animals both whined. "Do Wilbur and Ginger have mates in their packs?" More whining. No, they did not. "Do Wilbur and Ginger have potential mates in their packs?"

A few chochos and ocellars trotted over, looking rather eager.

"That's more than 'a' mate each," Jeff said. "That's a good seven other chochos and ocellars, each." He groaned. "I know what's coming."

"They need to be immunized to ensure they don't bring in alien diseases, and vice versa," Chuckie said.

"We can arrange that," Rohini offered. "It will be ready before you all return to Earth."

"Then, yeah, let's bring the menagerie. We need to ensure that whoever just lost their chochos and ocellars gets reimbursed for their loss, however."

"We will see to it," Fancy replied.

"Will this create a problem on Earth, though?" Tim asked. "I'm not saying to leave the animals, or Clarence behind, but Poofs and Peregrines are one thing. Chochos and ocellars are another. A very visible other. Same with bringing back someone from the dead."

Shrugged. "Let's phone home and ask."

CHAPTER 101

ALEXANDER HAD set up a feed with Hacker International. We had to go up to his ship to talk to them, but we'd been gone so long that we all wanted to anyway, regardless of the Clarence Clone and Alien Animals Questions.

Pretty much everyone who'd been in the room when we were taken was now packed into the computer lab where Hacker International lived. We also had President Armstrong in attendance, and, to my surprise, Gideon Cleary.

We'd updated everyone days earlier, but we hadn't been ready to leave the planet. We were ready now, as long as our new residents were approved.

"I don't have any problem with you bringing the animals back if they won't make anyone sick or get sick from coming here," Armstrong said.

"The Shantanu will guarantee both," Rohini said.

"Mister Valentino is another thing, though." Armstrong shook his head. "I'm not going to tell you how to deal with your family, Jeff, but are you sure bringing in a copy of your late brother-in-law is the right thing to do for your sister and her family?"

Jeff ran his hand through his hair. "Honestly, Vince, I'm not sure. This Clarence is more like I remember the original one being before my Aunt Terry died. We get nothing evil from him."

"I think he can help us with our Mastermind problem, in a lot of ways."

Cleary nodded. "You want to use him to lure Stephanie home, don't you?"

"Yeah, I do. Richard, Malcolm, and Night Crawler, what do you guys think?"

"I think it's sound for a lot of reasons," Buchanan said.

Siler also nodded. "Stephanie's gone to ground. While you've all been off partying in another universe, we've," he indicated himself and Buchanan, "been searching for her and coming up with cover stories for where you are and why the governor isn't upset that Kyle and his small team went to Florida instead of the Vice President and his wife, as requested."

"I agree with Malcolm and Benjamin," White said. He and Rohini were getting along swimmingly, which wasn't all that much of a surprise. Figured White was going to want to take a trip to the home system soon, just to hang out with his Penguin Counterpart.

"I also believe you all sell Sylvia short," White went on. "She is more than capable of making the distinction between clone and original, but she may not want to. We mate for life, if you recall, and while one can move on after a spouse's death, it takes us many years. Sylvia has not yet moved on. Why not do her and this new Clarence both a kindness and allow them to begin a new life together?"

"And hopefully he'll be able to help us find Stephanie," Cleary added.

"I agree about Sylvia. However, this Clarence won't be ready for Stephanie for a while. He's still . . . simple. Not stupid, his brain works well, but his experiences are limited. It's going to take some time."

"We have it," Armstrong said. "While I'm sure you'd all like to find the young lady sooner than later, we aren't ready to move against Goodman yet anyway. We've all agreed that allowing Goodman to know that we know what he's up to is counterproductive. I'm going to be moving him to another position—one where he has no day-to-day with American Centaurion or the C.I.A., and little contact with the Vice President, too. He'll be busy, feel he's moving up in the hierarchy, but be in a place where he can and will be watched."

"What about his relationship with Chuck?" Christopher asked. "We can't expect Chuck to act like Goodman's his best friend anymore."

The others nodded, both on Alexander's ship and in

Hacker International. Good to know Chuckie had plenty of support.

"We can use the truth," Chuckie said. "I was hurt when we were here, and I'm having terrible mood swings I can't control. That explanation will cover for me being angry with him. I can control myself from killing him or telling him what we know he is and has done. It'll work for long enough."

"How long do you figure for the clone to adapt and become useful?" Cleary asked. "And before you all shoot me the death glare, I'm not trying to be insensitive. But we need to know the timeline so we can adapt what we're doing and saying about Stephanie, among other things."

"Nine months to a year," Jeff answered before anyone else could. "Nine months would be the absolute soonest. I'd plan on a year, a little more if we can do it."

"That makes sense," Chuckie said, just as quickly. "I'm sure we can fool Goodman for that long, or longer if we need to."

The rest of the discussion was mundane and I focused on getting time to say goodbye to everyone—it was clear we were heading home soon.

The less said about the many tearful goodbyes we did once we were back on Beta Eight the better. Managed not to cry when we said goodbye to Patrina and Pretty Girl, who had come to visit and bonded with Jamie and Mous-Mous. The girls were clinging to each other and Patrina's mother and I finally had to pry them apart.

"We'll come back," I told Jamie. "I promise."

"You will," King Benny said, antlers proudly back in place. "It has been foretold."

Hugged him so hard his antlers wobbled. And I didn't even want to laugh.

How we were getting home was the big question. By ship had been suggested and vehemently vetoed by Jeff with massive support from Chuckie, Jareen, and Neeraj, which made no sense to me. But they were so against it I didn't argue.

Asking ACE was out, and no one felt that Abigail was ready to warp all of us that far, including Abigail.

This left going back the way we'd come. No one was all that much of a fan, but the history of success the Alpha Five transport system had was undeniable.

It was felt that we would have the safest trip if we beamed from the top of the All Seeing Mountain. So, entourage in tow, we zipped up there, some via hyperspeed, some via the Rapacian shuttle, which really was super useful. 2.0 had asked for and been given permission to keep it.

He hugged me tightly as we got ready to get into beaming positions. "Thank you. For giving me a chance to be a better person than my original was. I won't let you down."

Hugged him back. "I know you won't, Ronnie." I did, too, for some reason.

"Don't be a stranger," he said. "You'll always have a home here, if any of you ever need it." The rest of the Beta Eight folks nodded.

Last hugs all around, then we stepped as a group into the middle, Jeff holding Jamie, animals next to people. Serene and Rohini had figured out how to move the telescope, so it was to the side, politely waiting for us to leave so it could go back into its place of honor.

"Everyone be good and, next time, call before you come to visit or bring us out to save the day, okay?"

Everyone laughed and as they were saying okay and waving goodbye, the transfer hit.

This was far more like *Star Trek* than our first experience. We were all pixelating quickly, animals included. There was a bright flash of light and I saw us, all of those who were called Gods on this world, in a circle, once again talking to Beta Eight natives we didn't know.

As the déjà vu hit, there was another flash of light, and then we were gone, both versions of us. A third flash and we were in the second floor of the Zoo, which was the area in our complex with the least stuff in it.

"Whoa, did you guys see something . . . weird when we were pulled?" Brian asked.

Not everyone nodded—only those of us considered Gods on Beta Eight.

"What was it?" Kevin asked. "I feel like . . . I remember things I can't possibly remember." Again, only the Gods of Beta Eight nodded. Everyone else looked at us like we were crazy.

"It's just a side effect of the transfer," Chuckie said. "Nothing dangerous or long-lasting. We're home, we're all alive and most of us are reasonably well." He smiled wryly.

"So, let's go see everyone else and do the same thing we just did on Beta Eight."

"Hug, kiss, and cry?" Walker asked.

"Sounds about right," Serene said. "I personally have a child to get my arms around, and I know I'm not the only one."

Heard the sounds of running feet as Patrick, Ross, Sean, Raymond, and Rachel all came running across the walkway and flung themselves into their respective parents' arms. Denise Lewis was right behind them, and she joined her children in flinging herself at Kevin.

White and Amy were next, grabbing Christopher, then Gower, Abigail, and Reader. Mom and Dad were right behind them, hugging me, Jeff, and especially Jamie.

Chuckie looked funny, but before he could move off, Dad grabbed him and pulled him into our family hug. Felt him relax and saw Chuckie's expression go back to what I considered normal.

The rest of the Embassy and related family members came in, including Jeff's parents, Alfred and Lucinda, and Sylvia. Sylvia saw The Clarence Clone and stopped dead.

"Is it really you?" she asked.

The Clarence Clone looked at her for a few long seconds. "Sylvia?" he asked finally. "Are you . . . are you my wife?"

She burst into tears, ran to him, and threw her arms around him. "Yes. And you're my husband."

He hugged her and looked at me. "Thank you . . . Kitty."

"You're welcome, Clarence. And welcome home."

And then it was one gigantic hugfest for a long time.

But it really wasn't long enough.

CHAPTER 102

JAMIE WAS ASLEEP in her room with the cats, dogs, a large number of Peregrines, Bruno included of course, Mous-Mous and every unattached Poof we had, and all the ocellars and chochos as well.

Amazingly enough, our cats and dogs had accepted the new additions without too much complaint. Jeff having given them even more treats than the new animals probably helped, but the Poofs and Bruno were most likely the real reason for insta-love.

It was almost impossible to walk into her room without stepping on paws or tails, but Jeff and I had done our best. Mercifully, the Alpha Four Poofs had all stayed in their system, at least as far as I knew. Never thought I'd ever feel we could have too many Poofs, but right now, we had so much fur in our home we were maxed out.

Now we were lying in bed together in the happy afterglow of We Made It Home Safely sex. My head was on his shoulder, and my hand was stroking the hair on his chest while he stroked my arm.

"You know, I have a question."

"Yeah? What about, baby?"

"I've been thinking about the timeframe you laid out for when our New Clarence would be ready to help us find Stephanie and bring her in from the cold. He's pretty smart and very willing. I think he could be ready far earlier."

"Don't care. We're not taking any action against the Mastermind for at least nine months to a year. Longer if we can get away with it, though I doubt we can. Let Clarence have all the time we can give him. Maybe Stephanie will come home on her own when she hears he's alive. Maybe she won't. But we're going to take the time."

This wasn't like Jeff. He'd accepted that Stephanie was a traitor but he still wanted to bring her home, get her back on the side of right, save her. Just saying she could deal and *que sera sera* seemed out of character.

"Chuckie supported that idea . . . almost immediately . . ." And he'd seen everyone in the solar system, possibly the galaxy. I thought he'd seen them as energy signatures like I had, but maybe he'd seen them in a more in-depth way. I hadn't asked, after all.

"Yeah, so what? Chuck said I was right, why are you arguing?"

"Because that's also out of character. He gave no real explanation for why . . ." Thought about it. Really thought about it, about why both Jeff and Chuckie would say "we're taking our time," especially under the circumstances, and, in particular, the amount of time they were saying we needed. Plus, Jareen and Neeraj had been adamant that I not travel in a warp ship. "Oh. Um, really?"

Jeff chuckled. "Yes, really."

"You're sure?"

"Very. I'm assuming the oxygen-rich atmosphere helped. Not that we really had trouble before, but still, it's been four years since the last time."

"You mean I got pregnant on Beta Eight?"

Jeff rolled onto his side and kissed me. "You did. In the middle of Haven. But you're not allowed to name the baby Fancy or King Benny or anything like that."

"Hey, I'm Shealla, the Name Giver. I get to name the baby whatever I see fit."

He laughed. "We'll discuss it. And we're also not going to do anything to put you into action until the baby is safely here."

"We may not have any control over that, you know."

"I know. But I'm the Vice President and the Leader of the Gods. So I say that's how it's going to be."

"And who am I to argue with the Leader of the Gods?"

Jeff rolled on top of me, propped himself up on his forearms, and stroked my hair. "You're the most amazing woman in two galaxies."

Available December 2015,
the twelfth novel in the *Alien* series
from Gini Koch:

ALIEN IN CHIEF

Read on for a sneak preview

"**M**OMMY, why is that car floating?"

For some mothers, this question would be answered by the term "special effects" and/or "just watch the movie, honey". For me, it required a different explanation.

"Ah, Jamie, well ... I think it's because your little brother, um, wants it to. Charlie? Charlie, honey, put the car down, please. Now."

Thankfully, the car in question was one of the toy cars that my son was far too young to play with. That didn't stop him from wanting them, however. And, because he wanted them, well ... Charlie took them. By making them come to him.

In the past years I've gone through so many changes that you'd think change would be commonplace, something I didn't even think twice about.

You'd be wrong.

Becoming an alien superbeing exterminator? Handled like a boss. Becoming the Ambassador for an alien principality? So four years ago. Being the wife of a still-unwilling but going to do his best for his people and country politician? Got it covered. Finding that the Mastermind of the majority of our problems on Earth was a good friend? Still plotting the revenge. Swapping places with another me and visiting another universe? Check. Averting a solar system civil war? Double check.

But none of these changes prepared me for my biggest battle.

Being the mother of two.

Two alien hybrid children with, oh, shall we say, unusual abilities. Don't get me wrong—I love my children. They're great and, frankly, I have tons of help, a super supportive husband, totally there parents and in-laws, and a plethora of Secret Service agents following us everywhere. I mean, I have no right to complain at all.

I just have to say that sometimes it felt like averting an alien civil war was a lot easier than parenting. Times like right now, for instance.

My daughter Jamie of course knew why the toy car was floating. She was just asking so that she could point out that her little brother was doing something I didn't want him to in a way that might mean she wasn't a tattletale.

Of course, since Charlie's birth six months ago, we'd actually needed Jamie's tattling, because Charlie's very unusual talent had manifested at birth.

Being the family of the current Vice President of the United States meant that we were under microscopic scrutiny. Seeing as my husband, Jeff, was also an alien whose parents and family were originally from Alpha Four of the Alpha Centauri system meant we were under scrutiny far more in-depth than microscopic.

The A-Cs, as they called themselves on Earth, were religious refugees when they came in the 1960s. And they'd integrated into the world, sort of, and stayed hidden, almost completely, as citizens of the United States first and the world second. Now, thanks to a just-barely foiled alien invasion, the entire world knew that aliens were real, and that the best looking ones in the galaxy had chosen to live with us.

Perks aside, our A-Cs were here to protect and serve. Could not say the same for at least half of the alien races out there we'd encountered so far.

The A-Cs had two hearts and this gave them faster regeneration, hyperspeed, and superstrength. Some of them also had special talents, like Jeff, who was the strongest empath in, most likely, the galaxy. In addition to the empaths, there were imageers, who could manipulate any images, static or live or whatever, dream readers, and troubadours, who were the actors and public speakers of the bunch.

Our female hybrid children, of which we didn't have all that many, were all specially talented, with skills far surpassing the norm. But no hybrid boy had been exceptionally talented until Charlie showed up. And telekinesis wasn't an A-C trait.

I'd gotten pregnant on a world where telepathy and telekinesis were normal, though, which was the only explanation we had for Charlie's abilities.

You'd think that, with all the other things the A-Cs could do, Charlie being telekinetic would be no big to anyone in the A-C community.

And you would be wrong.

The car was still floating, and now it had company. "Charlie, put the cars down, please and thank you." He grinned at me—he totally had his father's smile—and yet the cars continued to fly away from the other kids in the American Centaurion Embassy Daycare Center and fly right to Charlie. "All the cars down, please, Charlie. Now."

Counted to ten. Cars were still flying. It was time to channel my mother. "Charles Maxwell Martini, you return those cars and put them right down this instant, young man."

No more grinning from my son, but the cars zoomed back to the kids who'd been playing with them and landed nicely. One for the win column.

Denise Lewis, whose husband was my mother's right-hand man and our Embassy's Defense Attaché, smiled at me. "Good job, Kitty."

Managed not to say that Jamie hadn't been this much work. She had been, she'd just been different.

Was saved from having to respond in any way by Kyle Constantine and Len Parker sticking their heads in. I'd met them when they were still playing football for USC and they'd helped me out in a big way. They could both have gone pro, but instead they joined the C.I.A. right after they graduated. Len had been assigned as my driver and Kyle as my bodyguard and they'd done a great job.

But right before some of us took a trip to the Alpha Centauri system to avert a variety of civil wars, evil plots, and yet another alien invasion, Kyle had been put in charge of the Second Best Lady's Cause.

Actually, I still had no idea what my official title was as the wife of the VP. No one around seemed to know, or care. I'd searched the papers for clues, but stories written about me tended to focus on all the madness that surrounded us on a daily basis and the adjectives tended more toward "outspoken," "blunt," and "trigger-happy."

Anyway, a politician who'd been aligned with all of our enemies during the presidential campaign that had put Senator Vincent Armstrong into the White House, dragging Jeff along kicking and screaming, had somehow managed to become our ally. The slipperiness of political bedfellows and changing alliances never ceased to amaze me. It truly made fighting alien invasions, mad super-geniuses, and crazed megalomaniacs seem like such clean work.

"Kitty, Gideon Cleary's here," Kyle said. Speaking of the devil I'd just been thinking about. "We need to brainstorm the next ad campaign."

Mommy Time was over. Time to get back in the saddle and handle grown-up things.

"And," Len added, "we have news, too. News you're not going to like."

Hugged and kissed Jamie and Charlie, handed Charlie to Denise, petted all our animals—of which we had so many, both Earth and alien, we'd all lost count—grabbed my purse, and headed out.

"What's going on?" I asked as we got on the elevator and headed down for the meeting. "New issues with The Cause?"

The Cause was protecting campus coeds from being attacked and raped. When we'd met, Kyle had been drunk and suggested that I might like to get to know half of the Trojan football team intimately. Len had stopped that— well, Len and Harlie.

Harlie was a Poof, aka the best wedding gift ever. Poofs were alien animals that looked a lot like tiny, fluffy kittens with no ears or tails, but with shiny black button eyes. They were fluffy balls on tiny legs and paws and I and everyone else loved them. They were also incredibly great protection because they could go Jeff-sized with tons of razor sharp teeth when danger threatened, so they were wonderful personal protection bundles of cuteness.

Supposedly they were solely pets for the Alpha Four Royal Family—which I'd somehow married into—but the Poofs were androgynous and mated whenever a royal wedding loomed. Supposedly.

In reality, the Poofs were Black Hole Universe animals and apparently our Poofs had decided to go forth and multiply. We had tons of Poofs and more seemed to show up with a lot of regularity.

In the Poofs' world, if you named it, it was yours. And the Poofs sort of chose what they considered a name—and therefore who they considered their "owner"—so a lot of people had Poofs simply because they'd said something like, "Look at that, how adorable is that?" Which is how one of our friends, Representative Nathalie Gagnon-Brewer had gotten a Poof. She called hers Dora for short.

Harlie had gone large and in charge way back when and scared Kyle straight, and to prove it, totally without my even knowing, Kyle had started a Take Back the Night program while he and Len were still at USC, which created a service where anyone could call to get a security escort throughout the campus back to wherever they lived, as well as doing community service teaching girls what to look for to avoid a date rape situation and also what to do to get out of it safely.

Many colleges had these programs in place, but Kyle's had been particularly effective, in part because he'd gotten all the jocks involved in a positive way. He'd been one of the representatives for USC's sports program's preventative counseling service that worked with athletes to keep them from becoming the kind of men who thought women were there as things for them to play with and dominate, and he'd been, from all Len said, quite intense about it.

All this had made him the man for the job when Cleary had come to us asking for support with putting a similar program in place in all the colleges and universities in Florida, where he was still governor. He'd also suggested it as my Cause, and I honestly had no objection.

Cleary had thought up The Cause, however, because he was intimately involved in a scandal that we had, so far, managed to keep under wraps.

"No, not with The Cause," Kyle replied. "I think we have a hit on Stephanie."

"Really?" Think of the scandal and it appeared. Or something like that. Maybe I still had some telepathic resonance from Operation Civil War. "How confirmed a hit?"

"We're not sure," Len said, as the elevator opened and

we headed off for one of the smaller salons. "Governor Cleary didn't want to tell us a lot without you in the room."

"For a guy whose state isn't next to the Beltway, he's sure up here a lot."

"He's going to run for President again," Len said. "We all know it. He's keeping his ties tight. Can't blame him for that."

"I can guarantee he wants to activate Clarence, though," Kyle added. "So if you still want to tell him no, you'd better call Jeff."

"Why?"

"Because Mister Reynolds sounds like he's on Cleary's side," Len said. "Not sure why."

Speaking of one of my son's namesakes and my best friend since 9th grade. "Chuckie's here? When did he get here?" Normally I knew when he or Jeff were coming to or in the Embassy during the work day.

Chuckie was the head of the C.I.A.'s Extra-Terrestrial Division and, based on what we came back with from Operation Civil War, the Golden Boy of the Agency. Which meant that he had even more enemies within the Agency than he had before, in addition to all the enemies he already had.

Chuckie lived in the Embassy now, but that was because his apartments kept on getting trashed by people trying to kill him. And his emotional state hadn't been stable since we'd gotten back from Operation Civil War, because of the horrible things that had happened to him during that war and the fact that the guy he'd thought was his best friend had turned out to be the Mastermind and therefore the guy directly responsible for the death of Chuckie's wife. Crap like that can affect a person for some reason.

"He came with the governor," Len answered as we reached the salon. "And they came in with Mister Buchanan. And they were all vetted by the Secret Service."

We had a lot of Secret Service agents with us, more than the VP normally got. Because of me. Oh well, I was keeping people employed. Go me, making jobs. We had less Secret Service tailing us inside the Embassy because we were in one of the most secure buildings we could be, and because we had other internal protection.

Malcolm Buchanan had been assigned by my mother to

be my personal shadow and bodyguard when we'd first come to D.C. And there wasn't a day I wasn't grateful for Mom's prescience. I insisted Buchanan had Dr. Strange powers because he came and went like the wind and if the man didn't want you to see him, you didn't see him.

I saw him now, though. He was standing at the back of the room, clearly on guard, leaning against the wall in a way I knew meant that he could propel himself wherever instantly. The boys moved to similar positions within the room.

Chuckie and Cleary were sitting, and they both looked rather stressed and grim. So, it was going to be that kind of meeting. Oh, goody.

"Missus Chief," Buchanan said with a small smile. "In case you haven't already guessed . . . we have a problem."

"I took the leap, Malcolm. Chuckie, Gideon, why so serious?"

"Someone just tried to kill me," Cleary said, voice shaking. "And I'm pretty sure it was Stephanie."

Stephanie was Jeff's niece, his eldest sister's eldest daughter. Her father, Clarence Valentino, had been an A-C traitor of the highest order. And I'd had to kill him. But not before he'd turned Stephanie.

Understandably, she'd blamed us for her father's death and joined the Mastermind's team with gusto. She'd also started sleeping with said Mastermind. And then he'd had her kill eight of our Secret Service detail during Operation Bizarro World.

Stephanie had freaked out and disappeared. There were two points of view about her disappearance. One was that she was faking us out, so that we'd come after her and then be trapped. The other was that she was afraid of the Mastermind, and hiding from him. The longer she was gone—and she'd been gone for over a year and a half now—the more credence the second point of view gained.

There was also the point of view that said Stephanie was dead, killed by the Mastermind. While we never discounted that one, if she'd been sighted, that would be a good thing. Barring her once again trying to murder people.

"Are you sure it was her?" I asked as I sat down at the small conference table we had in this room.

"Fairly sure," Chuckie said.

"Very sure," Cleary said.

Looked to Buchanan. Who shrugged. "I didn't see any of it, Missus Chief. I was just near enough that when Reynolds called I could get to them the quickest."

Wondered why Buchanan had been near to Chuckie, versus near to me, for this particular situation. Chose to table the question for later. "What happened?"

"The governor was finishing a meeting with several lobbyists," Chuckie said. "I was . . . observing the meeting."

"He was spying on us, he means," Cleary said, without a lot of animosity. Chuckie just shrugged.

"What was the meeting about?"

"Whether or not to close NASA Base," Cleary replied.

Well, that was new. And now it made a lot of sense that Chuckie had been "observing" this meeting. "Why would anyone want to close NASA Base?"

"I have no idea," Cleary said. "I certainly have no desire to do so."

"But you did, during your presidential campaign," Chuckie pointed out. "And the people who you met with are still on that platform, even though you're shifting to have a better chance of success in the next election, or the one after."

Cleary nodded. "That's very true. At any rate, we finished the meeting, and as we were leaving the restaurant, I saw Stephanie across the street. As soon as she saw me she disappeared. I thought she'd run away from me. But then someone took a shot at me."

"Excuse me? No one's mentioned that Florida's governor was attacked on our streets."

"The restaurant lets out into the back, where there's an alley and a small parking lot," Chuckie explained. "So that people can leave without being seen together, if needed."

"Gotcha. But still, shots tend to draw attention."

"Not," Chuckie said dryly, "when they're done with a bow and arrow."

Gini Koch lives in Hell's Orientation Area (aka Phoenix, Arizona), works her butt off (sadly, not literally) by day, and writes by night with the rest of the beautiful people. She lives with her awesome husband, three dogs (aka The Canine Death Squad), and two cats (aka The Killer Kitties). She has one very wonderful and spoiled daughter, who will still tell you she's not as spoiled as the pets (and she'd be right).

When she's not writing, Gini spends her time cracking wise, staring at pictures of good looking leading men for "inspiration," teaching her pets to "bring it," and driving her husband insane asking, "Have I told you about this story idea yet?" She listens to every kind of music 24/7 (from Lifehouse to Pitbull and everything in between, particularly Aerosmith and Smash Mouth) and is a proud comics geek-girl willing to discuss at any time why Wolverine is the best superhero ever (even if Deadpool does get all the best lines).

You can reach Gini via her website (www.ginikoch.com), email (gini@ginikoch.com), Facebook (www.facebook.com/Gini.Koch), Facebook Fan Page: Hairspray and Rock 'n' Roll (www.facebook.com/GiniKochAuthor), Pinterest page (www.pinterest.com/ginikoch), Twitter (@GiniKoch), or her Official Fan Site, the Alien Collective Virtual HQ (thealiencollectivevirtualhq.blogspot.com).

Gini Koch
The Alien *Novels*

"Gini Koch's Kitty Katt series is a great example of the lighter side of science fiction. Told with clever wit and non-stop pacing, this series follows the exploits of the country's top alien exterminators in the American Centaurion Diplomatic Corps. It blends diplomacy, action, and sense of humor into a memorable reading experience." —*Kirkus*

"Amusing and interesting...a hilarious romp in the vein of 'Men in Black' or 'Ghostbusters'." —*VOYA*

To Order Call: 1-800-788-6262
www.dawbooks.com

DAW 160